By the same author:

Mistress of the Streets

Mistress of the Boards

Mistress of the Boards

Richard Sumner

Random House
New York

Copyright © 1976 by Richard Sumner

All rights reserved under International and Pan-American Copyright Conventions. Published in the United States by Random House, Inc., New York.

LIBRARY OF CONGRESS CATALOGING IN PUBLICATION DATA

Sumner, Richard, 1949–   Mistress of the boards.

1. Gwyn, Nell, 1650–1687—Fiction. I. Title.
PZ4.S9565Mh3 [PR6069.U45]   823'.9'14   76-14183
ISBN 0-394-40857-8

Manufactured in the United States of America
2 4 6 8 9 7 5 3
First Edition

To Dorothy and Stephen

'As I have had two lovers of your name before, you will have to be my Charles the Third.'

—*Saying of Nell Gwynne
to King Charles the Second*

Part One
Charles the First

*A Play-House is become a mere Bear-Garden,
Where ev'ryone with Insolence enjoys
His Liberty and Property of noise.*

My Lord of Rochester

One

London—April 4th, 1665

*When Princes love, they call themselves unhappy,
Only because the word sounds handsome
in a Lover's mouth.*

—*John Dryden*

On the fourth day of April in the year of our Lord 1665, London dreamed lazily in the warm haze of a somnolent spring afternoon. The bright sunlight caught the curving ribbon of the Thames with glints of gold which belied the muddy water beneath as it took its way from the quiet mossy banks at Richmond to eddy and wash around the great piers of London Bridge and bubble down to the Palace of Whitehall.

The weather was fine enough to draw out London's citizens, whether to sip at jocolatte in Monsieur Roche's shop in Queen's Head Alley, to take a measure of malmsey at the Dolphin in Tower Street or a humble pot of Bide's ale at the Black Boy in Scalding Lane. The breath of whispered spring even penetrated the overhanging eaves of the tall timber houses, refreshing the stuffy narrow streets and alleys beneath with light and gentle breeze, so that the painted craftsmen's signs creaked gently as they swung over the heads of the thronging populace. These were the veins in the body of London—a capital of pageantry and squalor. Far above, piercing the skyline, soared the spires of a hundred or more churches, investing the city with a distant and deceptive cool splendour.

The sun took the gilt pinnacles on the corners of the roof of Old St. Paul's and made them glitter as if they were made of molten fire, standing out above the packed warren of russet tiled houses running up Ludgate hill and across, down to the swift-flowing river. The watermen who plied their wherries up and down the broad highway of the Thames sweated as they pulled at their oars and thought longingly of a whiskin of strong ale at the nearest ale house, which could not be theirs until they landed their passengers safe at Paul's Wharf.

Yet at the Cock and Pye tavern in Drury Lane all was not well. A shaking, gesticulating figure, hollow of eye and rag-clad, disturbed the repose of the company with a loud denunciation. For an old man his voice throbbed with a surprising vigour of passion. ' 'Tis God's curse on the sins of us all. 'Tis the Lord's hand on this Sodom of a city,' he shrieked as his eye swivelled to a solitary rat scuttling under the wainscotting in the corner of the taproom.

'Doom, I tell ye, doom is coming. There is no escape.' His voice rose higher. 'Therefore the Lord, the God of Hosts, the Lord saith thus: "Wailing shall be in all streets; and they shall say in all highways, Alas! Alas!" ' The words filled the low timbered chamber above the laughter of the little groups of men around the tables and the rattle of pewter tankards. A few heads turned, surprised, in the speaker's direction, but most people in the Cock and Pye continued to down their ale indifferently, with only one exception.

'Odsbud, man, cease your blethering! You fair addle my brains wi' your rantings. Save them for the Presbytery before you sour the ale.' A stocky man of mature years frowned over the rim of his mug.

The old man glanced nervously round. His hands plucked uneasily at his scanty beard and there were little beads of sweat upon his brow. His eyes held a fevered look. ' 'Tis the Lord's work and it is wondrous in our sight.'

' 'Twill be wondrous that you don't end wi' your snivelling nose in the gutter an' you cease not your moaning, and that I promise you!' retorted the stocky gentleman. 'You carry the stink o' the charnel house in your rags.'

A trembling finger levelled at his stolid form. 'The Lord hath spoken to thee, master: "Thou fool, this night thy soul shall be required of thee: then whose shall those things be, which thou hast provided?" '

Robert Duncan gazed, slightly mystified, at him. A capable square hand loosened his neat linen band as he regarded the soothsayer. To a Scottish merchant more used to the orderly bustle of the Royal Exchange and the business talk of the St. Michael's Alley coffee house, such revelations were a new experience. Duncan's prosperous air, his regular-featured ruddy visage and his thick red hair greying at the temples indicated a man to whom such prophetic matters were beyond comprehension. They spoke the voice of Bedlam.

From outside the breeze wafted through the small leaded casements of the Cock and Pye, and with it came the vociferous noises of 'prentice boys outcrying each other with offerings for sale: 'What d'ye lack, my masters? What d'ye lack?' Past the entrance to the tavern rumbled the town coach of my Lord Craven proceeding down Bridges Street into Drury Lane, preceded by a running footman with his long staff shouting to make way, weaving through the press of pedlars, street vendors and citizens, and bawling at an old itinerant pastry seller to get out of his path. Round the corner from Maypole Alley came a burly water carrier, with his customary cry: 'Thames water . . . bright fresh Thames water—penny a buck-et!' From the noise in the tavern to the hubbub outside it was obvious that London was proceeding along her usual boisterous, busy path. Looking from where he sat in the window down Maypole Alley, Rob Duncan sighed as he squinted at the gilded crown atop the tall maypole clearly visible in the Strand. Such a fine day to talk of misery and death! He shrugged and finished his ale.

The stout innkeeper strode to the door and kicked it open, jerking his head to the street outside as he turned on the agitator in his tavern. 'You can take your woes to the Rose in Vinegar Yard, my bully—aye, so you can—or fall abed and take suck from a biberon. But leave you will!' A hearty thrust from a brawny arm expelled the ragged figure and the door latch clicked back.

'You don't want to take no notice of old 'Arry, your honour,' advised the innkeeper. 'He's been telling us the same story this five year or more. Comes in for a pot of small ale and gives us the jerks when 'e gets one of 'is turns. Never so 'appy as when 'e's miserable. I warrant his was a different errand from yours. I've just sent my good wife to tell 'er you're waiting. She'll not keep you.'

Duncan grimaced. 'I hear the hinnie keeps many a one waiting nowadays at her pleasure. His Grace of Buckingham, my Lord Mulgrave . . .'

'Aye,' nodded the innkeeper. 'My hostelry is honoured indeed. All London talks of 'er, and she but a young girl.'

'A girl with a difference, fellow. The boards of the Theatre Royal have never seen such a one, forbye. So she grows nifty in her cock loft, does she?'

The innkeeper shook his head violently. 'Nay, sir! Never that! To be sure, she keeps 'em dangling, but no doubt it does 'em good. 'Tis not rank that recommends 'em. I've known her dally many a long hour with some rag-tag in my kitchen while she disdains the company of the quality. In fact, I well remember how she sent my Lord Babington to the devil t'other day to consort with that one-legged cutpurse beggar friend of hers. *He* has little need to beg now with the flood of groats she gives him. I swear he'd be lodged here if she had her way. But she hardly favours any on 'em. Only to *one* of late has she shown some marked attention.'

'Who is . . . ?' prompted Duncan.

'Nay, sir, I'm mum,' responded the innkeeper with a grin. 'The scandalmongers will tell you soon enough if you've a mind to hear. I swear from 'ere to Temple Bar the talk is of little but the Dutch war and the dallyings of Mrs. Nelly.'

'Tales heard only by those pox-ridden cheesecurds with their ears in the gutter!' a voice came in clear rebuke.

The noise in the tavern dropped slightly and some heads turned to the stairs. A small slender figure stood looking down at them with a glint in her eye. It was a young girl with long tawny waves of hair, dressed simply, which fell in ripples over her slight shoulders and framed a face of startling loveliness. She had wide long-lashed hazel eyes above a straight little nose and a curving bow of a mouth now parted in laughter to reveal perfect white teeth. Her complexion was of a flawlessness which owed nothing to ceruse or livenwort and cream—smooth and very pale, with a becoming blush of freshness. She was dressed plainly in a wool russet gown with smock sleeves and bodice which amply displayed the firm shape of her young breasts. Now she looked down at the innkeeper, her slim arms on her hips, an expression of mock severity on her face. 'Hang you with polecats, Tom Jackson, for a scurrilous rogue! What do the gutters say of Nelly Gwynne?"

The innkeeper looked embarrassed. 'Lord, Nell, what should they say? Rumour couples you with every great name in Whitehall.'

'And adds I couple with *them*, I dare swear.' Her eyes twinkled. 'Not the backside o' the truth if every man's inclination came true, which'—she came down the stairs with a light step—'I am glad to say is not so yet.' She looked quizzically at Robert Duncan. 'Have you come to join my court, Master Duncan? Master Killigrew tells me that but for you I should never have trod the boards at all. I'm told you verily forced him to take me into the company of the King's House. In fact, Tom Killigrew added that but for you I should be out on my arse in Lincoln's Inn Walk.'

'An exaggeration, Mistress Gwynne. Master Killigrew knows his business or he could not run the King's Players at Drury Lane so well as he does. He noticed you, I believe, before I did.' As he took one slender hand to kiss, he reflected it was no wonder.

She burst out laughing. ' 'Oons, hardly a good beginning, sir! I lost my temper because he would not help my sister Rose out of Newgate prison for debt. Not that it was his fault the silly bitch found herself there.' She gurgled. 'I think I called him . . .'

'A greasy pimp, a scrawny coxcomb and a curs'd jackdaw,' supplied Duncan amiably. 'He said you were . . . memorable.'

Mistress Nell Gwynne had the grace to blush. 'My language you must excuse, sir. My origins again betray me. I was, you recall, but born in the Coalyard and brought up in a bawdy house serving strong waters to the gentlemen.' She turned to the innkeeper. 'A pottle of whit, Tom, if you please. My mouth's as dry as Dutchman's powder.'

'Did he help Rose out of prison?' enquired Duncan.

'He did, as he is a gentleman. And Rose resumed the path that had first taken her there—the malapert slut—though pox take her, she's been the merrier since that rogue of a husband ran off and left her free.'

'And you entered the Theatre Royal as an orange girl.' She turned round to the counter to pick up her ale and there was a pause as she took a deep draught. 'Eventually,' she agreed in a quiet voice. Her eyes seemed to cloud and Duncan saw her face whiten suddenly. He directed a searching glance at her. 'Are you well, Mistress Gwynn?'

She shook her head slightly and smiled. 'A trifle parched, that is all. Shall we sit, sir?'

They took a settle in a corner and Nell looked down at her hands cupping the tankard. Awkwardly Duncan attempted to break the distance that seemed suddenly to have fallen between them. 'I saw you first as an orange girl, my dear. Or rather, I saw you first breaking your orange basket over the skull of a member of the audience. I recollect you actually stopped the performance.'

There was a sniff. 'Marry and Amen, Jem Curd had a skull like a Barcelona walnut. He used to terrorise us orange girls till we were with child to be rid of 'im.' Duncan saw that the cloud had passed. There was a distinct glint in her eye once more. 'You make me sound a veritable harpy, Master Duncan.'

'No, child, merely an imp of much spirit. You have trod the boards a bare three months. Already you have caught the acclaim of this city, the devotion of Mr. Dryden and the eye of his Majesty the King himself. He has been to see you now three times, I am told. And tales tell of more *particular* devotion . . .'

'As they always will,' she finished lightly. 'London and applause is nothing, I dare swear, to the approval of Master Killigrew. Fortune smiles on me indeed!'

'Fortune is a plaguey unreliable thing, Mistress Gwynne, and all is not always as it seems. I find both good and ill fortune a poor illusion. It exists only in the minds o' the envious. I mind when I was a lad we were gae poor but I was happier then, I think, than now. And look at me now.' He patted his stomach covered in good English broadcloth and laughed. 'Whoever would have thought that wee Robbie Duncan frae Dunblane would end a merchant of the City of London and a member of the Worshipful Company of Goldsmiths wi' a fortune that would buy a dozen lairdies and a hawkit cow for every man, woman and child in my ane village.' His voice was suddenly bitter. 'Whoever would have thought my only son, Hamish, could have survived a' the wars to die frae the bite of a mongrel cur the month after he came home to me. A brisk and bonny lad to be sae cut down.' He ran his hand wearily through his greying hair. 'Nay, lassie, fortune brings you up only to dash you down. I dinna wonder men gi' her the woman's name.' A gold coin bounced on the table. 'So—I have a' the money a man could want and folk'd deem me a success, I dare swear. Nae doubt I'm getting sentimental in my old age, for I run on like a feckie. How can a child like you know of such things?'

'I know.' Huge hazel eyes below a tumble of tawny curls gazed back at him gravely.

'How?'

'You tell me all is not always as it seems, Master Duncan. Do you think me untouched by living? I have no father and I never knew him. I first learnt to walk in the alleys of St. Giles. My childhood was spent at a whorehouse in Lewkenor's Lane with that flesh fly Ma Ross trying to persuade me into a man's bed for profit.' He felt her hands impulsively come out and cover his own. 'I've seen stranger things than you'd credit, Master Duncan. What d'you think lies behind the paint of an actress at the Theatre Royal? Do we have a life of glitter with hopes of marrying into taffeta? Haply. I see their faces in the pit and I know what they're thinking: "A fine face, but a whore under her petticoats." No . . . ?' she retorted to Robert Duncan's vociferous protest. 'I think you have not been in the Women's Shift of late, sir. My best hope is one day for a huge farmer to plant himself in the tiring room and say, "Nelly Gwynne, marry me! You're a fine wide-hipped woman and I warrant you'll be a happy breeder." I'll faint into 'is arms, I promise you.'

Robert Duncan laughed, but he shook his head disbelievingly. 'I'll no' believe those pretty eyes have not brought a lad or two, Nell. Or even three or four, I make no doubt.'

'Aye.' She placed her tankard down on the table. 'But where do those encounters lead me? I've seen my sister Rose succumb to the heat of a man's passion and then he left her, alone with a great belly and a mountain of debts to remember him by.'

Robert Duncan looked up, startled. She continued almost as if he weren't there. 'I see what life has done to my sister. Now she sells herself carelessly, as if her heart had died within her. Perhaps it has. It all began because she was poor and hungry and forgot she was a warm breathing woman with love to give and a right to love; because it was more important to fill her belly than wait for a dream that was as like as not a story to tell children. And when she thought it had come true, it turned into a nightmare. Rose's heart died in a winter of loneliness and grief. It is not a mistake I am minded to make.'

Duncan was amazed at the quiet force of her voice and the brightness that stood on her lashes. 'Child, I never thought—'

' 'Oons, Master Duncan, how should you? No more can any man.' She stood up and shook out the creases in her skirts. ' 'Tis spring, after all, and life returns and *I will live*. 'Tis spring, the sap runs high in the blood. Who could be sad in England in tart and cheese-cake time?'

At the top of the stairs appeared a small maid in a mobcap holding a cloak over one arm and waving wildly. ' 'Ere, Nelly, you forgot this.'

'S'life so I did, Mit.' She ran to the stairs and the serving maid draped the cloak round her. Tying the ribbons, she came back to Robert Duncan. 'If you can wait, sir, I will join you. I must be at the theatre within this half-hour—the performance starts at three o'clock, and you know how the vizards and oglers throng round so we can scarce get dressed. Only an execution draws 'em off and there are none today, I believe. Do you come this afternoon or do you fear your name to be coupled with mine?'

Duncan bowed. 'Did I not say I was one of your court, Mistress Gwynne?' he asked, his eyes twinkling.

'Truly you did, sir, and I thank you.' To his surprise she kissed him on the cheek softly. 'I need not Master Killigrew to know what I owe to you, sir. Shall we take a chair together? Of course, for a lady to be seen with a man in a hackney coach is ruinous. But nothing but the behaviour of a bawd is expected of an actress at the Theatre Royal. The world knows 'tis as hard for a woman to keep herself honest in the theatre as 'tis for an apothecary to keep his treacle from the flies in hot weather. And you know how the city sees *me*, Master Duncan.'

'No, Mistress Gwynne.'

She glanced mischievously at him. 'Why, the veriest bawd of London.'

The tiny Women's Shift at Drury Lane was crowded with milling gentlemen of all classes and estates in life. Fastidiously dressed noblemen rubbed shoulders with plain-clad citizens and ill-dressed, open-eyed 'prentice boys. The room above the stage was but small, it was cluttered with stage props, and the crowd pressed so hard it was difficult for the actresses to move to fasten their costumes or apply their paint. The continuing state of undress in which they remained appeared to afford the crushed spectators some little interest.

The gentlemen perched on the tables amongst the unguents and bottles of Hungary water or leant against walls eying the charms of each beauty in her shift before she transformed herself for the stage of the Theatre Royal. The atmosphere was somewhat stale and heavy and the noise deafening. Yet somehow the actresses of the King's House contrived to don their finery and exchange fragmented conversation with the gentlemen who pressed so eagerly round.

'God's death,' complained Bab Knipp, 'as well be in a baker's oven here. I protest, my Lord Ossary, you've sat in my bottle of Neroli, pox take you. It cost me three guineas at Madame Perineau's at the Exchange. Take your breeches off me table, sir—I swear you've now the sweetest rear in London.'

Laughing, the gentleman lounged to his feet. There was a noise of derision as my Lord Ossary brought a wet hand from feeling behind him. 'Enough, Mrs. Knipp. How can I repay such a compliment? At least let me recompense for another visit to la Perineau.' There was a clink as five gold coins dropped neatly down the lady's bodice.

'Pink you for an arrant rogue, Ossary. I'll live yet to see you go up Tyburn hill.'

'You're out, Knipp. He'd lose his all on the block. A perquisite of rank, you understand.'

'His all? I thought 'twas his *head* was cut off.'

'Save your sallies for the Shoe Lane cock pit where they belong, Mrs. Knipp, if you please. The Theatre Royal may resemble a Fleet Alley bawdy house in the afternoons but was once a place of drama not so long ago.' A buxom lady with a peevish expression sniffed as she placed a taffeta 'mouche' at the corner of her mouth. 'I vow and swear, since Mrs. Gwynne took prime notice at the King's House 'tis no better than a market for whores.'

'Perhaps there was no merchandise to market before she came, Mrs. Weaver,' retorted fat Kate Corey by the door. Mrs. Weaver bridled and turned to deliver a crushing riposte, but before she could speak, a small, delicately built personage, sumptuously dressed in a flowing robe of embroidered velvet with a tall spiked crown upon his head, appeared, flicking frantic fingers and moaning.

'King Montezuma of Mexico, I deduce,' drawled a voice by Mrs. Weaver.

The figure appeared distracted. 'Ladies, please! I pray your aid! Disaster ever strikes at the eleventh hour, and this on a day his Majesty graces us with his attendance. Have you seen my fan?'

'Your *fan*, Major Mohun?'

'Aye. Let me perish! I swear I cannot stir abroad without something is missing when I return! 'Tis as tall as I am, you recall—green feathers on a gilt stem. Lord, you *must* have seen it. 'Tis twice the size of Beck Marshall. The hour lacks only ten minutes; Master Lacy is with child as Mrs. Nelly has not yet arrived and some pocket tipstave has made off with my fan!'

'Cannot King Montezuma enter minus his fan?'

'An actor can cope with anything, my Lord Mulgrave,' said Mohun coldly. 'But that is hardly the point. The directions say, "Enters, fanned gently by slaves." How can I be fanned gently by that provoking minx Beck Marshall when there is no *fan?*' His voice became a wail and he began to scurry round the Women's Shift, turning over stools and pulling out costumes in search of the relict, ignoring the protests of the actresses. Mrs. Weaver poured out a string of unbecoming oaths as he jogged her arm and sent a squirt of Amber water into one eye.

'Is this yours, Mohun?' A rich resonant voice carried above the hubbub in the tiring room. Charles Hart, leading actor of the King's Players and great nephew of William Shakespeare, stood in the entrance idly swinging a long gilded pole between his fingers. He was a tall dark gentleman of imposing presence and patrician profile.

'I gather Master Kynaston found it—or rather, it found him. Orange Moll was lambasting one of the orange girls with it and he walked into it as he—'

Michael Mohun uttered a squeak of relief and grabbed the fan from him. '*Lambasting?* How . . . who could have . . . ? When I find . . .' Major Mohun's voice spluttered in disjointed outrage.

From the door came a peal of laughter. 'You will have no time I fear, sir. We both have but three minutes to assume our regal states. I might suggest you take your fan and revive Master Lacy. He swoons with relief at my arrival.'

A chuckle ran round the Women's Shift, and Major Mohun turned and smiled as he saw who it was. 'At last, a fellow artist! My royal daughter Cydaria. I give you good day, Mistress Gwynne.'

Outside in the pit a boisterous, restless crowd fidgetted uneasily on their matted benches as the hour of three drew nearer. Beneath the glazed cupola over their heads the bright sunlight diffused in airy patterns, playing on the green and brown hues of homespun and the pale faces of the vizard-masked ladies, seated cheek by jowl.

Above them lounged the 'prentices in the cheaper seats of the middle gallery, shouting and calling for the play to begin. Indeed, should the Theatre Royal be late in commencing its performance, they had been known to relieve the tedium of waiting by pouring their pots of ale on the unsuspecting beneath. Yet further above them, in bewigged and feathered splendour, winking jewels, sprawled the members of the Court of King Charles the Second. Elaborate curled periwigs brushed across silk shoulders of violet or maroon, suits of richest velvet, satin and gold. Mingled with such heavy richness was the delicate lace-edged toiletrie of ladies, lightly clad in flowered silks or soft glowing damask, faintly perfumed, displayed below exposed white shoulders and bosoms scarcely less exposed. Many amongst them wore one of the large flat-brimmed hats recently imported from France and known as 'cartwheels.' Tied with ribbon and sporting huge feathers of all colours, they effectively shaded from view the faces of the wearers beneath. In simpering spurts of polite conversation they awaited the beginning of the play.

All the restricted space of the theatre at Drury Lane was crammed with close-packed humanity, save only the upper gallery under the eaves where the lackeys of noble patrons were admitted free to view the last act.

In a box at the side, overlooking the stage, in solitary if informal grandeur, sat his Majesty King Charles the Second himself, with his brother James, Duke of York, and his natural son, The Duke of Monmouth. Gorgeous in black velvet slashed with white satin and silver lacing, the King lounged nonchalantly, occasionally raising his hand in amiable greeting when challenged by some loud voice in the pit. He was tall, dark and swarthy. His black curled periwig and black moustache contrasted with the sensual, somewhat heavy features of his face and dark complexion to show that he had inherited all the passionate qualities of his grandfather, Henri of Navarre, and his Medici ancestors.

He too awaited the start of the play but appeared not to be impatient. Rather, his dark luminous eyes gazed with interest about the theatre and stopped from time to time when they alighted upon a damsel of more than passing beauty of face and figure. His harsh features were entirely changed when he smiled and his cynical expression was shadowed by more than a hint of wicked humour.

'I rather hoped Miss Davis might have come with me today to see her new rival of the King's House, but I fear me she imbibed too heavy of the burgundy last night and is in no fit state to leave her bed,' observed the King. 'Ever since Buckingham told her that spirits would ruin her looks, she has turned to wine with a vengeance. The morning found her untimely.' He smiled. 'A pretty creature but lacking wit.'

'Could you not revive her with Dr. Goddard's drops, sir?'

'I fear she was even beyond that, my son,' murmured Charles as he glanced interestedly down the bodice of an orange girl leaning against the apron stage. 'An eternal problem of women, James. They either have looks or character. Never both. Look at Barbara...'

They stared across at the upper gallery where a lady reclined, surrounded by a small group of admirers. A cartwheel hat hid her face from view. But as Charles looked at the woman who had once been his mistress and favourite, his expression was disenchanted.

'I grant you Frances Stuart is virtually a lackwit,' conceded the Duke of York, 'but my Lady Castlemaine is still a damned fine set-up woman, Charles.'

'She has a tongue like a fishwife and the greed of a turnkey.

And I suspect that if her bolster could talk, it might tell a tale or two. Aye de me—women, what a blessing and a curse they are.'

The Duke's voice was tinged with light sarcasm. 'I wonder they interest you so, in that case, my liege.'

Charles shrugged slightly but said nothing.

Some gentlemen began to take their seats in the row which stood on the stage itself. Onto the boards strolled a tall, thin figure clad startlingly in a puce velvet coat garnished with turquoise ribbons, carrying a gilt-knobbed cane at least six inches taller than himself. A set of turquoise ruffles and waistcoat contrasted sharply with black ferrandin breeches with close knees. His periwig was of fair hue, swept up into two high wings at the front and cascading in elaborately arranged curls into twisted plaits down the back. Irritably he flickered his kerchief at the dusty seat before reclining with a sigh. His expression was one of weary boredom. Several amazed faces looked aghast at his costume, but the gentleman seemed all unaware.

'Charles, who *is* that extraordinary fellow in puce velvet with the enormous perruque?' asked the Duke of York.

'That, my dear brother, is Perfection Fox, known to the world as Lord Stephen Fox. 'Tis a gentleman of much affectation but a gentleman of much courage withal. He has but lately returned from Paris, I am told.'

'Does he always dress so . . . so . . . noticeably?'

'He thrives upon it, James. He was at Worcester fight with me and gossip hath it that when we all fled the beleaguered city—myself to skulk in ill-fitting shoes in the mud of the Severn—Perfection Fox found a large comfortable hackney and drove in easy stages back to the Scots border. He slept each night, cool as you please, in the best inn that could be found.'

James's brows rose. 'Did none challenge him?'

'Who would have thought a gentleman who travelled with two coaches of baggage, a valet and an incessant demand for eggs boiled soft could be a fugitive malignant? I am told he complained the sheets were not sufficiently aired when he lodged at the same hostelry at York with Hewson's cavalry troop.' Charles gave an appreciative chuckle. 'When he got to Paris shortly after me, he brought with him £5000 in gold—God knows where he got it from—and told me he had been rattled to death on the roads and frozen to the marrow a' board ship. He gave £500 to Mam to heat her apartments in the Louvre—said he couldn't abide the draught when he paid her a call. 'Tis the only time I've seen Mam at a loss for words; she didn't know whether to be grateful for a gift or outraged at an insult.'

The Duke of York gave a gasp of mirth. 'Does nothing unnerve him?'

Charles's voice was thoughtful. 'Oh yes, I once saw a lackey spill claret on his small clothes. The expression of horror on his face lingers with me still.'

A herald walked slowly onto the apron stage in front of the proscenium arch, and raising a trumpet, blew a long, sustained blast. Those near to the gentleman in puce may have observed him to wince. With a double flourish of his trumpet the herald announced: 'The Company of the King's Servants of the Theatre Royal humbly beg the attention of the audience for a tragic drama by Master John Dryden entitled *The Indian Emperor,* or *The Conquest of Mexico by the Spaniard*s.'

The light that filtered through the leads of the cupola over the pit had dimmed by the time Charles Hart finished the play by clasping Nell Gwynne to his chest, declaiming the closing lines.

Inside the theatre an intimate atmosphere was engendered by the lighting of the candles in sconces around the stage, so that the players were bathed in an arc of soft beams that flickered slightly in the draught around them. Nell found herself looking into the intense blue eyes of Charles Hart as he told her, 'I loud thanks pay to the powers above, thus doubly blest, with conquest and with love.' Nell had been clasped to his breast before, had heard those words before, and the feeling had been growing on her of late that the intensity with which Hart thus addressed her spoke of more than dramatic passion. He had started to frequent the Cock and Pye in an evening more often of late and Nell had allowed him into her private chambers—to the evident notice of Master Tom Jackson and others.

Now he held her close and drew her to him smoothly. She gave a little gasp, and then something happened that had never happened before. Charles Hart forced up Nell's chin and she felt his mouth close upon hers. Cheers swept the audience, and then, with them still ringing in her ears, Hart drew her off the stage. Clapping filled the pit and calls and bangings of tankards on benches drew them back onto the stage. They bowed and the play was over. But as they left the stage and the tumblers came on to usher in the farce, many in the pit noticed that Charles Hart still held Mrs. Nelly Gwynne's hand quite firmly.

As they reached the wings, Charles Hart stopped and turned her to face him. 'I dare not be too busy in my praises or you will think me but a vain flatterer, Mistress Gwynne.'

'So you are—as all the company knows.'

Hart's eyes brimmed with laughter. 'Then let me flatter you the more. Let me flatter you this evening—to Spring Gardens for neat's tongues, trifle and tarts, and stay till midnight.'

'I know,' said Nell to Hart. 'And after midnight?'

'That will depend on the moon and you.'

She shook her head slowly.

'I had good hope that fantasy and fact might merge, Nelly,' he said reproachfully.

'Sometimes they do. But many a maid has found her sweet fantasy becomes cruel fact all too soon and she a matron within the year.'

'You are no maid.'

She smiled a little at that. 'Nor wish to be a matron. Are you a scholar of such things, sir?'

An explosive, tetchy voice from behind interrupted them. 'God's wrath, Nelly! You're back on after the farce; this is no time for dalliance. Away with you, gel!'

'Coming, Master Lacy.' She turned back to Hart. 'Look for

me if you will this evening at the Cock and Pye, but I cannot swear to be there for you, Master Hart, you understand.'
'Charles,' he corrected.
'Charles.'

As the tumblers turned the last cartwheel, the burly figure of actor and playwright John Lacy appeared. He made a deep bow to the King in the royal box, with whom he was something of a favourite, and declaimed in tones of great solemnity, 'The Theatre Royal is overwhelmed to admit the presence of a personal emissary from his Most Christian Majesty, the King of France.' There was a pause as cheers and boos drowned his voice. Lacy put up his hand for silence. 'Hearing of our valorous fight against the Dutch, his Majesty has despatched a lady' —another pause—'a *beautiful* young damsel named Mademoiselle Grosse Poitrine to aid our morale and offer his advice. I offer *you* . . . Mademoiselle Grosse Poitrine!'

The curtains at the rear of the stage lifted and an enormous cartwheel hat appeared and wafted across the stage, dragging at the edges. It had a bunch of violently purple ostrich feathers in a plume at the front and a froth of netting covering it in a cloud. The audience greeted it with shouts of mirth. The lady beneath lifted up the flopping brim with one pretty hand and reproved them. 'I'll thank you scurvy fleaks to keep a civil tongue in your heads. You just don't know Quality when you sees it. 'Ere's me, come over 'ere h'at great *expense,* and all you do is burble like parrots!' Cheers swept the pit and the King was seen to rest his chin on his hand, a look of vast amusement on his face.

Mrs. Nelly Gwynne gave a jerk to her bodice. Her bosom was stuffed out to huge proportions and swayed perilously as she moved. 'I'll 'ave you know that in Paris I'm reckoned all the rage. With this lot on, you could sell me as I am in St. Martin-in-the-Fields for a ten guinea!' She minced forward, swinging her hips exaggeratedly, and curtsied in impudent fashion. ' 'Ello, mon sewers—that's French for what 'is Majesty thinks of you. I've come *all* the way over from Paris—and I've been bloody seasick all the way—just to sing you this little song. And as you're all so poxey ignorant, I've had it turned into English . . . h'at *great* expense.'

She seated herself on the apron stage on a stool and pulled back her skirts, as she crossed her legs, to expose one pretty ankle and leg up to the thigh. 'Now you'll 'ave to wait till I get rid of this curs'd boat of a hat; I can't play a note while it's sitting on me nose.' She flung the hat out into the pit and drew her hand across the strings of a dulcimer. Her clear voice filled the theatre and silence fell.

> 'To all the ladies now at land
> The men at sea indite;
> But first would have you understand
> How hard it is to write
> Our paper, pen and ink and we
> Roll up and down our ships at sea
> With a fal la la la la . . .'

'That's Buckhurst's song!' declared his Highness of York indignantly. 'That's not French . . .'

But his royal brother was not listening. King Charles the Second scribbled something on a piece of paper and beckoned to a servant. 'Dalton, when the lady finishes, take this and give it to her, and await her reply.'

James, Duke of York, sighed.

Two

Make much of every buxom girl,
Which needs but little courting,
Her value is above the pearl
That takes delight in sporting.

—*Sir George Etherege*

'Mordieu! I vow and swear, Sam Pepys, you wouldn't care if I nevair left the 'ouse for a twelvemonth!' A small lady, eyes bright with unshed tears, stood erect and indignant in her small front parlour in Seething Lane. Opposite her, a modishly dressed gentleman in a black silk camelott suit with gold buttons and gold broad lace opened and shut his mouth in frustrated and mounting fury. Heartened by his silence, the lady pressed home her advantage in pretty French-accented tones, and stabbing gestures of accusation. 'You nevair take me out; you nevair wish me to stir abroad without you—eh bien! 'Tis no better than a prison this—this Seething Lane! You grudge me any companions; you forbade le pauvre Monsieur Pembleton to come 'ere.'

A fervent protest rose to the gentleman's lips. 'Aye! Let us take Master Pembleton! An assiduous rogue of a dancing master! Two visits a day he came. I warrant if he led you a dance, he led me a finer one! I have no mind to wear the horns of a cuckold.'

'How dare you! What about *you* and la belle Madame Bagwell?'

'That was close on a year ago and naught but harmlessness, save in your mind, Lizbet! She is the wife of one of our carpenters. I merely went to her house for—'

'Kissing, tousing and tumbling! Me, I *know*.' Mrs. Pepys nodded her pretty head emphatically and turned away with a swish of skirts.

Her husband endeavoured to assert himself. 'God's death, woman, the country is at war, the Dutch might sail up the Thames at any time. I am Clerk of the Acts to his Majesty's Navy. I have the task of finding enough ships and men to stave them off and little time enough to do it in. When I come home, fatigued and chilled to the bone, I might expect some wifely sympathy. But all you can greet me with is this damned caterwhaul about needing a new gown and some amusement!'

The tiny figure of the lady suddenly drooped. She fished ineffectually for her kerchief and her voice came trembling and muffled over her shoulder. 'I s'ink that is just as excuse, Samooel. You 'ave not the love for me that once you 'ad. Once not dix mille Dotchmen could 'ave distracted you. No, you 'ave changed, I know it well. When you go to the theatre you do not take me. I am forgotten, bien sur. You make me triste en bas du coeur.' There was a sob.

All at once the angry expression faded from the face of Mr. Samuel Pepys. He strode across the room and gathered his wife to him. 'There, my Lizbet, don't cry. I am peevish, I know, but I have endured all day on naught but a crust of rye bread and a glass of mum.' He kissed the top of her head, which was just level with the lace of his jabot. 'Oddso, my dear, you smell a deal sweeter than tar. I came home in particular because you seemed out of sorts and I wished to see how you did. I bring some powder of bezoar stone and mithridate for your melancholy. Also, I bear an invitation from my Lady Batten for a dinner tomorrow. I wondered if you would like to take Jane to the Exchange and buy a new moyre gown, since you say your old one is in—ah—tatters?'

She raised her face to him and clutched at him forlornly. 'And you are not ennui with me?'

He flicked at her chin. 'Not though a hundred thousand Dutchmen arrive and burn London to the ground. Indeed, my love, you must forgive my shortness of temper. The fleet is due to sail in ten days and yet we lack supplies: rope, tar, powder and sailors most of all. My Lord Chancellor lies moaning with gout and berates me: Why have we not enough of this? Why have I not procured any of that? 'Tis hopeless to keep repeating we lack money and what we have is embezzled by those rogues who are supposed to supply us.'

'But surely, the Navy Board, they know this,' she ventured.

He looked resigned. 'I shall go again this afternoon with my lists of unfinished work and that damned wittol coxcomb Sir William Penn will look across the room at me in that insolent way he has and drawl that the Commissioners of his Majesty's Navy cannot understand how I have failed to oversee such things! I would love to wipe that smug smile away with the heel of my shoe—aye, marry would I!'

Mrs. Pepys searched his white, careworn countenance. 'I s'ink, Samooel, you worry too much and that makes you so maladroit. You want to make your way in the world and this possesses you. Is it not so, my heart?'

'I would I could be a knight and keep my coach, Lizbet,' admitted her spouse. 'But what with my nifty sister Paulina who lacks dowering and your shiftless brother Balty, I cannot see how 'tis to be contrived. I could not maintain the estate even were I offered it, as I might be.'

'We 'ave come a long way since those days in Axe Yard when we dined on hog's harslet in a garret, ma mie. You are cousin to milor' of Sandwich; you 'ave the friendship of his Highness of York. What of the hatred of such as Sir Penn? He matters no more than . . . that.' She snapped her fingers. 'Be patient and I doubt not one day to see you un grand seigneur du cours and I shall be . . . my Lady Pepys.'

Mr. Pepys smiled slightly but loosened his grasp. 'I must not dally, my dear. I have to attend his Majesty and the Duke of York this evening with Sir John Minnes to account for our naval repairs. His Majesty orders tomorrow as a fast day for all the kingdom against the war.'

His wife stood on tiptoe, so that his dark curled periwig brushed her nose, and planted a kiss on his cheek. Then she stood back and looked at him critically, her head on one side. 'Me, I think you look prodigious modish, Samooel. Nothing less than an earl in finery. Un veritable flameur! Enfin, go and attend your King. At least I cannot be jealous while you are there. His attention is firm fixed in another direction.'

'Do you refer to my Lady Castlemaine, to Frances Stuart or to Moll Davis from the Duke's Theatre?'

'To all of them, my 'usband. He has a big heart your king and there is room for them all. He suffers from a malady—these ladies are but symptoms.'

'What is the cure, my flower?' Mr. Pepys's tone was light.

'I fear a shock only could cure him—like hiccups, you know.'

'Like *hiccups*?'

Mrs. Pepys nodded firmly. 'Yes. You will see.'

Much later that same evening, as a cloudy moon sent pale beams of light into shadow beneath the overhanging eaves of Drury Lane, a plain hackney coach came to a halt outside the Cock and Pye tavern. From behind the shutters that hung ajar came the sound of singing mingled with the plaintive notes of a distant flageolet. A cloaked and hooded figure slipped from the gloom to greet the bowing lackey who awaited her. There was a fine drizzle which spat on the cobbles and soaked the downward drooping feather on his hat as he ascertained the identity of the lady. 'Mrs. Eleanor Gwynne?'

He caught the glimpse of a slight smile, but she answered softly, 'The same.'

He helped her into the coach, surprisingly upholstered in luxurious deep velvet, and the door shut as she settled back into the cushions with a sigh. The hackney clattered off down the Lane and turned abruptly at the corner, so that Nell had to hang on to the strap to save herself from falling.

Why had she come on this journey? she asked herself. Why had she agreed to the terse message delivered to her only that afternoon? She still clutched the billet of paper in her fingers, turning it restlessly as the hackney rumbled along and a whiff of air through the window told her they were passing down Fish Street. Certainly it was not because she did not know what the message meant.

Any actress of the King's House in Drury Lane knew what a summons from the King meant—if the chance were taken and properly exploited, it could mean fame and fortune beyond any girl's wildest dreams. Moll Davis of the Duke's Theatre already lived openly under the King's protection, and Nell recalled the tales she had heard in the Women's Shift of the luxurious style of life enjoyed by that lady.

Yes, she knew exactly what the summons meant, and now she went the same road—through a king's bed to a chance of security. For she did not love Charles the King. He was attractive, of course, with that dark sardonic countenance and those smouldering eyes which gave him an ugliness that was perhaps even more appealing to a woman than true beauty. But if she was flattered at his notice, she was not overawed. She remembered those words she had heard so long ago: 'Rank does not stop a man from noticing a pretty face, my dear, or a well-turned ankle . . .' She had remembered it before when she had first trod the boards and sank into a deep curtsey under the King's interested eye, and now she remembered it again. She had been anxious that day to win his notice and she had succeeded. And now . . .

To a girl of Nell's upbringing the summons was akin to the grant of a dukedom. To a child brought up in the fetid alleys of St. Giles it symbolised what every girl wanted. Not the thrill of passion; Lord knew, that wore off with the fourth brat when it came. No, it was security that it meant. Immediate comfort and the knowledge that a meal would arrive the next day and the day after that. A life that promised more certainty than the gay tinsel existence of an actress at the Theatre Royal. Why, then, did she feel so strange?

A sudden jerk told her that the coach had come to a halt, and as the door opened and the steps were let down Nell felt the clammy touch of the mist as it mingled with the drizzle on her cheeks. The sound of water rippling below caught her ears as it slapped against the landing place. They were at the secluded river stairs of Somerset House.

A link boy appeared and his flaring torch was held aloft to guide her down the narrow steps to the little platform at the water's edge. Gingerly she settled herself in a waiting wherry and the boatman bent to his task, taking the boat smoothly and silently out into the middle of the dark moving course of the Thames. She was alone, apart from the boatman; the link boy remained behind, and the glimmer of his torch was soon swallowed up as the barge was taken by the swift current deeper into the cool velvet darkness. Through the still night air she could hear the muffled *doom, doom* of the drum being beaten at Westminster Stairs to guide the boatmen in through the mist.

The air was cold but fresh, a deal fresher than the odorous atmosphere in the streets and alleys of the capital, which was tinged with the smoke of the sea coal used by most Londoners. The drizzle had stopped, and when the mist lifted slightly, she could see the glimmer of lights on the bank on her right as the boat glided by. They came from lanthorns standing on the private landing stairs of the stately mansions set in their own gardens stretching down to the river. Nell caught the rustle of the wind in the leaves as the boatman eased the wherry over to the right-hand bank. They drifted past, the golden points of light from the lanthorns dancing on the ripples of the running black water. Nell gazed up and saw the huge tall mass of Suffolk House and York House loom up behind the trees and then disappear around the bend in the Thames.

The boatman rowed softly on, his oars making barely a sound as they dipped regularly into the water. She found her heart beating fast as the boat neared the end of its journey, for Nell knew nobody who had taken this path and returned to tell of it. Perhaps, she decided, this was why she had come.

All at once tall tiers rose out of the gloom to greet them, and the boatman drew the boat over to where a solitary lantern hung out over the river. Nell was helped from the bobbing wherry onto a small wooden platform by a stiff, correct manservant who bowed before her impassively. 'Have I the honour of addressing Mrs. Eleanor Gwynne?"

'The same, sir.'

The man lifted the lantern for a second and looked into her face. 'My name is Thomas Chiffinch, ma'am. I am the Page of his Majesty's back stairs. Would you please to follow me?'

Picking up her skirts, Nell followed his erect shadow up the steps, the wind flapping her cloak against her ankles. Anxiously she caught up with Master Chiffinch. 'Where . . . where are we?' she gasped.

'We are ascending the Privy Stairs of Whitehall Palace, madame. Yonder'—he pointed to a row of tall leaded windows on the right looking out over the river—'lies her Majesty's apartments.'

Nell looked intently at the curtained windows, but there was no sign of life apart from a faint glimmer behind the still hangings. Beyond them in the dark, as far as the eye could see, sprawled the mass of buildings which housed the royal household and the web of intriguers, place seekers, procurers, prostitutes and pensioners who fought and squabbled in the Palace of Whitehall.

'His Majesty's lodgings lie to our left,' added Chiffinch.

Nell wrapped her cloak around her as they passed under an archway into a neat courtyard garden lit at intervals by lamps hung from brackets on the walls. Master Chiffinch motioned Nell through a side door. 'May I conduct you through my own humble apartments, ma'am, as they lie in our way.' She followed him through three unlit chambers, and out along a narrow paved corridor.

Chiffinch nodded briefly at a door set in the wall ahead of them. 'Yonder lies the apartments of her Majesty's Maids of Honour. By some—er—misarrangement, they seem to lie nearer to the King than to the Queen.'

Nell could not see his face as he led the way, so she could not tell whether this correct personage allowed himself a smile. Suddenly Chiffinch stopped at a low door, which he unlocked. After a cursory look up and down the deserted passage, Nell was ushered through. There was no light but the flicker of a candle as they climbed around and around up a spiral staircase until they reached a tiny landing.

Master Chiffinch retreated, clutching his lantern. Nell heard his footsteps clatter down the stairs, and the light receded with him. She was in total darkness. Then, as her eyes became accustomed to the gloom, she saw a ray of light showing from under a door in front of her. She turned the knob slowly, her heart in her mouth, and opened the door. Light streamed out on her from a cosy, well-lit room richly panelled in dark oak. An enormous Turkey carpet spread beneath her feet across the oak floorboards. Before her stood a huge fourposter bed of deep incarnadine velvet embroidered in crimson and gold with valances and curtains of cloth of gold. Two embroidered armchairs and footstools stood in front of an enormous roaring fire and on one of them a couple of spaniels lay asleep, their noses twitching slightly in the heat. Beside a long seat in the window embrasure was a low table set with a crizzled glass serving bottle, two cups of silver gilt and various cold meats. Slowly she trod into the room. She was in the King's bedchamber.

The clock on the clock tower had just struck one when James, Duke of York, caught sight of his royal brother swaying slightly as he proceeded down one of the walks of the empty Privy Garden. The King waved his cane amiably as York caught him up, and James put out an anxious hand to his elbow as Charles stumbled a little.

But the King quickly recovered his balance. 'No, no, James, not cooked through. Just a little overdone—a long night with Buckhurst, Etherege, Sedley and that young rogue Rochester.' He straightened his periwig firmly and strode on with deliberation. 'The perfect antidote to an endless meeting with the Navy Council. D'you know, I swear Sedley breefs his cards. They're like a pack of fishwives.'

'Who? Sedley's friends?' asked James, bewildered.

'No, no, that damned Navy Council. It's like a hive of bees

ruled over by that press— presp— preaching old fool Clarendon.' Suddenly the King gave vent to a loud roar of laughter. 'Odsfish, he tells the filthiest stories!'

'Who? My Lord *Clarendon*?' James was incredulous.

'No—Rochester. You're not attending, James.'

Now the two royal brothers passed into the deserted length of the Stone Gallery. Charles breathed deeply as they walked, their steps echoing out down the length of its empty vastness. Suddenly the King's cane tapped angrily at the ground. 'I'm sick to death of Clarendon's pro—posing. We all know we were beaten to flinders at Guinny, December last, and our humiliations haven't stopped since, but to hear your father-in-law talk, James, you'd think I'd personally steered each ship into the Dutchmen's fire.'

'One of those meetings, was it?' asked the Duke sympathetically.

'Odsfish, James, you should have been there—'twas better than a play. There's my Lord Chancellor lying on a couch, groaning with his gout and being rude to me in the most frigid polite way. There's my Lord Southampton mopping his brow and moaning like a pregnant woman. And Rupert standing in a corner swearing he puts it all down to spies in our midst and vowing to keelhaul anyone he chooses! My lord!'

'It seems I was favoured, being down at Deptford.'

'You were,' said Charles feelingly. 'God knows I would do anything to save those poor wretches of sailors being impressed, but what am I to do? The Parliament will not grant me funds; the conditions are bad; I have spent all possible and I have no more to give. I tell you, James, Clarendon and Sir George Carteret will drive me to enlist, if only to escape their nagging tongues.'

The Duke of York laughed.

'Aye, you may titter, brother, but what's to do? The merchants of the city will not lend to the Crown with only the fortunes of war as security—though the war be in their own defence. Only that stubborn old mule Albemarle gives me good advice; he is hardly polite to me, but then, he's not polite to anyone.'

'The war has had a bloody beginning,' commented James. 'We have gained no glory but hundreds of dead and wounded.'

'You need not tell me, brother,' said Charles wearily. 'Master Evelyn comes almost daily to beg money for housing wounded men and succouring widows and orphans. I would give if I could but I have no more for him; this war is costing £1000 each week and the Crown is destitute. In the end I have to tell him to apply to my ministers, and both of us know that road leads precisely nowhere. I see the look in his eye and I know what he is thinking—what a prodigal spendthrift rogue of a king he has. Perhaps he is right, but I cannot screw more gold out of the Parliament. I am surrounded by fools! Fools! I dare swear, of the lot of them, only a handful know what's amiss.'

The Duke of York smiled. 'You and Mr. Pepys appear to be of one mind.'

'Mr. Pepys?'

'Yes, that tubby little man who is Clerk of the Acts. A truly indefatigable worker, I give you my word, and worthy of advancement. Indeed, I have recommended him for the post of Treasurer of the Tangier Committee.'

'I remember—Sandwich's cousin. I fear you underrate him, brother. I think your Mr. Pepys is almost unique in his virtues.'

'How so, Charles?'

The King's eyes showed mock astonishment. 'I believe he is that rarest of animals—an honest man.' He led the way towards the royal lodgings. 'What do you here at this time, James? I hear ever since Mistress Arabella Churchill fell off her horse and displayed uncommon slender legs, you have been seen more often of late at Whitehall, particularly near the apartments of the Maids of Honour.'

'Rumour, Charles. And you wrong me. I had to see Brouncker on naval business.'

'Till this hour?' Charles raised sceptical brows.

James groaned. 'No, I confess. I should have known better,

but I accepted an invitation from Frances for a party tonight. We spent most of it playing blind man's buff and hunt the slipper! The girl's as innocent as a five-year-old!'

'It is her innocence I find alluring, James,' retorted the King. 'One does not encounter it often in Whitehall.'

'More like imbecility, Charles. You know what Courtin finds so fascinating in Frances Stuart? He says he has never found so little wit and so much beauty both in one woman. I feel I must agree, though I declared myself her Valentine but two weeks past.'

The King appeared thoughtful, even depressed. 'You should know by now, James, women are always a disappointment. You think you've found a treasure and you've found an empty casket. There's always a catch. Either they're not worth having or they want to own you body . . . and soul.' He turned a flushed face to the Duke of York. 'Either they disappoint you or you're a disappointment to them. Barbara disappoints me and I . . . I disappoint my wife.'

'Nonsense, Charles.'

'I always have disappointed her and I suppose I always will.' The King's eyes, dark and intense, held a blank look. 'She wants to hold me and stifle me in her arms. I can't feel like that—I never could. And she can't feel anything less. Pray that you die before me, James; you will find it a lonely task to be King.'

'Pox take it,' murmured James in embarrassment. 'Look here, Charles, don't you think you'd better get to bed?'

But the King put his hand on James's arm, until the Duke felt the grip hard through his velvet sleeve. 'Don't you know what is wrong with her, this woman, my wife? Don't you? I will tell you. She has committed the one unforgivable sin: she has fallen in love with me. God, how I wish—*wish*—she had not. She condemns herself to pain and me to perdition . . . Barbara keeps her jewel casket by her bed and under it a dish of Venus cockles to kindle her appetite should it wane. My Queen has a prie dieu and a stoop of holy water. James, I ask you, how can a man fight that? Damn it, man, how can he, plague take it? I can take Barbara, aye, and leave her when she casts her shoe at my head. But my little Catherine . . .' Charles swayed ever so slightly.

With relief, James saw two lackeys standing immobile at the doorway to the King's own suite of apartments. He took his brother's hand and brushed it formally with his lips. 'My liege, I bid you a very good night.'

With a mocking smile, Charles saw his brother hurriedly depart. 'Never could stand me bosky—poor James,' he said softly.

Ten minutes later, clad in a dull maroon gown of satin trimmed with gold lacing and twist, the King trod up the stairs to his private bedchamber. When he opened the door he saw a sight which surprised him. In one of the armchairs in front of the fire a young girl was curled up with one spaniel on her lap and another festooned over her feet and the footstool. With one slender hand she absently stroked a dog's ears and with the other she sipped at a glass of Rhenish. She was dressed very simply in a plain amber woollen gown and her hair fell in a tawny mass down her back, the candlelight catching the glints in the loose waves at the edges and making them glow with an aureole of liquid fire. Her delicate features were well known to the Theatre Royal and most of London, and bereft of her stage paint she looked at once far younger and more beautiful. She turned a grave, faintly startled gaze upon him and he saw two huge hazel eyes set in a face of elfin loveliness—pale and compelling.

'Odsfish!' ejaculated the King. 'I had clean forgotten about you!'

Three

Fantastic Fancies fondly move;
And in frail Joys believe;
Taking false pleasure for true love;
But Pain can ne'er deceive.

Kind Jealous Doubts, tormenting Fears,
And Anxious Cares, when past,
Prove our Hearts Treasure fixt and dear,
And make us blest at last.

—My Lord of Rochester

She stood up and a spaniel slid off her lap with a grunt of protest. Then she dropped a curtsey. 'Sire.' As she looked up from her obeisance she saw that his eyes glittered and he swayed a little as he stood. She knew the signs well.

' 'Faith, my dear, no 'Majesties' here, I beg of you.' Charles strolled easily across the chamber and poured himself a glass of Elstertune Rhenish. 'I fear you have had a sorry time a'waiting. Affairs of state, I assure you, and nothing less must have taken my mind from you.'

'Indeed?'

If the voice was sarcastic, the King did not appear to notice. He drank the glass at a gulp and immediately poured another. 'If you would care to make ready, my pretty, all is prepared.' He gestured to the bed, whose coverlet was turned back, blood-red satin sheets exposed. Jerkily he raised his hand and the wine slopped over the rim to stain the carpet.

'I am a King's Servant. I am at your service, Sire, and my *body* is yours to command.'

'Eh?' This time Charles had noticed the tone of her voice. It was icy and cold, hardly that of invitation. He turned and found himself being regarded by the direct stare of two hazel eyes bent haughtily upon him from under straight dark brows.

Charles was bewildered. The ladies Chiffinch brought him did not usually behave in this way. Most of them were overcome at the honour done them and he had the agreeable task of teasing away their shyness. Others were frankly eager and doubly exciting. He was not used to ladies who stood rigidly in the center of his bedchamber and raked him with scornful eyes, seemingly unimpressed by his regal state. The fogs of the evening seemed all at once to press upon his brow and the second glass of wine went the way of the first.

'Odsfish,' murmured the King. Suddenly he had a thought to explain this strange reluctance. 'Under whose protection are you living, m'dear? I dare swear you worry at my lord catching his bed empty tonight and yourself with a black eye on the morrow. You have no need to worry, I assure—you may pass from one man to another as easy as balancing on kerbstones.'

Her eyes flashed at that. 'You mistake, Sire. I am free as any woman in London. You have purchased me at the whore market of the Lane, as you are aware.'

'Pardon, mistress?'

'London offers the whole range to choose from, as you must know, Sire. There are the whores of the Fleet ditch or Dog and Bitch Yard for the vulgar; the wine shops of Moorfields for the merchants and the salons of Whetstone Park for the enjoyment of gentlemen. You may take Betty Buley's hospitality or Mistress Moseley's—a madam-whore or a drab.' She put the glass down. ' 'Twill depend only on the size of your pocket. Those you choose cannot complain—after all, they are paid for what they do. What feelings can they have? 'Oons, 'tis not as if they are *human*. They come from the gutters like the rats in the city and are worth no more.'

'I did not ask for a whore, my child. I merely requested the company of a lady.'

Nell's eyes wandered significantly to the bed and then back again. 'Whores are ladies, Sire, though perchance they are usually more beautiful.'

Charles blinked. The tenor of this message was not lost upon him. He put his hand in the pocket of his robe, and drawing out a snuffbox, took a sniff, inhaling gently. 'I take it someone has offended you, my dear. Who? A saucy page, haply —tell me his name and he shall suffer for his impudence.' He dug in his other pocket and brought out a flat packet and opened it. Lying on a bed of crimson satin a bracelet of diamonds winked in translucent light. Charles picked it up and dangled it before her. 'A peace offering,' he said.

She shook her head. 'No.' she said quietly.

'Odsfish, my dear, let's not have a melodrama,' he begged with a touch of exasperation. 'Let's mend our differences in bed.'

'With you in the state you're in, there's not much point, is there?' She pointedly eyed the wine stain on the carpet. 'I doubt you could raise much interest tonight.' Charles looked at her in amazement. 'Aye, I know. They call you Old Rowley, after that goat in the park, don't they? Still, I doubt if even he ever quaffs a cow's whiskin to equal what you've just had.'

'I may have imbibed a little too strong . . .' said Charles faintly.

'You're pissed as a newt,' came the firm reply.

He regarded her with interest. A refreshing quality of honesty not often found in those around him, he thought. However, he did not change his opinion of her: the actresses of the King's House were used to dealing with a crowd of men in the pit at Drury Lane and even more pressing attentions in the tiring room behind the stage. Charles decided to solve the impasse in the usual way. 'I have it in my mind to soothe away your temper, my pretty, like—*this*.' He put out a hand and grabbed her.

With a shock of dismay she felt herself drawn into his embrace with an iron grip. A ruthless hand took her chin and forced it up. She saw his face, swarthy and sardonic above the dark slash of moustache. His mouth came down hungrily on hers, so tight the hold he had on her that she felt she would be bruised by his fingers. Her lips met his in a detached cool way, unresponsive as a statue.

Abruptly he put her from him. She began to speak, but he interrupted harshly. 'I won't be made a fool of, mistress.'

Sharp as a sting, back came her reply: 'I rather think you have just made a fool of yourself.' Impassively, her arms still at her sides, the girl stood motionless. The look in her eyes startled him. He stood back, and as he watched, tears ran silently down each cheek. But her voice spat with passion. 'You scurvy fleak! You think just because you're the King you can buy me with tawdries, don't you? Go and buy a whore with your money, but you'll not buy *me*. I care not if you be a king or the cham of bloody Tartary . . .' Her eyes slid over him. 'You know where you can put your crown, orb and sceptre—*Sire*!' She dragged at the lacing on her bodice. 'I do not need your jewels; I already have one. Look—' She drew out a glittering pendant of precious stones that winked and flashed in the candlelight.

He took it and traced the legend that ran around the rim engraved with diamonds: *Charles Rex*.

'You gave it to a previous lady as a gift of favour, and as a gift of favour it came to me. My ownership came via a successful mission at Shoreditch turnpike: a present from the underworld of London, a gift from the gutter, you might say.'

Charles shook his head in wonderment. 'Ods my life. It seems that we have something in common at least. Poor Barbara . . .'

She rounded on him. 'We have nothing in common! You were born in a palace, petted, crooned over and lulled to sleep on down pillows. I was born in the gutter and brought up in a bawdy house, with rufflers, Abram men and clapper-dogeons. The only lullaby I ever heard was Mam spewing 'er guts up when she came home from the Leathern Bottle. Life's cheap where I come from. If the sweating sickness don't get you in the summer, then the toppin' cove will come autumn.'

'Toppin . . .?'

'The hangman.' She bent and picked up her cloak, draping it round her shoulders. He caught the last flash of fire from her eyes. 'My sister has lodgings in Paternoster Row. She sells the only thing she has, the only thing she truly owns—her body. That is what brings a man to her chamber at night and money to her purse. And when morning comes she knows that night may not bring him back to her, for he does not bring love with him when he comes. That is left at the door. She ended in Newgate for debt when her man deserted her. She sold her body to a fine noble gentleman and it fetched the price of her release. What do you understand of that, *Sire*?'

All at once the fire died out of her eyes and she seemed to shrink before him. 'I'm sorry. I—I—shouldn't have come. Pray excuse . . .' Desperately she caught at her lip, but it was no use. Before Charles's astonished gaze, she sank into a faint at his feet.

Shortly afterwards Nell came to her senses but with head swimming, to find the King forcing down her throat a fiery liquid which set her coughing and spluttering as he cushioned her firmly against his shoulder on the bed. With the return of senses came also the return of memory. She struggled to rise, murmuring, 'I . . . must go. Pray excuse me, Sire. I . . .'

'You will do no such thing, Mistress Gwynne. I shall, however, place you between the royal sheets with the hasty reassurance that my royal carcase will remain outside it. Come, my dear.'

Gently he took off her shoes and slid her into bed, drawing the coverlet over her. Then he went across the bedchamber and came back to her, bearing a plate and a glass of Rhenish. 'Drink this, my child, and take some neat's tongue. Haply you will feel better anon. Yes—*down*, Susie . . .' this to the spaniel, who with shrill yelps endeavoured to grab at the King's coat.

Nell sat up in bed and slowly sipped at the wine. 'I fear I lost my temper, Sire.'

Charles sat down on the edge of the bed. 'I fear you did, Mistress Gwynne—perchance with some reason. I swear, at one point I thought you might commit high treason.'

'Sire?' She looked puzzled.

'Clout me one, my dear. It still remains treason to lay hands on my sacred person.'

Despite herself, Nell giggled slightly and choked as the wine went down the wrong way.

'That's better,' said the King encouragingly.

'I fear me I should never have come, Sire . . .' she faltered.

' 'Oons, you had no choice. I sent you a royal command, did I not, and a royal command has to be obeyed. As you said, you are a King's Servant and have to obey my every whim.' His dark eyes twinkled.

'I said a lot more besides.'

'Yes, I do not wonder that you are an actress, Mistress Gwynne. I swear, you put the fear of God into me.'

She smiled tremulously, her tumbled hair pushed back from a high pale brow. Watching her, Charles felt curiously touched at her smallness of size and her vulnerability as she lay still against the satin pillows, nibbling at a neat's tongue. He remembered her stream of accusations and a cynical smile lit up his dark visage as he watched the flickering flames.

'I fear you wronged me in some degree, Mistress Gwynne. I am not quite the pampered lapdog you think me and I have not led a lapdog's life. You spent your childhood in a bawdy house; I spent mine on the battlefield. Unlike you, I knew my father—but they cut his head off in front of an ogling crowd of people despite all that I could do. We lost our kingdom, our title, our wealth—everything—before I was nineteen.' There was a hiss as a log suddenly caught fire, and a flame leapt upwards, casting dancing shadows across the room.

'When I was twenty-one I was up to my waist in icy water on the Welsh border, hiding from Noll Cromwell's troopers. I spent ten years wandering around Europe, with scarce a welcome wherever I went, but polite demands that I leave the country to relieve 'em of the embarrassment of harbouring me. Your sister was in prison; so was my brother and sister, and now they're both dead of the smallpox. I never see my other sister, as reasons of state married her to a malignant little snake of a Frenchman who won't let her out of his sight, though he has more use for painted boys than for her. Look behind the glitter of the Crown, my dear, and see the truth.'

'I implore you to forget what I said, Sire. Please,' she begged him.

'Odsfish, my dear, there's no need to sound like a Puritan beldame. You're not a Puritan, I suppose?'

She shook her head.

'Thank the Lord for that!'

She found his eyes fixed on her and blushed a little under his scrutiny.

Charles looked puzzled. 'Tell me, child, how comes it you speak so well—you who tell me you come from the gutter?'

'For that you must praise Master Killigrew, Major Mohun and Master Lacy, Sire. They have taught me the ways of a lady. I may not speak Master Dryden's lines like a parrot, or 'twould be apparent.'

'I might also praise your own native wit,' added the King.

She blushed and turned from him, fiddling with the hem of the coverlet. 'Aye, you might.'

Charles smiled a little but said nothing. He got up and went over to the fire, holding his hands out to the warmth. 'I fear me we have more in common than I even at first realised. Both of us live on the same public stage; both of us hear the same adulation; both of us know the total hypocrisy of what we hear.'

'Not always, Sire.'

'Oh, come, Mistress Gwynne.' The King turned and surveyed her ironically. 'You have told me yourself that London sells women like so many cattle.'

'That is so, Sire,' she agreed. 'But the cattle may still have feelings and not all who come to buy are flesh flies.'

'I am relieved to hear it,' he said politely.

'Oh no, Sire!' Her voice was clear and firm. 'I have known

much kindness in my life, Sire, from that same bawdy house, and even love.'

'*Love?*' said Charles. 'A much used and little understood word, my dear. 'Tis an exhilaration reserved only for transient youth.'

'Why become old and bitter before you must?' countered Nell.

He shook his head slowly, and she saw the lines, deep-scored as by a sculptor, running from nose to mouth. 'No, child, we do not become bitter. Life makes us so.'

'No, Sire,' she said earnestly. 'You but deny the love in yourself. Each of us carries love within us. It is like water, it must find somewhere to go. It cannot be dammed up forever. You know that you are needed, you are loved—and it is enough.'

'If it can be found,' agreed Charles. 'But then, life hardly ever does give you what you want, does it?'

'If you really wish for something, then it will be yours—if you're prepared to fight for it.'

He leant against the mantle with one arm spread out along its length. 'I wonder,' he said. 'Perhaps that is merely the fond diddly of human kind. I believe if you expect nothing from people, then you are never disappointed.'

She shrugged. 'And never very exhilarated either. Would you have people angels, Sire?'

He was silent for a moment. Then he added, 'I find I love only until I possess. But once I possess, I grow indifferent.'

She lay on one elbow, watching him. 'I would say, Charles,' she said softly, 'that you do not love at all.'

'How can you make yourself love someone, my dear? Tell me that. A trick of necromancy.'

She put out one hand to feed a tit-bit to the spaniel, who snuffled a wet nose between her fingers. 'Faith, I know not. 'Tis not something you want, it just happens to you, and when it does, you stop caring about anything else. Some people might say you should stay in control and not let yourself be carried away. Some people might say it was folly. But when it does happen, you know you've never been alive until that moment.'

Charles made a hopeless gesture with one hand. 'Why coax your heart to life, to have it ripped from you and leave you wounded to the soul?'

'Anything worth having has a high price. If life is cruel, it needs a little loving along the way. Ods my life—' She broke off. 'I swear, I run on like a rattlepate, Sire. I doubt you need my strictures. What can I teach the King?'

'You mistake, Mistress Gwynne,' said Charles quietly. 'Haply you have taught him a great deal. Tell me, however, does it not destroy you, this love?'

She shook her head. 'Never.'

'My father would have agreed with you,' he said, nodding. 'He held that a man endured like the head of a pike—the truer the metal, the hotter the firing.' He poked at the fire with his foot, so that a log sent a flight of sparks up the chimney. 'I doubt not some of us seek to escape the heat.'

There was a strange discordant sound in the distance as several clocks of various timbre gave out the information that it was three o'clock in the morning. She looked surprised. Charles smiled at her. 'Merely the clocks in my Closet, my dear. I have a number and they make a racket.'

Nell slid out of the bed and picked up her cloak. 'I must go, Sire.'

Charles came forward and draped her cloak around her shoulders. 'I fear you take with you a ruined reputation, child. You have spent half a night in the King's bedchamber. 'Tis something the gutter is not like to miss.'

She turned, and he saw her eyes twinkling mischievously. 'I am an actress of the Theatre Royal, Sire. I have no reputation to lose.'

The King looked searchingly over her as she stood before him, and his hands rested lightly on her shoulders. 'I think you are a very remarkable woman, Mistress Gwynne.' He strode over and gave a tug to the rope which hung by the bed. 'Chiffinch will see you home safe,' he said.

'I do not doubt it, Sire. I warrant he has done it times enough.'

Charles chuckled. 'Never with such a redoubtable lady, I'll swear to that.' He came back towards her and took her hands in his. 'I sent for you this evening, Mistress Gwynne, and I fear me you have deemed yourself insulted.' She began to vehemently protest, but he continued calmly, 'What say you we strike a bargain, you and I? We will pretend this evening never happened and I will see you once more only when *you* wish to come to *me*. You have my word that you will not be importuned again. I want you to know meanwhile that this provant rogue of a king will ever be ready to render you service should you need it.' Nell felt his warm clasp on her fingers. 'You may never come to me, but if you do, you must know that my—ah—interest will be unchanged.'

She nodded and smiled shyly. He bowed very low over her hand and kissed it as punctiliously as if she had been a lady at his Court. Then he straightened, and she saw a laugh deep in his black eyes and a slight smile crinkling his lips, as though to show her he could still command some dignity. Formally he conducted her to the door of the bedchamber and held it open. 'Until we meet again, Mistress Gwynne.'

The first pink streaks of dawn had begun to touch the house-tops when Nell wearily lifted the latch of her lodgings at the Cock and Pye tavern. No one was abroad yet and the closed door of the tiny room on the right told Nell that Mit, her maid, was still abed and asleep. She took off her cloak and hung it on a hook. A voice said, ' 'Tis now gone midnight, Nelly, and I still lack an answer.'

She whirled round in dismay. Charles Hart got to his feet from the settle in the corner. 'I must have a more tenacious nature than I knew. Eight hours waiting and you off to Whitehall Palace. No, don't worry. Mit told me, and I can be plaguey discreet if need be. Tell me, have I the honour of addressing the King's whore?'

'You have not. We spent the time talking.' She moved over to the mirror on the wall, and taking a brush, began to tease out the tangles in her hair.

Hart chuckled. 'God's death, Nell. You don't seriously mean to tell me you have been in the King's bedchamber at Whitehall till this hour and expect me to believe you spent the time *talking*!'

She shrugged and answered him briskly. 'His Majesty is a gentleman. The night was hot and I was took faint. He was very kind to me and . . . well . . . yes, he was very kind.'

'So you now trade under the Crown, do you?' whispered Hart as he took the hand that clutched the brush and held it fast. 'When do you go again to see the Black Boy in his lair?'

She dragged her hand away. 'I do not go again—ever.'

Hart's brows rose in surprise. 'I have never thought myself a fool, but I fail to see why, if he was kind, you should not wish to see him again.' A blush rose to her cheeks, but if Hart saw it, he affected not to notice. 'I might merely conclude,' he added gently, 'that this news arouses hopes so manifestly dashed by Mit's information a few hours before.' He drew her back to him and dropped a kiss on her forehead. She trembled a little in his arms. 'You would have done better to have come to Spring Gardens with me, Nell,' he murmured.

'I told the King I was a free woman—not one to be bought or sold,' she said unsteadily.

'God's death, I don't want to buy you. I've never bought a woman's favour yet and I don't intend to start now! You will remain free just so long'—his hands crept round to cup her breasts—'as you wish to be free.'

She jerked her head away from his lips. 'I do not love you, Charles.'

'Ods my life, my dear. Shall that stop you? One of us may have love and enough to spare. I will not deceive you, Nell. I an an indifferent and prodigal sinner. I have lain with a variety of beautiful women and I have enjoyed them all. I may love more tomorrow—but now, tonight, I love you, I want *you*, Nell.'

She sat still, gazing unseeing into the mirror.

'Love is a powerful pleader, Nelly, and my love, my life and my fortune lie at your feet.' As he spoke he pressed hot kisses into the exposed hollow of her neck where a little pulse beat dizzily. 'Are you so cold, my dear? I wonder . . .' She saw his dark handsome face above hers in the mirror. Charles Hart smiled. 'One has to take what one wants in life, Nelly, and not be afraid to do it. Can we not love and enjoy each other and banish care for a while?' His hands moved away.

She felt hot breath on her shoulders. All at once there was a ripping noise and she gave a little cry as buttons dropped onto the floorboards. His hands slid over her skin and down to fondle her naked breasts. 'You forget what life has to offer, sweetheart. I would rather bed you willing—but, willing or no, I am going to bed you tonight, Nelly Gwynne.' His grip tightened.

She quivered a little at his touch but did not struggle, and then he lifted her to her feet and her dress crept rustling to her knees. He drew her over to the bed, and as if in a dream, she felt him lay her on it and his touch was hot under the lacing of her shift. She was quite motionless, staring up at him, offering no resistance, making not a sound. The last thing she saw was his eyes—blue, intense and almost hypnotic—looming over her as his mouth closed over hers. It seemed as though a wave of warmth flooded through her body—her whole being stirred as though awaking from a deep sleep. The warmth spread tingling to every part of her as she was swept away. She felt him inside her, potent, bruising, demanding, pushing her to the brink of consciousness.

Suddenly, to her own surprise, she felt her arms cling around his shoulders, and a little moan escaped her. She never knew afterwards if it was one of fear or of joy.

Four

*This day, much against my will,
I did in Drury Lane see two or three houses
marked with a red cross upon the doors,
and 'Lord have mercy upon us' writ there;
which was a sad sight to me ...*

—*The Diary of Samuel Pepys
June 7th, 1665*

As spring merged into summer London endured a lengthening strain of close weather. May passed into June and the city sweltered under a succession of hot days that left the twisting streets stifling and airless and the people parched. In the scorching temperature the houses steamed gently like pies in a cookshop.

The supply of fresh water in the conduits ran to a trickle and many unfortunates were reduced to a cupful of tepid, brackish water each day unless they braved the penny buckets of the Thames water-cobs. With the baking heat, the stench from the garbage in the alleys reached a new height and citizens could be seen clutching kerchiefs or stuffed onions to their faces as they hurried by, dust blowing under the hot feet which tramped the cobbles. So enervating did Londoners find life that they could barely find interest in the scandalous behaviour of my Lord of Rochester, but a year at Court, who held up the coach of the beautiful and wealthy Mistress Mallett to make off with her. He achieved his goal, only to be pursued by the King's justice and apprehended. He too sweltered from the close confines of the Tower, where he was lodged for his passions.

Summer saw the departure of many gentlemen to join the fleet under his Highness of York, which sailed with the Lord Admiral's promise that he would sink the Dutch where they floated. London emptied of gallants as they left to volunteer for war—even gentlemen of the most unlikely sort. My Lord Buckhurst left his gaming and wenching to take up arms; my Lord of Rochester was released from prison to sail in the *Royal Katharine*, and even his Grace of Buckingham roused himself from his customary lethargy to take service aboard *The Prince* when she sailed.

London was amazed, at the end of May, to see the departure of my Lord Fox for the tribulation of war, leaving London with a Berlin heavy-laden with baggage and two valets, with a pomander pressed firmly to one delicate nostril. He said, indeed, that he left the metropolis only because the heat had made life there insupportable, but his determination to face the rigours of a jolting coach journey to the coast could not but arouse admiration in the eyes of those of his acquaintance who saw him go.

For those who were left, the suspense grew. One June morning brought the distant sound of cannon with the wind up-river and citizens stopped, listening, knowing that the fleets must be engaged. But no news came. The exodus of the gentlemen of the Court led to empty spaces in the pit of the Theatre Royal and the loss of trade at the Royal Exchange, while many a Fleet-ditch drab and rogue of Alsatia bemoaned the loss of rich pickings and called down imprecations on the rascally Dutch. Some found the times particularly hard and were driven to seek temporary assistance in Drury Lane.

Prudence Hope-to-be-Saved Brewster, known to all the

world and her mistress Nelly Gwynne as simply Mit—the origins of such a name lost in the mists of time—was beating out a stout broom on the lintel of the Cock and Pye tavern when a poke from a crutch nearly sent her flying. 'My Gawd . . .' she began and turned to see a one-legged beggar looking quizzically at her out of a pair of rheumy blue eyes above a wispy grey beard. 'Oh, it's you,' she said crossly, turning back to her task of hitting the broom against the timbers. Dust flew in clouds. 'I thought you was off on the dommerar run this mornin'. I s'pose you've come round sniffing for a bite of my mutton pie again.'

'Now, Mit,' protested the beggar, 'I ain't no ruffler nor no angler—and I'm a sight too ancient for the kynchen lay an' all!'

To this obscure speech Mit merely sniffed. 'I'm sure what you do is none o' my concern, Hobey,' she said. 'P'raps you ain't on no priggin' lay. But you gets our Nelly a bad name 'anging abaht 'ere all day long, as you well knows. Looks like you might be a fencing cully and she your lady-mort choose 'ow. We don't get quire birds in Drury Lane. This ain't the like o' Seven Dials, you know. We're more used to seein' my Lord Buckhurst or Sir Charles Sedley or my Lord of Craven being carried home than a rum mort like you.'

'You button your lip, my girl,' retorted Hobey. 'Nell ain't gone all satin drawers on me, nor is like to. I've known 'er since she was 'alf the size o' that broom and she don't forget it. She's not the sort, bless 'er 'eart. You ain't got cause for the nifties either,' he said roundly. 'You've changed since Nelly took you from scouring the pans at Ma Ross's bawdy house in Lewkenor's Lane, and no mistake. Nor I ain't no ruffler neither. I lost my prop on an h'expedition to La Rochelle wiv 'is Grace o' Buckingham's dad—and 'e weren't too top-lofty to take me. Not my fault I've come down a trifle.'

'Oh, come and sink your chops in a pasty,' interrupted Mit, raising her eyes to the heavens. 'I should have known better than to argue, you old bellows pipe.'

He caught the look in her eye and grinned. 'Oh, you're horl right, my dear. Jest a bit vinegary in the mornin's, I make no doubt. You lead me to your pasty, see. That's something I *won't* argue about.'

She tutted at him but led him through the taproom and up the stairs. As she went up the steps before him a neat thwack of the crutch caught her on the rear and she screamed.

'Gawd, what I wouldn't do if I 'ad *two* legs,' said Hobey with relish. Mit ushered him in. Hobey shook his head at the cosy chamber with its green serge hangings on the walls and gilded leather-backed chairs. 'Ho, it's all quince pies and banberie cakes 'ere an' no mistake, ain't it!'

'The 'angings are new-come from the Exchange,' Mit informed him proudly. Sitting him down at a table with a huge hunk of pie before him and a tankard of small ale at his elbow, she watched the beggar compensate for a day and a half without food. Only after a good twenty minutes did he lean back with a sigh and begin to pick his teeth with one black fingernail. 'Sure you wouldn't like a gnaw at the table now?' asked Mit sarcastically.

The beggar winked at her. 'Where's Nelly?' he demanded.

'Gorn wiv Rose to see 'er mother,' answered Mit. 'Seems she got the jerks when the 'ole family next door to 'er in Bell Alley took the sickness. She says all on 'em 'ave been shut up in the 'ouse for forty days till the danger of infection's over. 'Tis the new order o' the Lord Mayor hisself.'

'They'll all be dead as nails afore the forty days is up,' said Hobey gloomily.

'Aye—well, 'tis the only way, ain't it,' commented Mit uneasily. 'I reckon when Nell moved 'er old dam from that flea-pit in the Coalyard to Bell Alley she thought she was doing 'er a good turn. It's only a short step from Whitehall, you know. Sir Thomas Ogle lives next door on the other side. But there's no telling when the plague takes root, it strikes anywhere it pleases.'

' 'Ow is Nell's old mother?' enquired the beggar. 'I ain't seen her for a twelvemonth or more. Is she still 'itting the gin like she did, the old bawd?'

Mit grinned. 'Not now she ain't. Nell wanted to stop 'er guzzling, so she went and lodged 'er with a family of Quakers.'

'Quakers?'

'Aye, she moved 'er out of the Coalyard and told 'er she could 'ave a bit o' money for 'er keep and enough for a tipple jest so long as she stayed wiv this family, the Fletchers. S'life, Hobey—talk about laugh! The pore old crone 'as to be in the 'ouse afore midnight and upright as a judge. Mistress Fletcher's kind enough but she's as big as a barn door and she keeps old Madam Gwynne on the rightabout. 'Ere, I 'ope *they're* all right.'

'You know what they say about the plague—first off, one dead; last off, all dead,' mused Hobey. 'I don't remember it starting so early since '37, and *that* was a year and no mistake. You mark my words, Mit, you ain't seen nothing yet.'

'Leave off, Hobey,' said Mit pettishly, touching the haresfoot hanging from a riband round her neck. 'We've got enough with the war an' all without the black spot to add to it.' She paused by the open casement in the overhanging first storey which leaned out over the street. In the lull of noise from below came again the sounds of distant booming wafted up from the river like far-off thunder. 'Nelly says Rose ought to take 'er mother off to Chelsea village while the sickness lasts. Chelsea should be safe; it's way and far off.'

'Not much for Rose to do out there, is there?' jeered Hobey. 'She needs men and plenty of 'em. I wonder *she* didn't volunteer to go to sea. Marry and I do.'

'I reckon Rose likes 'er freedom,' countered Mit. 'Since 'er rotten pricklouse 'usband ran orf, she's not stuck wiv anybody for more'n a month. She's got money enough, Lord knows.' She moved over to make the bed.

'More than 'er sister,' agreed Hobey. 'But it's *Nelly* what keeps 'er old mother. Always been the same—tight as a Puritan's purse that girl Rose is. I s'pose Master Hart went with 'em both.' He eyed the bed.

'Ole puff-paste!' said Mit disgustedly, plumping pillows with a forceful hand. 'Full o' wind and bounce *'e* is! Finelooking, I grant you, but 'e's as vain as my Lady Castlemaine. You should 'ear 'im carrying on—"I fear me we shall have a belated h'arrival, my dear, if we do not remove upon this h'instant." La!' She shrugged. ' 'Tis enough to make you as drowsy as prayers when 'e starts. I don't know what Nell sees in 'im. I make no doubt he's kind enough to her—anyone can see he's mad as fire for 'er. But 'e don't care about 'er more'n a flea's arse. The only person 'e cares about is 'imself. It's "I want this" and "I want that." Gawd! You'd think 'e was still on the stage! He's a rogue in the bud and no one'll tell me different! It must be like lying with a peacock in bed. I'd ruffle 'is feathers with a dousing from my pisspot if I 'ad my way!'

'You know what, Mit—' Hobey interrupted her. 'I reckon the Duke of York might win this war yet.'

She looked at him suspiciously. 'If he sent *you* to fight the butterboxes, I dare swear they'd sue for peace within a week...'

Nell clasped the ample form of her mother in a fond embrace and heard a clink of glass as a heavy weight hit her knee. 'Ma, you promised,' she said accusingly.

Mrs. Gwynne looked at her daughter sidelong from beneath a bird's-eye hood and grimaced. ' 'Tis only for the journey,' she argued. 'A little o' sommat to keep the cold out.'

'In *this* weather?' retorted Nell, ruthlessly plucking two gin bottles from a capacious hidden pocket in her mother's cloak. 'Shame on you, Ma!'

Beneath the gateway of the Bell Inn at the Maypole in the Strand three figures stood waiting for the coach to leave. Mrs. Gwynne cast a wistful look at the taproom as they waited in the courtyard. 'Just time for a quick snifter before Rosie and me goes off?' she asked hopefully. 'What about it, Charley boy?'

Charles Hart very properly ignored this appeal, staring into the middle distance and tapping his cane on one elegant boot. But a tall raven-haired lady, clad most becomingly in flowered ash silk with a huge feather-brimmed hat, turned and frowned at her mother. 'Pox take it, Ma, don't you ever give up? I warn you, if you're going to carry on like this all the way to Chelsea, I'll *force* two bottles down you to make you sleep!'

Mrs. Gwynne's eyes brightened. The prospect did not seem to daunt her. Rose Gwynne cast her a withering look. She was a most beautiful girl, with huge dark eyes set in a delicate heart-shaped face. Only a somewhat tight look around the mouth gave an indication that such beauty might be flawed. Now she dabbed delicately at her nose with a kerchief soaked in Hungary water.

'Pho,' she complained. 'The stink in this courtyard is enough to make one retch, I swear.' The words were pronounced with a deliberate care. 'If this heat continues, I shall be fairly broiled before I come to Chelsea.'

'Better broiled than dead, ma'am, I might suggest,' urged Hart.

'Oh, nonsense!' tinkled Rose. 'You surely don't believe that the sickness will last, do you? I am told there are always odd outbreaks at this time of year. I am merely taking my departure because I have promised myself a holiday this month past. London is so overpowering at this time of year, do you not think?'

Charles Hart nodded politely and beckoned over a potboy carrying a tray of foaming ale. As he drank it down, the coachman appeared, wiping his mouth on his sleeve.

Nell dropped a small purse into her mother's fat hand. 'And *don't* spend it on ruin, Ma,' she whispered.

As the potboy turned to go he tripped and sent a stream of small ale over the delicate silk of Rose Gwynne's dress. For a second she stared open-mouthed and speechless at the dark spreading stain on the material. Then she went for the potboy, eyes blazing. 'You lump of steaming cow's dung!' she stormed. 'Look what you've done! I paid a ten guinea for this at Unthanke's but two days past! It's ruined! You lousy misbegotten spawn of a black-souled bawd!'

Charles Hart raised his brows in faint hauteur. Several interested eyes turned on Rose. 'Are any o' you for St. James's, Tothill Fields or Chelsea village?' enquired the coachman placidly. 'Aye,' said Nell hurriedly. 'Get *in*, Rose.' She pushed her mother and sister into the coach while the potboy, a pimply-faced youth, stood looking open-mouthed. Rose leant from the window to deliver her final thrust. 'Pox take you, you weak-chinned whoreson!' The coach drew off with a jerk and she was lost to view, still mouthing obscenities.

Nell watched her go and clung to Charles Hart, shaking with laughter. 'I told you,' she gasped. 'When you took up with me you took up with Quality, Charles!' He looked pained, but his expression softened and he kissed her.

Ten minutes later both of them were seated in a hackney which endeavoured to make its way through the thrusting, complaining press of traffic down the Strand to Drury Lane. The overwhelming noise, the rattle of the coach over the cobbles and the deadening heat which the lowered window failed to alleviate drew a weary complaint from Hart. 'God's death, Nelly, I wonder we stay in this city—'tis like an oven!'

'As long as the Theatre Royal remains open, we have no option. We are members of the King's House and the theatre is still open to the public.'

A shouted altercation between two chairmen and a coal waggoner who had deposited half his load in the way of the traffic drowned her voice. Eyes alight with mirth, she stuck her head out just in time to see a grey-flecked grizzled head emerge from the lowered chair. 'Master Duncan!' she said in pleased surprise. He looked up and waved and came up to their coach, puffing slightly. 'Is it you, Nelly?' he queried, mopping his brow. 'Och, 'tis real cookshop weather we're having. I sweat like a cheese. Oh, I give you good day, Master Hart.' Charles Hart inclined his head coolly.

'Come and join us,' invited Nell. 'We're off to the Lane. Haply we could drop you somewhere.'

'I am on my way to Westminster Stairs, hinnie. Aye, 'tis no weather for walking. I have n'ae the stamina for this at a'.' Grunting, he heaved himself into the coach and sat wheezing stertorously. 'Ah, 'tis nothing less than purgatory in this heat,' he repeated. 'I wonder to see you remaining in the city at all, especially with the reports of the sickness spreading.'

'Mistress Gwynne has just reminded me,' said Charles Hart. 'We have our duties as members of Killigrew's company. All must needs stay so long as the theatre remains open.'

Duncan loosened the linen band at his throat. 'Tom Killigrew might not be able to keep his theatre open much longer,' he told them. 'My Lord Mayor is frightened at the spread of the sickness. He has prepared plans to combat the pestilence. Men are being hired to kill all the dogs and cats they can find at twopence a head—'tis said they spread the disease. And that is not all. The City Council plan to close all theatres and prohibit public gatherings to stop the danger of infection. They're setting up pest houses in Southwark for the sick a'ready.'

'Charnel houses, more like,' grunted Hart.

'Aye. The puir souls,' nodded Duncan. 'I dinna like to see *you* still here, Nell. Can you no' go?'

She shook her head, smiling.

'Well, promise me you'll go as soon as the theatre is closed. Promise,' he urged.

'I promise,' she told him. 'Both Charles and I will be out of this city as quickly as a Puritan in a theatre!'

Duncan grinned. 'I have it in mind to go mysel',' he went on. 'So I've hired a private coach to take me when I want to get out o' the city. I have it in my mind to take the sea air. Have you ever been to Brighthelmstone, Master Hart?'

'No.'

'It's a gae huge coach I have ordered. What say you to joining me down by the sea for a spell? It's a deal healthier than London, I promise you.'

'But you must want to go now, surely,' protested Nell. 'You won't want to wait for our convenience. The theatre might not shut for ages. Master Killigrew will not close until he is forced.'

'Oh, as to that'—Duncan shrugged—'it doesn'a matter either way. I still have business to finish, and I can go at any time.'

She leant forward and laid her hand on his. 'I thank you for your offer. We should be glad to go with you, Rob. Wouldn't we, Charles?'

'Yes, indeed,' said Charles Hart politely.

'Whenever you want the coach, you just send word to me at my lodgings in King Street and I will order it within the hour.

If you both come to the Bell posting inn at the Maypole, I can whisk us all off to Brighthelmstone within three days—'tis a fast coach and six, you understand.'

'That is monstrous kind, Rob. How can we thank you?' asked Nell.

'Nay,' grunted Duncan. 'That is just foolishness. I was going to Brighthelmstone anyway. A coach and six can take one old man like me and leave ample room to spare.'

'Aye,' she murmured. 'In that case, one wonders why you ordered one, sir.'

Duncan grinned. 'I dinna like to think what the city is going to face in the next few months. Trade is bad because o' the war; the sickness drops a shadow over all of us. But there's a worse thing yet.'

'What?' asked Nell, alarmed.

'When my Lord Mayor closes the Theatre Royal, London will be without Nelly Gwynne at Drury Lane. I daurna think of the effect on the city.'

Nell burst out laughing and dug him in the ribs. 'You're a gae flatterer, Master Duncan.'

A few moments later the coach left Duncan at Charing Cross and continued up to Bridges Street and the entrance to the Theatre Royal. As it rolled around the corner, Nell watched Hart's profile. 'What's amiss, Charles? Do you not wish to go to Brighthelmstone?'

Hart slewed around to face her. 'I mislike yonder fellow's meddling!' he said furiously. 'He thinks because his pockets clink with gold, he owns the Theatre Royal and all who serve in the company.'

'Why did you not refuse him, then?' asked Nell.

'Oh, use your wits, Nell! If I said aught against Master Duncan—Master Moneybags—I should lose more than a coach trip. I should lose my livelihood, I make no doubt!'

'No, Charles!' exclaimed Nell. 'You wrong him—indeed you do! He but seeks to help.'

'To help who?' retorted Hart. 'Not me, I'll warrant. Master Duncan has a wish only to help you, and I know why!' He sneered. 'Such a chivalrous Scots gentleman it is. He puts one in mind of a melodrama or a play. Such a smooth, plausible manner. Quite like Macbeth—do you not think, my child?'

'No, I do not, and I think you are—'

'What? What do you think I am?' Hart was shouting by now, his hands clenched and his eyes burning with anger.

'I think,' said Nell quietly, 'that you are utterly wrong, Charles.'

The succession of days of airless heat found the company at the King's House increasingly depressed and quarrelsome. Playing to half-full houses, with people sitting as far apart from their neighbours as they could, holding stuffed cloves or onions to their faces—'like a row of turnip tops,' as Beck Marshall commented morosely—did not make for happy relations in the company. Whispers of Nell's billet from the King had led to excited speculation in the Women's Shift and eager expectation from Master Killigrew for increased royal patronage in the future. Neither hope was to be fulfilled.

The Court removed itself to the Palace of Hampton Court and his Majesty came no more to grace the theatre with his presence. Takings fell and Orange Moll was driven to hawking roll-tobacco in the streets to eke out a dwindling income.

The company was aggrieved. 'We *are* the King's Servants, are we not?' complained Ann Marshall, Beck's sister. 'Surely we may depend upon his protection and his attention!'

'*Some* receive more attention than others,' observed Bab Knipp drily. 'For most, to be one of the King's Servants means naught but your wages in arrears with the rest of his Majesty's creditors.'

'But for others . . .' prompted Edward Kynaston, seating himself on the apron stage.

'A demand for services most singular,' Bab answered demurely.

Beck Marshall spoke bitterly. ' 'Tis certain Nell has not brought that demand—small surprise, with 'er finicky ways and 'er drab's figure. I warrant when 'is Majesty got 'er clothes off 'e took ill of the megrims. *That's* why 'e's gone to 'Ampton Court and left us empty as a drum!'

'She was invited to supper by the King—and went!' countered Edward Kynaston.

'Aye,' sneered Berk, her thin, sharp little face looking contemptuous. 'But since that day—that night—she goes no more to Whitehall and his Majesty comes no more to the King's House.'

Bab Knipp rested one leg on her knee and unbuckled her shoe. 'Haply Nelly found his Majesty lacking?' she ventured mildly.

There was a stunned silence.

'*She* found . . . ?' murmured Ann Marshall incredulously. 'Have you just dropped from the womb at midnight, Mrs. Knipp? Do you mean to suggest that Nelly Gwynne refused the *King*! As well ask me to believe 'is Majesty's become a Presbyter! His Majesty . . . *lacking*? My Lord! Rather the other way about, *I* should say.'

Bab Knipp shrugged. 'Well, if she's been laid or no, she keeps her counsel. 'Tis evident if she has lost one *heart*, she has gained another.'

Edward Kynaston grinned. 'Aye—to the exclusion of the rest of us. I swear, if anyone turns so much as an eyelash on Mrs. Gwynne, he can expect a dagger in his ribs that same night on his way home. I hardly dare poke my nose in the Women's Shift any more. Master Hart has a jealous nature withal.'

'Damned top-lofty if you ask me,' sniffed Beck Marshall. 'Looks at you like you was a worm or a flea. They say he has a rival in Master Duncan. There's more sap in *that* old turn-me-over than you'd think. They say he goes up to Moorfields every week for a quick dabble or two.'

'*They* say a great deal,' interrupted Bab Knipp. 'Master Duncan's a gentleman—and 'e's old enough to be Nelly's grandfather.'

'Tell it to Master Hart,' jeered Beck. '*He* might believe you, but I never will. The old ones are the worst, God knows.'

Kynaston coughed nervously. 'That does not solve our problems. Do we know aught more of Nell's visit to the King? Will he return and bring the Court back to London or not? If he comes, does he come to the theatre or not? Haply his absence is simply due to the sickness. 'Tis said it has started earlier than ever before and grows more intense by the day. Gossip hath it that the city is already stricken to the tune of a hundred deaths a week.'

'Ods my life,' said Ann Marshall airily. 'The summer always brings the sickness to London. Wait a week or so and you'll see it disappear. 'Tis the heat—brings the humours out of the ground. They say the only sure way to protect yourself is to take an infusion of entrails in spirits of wine.'

'Entrails?'

'Aye, my grandam swore the only way to avoid the black spot was to take the brains of a murdered man stewed with his backbone, marrow, guts and nerves, digested for six months in spirits of wine.'

'S'life!' exclaimed Bab Knipp, appalled. 'I wonder she thought you'd survive at all! Where in Bedlam did she get a murdered man?'

'I never asked her.'

Beck Marshall looked nervous. 'Major Mohun says if you tell a charm, you'll not catch plague nor the sweating sickness. They say they've avoided pestilence in Paris for more than thirty years with it. 'Tis a jumble o' words: "Voosy un cors mot..."'

' "Voici un corps mort" ' came a cool voice in impeccable French behind her. ' "Royde comme un Baston. Froid comme Marbre. Leger comme un esprit. Levons te au nom de Jesu Christ." No doubt as sure a cure as any, but I beg you ladies not to trust to its infallibility.' Small and slight but invested with a certain dignity, Major Mohun strolled towards them. 'Put it down to night air or the Papists, it makes no odds,' he said lightly. 'Either way, there's no cure.'

'Hen's dung, dried and powdered,' said Mrs. Knipp firmly.

'I beg your pardon.' Major Mohun blinked.

'That's the only sure cure—'tis well known.' She stood up, brushing at her gown.

There was a loud slam of a door to the right of the stage and around the corner of the apron stage strode Charles Hart with a face like thunder. He scowled when he saw the small group sprawled in the pit in front of him and made as if to avoid them. Bab Knipp tripped up to him. 'What is your favourite cure for the plague, Master Hart? Do you know of an effective one?' He looked her up and down witheringly, spat an oath, and then turned on his heel and walked off, pushing one of the benches over as he went. Mrs. Knipp raised her eyebrows and whistled.

' 'Tis the green-eyed monster that doth mock the meat it feeds on,' murmured Major Mohun as he watched the back of Charles Hart depart.

'Eh?' queried Beck Marshall. 'Master Hart has blue eyes, sir.'

'Tut, tut,' said Major Mohun reprovingly, 'and you call yourself an actress, my girl?'

Bab Knipp opened the door that had just slammed, and tiptoeing up the narrow steps that led to the small tiring room behind the stage, found a small figure, head in hands, slumped before a mirror. Bab saw that it was Nell, dressed in a beautiful costume of tawny yellow silk with a half tunic of white gauze embroidered with pearls which seemed to literally float about her fragile limbs. A huge fan of yellow feathers lay forlornly across her knees. She looked up, sniffing valiantly, and visibly relaxed when she saw who it was. 'Thank the Lord it's you, Bab. I don't think I could have stood Lizzie Weaver's eager prying eyes or Beck Marshall's tongue just now.'

Bab Knipp snorted. 'Ods my life—you don't want to take any account of them. Lizzie Weaver's naught but a walking pease-pudding and Beck Marshall 'as as much brain as a plucked chicken. They'd both be better for a dose of ratsbane. What's the matter? You're not taken ill, I hope.'

She shook her head. 'No, no. I'm afraid Charles—Master Hart—has taken offence at . . . this.' She stood up and the light drapery sank into feathery order about her.

'How so?' queried Bab. ' 'Tis a little scanty, but you've trod the boards in worse.'

'No, 'tis not what it looks like. 'Tis who it's from.' She fumbled amidst the bottles on the table and handed Bab a card with neat, firm writing upon it. 'Read that,' commanded Nell.

My Child . . . You once Said that You never had a Father, and I never had a Daughter. It may be that London will shortly be deprived of your Talent for a Season. I should be grateful if you would Accept this from someone who likes to think of himself as in some sense your Father and ensure that London does not Forget you for Many a Year.
        Robert Duncan, Merchant

Bab Knipp shook her head. 'I see no problem here, Nelly. Odsbud, Hart didn't take objection to this, did he?'

Nell nodded mutely. 'I put it on and showed him, but when he found out who it was from he fell into a thund'rous rage and threatened to rip it off my back. He wouldn't listen to me at all. I tried to read him the card but he just brushed it aside and left me. I've never seen aught like it. He ranted and stormed like a man crazed, accusing me of lying with the oldest goat in the field. He *knows* it all to be false! He was in a royal temper, Bab!'

Bab Knipp nodded understandingly. 'Aye, I know. What are you going to do, sweetheart, send it back?'

'God's death, no!' Nell blew her nose fiercely and looked up at Bab with a hard glint in her eye. 'If he thinks I'm going to cast this into the face of an old gentleman to satisfy his vanity, he's out, Bab! Master Duncan's worth more than that. I couldn't do it.'

'Haply you'll hurt Master Hart if you wear it, Nelly.'

'Oh, pho!'

Bab wandered over to the table and began to play idly with the paint bottles and lotions there. 'There's talk, Nelly, I think I should warn you. Beck Marshall's saying you're to blame for the emptiness of the theatre these days.'

'That's the plague, Bab. How can it concern me?'

'Beck's saying that since you returned from Whitehall the King's not returned to the theatre. She says you obviously offended his Majesty so that he is determined to ignore his Servants at the Theatre Royal.' Bab saw Nell's knuckles whiten on the brush handle she was holding, though her face was in shadow.

'That's not true, Bab! The King and the Court have removed to Hampton Court because of the sickness.'

'Aye.' Bab carefully rubbed eye kohl on her lids. 'But you have never returned to the King, Nelly. Have you?'

Nell sat looking down at her hands. 'No, Bab, and I won't.'

Bab shrugged. ' 'Tis none of my business, sweeting. I am but warning you of what tongues are clacking.'

'I know.' Nell walked slowly over to the door. 'But I tell you this, Bab. They may clack as they will, but what happened that night remains a matter 'twixt me and the King himself.'

As Nell left the Women's Shift she encountered Beck Marshall, who dropped an insolent mock curtsey. 'Good afternoon, Madam Fantail. Whither away? If you have come in search of an audience, I fear me you will be disappointed. Somehow they just seem to dwindle away. Perhaps you haven't noticed. We are the King's House and yet we have not seen the King for eight weeks at the play.'

Nell shrugged in a gesture of boredom. 'I fail to see, Mrs. Marshall, how that should concern me.'

'Perhaps,' Beck hissed, 'you can cast your mind back to the last time his Majesty attended the Theatre Royal. At the end of the performance you received a request for your company. Since then you have never returned to Whitehall, and his Majesty has treated all of us as though *we* had the black spot!'

'I might tell you to mind your own business,' Nell said softly, 'or if I thought you would understand, I might say that you intrude on my private affairs. But I must use words you will take note of, Beck. So I have but one thing to advise.'

'What is that?' asked Beck.

'Voyage away, Beck, and a fart fill your sail!' said Nell cheerfully. She pushed past Beck before the girl could collect her wits, and the door banged behind her.

Outside she found a man waiting in the corridor. 'Can you

come to the pit, Mrs. Gwynne? Master Killigrew has arrived and wishes for the attendance of the whole company.'

Nell made her way to the front of the apron stage, and the whole company, chattering, assembled, shortly after joined by Mrs. Knipp and Beck Marshall, until the familiar angular figure of Thomas Killigrew walked easily on to the stage and held up his hand for silence. In one hand he carried a large and official-looking document. Killigrew's face was thin and tired and there were worried lines about his mouth. His voice, when he spoke, was calm but sad. 'This must be a melancholy meeting, my friends, one which cannot but strike a blow at the vitals of the Theatre Royal. As you know, the war and the spread of sickness have torn holes in the crowd we are wont to see pack our benches of late . . .'

'And *other* causes,' said Beck Marshall in a deliberately audible voice.

Master Killigrew gazed mildly at her. 'Do you wish to address the company, Mrs. Marshall? No?'

Beck subsided into muttering silence. Master Killigrew's lazy eyes flickered over her for a moment and then he continued. 'I have here,' he declaimed, waving the scroll, 'an official communication from my Lord Mayor and the city aldermen. It is countersigned by his Majesty the King: "In view of the spread of the pestilence, it is the command of the King that the Theatre Royal at Drury Lane be closed until further notice to prevent the risk of infection." Ladies and gentlemen, I regret being the bearer of ill news, but I fear the theatre is closed.'

There was an astonished hush in the pit and then the clamour broke out—voices demanding how long the theatre was to be shut, Kate Corey weeping gustily into a large and dirty kerchief, Lizzie Weaver demanding in her strident voice how she was to be expected to survive deprived of her living, Major Mohun picking his teeth elegantly with a gold toothpick, and advising her in a quiet whisper, quite missed by that matron, to live off her fat, which could be depended upon to keep her for six months at least.

Master Killigrew quelled the riot of voices with one upflung white hand. 'I need not add,' he said patiently, 'that as we are all King's Servants here at the King's House, all salaries will continue to be paid as usual until such time—as yet unknown—when the Theatre Royal shall open again.' He paused. 'I might add a personal note of advice to you all—leave London as soon as you can. This sickness is no ordinary one and it is spreading fast. Remember: the plague is no respecter of persons; male and female, fishwife and countess, actor and duke, all are equal to fall before it. Leave London, and I pray when the pestilence ceases its ravages, we may all meet once more, a company of players again.'

Nell pushed away through the cluster of actors and actresses, her mind awhirl. Charles Hart was nowhere to be seen.

Clutching a gilded glass bottle of amber perfume to her nose, Nell followed the torch of a link boy home from an evening spent with Master Lacy and Bab Knipp at Lacy's untidy lodgings around the corner of the Lane in Cradle Alley. At an alley further down Nell bade goodnight to Mrs. Knipp, who was speedily swallowed by the gloom as she made her solitary way home without the comfort of a link boy's light. Nell and Lacy knew something few in the company knew—that Bab Knipp, for all her brave show and sparkle of gaiety, led a miserable life, married to a drunkard who took her money and beat her into bruises as recompense. Nell shook her head as she watched her friend depart. How, she asked herself, could someone like Bab afford to leave London? Come to that, she reasoned, how could most of the Londoners afford to leave their homes and jobs to escape illness? The answer was a simple one—most of them could not. They were too poor to quit their flea-infested homes and must rely upon the dubious protection of turpentine pills or 'plague water.' And most of them would die if the plague spread.

She thought again of Master Duncan's offer. Should she go to him and ask him to order the coach he had promised? She had not done so and still she hesitated. How could she coldly arrange to leave when Charles would not go with her, indeed, had stormed off in a rage at the very mention of the name Robert Duncan.

She sighed and pressed back under the gabling at the link boy's warning cry as a maidservant threw open an attic casement above and disgorged the contents of a chamber pot in a stream, drenching the cobbles below. She trod after the link boy, pondering once more the unfathomable emotions of the male of the species, far more intangible than the legendary volatility of women.

As flickering flame led her down the winding length of Wych Street, Nell felt a sense of something behind her, an echo of some sort, sounding in a dull muted whisper, falling a second after the clack of her wooden pattens upon the cobblestones. The sound came closer, and at the second she looked around in alarm a whining voice greeted her. 'Spare a groat for a pot of ale, Mistress. Spare a penny for a poor old man.'

There was a familiar resonant depth to the low whisper. Suspiciously she peered at the bent figure in the shadows. 'Pox take you for a pricklouse, Charles! I took you for a highwayman.'

There was a smothered laugh as the link boy turned to see what had happened. Charles Hart straightened and threw back the hood that had covered his face. He grinned at her with a flash of white teeth. 'Not so far from the truth, my child. If I am no highwayman, I seek to take the hymen way with you.'

The amused expression faded from her lips, to be replaced by one of troubled indecision. 'You took that way some time ago, Charles. You, and only you, have taken it, as you well know, these last three months, and yet you hurl insults at me not to be borne by any Billingsgate fishwife with an ounce of good red blood in her veins.'

She saw a tremor pass over his face and when he spoke his voice held an unaccustomed note of pleading. 'God's death, Nelly, can you not forget my curs'd temper? You know how I—how I—I swear I did not mean, I *never* suspected . . . Oh, pox take it, Nell, can you forgive me?'

'You've a tongue like a whiplash and a choler like a

drunken Dutchman,' she told him tartly. 'I suppose you know half the company at the King's House saw our little affray.'

'Aye, I know,' he mumbled. 'That is, I met Kynaston at Will's and he told me of Master Killigrew's announcement.' He strode forward and called the link boy, tossing him sixpence. 'I will see the lady home, lad.' The link boy looked anxiously at Nell, but on seeing her nod, prepared to depart. 'Here—leave me your torch.' Hart tossed the boy a shilling and he bowed before running off, leaving them together.

The torch cast an eerie light around them. It was a still hot evening as they picked their way round the corner of Maypole Alley into Drury Lane. The air was rank and stale beneath the overhanging rooftops. Heaped against the wall of one house was a pile of stinking refuse which spread out across the cobbles until it mingled with the filth in the open gutter that ran down the centre of the street. Nell put her perfumed bottle to her nose and scrambled over the slippery cloying mass of slops and rotting vegetables. Charles Hart offered her his arm. 'What's to do now, my life?' he asked. 'It seems all at once everyone is leaving London. Even Will's coffee house is closing down. Imagine! Master Dryden will be lost without his seat by the window. And Kynaston tells me the infection spreads further despite leaving all six of the great Bibles in St. Paul's open to Lamentations to turn the wrath of God. It seems He has not yet attended to the plea. Are we to leave London too?'

She did not look at him. 'That depends, Charles. I had no mind this afternoon to return that costume to Master Duncan to satisfy your vanity and I have no mind to leave London now lest Master Duncan find I have spurned his offer. He expects us to travel with him and I told him I should go, when I went, in his company and yours. I will not spit in the face of that old man to please you, Charles.'

There was a short silence.

'You know, Nelly, you are destined for great things. When you speak like that, strike me dead if I couldn't believe it was that haughty dame Castlemaine talking. Surely we can . . .'

A loud croak of a voice and the dong of a bell interrupted

him. Swinging into view came the familiar figure of one of London's night watchmen, his grey felt hat jammed down over his nose, his bell clanging rhythmically to the even tone of his voice. He appeared to weave about slightly as he walked, putting out a hand to save himself from tripping as he jerked at his bell. 'Twelve of the clock. A fine hot night and all's . . . well.' His voice died at the end of the sentence and they saw one hand go up to wipe his brow. Then the bell rang again, but this time discordantly, harshly as it fell with a clang on the cobbles and the staggering figure tried desperately to begin his call again. 'Twel . . .' He staggered, coughing, lurched to reach for his bell and fell headlong in the gutter.

'Poor old sot,' murmured Nell sympathetically and made as if to go and help him up. 'He must have had a drop too—'

'No!' shouted Hart and dragged her back.

Amazed, Nell looked up at him, but Hart shook his head and led her over to where the hunched watchman lay. Gently he turned him with his boot and then held the torch high over the lolling face. The lips were drawn back in a hideous grimace, the eyes stared up unseeing, the pupils rolled back sightless and empty as eternity. From the mouth a black trickle of blood spread across the jowl below a mass of dark festering sores. The watchman was dead. Horrified, Nell stepped back.

' 'Tis the plague, Nell—the black spot,' said Hart calmly. He raised his torch and the flames picked out the wooden door by which the victim had fallen. It was bolted with a heavy chain and the shutters of the windows were closed. As Hart and Nell moved nearer they could see a cross and beneath it faint words daubed in rusty dried blood on the boards. Tall and flickering in the torchlight, dancing as it seemed with an almost malignant intensity, they spoke the hopeless words of death: *Lord have mercy upon us.*

'We leave London at once,' said Hart tersely. 'Send word to Master Duncan. We leave tomorrow!'

Five

*He's most in debt who lingers out the day,
Who dies betimes has less and less to pay.*

—*Seventeenth-Century Sampler Legend*

Once again a coach waited in the courtyard of the Bell Inn as the sun rose over the city to bake the cobblestones and bead the brows of London's long-suffering citizens. But today at least the concerted ringing of church bells from every part of London—ringing out continuously and triumphantly—indicated that England had cause for rejoicing.

All the previous night they had rung, banishing sleep for the city and tempting even the nervous to light bonfires in the streets to toast with wild enthusiasm the defeat of the Dutch. Now, in the sunshine, captured Dutch flags drooped from their masts on the Tower wall. Up and down Ludgate hill roamed bands of 'prentices calling damnation down upon the Dutch and cheering the glorious victory just won by that valiant gentleman the Duke of York—the greatest victory, they boasted, ever known in the history of the world.

The regular joyful pealing of the carillon bombarded Charles Hart's ears as he perused a broadsheet with details of the battle. ' 'Tis a complete victory.' he declared. 'It says the Dutch are utterly routed—some forty ships fled into the Texell and they have lost at least five thousand men! What say you to that, Nelly?'

But he addressed deaf ears. Inside the imposing equipage resting behind six champing, snorting horses, two ladies craned their necks to see under the gateway of the inn whether anyone had just arrived. 'Where is 'e, Nelly?' demanded Mit. 'He ordered the coach for seven of the clock and 'tis now nine. He did say 'e would come, didn't 'e?'

Nell nodded worriedly. 'Haply the press of business has held him up . . .' She heard the clop of hoofbeats drawing into the courtyard, and a plainly dressed man on a handsome cob edged his way past two dray carts and came up to the coach, touching his forelock.

Mit watched while Nell unfolded a crackling sheet of paper. ' 'Tis Master Duncan,' she sighed. 'He says the sudden news of the victory over the Dutch has given him a quick chance for some new business enterprise. "I must implore your . . . I hope to . . ." ' She studied the letter. 'He says he will be about his business for a se'enight and will join us at Brighthelmstone two weeks hence! Oh, hang 'im with polecats!' The gentleman on the cob blinked. Nell turned to him. 'You take this message back to Master Duncan and repeat it word for word: "Mrs. Gwynne thanks him for his letter and tells him to his face he is a fool to linger longer in this Godforsaken city. She would rather receive him penniless and whole than rich and dead!" Have you conned that, sir?'

The man nodded dumbly and Mit hid a smile behind her hand. Nell gave him a groat and he departed. 'Pox take him!' she said furiously. 'The fool—the stupid, thick-skulled fool. Devil take him!' She tapped the paper irritably against her teeth. 'I've a mind to go and drag him forcibly from his banking house and tie him to this coach with my own hands.'

Charles Hart leant against the coach door. 'He'll not thank you for poking a nose into his affairs, my dear. Do you know how closely you resembled your sister just then? Mit looked terrified, I swear!'

Nell smiled a little at that. 'Pox take you too, Charles, for a jesting cheesecurd. I wonder, should we wait further?'

'What, for a se'enight!' exclaimed Hart.

'No, no. Just for an hour or two—in case Master Duncan should change his mind.'

Charles Hart climbed into the coach and shut the door. 'You overrate your powers for once, my dear. Master Duncan is a merchant first and before all else. He will not come.'

She began to protest, but Hart took his cane and tapped it peremptorily on the ceiling of the coach. Her voice was drowned by the jingle of harness and the rattle of wheels as the coachman gave the horses their heads and they plunged forward under the archway.

Not for the first time, Master Trott, landlord of the Ewe and Lamb at Brighthelmstone pondered the strange ways of folk from foreign parts. He stood behind his counter, tending lovingly to his proud array of silver and pewter tankards and mused on the peculiar customs of folk from London. It was not, he comforted himself smugly, that he held aught against them. They brought him trade, and Master Trott was not a man ever to turn trade away. But *no one*—leastways, no one of his acquaintance—could find his guests from London anything other than mighty queer.

These Londoners—foreigners, more like—sniffed the innkeeper, with their nifty ways and their requests for chines of beef and a hash of rabbits at midnight when all honest folk were abed and asleep, as he well knew! Take the gentleman and his lady upstairs. An actor he was supposed to be. What sort of a job was that for a man? Painted and prinked, dancing about on a stage like a puppet for all to see. And he had heard they had men playing women's parts on the stage in London! Master Trott shook his head. Heathen it was, he decided. Not but what the gentleman seemed open-handed enough. As was his lady . . . Master Trott cast a sardonic look upwards as he gave a brisk rub to his best silver flagon. Man and wife they might call themselves, but he knew different. No couple who were married behaved as free as these two, Londoners or no. Never in all his born days had he come across such a strange couple. A good three months they had been with him, and something was wrong, he swore, or his name was not Jeremiah Trott!

Within a few days of their arrival the lady appeared to become preoccupied, 'her feelers otherwise,' as Master Trott put it to himself sagely. As though she had something on her mind and was never really listening, try as the gentleman would. There was an ominous quiet about the two of them, and Master Hart began to look tight about the lips and answered the innkeeper irritably when addressed. The lady seemed eager all the time for news from London and pestered Master Trott for a letter almost every day.

No letter had ever arrived, and the innkeeper found the lady waxed more nervous and preoccupied than ever. A pity, he decided, for never had he seen such a taking wench, with her creamy skin and big dark eyes. No doubt fretting for relatives in the metropolis, he told himself, for certainly something serious ailed her.

And then, all at once, as if the tension were too much for the pair of them, the quiet snapped like a boy's catapault and the whole of the Ewe and Lamb had rung to the shouts, curses and imprecations of their quarrels. Even through two doors he had heard them, and such language as he sweated to remember, from the lady as much as the gentleman. Each of these sessions was followed by equally passionate reconciliations, and Master Trott and the Ewe and Lamb had goggled mystified at the firm-closed chamber door of their peacemaking. Such goings-on! He tutted as he carefully hung his tankards up above his row of gleaming taps.

Master Trott counted himself lucky he had only four of them staying at his inn. *That* was four too many, he considered, for all that two of them were dowager ladies of ample means and respectable habits. Master Trott distrusted new ways and he had encountered too many in the short space of a few weeks for him to adequately digest. He marvelled at the prodigal spendthrift habits of the wealthy. My Lady Bridge, for instance, he ruminated, as he arranged his best blue galleyware on the shelf. She seemed to live on nothing but sherris and soft biscuits morning, noon and night. And as for her friend Lady Appleby—what sane mortal, he asked himself, called the chambermaid upon retiring to open the windows at night? 'Twas well known fresh air was positively dangerous and night air the worst of all! But there was no telling her—there was no telling any of them.

He fixed his professional smile on his fat face as he espied the two ladies followed by their black pages entering his taproom. He bowed, clasping his napkin to the rotund expanse of his stomach, and humbly asked their pleasure. The first of them, a small plump lady with a pronounced stubbornness about the chin, considered him for a moment before replying.

'Two glasses of sherris and a dish of macaroons,' she said sadly. She turned to her companion. 'Not that it will be like those beautiful confections of Master Scrivener's. I swear I die at the thought of his pastries. How much longer must we endure this . . . this *exile*, I wonder.'

The tall, thin lady behind shook her head in sympathy. 'Some while longer I dare swear, dear ma'am. They said in the last news from the city that the death toll has reached seven thousand a week.'

'Seven thousand a week!' exclaimed her companion. '*Now* tell me, if you dare, dear Lady Appleby, that it isn't a plot of the Papists. 'Tis as clear as the nose on my face. They plan to destroy us all!'

'But,' countered her companion firmly, 'there is not the *slightest* evidence that the Catholics have anything to do with the plague; indeed, I do not see how they might have. Catholics and Protestants are dying alike in London, you know.' Master Trott discerned a distinct gleam in her eye. 'Perhaps you are forgetting, *dear* Lady Bridge, that my late husband's family have long been counted amongst those of the old religion. I myself have known several delightful people of the Papist persuasion, especially in Paris when I was taken on the Tour with my brother.'

My Lady Bridge's voice was deceptively sweet. 'Alas! I cannot match your travelling experiences, ma'am, for my family was so impoverished through supporting the Royalist cause, it was as much as we could do to find a crust to eat. *Your* father of course compounded with the regicides . . .'

Lady Appleby, a dangerous flush upon her cheek, sought to bring the conversation back to its original point. 'I fear we wander, dear ma'am. I still fail to see how you can accuse the Papists of causing the plague. Surely 'tis miasmas and humours in the ground, an infection of the air, you know.'

'Exactly,' said Lady Bridge darkly. 'And *who* produces these . . . miasmas?' Without waiting for an answer, she proceeded up the stairs to her room, followed by a frustrated-looking companion.

'My Lord!' murmured Master Trott.

Nell would have been surprised at the depth of Master Trott's interest in her had she been aware of it. But in fact she was hardly aware even of the crash of the grey waves on the September shore below, as she sat in the window at the back of the inn which looked out across the quay. Neither the haze of sea spray which came in through the open window nor the scream of the gulls outside could rouse her interest from its one consuming fixation.

Where was he? she asked herself. Why had he not come? She had waited, she had sent letter after letter to him, but she had received no reply. A horrible fear, hardly articulate or possessed of definite shape or form, turned insidiously within her, rousing her to a fever of nameless dread. Always came into horrid focus the face of the dead watchman lying in the gutter of Drury Lane. Only suddenly, mysteriously and frighteningly, his face would become the face of Robert Duncan and she would wake in the night with a sudden jerk and lie sweating and trembling in the dark. Each day she wondered if the next day he would arrive and laugh away her old worries with his wheezy chiding and tell her she had been fashing and greeting like a mauken. How she longed to hear his voice scolding her to brush away her fears. But he did not come. Charles Hart was like a being apart. At first when she voiced her worries he merely laughed away her suggestions, then, when this proved inadequate, he tried arguing, pointing out that she did not know where he was, whether well or ill, and could do nothing therefore to aid him.

For some time his argument sufficed. She believed Duncan might have gone away on business and forgotten or failed to send her word. But as the weeks passed, the nameless tension that rose unbidden in her breast and made her heart jump suddenly at any odd time of the day or night became a living presence always with her, shutting her off from Charles and his reasoned talk. The nameless fear took shape and became certainty. From that point on, each second spent in Brighthelmstone was torture to her. She pictured Duncan lying ill and alone somewhere in London and she knew she could not rest until she tried to find him.

Nell's aloofness, her hidden thoughts, led Hart to abandon reason and attempt to ignore the thing that lay between them. When he tried to make love to her, he found her cool and unresponsive; he attempted to remonstrate, and the result had been those passionate outpourings of repressed tension that had caused the shocked disapproval of Master Trott. For a long time Hart held her with his sensual possession. For a longer time her own feeling of helplessness prevented her from doing more than write feverish letters to Duncan's lodgings in the city, letters that brought no answer, save relief to her nerves.

But as she sat gazing unseeing at the sea, she knew the moment had come when reason was past; when, even though she might not be able to find him, she had to return to London to look for Robert Duncan. Nell wondered how to tell Charles Hart—the very mention of the name now drew from him a bitter half-mocking stream of incisive sarcasm, either that or a furious oath and a slammed door. Nell knew he would tell her she was a fool; she could not go back to London to search for someone who might not even be there. She knew, but...

The door opened and Charles Hart strode into the room. 'I have a letter from Killigrew, Nell,' he said, waving a scrap of paper. 'He says the Court is expected to remove to Oxford next month. All the company are commanded by his Majesty to attend him there to present a play in honour of the birthday of the Duke of York. If we're all lucky we might get the arrears of pay due to us and leave to stay past Christmastide. D'you know Kynaston is over six months in arrears with his salary?' He stopped suddenly, aware that Nell was not attending.

'I must go to London, Charles,' she said in a low voice, looking out of the window.

Hart stood quite still. Only by the quick throbbing of a vein in his temple was it possible to tell that he was labouring under intense strain. 'This is really most affecting, my dear,' he said coolly, 'but I believe entirely unnecessary. Master Duncan has obviously disappeared on a business enterprise—haply abroad—and his apologies have gone astray. Is that so improbable in the present situation in London?'

'I do not believe you. Robert Duncan is ill, he is in some terrible trouble and he needs me.'

Charles Hart delicately inhaled Melilot snuff. 'Perhaps he is—but how may you help him without knowing even where he is?'

'I will search, and if he is to be found, I shall find him.'

'How very redoubtable,' said Hart, his voice silky, 'but I regret I must prevent this dramatic self-immolation on the altar of—ah—friendship.' He turned on his heel and went over to pour out a glass of claret. 'I dare swear we shall have to remove in a week or so.' He sipped at the wine. 'Killigrew says he will send another letter when 'tis settled. He is staying at Salisbury with the King.'

'I said I must go to London. I must—'

'I heard you!' shouted Hart and he flung the glass across the room at her. It broke into a thousand splinters at her feet, the liquid staining the carpet. 'I have listened to you long enough. For weeks and weeks I have heard naught but Robert Duncan, Robert Duncan—until I am near mad with the name. I have tried to tell you, you can do no good in seeking him—you do not listen. I have told you there is no proof he is yet in the city—you ignore me. I have told you that if he has the plague, he is as good as dead—you repeat you want to go. God's blood!'

He came towards her, livid and taut with fury. 'I have suffered *you* for long enough. How you came to ensnare me thus, I shall never know. You are naught but a painted drab with flesh as cold and dead as those rocks out there. A little slut from the gutter with the brain of a chicken who grows stale with bedding. Go, if you prefer Master Duncan—a damned merchant, an apron rogue with greasy paws. Go, if you wish to take the plague. Go and be damned! But remember'—he flashed the words at her, half threat, half plea—'once you leave through that door, all is over between us forever!'

She looked down as he stood over her, breathing heavily, his face flushed and his hands trembling, and her voice was a whisper.

'I shall leave in one hour.'

Six

Nor Censure us, You who perceive
My best belov'd and me,
Sigh and Lament, Complain and grieve,
You think we disagree.

—*My Lord of Rochester*

Queen Catherine of Braganza looked breathless as she finished a single coranto in the arms of her royal husband at the head of a row of lords and ladies of the Court. Her piquant little face looked mischievous in the candlelight as she bent towards him. 'I t'ink, Charles, you dance much better than James, who dances so much while you dance so little.'

Charles laid a hand over his heart. 'Have a care, m'dear, I am growing old, you know. My dancing days will soon be done.'

'Nonsense!' She rapped her fan on his knuckles. 'You are naught but a boy. I warrant I should be grey-haired before *you* would settle to be a complaisant dotard of a husband.'

He caught the twinkle in her eye and smiled. 'You will never grow old, Catherine, you will always be a child in spirit.'

'Do you really t'ink so?' Her face lit up and her eyes sparkled. 'I t'ink you are ver' kind tonight, Charles. First you dance wit' me, then you give me compliments.'

The King led her back—through a line of curtseys on one side and low bows on the other—to sit on a raised dais. Together they watched the ebb and flow of the dancers as they trod in stately measure under the light of a myriad candles scattered in sconces down the long ballroom. Catherine sipped at a glass of malmsey, then said, her voice concerned, 'I like it here at Salisbury, Querido mio, but I would be back at Whitehall. I cannot help t'inking of those wr-retched people in London enduring the heat and the sickness. The Duchessa Alber-r-marle tells me her 'usband writes of the pest houses full to overflowing and deaths rising by the day. It seems were it not for the Duke of Albermarle and my Lord Craven, the city would be in chaos by now.'

Charles nodded. 'Craven served my father well and serves me also. It is upon such men that the destinies of kingdoms rest. But what of us? Shall we return then to Whitehall, Catherine? Shall we order all those gaily dressed butterflies to follow us back to London, and see how many sicken and die?'

Catherine's brows wrinkled. 'No, we cannot,' she said decisively. 'We cannot be res-s-ponsible for their deaths. I do not mind for myself. They say in Portugal, death knocks only once on your door. He knocked on mine two years ago and I survived.' She squeezed his arm. 'Because of you.' Charles shook his head. 'No, it is true. It was you and not those bastardos of doctors who cured me. I survived then so I should not die now. You see, I will live to be a dow-ager!' She took a piece of marchpane from a comfit dish. 'But we cannot lead these people back into the jaws of death.'

'I wish I did not have to skulk here, my dear, like a whipped cur. What must the Londoners think of me?'

Catherine bit into a comfit with her slightly protuberant teeth. 'What they have always thought—that you are a king who does what he cannot prevent and does not do what would lose him his t'rone. What else does any king do?' She glanced up at him with a gleam of amusement. 'They might also say that as all the ladies have left town, so must your Majesty in their pur-purs-s-s-uit.'

'Odsfish, your Majesty, do you throw my affaires in my teeth?' Charles barked with laughter and took her chin in his hands, to the dismay of the Duchess of Penalva standing behind. 'You fence with wicked stabs, my Queen. Do you seek to make me blush? Confess and be hanged!'

'I cannot con-fess,' said Catherine, her Portuguese accent heavy on her tongue.

' 'Tis what all English ladies say to their husbands when they find them out. Say it,' insisted Charles with mock severity.

Catherine's eyes glinted back at him. She took a deep breath. 'Confess and be hanged!' she said in flawless English, with a carrying voice that floated audibly across the room above the music of a bransle.

The heads of the ladies and gentlemen turned, startled, in their direction and the orchestra faltered to a halt. Catherine turned pink and the hawk-faced Duchess tutted angrily behind her.

But Charles was not disconcerted. He rose easily to his feet and bowed to the company. 'My apologies to you all, my lords and ladies. Her Majesty but upbraids my acknowledged and besetting vice of mendacity. Pray continue . . .' He sat down with a flourish of his handkerchief, and the bransle continued its light pace. Catherine chuckled.

Before them, twirling down the room, came the gorgeous jewelled and lace-frothed figure of my Lady Castlemaine together with the young Duke of Monmouth. As they reached the end of the room before the dais they stopped and made their obeisance to the King and Queen. Charles and Catherine nodded briefly and the line of dancers continued turning, now in a line, now in a circle.

Charles's eyes were cynical as he watched the graceful movements on the floor. 'And so the dance of life continues,' he said reflectively, 'as ever it did. Look there. Do you see the lady in the lemon brocade, with her hair dressed vaguely à la bergère, talking with that wasted nymph who droops under the weight of those emeralds she is wearing?'

'Why yes, that is her Grace the Duchess of Buckingham and Lady Falconbridge,' said Catherine, puzzled.

'You mistake, my dear,' retorted Charles ironically. 'That is Mary Fairfax, daughter of the Lord General Fairfax, commander of the forces of Parliament against a malignant king. 'Twas the only way Buckingham could recover his estates, which Parliament had stolen. I am told they speak to each other but seldom. He bought his lands back and she—she bought a title.' His eyes mocked. 'They say she is a faithful wife but George is a neglectful husband. So virtue is a penance.' Catherine was seen to flush slightly, but Charles did not notice. 'The thin damsel in the emeralds is Lady Mary Cromwell, and *her* father needs no further exposition.'

'Oh,' said Catherine, looking troubled, 'I see.'

'Do you, my dear? What may we learn from such a sight? That life runs in seasons like the rest of nature; that we thrive or sicken according to the run of fate, sometimes basking in summer, sometimes shivering in winter. When we believe ourselves up, fate will pluck us down. My crown is no more steady on my head than the petals on that rose you have in your hair.'

Catherine looked worried. 'You sound peevish, Charles. Perhaps you are wearied—the damp of this Avon valley does not agree with you.'

'God's death, I think I shall go mad if I have to sit much longer, unable to fight the Dutch or the plague,' returned the King. 'And without the jests of that young blackguard Rochester to cheer me.' He twirled a wineglass between his fingers. 'I have a month's mind to leave my Court and go on my travels again, back through that countryside I last saw as a fugitive after Worcester. 'Twould be a trip back down ten long years . . .' He spoke his thoughts out loud. 'I wonder how the Penderels are? Do they all still live?' Catherine looked blank. 'Aye de me,' he sighed, ' 'twould be a change indeed from being forced to wait and watch my Court of cuckolds hard at work.'

'At play, Sire.'

Charles shook his head. 'Ah no, Catherine, you mistake, indeed you do. They merely appear idle. In fact, they are all active, ceaselessly intriguing for power, wealth and place with an appetite as insatiate as the sea. Come, let me educate you . . .' He glanced over to where the Duke of Buckingham was lining up for a gavotte with Frances Stuart. As they both watched, Buckingham pressed a kiss to the lady's wrist. Charles smiled. 'I see Buckingham is hovering around la belle Stuart like a bee around a honey pot. Methinks Barbara is not best pleased.'

Catherine saw my Lady Castlemaine pass the Duke and his partner and the flash of anger from her fine eyes directed at the Duke's impervious back.

'Do you think the Duke of Buckingham has suddenly fallen in love with Frances? Let me enlighten you. George is interested in controlling Frances because he hopes through her he might influence me—a vain hope, I fear. Barbara hopes that she might keep her influence at Court if she woos Monmouth, knowing my fondness for my son—a fondness that, alack for Barbara, does not extend to my son's wenching. Barbara and Buckingham are too much alike to agree for more than five minutes, but they are united with my Lord Bristol in a hatred for *that* gentleman.' He nodded to where a stolid figure sat in one corner looking without interest at the festivities over a glass of canary. 'My Lord of Clarendon,' explained Charles. 'They have so far tried to make me believe he is a traitor in the pay of the Dutch, a traitor in the pay of the French and an embezzler who used Crown money to build that pile of his at Clarendon House. A veritable rogue of a Chancellor!'

Catherine considered his swarthy profile with a new understanding. 'But you do not believe them?'

'No, I do not believe them. Their wishes are breeders of much wind and their wind can hate but never destroy. It merely buffets like a storm that is soon over.' His voice held an emphasis.

Catherine reddened. 'I know. But I fear they also hate a lady who is hardly a match for them in guile or wits.' She looked anxiously at Charles.

He stretched over and took one little hand in a warm clasp. 'But that lady has them routed on her own ground. She surpasses them in honesty, which is a quality beyond their understanding. The lady they hate is not only Queen of England but also the Queen of my heart.'

Catherine's face shone. 'Oh, Charles, how kind you are!' she exclaimed impulsively.

His face twisted in a wry smile. 'I wish I were,' he said gently.

To the strains of a gavotte the rows of courtiers leapt and turned before them. There came a click as a line of heels kicked in the air, then the partners kissed before whirling away once more. Charles's brows rose as he espied the slender legs of the lady partnering his brother of York. 'I believe James is reforming in his habit of wenching,' he said thoughtfully.

'How so, Charles? Has James become faithful?' murmured Catherine ingenuously. 'Anne has never—'

'No, dearest, but he chooses for once a lady of some beauty about the body. Mistress Arabella Churchill has the neatest-turned ankles that ever I saw. I swear, in the past James's mistresses were given him by his confessor as a penance!' The Duchess of Penalva froze into taut, outraged immobility at such loose talk. But Catherine laughed gaily, and thereby drew a wink from Charles. 'You're no sobersides, my life, for which I'm devoutly thankful,' he whispered.

Catherine's glance travelled over to the corner of the room once more. 'I t'ink James's father-in-law iss not so pleased as you are, Charles.'

'Clarendon worries too much,' said her husband irritably. 'He wishes James would be a faithful husband, of course, but what would you? Anne begs me not to let her husband go to sea and reproaches me when he stays at Court and turns to the ladies for amusement. A good thing she is indisposed tonight and not present to see her husband, methinks.'

'Clarendon also worries because your brother goes now to Mass, Charles.'

A shadow descended on the King's brow. 'I know,' he said heavily. 'If only James could be more discreet about his private life. He never is! All the Court knows as much of his flirtation with Papistry—saving your presence, my dear—as it does of his flirtation with Mistress Churchill.'

'James does not pretend,' mused Catherine pensively. 'He says his prin-ciples will not allow it. He holds one cannot do evil to keep the peace.'

'For which honesty he would be forced to go on his travels if he sat in my place,' retorted Charles. 'This realm has already been drenched in blood for the sake of *principle*. I thank God I am made of coarser material.' Catherine looked quickly up at him but said nothing. 'I think I prefer the open roguery of people like those gentlemen over there.' Charles gestured to a group of three playing Ombre under the flaring candles. 'Look at them. They'd dice their souls away if they could! Sedley, Buckhurst and that fat lecher Harry Savile. At least I know them for what they are and have no illusions.'

'You have honest men to serve you too, Charles,' reproved Catherine gently. 'There is my Lord Albemarle, my Lord Craven and that dear old man his Grace of Newcastle—all good, loyal men.'

'Aye. Unfortunately, it is not these "good, loyal men" my people think of when they think of my Court. It is not Albe-marle, Southampton or the Duke of Ormonde they think of, but Sedley's drunken excesses, holding his swilling orgies in front of all London on the balcony of the Cock tavern with that blackguard Ogle!'

Catherine leant towards Charles and lowered her voice so that her duenna could not hear. 'They . . . say . . .' she began falteringly. 'Or at least my Lady Suffolk told me that Sir Charles and my Lord Buckhurst and that other one . . .'

'Sir Thomas Ogle?' prompted Charles innocently.

'Yes, that is the one,' she agreed. 'They say'—she hissed the words hesitantly into his ear—'that they took all their clothes off before they addressed the crowd.' Her eyes were round as saucers.

Charles nodded. 'All quite true,' he whispered back. 'But you shouldn't listen to scandal, my Queen!'

Catherine was tapped peremptorily, if discreetly, on the shoulder by the Duchess of Penalva, and she straightened to see Frances Stuart awaiting, quiet, while she arranged her skirts about her on the window seat. In one hand she held a dulcimer. Catherine nodded encouragingly to the blushing girl. Drawing one hand across the strings, Frances began to sing a love song in French in a sweet, clear voice that drew respectful silence from all around.

Charles's eyes were moody as he watched her. Why would she never submit to him? he asked himself for the umpteenth time. He had offered jewels, trinkets, a title—all to no avail. Still she would have none of him. A virgin in Whitehall. Charles believed it despite the sneering remarks of my Lady Castlemaine. While he respected her in abstract, Charles was bound to admit he found her stubbornness exasperating. To see beauty such as that day after day but never to touch her or possess her ... 'Odsfish,' he said out loud. 'A woman, a dog and a walnut tree. The more they're beaten, the better they be.'

Catherine looked at him, surprised.

'An old English saying,' he explained. ' 'Tis advice on how to control your wife.'

'A monstrous barbaric saying,' replied Catherine coldly. 'No wonder they say the English are not civilised.' She saw his eyes flicker over Frances Stuart's exposed breasts in its low-cut corsage. 'I warrant *some* ladies can be more exasperating than others.'

With a last ripple of fingers across the strings, Frances finished her song, and flushing slightly, gazed up suddenly at the King.

Charles grinned and turned to Catherine. 'I will show you one more old English custom before we retire, my dear.' He got to his feet and held up a hand for attention. 'One last dance, I think, before the proceedings close,' he boomed, his eyes alight with mischief. 'One last dance to end with, my lords. Come join in "Cuckolds all Awry," the old dance of England!'

There was a titter from the ladies. As the courtiers moved into the centre of the long room Charles turned to hand Catherine down from the dais. She placed her hand in his and covertly dug her nails into his skin. 'You choose *that* to shock me, you rogue. I t'ink you are a ras-cal,' she scolded in a whisper. 'Confess! Confess and be hanged!'

His laugh sounded in her ears as the viols struck up their tune.

Seven

*... I have gained a knowledge how to distinguish
of love hereafter, and I shall scorn you
and all your sex, that have not soul enough
to value a noble friendship.*

—*Thomas Killigrew*

The solitary bell tolling from Old St. Paul's greeted the swaying market cart as it left the turning alleys of Southwark and crawled onto the cramped highway of London Bridge. Under the bridge gate it passed, and the light was still strong enough to pick out the row of wizened skulls that grinned down upon people below—an ominous symbol of entry into the city.

A few wisps of hay were jerked off the back of the cart, and they floated gently to the ground as it jolted its way between the houses and shops on both sides of the narrow street. It rolled past empty and shuttered dwellings which shivered silently on the huge buttresses of timber suspending them above the fierce currents of the river swirling beneath. No boatmen waited at the bridge foot, crying 'Next Oars!' The water flowed on; there were no wherries or barges touting for hire to disturb its peaceful rush down to Whitehall. Dusk was falling as the bell sent out its single monotonous note across the city.

Nell turned to her companion perched on the rough seat at her side. 'Stap me, this is a change from the bells that sent us out of London last time, isn't it, Mit?' Mit shivered and gazed about her with large and frightened eyes. The cart rumbled over the drawbridge and drew to the end of London Bridge, past the boarded-up front of the Bear tavern, but Mit's thoughts were still back with the gently rolling Kentish lanes through which they had lately passed. For a week and more they had followed dusty paths fringed with hedgerows of scratching hawthorn tendrils feathered with clusters of cow parsley, flaming dots of ragwort, ragged robin and the frosting of celandine. Only when they had come to London had it seemed as though that other world of laughter, colour and slow-spoken country folk had never existed at all. How could it be imagined in such streets as these?

Ever since they had entered the city on the cart Nell had bought from a surly farmer at Clapham village, Mit had begun to realise what she had taken on when she had insisted so fiercely on accompanying her young mistress on this visit to the capital. Still, she had sworn to stick like pitch and she wasn't turning back now, however mad she thought the venture. Mad—Mit repeated the word to herself as they drew up, but she tensed her fingers and said brightly to Nell, 'A good night's sleep, a quick visit to Master Duncan and we'll be on our way before the sun's high tomorrow, I make no doubt.' She touched the plaited straw hat, stuck with a sprig of wild rosemary, that sat upon her wiry curls. 'Pink me, if this don't suit me passing well. Still'—she sniffed at the horse's rump—'not much point being dressed up like a Moorfields trollop, there's precious few to see us.' She faltered at the lonely echo of the cart-horse's hooves as they crossed over the bridge and made their way into Cheapside towards St. Paul's churchyard.

The streets were empty. They had not passed more than half a dozen people since they felt the cobbles beneath the cartwheels. Those they had seen, pinched, white-faced, had drawn their cloaks about them and receded into the shadows to watch them go by. They were people, Nell privately thought to herself, who looked as if they had already taken leave of the world of the living. None of the noise Mit and Nell, both London bred, were wont to hear in the streets prevailed, no shouts of hawkers or pedlars, or furious arguments held in the press of traffic.

The silence was eerie and prolonged. Only once had it been broken, when a tottering drunk carrying a bottle had almost fallen under their wheels. He had lifted a grisly toast to them when he saw their cart coming. 'Bring out your dead . . .' He had giggled with a strange, nervous laugh. 'Bury 'em by night or day, you'll not bury 'em all! Bring out your dead . . .' His maniacal cry echoed in their ears, though they left him far behind.

They turned down the gloomy length of Thames Street and found themselves coughing at the fumes of black smoke that entered their lungs, stung the eyes and made them retch as they smelt the acrid vapour of vinegar and sulphur. At intervals all down the street stood bonfires of sea coal in front of almost every door, blackening the cobbles and lighting the houses with a macabre red glow as the citizens of the stricken city tried vainly to purify the air of the hidden poison that raged in her veins. Like propitiating incense the black smoke twirled skywards, carrying with it pathetic prayers for release and the aid of heaven.

Down the centre of the street before them, under the dappled rump of the horse, Nell could see grass impudently pushing up between the cobblestones, as if to herald the triumph of nature reclaiming what small mankind was unable to protect. Above odd doorways, as if to pacify the malevolent forces that sought to destroy them, people had draped bunches of hops, now sun-bleached and dead, across the lintels, a latter-day daub of immunity from the angel of death of Jehovah passing over in His thirst for souls.

Mit gave a choked cry and jerked suddenly at the reins. The cart came to a halt and Nell looked blankly between the shafts, following the line of Mit's trembling finger. A man lay sprawled face up, one arm loosely falling over the chain that was strung between the posts to protect pedestrians. His tongue hung black from his mouth and his breath bubbled in a trail of froth as he gasped away—all unseeing—his last grasp on life. Mit made as if to leap from the cart and help him, but Nell caught her in a tight grip of nails on the wrist. 'Leave him, Mit. You can't do naught save kill yourself!' She twitched the reins and the cart carefully manoeuvred around him.

Some twenty minutes later they passed over the Fleet and into Fleet Street. The measured mournful hollow dong of three or four bells sounded together with the rattle of wheels and the sound of footsteps. Nell drew the cart to one side and held her kerchief to her face when she saw what was coming.

A small procession of half a dozen men, led by a priest, proceeded in solemn silence—faces downward, staring—along the street towards St. Paul's. Each of the men carried a hand bell, which he tolled in unison with his neighbours. All were dressed in black. Behind them trundled a cart upon which reposed four coffins: two small and two large. As the sound of the bells and the priest's murmured prayers faded away, Nell found a small flask being pushed into her hand by Mit. ' 'Ere, drink this, Nelly. A spot o' ruin never gave anyone the plague. Leastways, if it did, the 'ole lot of us'd be dead by now, choose how!'

Nell took a sip at the brandy. 'Ods my life, Mit,' she murmured, 'I think I've brought you into hell and not into London at all.'

Mit shook her head decisively. 'Nah, Nelly, you're forgettin'. I was skivvy wiv Ma Ross at Lewkenor's Lane. Now *that* was 'ell on a Sat'day night after they'd lost their all at that crooked basset school.'

Nell smiled. 'Does nothing set your teeth on grinders, you lump of rock, Mit?'

' 'Tis only corpses,' pointed out Mit reasonably. 'We all comes to it in the end, I reckon.'

Nell nodded, but she did not notice how a sudden pallor had drained all the blood from her maid's features, nor how Mit's nails dug into her palms. Down the Strand they rattled and turned into the parish of St. Giles. The houses, gaunt and empty, seemed to dance before them, with red cross after red cross mutely affirming its message of inexorable doom: *Lord have mercy upon us—Lord have mercy upon us—Lord have mercy upon us—Lord have mercy upon us*—Time after time the words slid past Nell's eyes, until they became like a prayer dinning into the recesses of her brain. As she came to the corner of Maypole Alley where the conduit stood, she was so lost to the world around her that it took a twice-repeated cry to stop the cart. 'Nelly, Nelly! Dear God, is it really you?'

Nell looked down to see a girl's white face, her matted hair snarled around her shoulders, staring up at her. 'S'truth . . .' breathed Mit. 'What a turn-up for the book an' no mistake!'

'Sarah!' shrieked Nell, and jumping down from the cart, ran round to fall upon the neck of the shabby figure, bestowing kisses and tears in equal quantities upon one pale cheek.

Four hours later Sarah towelled briskly away at a falling mass of wet fair tresses while Mit stoked up the fire in the draughty attic chamber of an otherwise empty Cock and Pye tavern. A good scrub, a chine of beef, a sack posset and a dish of Dantzic gherkins to finish had made of Sarah a new woman.

Nell thought she had changed little since she had last seen her in the midst of a throng of men at Madam Ross's bawdy house in Lewkenor's Lane: still the same glint in her green eyes, still the white soft skin and the slender curves and the same sharp wit that had brought so many to Lewkenor's Lane in time past. In a moment Nell was back in her childhood, reliving the days when she had looked up in awe at Sarah and her beautiful compatriots, experts in the art of whoring. She and Martha and Edith—Nell wondered what could have happened to all of them.

'What's been happening, Sarah?' she demanded. 'How came you to be in such condition and still in the city when most others have fled?'

Sarah towelled briskly at one little ear. 'Plague and a black-blooded rogue, to be brief, Nelly, and naught else was necessary.' She transferred the towel to her other hand. 'Pox take me for a fool, but I didn't leave London fast enough when old Ma Ross died.'

'*Died!*' screamed two voices in unison. 'When?'

'Over a month past.' Sarah shrugged. 'Took sick one morning, spewed up blood, boiled with a raging fever and died afore nightfall—and none sorry to see 'er go, I swear, in all London.'

'Dead . . .' mused Nell grimly. 'Whoever would have thought the old flesh fly could die? She was indestructible, I always thought. London Bridge'd as soon collapse as Ma Ross.'

'Well, she's gorn,' said Sarah firmly. 'Dead as a doornail. Likely she'll never decay, more like pickled in 'er poxey coffin, the old toad!'

'Sarah!' exclaimed Mit, appalled.

Sarah began to wipe the creamy orbs of her chief pride and ignored her. 'So it's curtains for all of us at Lewkenor's Lane. They say Madam Bennet's took the sickness and died too. So the two of 'em went together, rivals to the end.' She laced up her shift and came to sit by the fire. 'It meant no job for me, of course, and I was out on my own for a bit o' custom. 'Ard times, you know—there wasn't a gallant in the city with an eye to look or a finger that itched. I swear I got itched myself something awful. Well, you're not used to it, are you? I'm not a Popish nun, but there you are. What a time to lose your post!'

'But,' interrupted Nell, 'what happed to all the others— Martha, Beatrice, Edith?'

'Ah,' said Sarah, 'that's a tale in itself. Martha's married. She took up with a Thames waterman, and 'e wasn't no fool nor 'e weren't born yesterday and he took off and married Martha for all she'd worked in a bawdy house. 'Ere, did you know your old mate Hobey still came 'anging about Lewkenor's Lane till recently. 'E's a fly one an' no mistake.'

'The others, Sarah . . .' prompted Nell gently.

'Yes, well,' amended Sarah. 'Edith got 'er heart's desire and took respectable three months back. 'Twas all on account o' some clergyman who came to Ma Ross's one evening with Sir Charles Sedley.'

'A clergyman?' exclaimed Mit. 'At *Lewkenor's Lane?*'

'Aye. He came with Sedley, sat down cool as you please and drank brandy all night without turning a hair. In fact, 'twas he who helped Sedley home, I remember—talk about stagger. Yes . . . Edith,' she hurriedly continued as Nell raised eyes to the ceiling. 'She was serving the ruin that night and this pulpit banger—Doctor Tenison, I believe 'e's called—got into conversation with her and . . . well, that's it.'

'Did he marry her?' asked Nell faintly. 'A clergyman?'

'No, no. He offered her the job of housekeeper that same night and she accepted. Good thing, really. She never 'ad the urge like me—couldn't put 'er heart into it, poor girl. Some are like that. She'll like being a housekeeper, I doubt not. He's vicar of St. Martin-in-the-Fields, I believe. He'll look after Edith.'

'And Beatrice?'

There was a prolonged silence. Sarah looked into the flames. 'Dead . . . Nelly. She took sick the day after Ma Ross died. She snuffed it two days later.' Suddenly Sarah turned and Nell saw her face was wet with tears. 'I did what I could, I swear I did. I bought plague water; I forced turpentine pills down 'er; I shoved unicorn powder down 'er, but . . . she died.'

Nell poured out a cup of sack posset and handed it to her quietly. 'Like so many, Sarah. There was little you *could* do.'

Sarah nodded as she sipped and sniffed valiantly. 'It was that made me decide to leave London, and I thought I'd leave for the country next day. But I met a gentleman'—she paused —'a covetous and ungrateful fulsamic fop, a scabbed sheep.'

'What happened, Sarah?' asked Nell.

'He laid me, deceived me and ran off with all my money and even took my paint pots with 'im. He told me he'd take me to the country, told me he was a baronet. I must have been a right healthy fool, as sound as a hog. Lies, all of it! I was looking for 'im when I bumped into you, Nelly. You've no idea how dangerous it is in the streets o' nights, let alone the clanger carts.'

'Clanger carts?' queried Nell, puzzled.

'Aye, they ring the bells to toll the dead to their graves, and when they bring the carts round for the bodies, they 'ave a bell mort dongin' away to let you know 'e's there. Not that you're likely not to know, it's about the only traffic to be heard in the street. It's got so bad now they're buryin' 'em in huge pits all thrown together, and they 'ad to lay on a day collection as well as one at night to collect the bodies, they pile up that quick. Lord! You should see the skull procession at noon through the city in Fenchurch Street on its way to the pits. 'Tis become so regular it almost becomes a public spectacle!'

'*Don't*, Sarah!' Mit shuddered, holding her handkerchief nervously to her mouth.

Sarah shrugged. 'We all might go tomorrow. No use pretendin' different. The quacks can't save you and you might as well nail yourself into your own coffin as go to a pest house. They're no more able to stop the sickness than tomorrow's dawn.'

'I don't understand, Sarah,' argued Nell. 'How are there all these deaths? When Mit and me came through the city we didn't see more than a dozen people all told. Where do the dead come from?'

'Odsbud, Nell, they're still in the city. It's just you don't see 'em. They hide in their houses with the rats. You've no idea how fearful people are, how they daren't venture abroad, and when they do, avoid everyone else. People are scared to their breeks. No one dares to buy a periwig any more for fear it is made of hair cut from the heads of folk dead of the plague. The Mayor has to pay collectors of bodies to get skinned as newts before they'll go on the round at all. S'life, even the pesthouse nurses are keeled over as saints! It's no wonder. If you take the sickness, they shut up your house, no matter who's in it, post a guard outside to make sure you don't escape, and lock you all in for forty days. By the time they'll let you out, you're all dead and no mistake!' She crunched on a Dantzic gherkin. 'People blame anything from the rats to the Papists.'

'Aye, I know,' Nell agreed. 'There was a woman at Brighthelmstone, at the same inn as Charles and me, swore 'twas the Papists who had caused the sickness, though quite how, I never found out.'

Sarah fixed an intent green glance upon her. 'What in hell are you and Mit doing in London?' she asked.

They sat around the fire while Nell told Sarah the whole story. She did not interrupt at all while Nell recounted the events which had led up to her return, but looked slightly startled when Nell announced her intention to seek out Rob Duncan on the morrow.

'You'll never find 'im, Nelly, or if you do, you'll take the sickness and die with 'im. Leave London tomorrow.'

Nell shook her head stubbornly. 'No, I'll go to his lodgings.'

'And what if he's not there?' Sarah rose and began to pace the room, her gown clasped about her. 'Let me think. I heard all the merchants have moved to the parish of St. Michael's Cornhill. There's not been a case o' sickness there all summer despite the rest of the city's stricken. 'Tis said they'll pay any price, even for an attic, if 'tis within the bounds of the parish.'

'It's right in the centre of London!' protested Mit.

'Aye, but it's free from infection for all that. God knows why, I don't. Some of them money coves are still in London. They value their lives less than the risk of their gold pieces going to looters and vagabonds.'

Dragging two pallets into the single chamber, the three girls settled down to sleep after Nell had shot the bolt and rammed a chair up against the door. As she lay dozing off to slumber there came a distant rattle of coach wheels coming around the corner of Cradle Alley. Nell sat up in bed, listening. The wheels came closer, metal crunching on cobblestones, and she heard the muffled dong of a hand bell. She shivered. A raucous voice called out, breaking the peace of the still night air: 'Bring out your dead . . .' it cried. 'Bring out your dead . . .'

The lackey who eventually answered Nell's repeated summons on the door of Robert Duncan's lodgings in King Street was supercilious, and indeed, little short of offensive. A small serving wench looking for a job, he doubted not. He was surprised when the small serving wench asked for the whereabouts of a respectable man like Robert Duncan. He stood well within the shade of the porch and sniffed at a pomander. 'I 'ave no h'idea where Master Duncan is at present. 'E left 'is lodgings h'at a moment's notice and gave no h'address. Now, if you will h'excuse . . .' He attempted to shut the door, but found the small serving wench's foot blocking its passage.

'You must know something,' she said firmly. 'Did Master Duncan not say even roughly where he was going?' Two gold coins dropped inside the doorway, and Mit hid a smile. 'Where is he?' repeated Nell tartly.

The lackey remained as impassive as ever, although he looked somewhat surprised. 'I will h'enquire,' he said loftily. A moment later he returned. 'I 'ave reason to think Master Duncan might be found h'at a hostelry at the sign of the Nodding Cow.'

'Where *is* it?' she pleaded.

The lackey shrugged. 'That I could not say, miss. Now, h'if you will h'excuse me . . .' He shut the door and this time Nell did not prevent him.

'Where is it?' she asked Mit helplessly. 'Where in the name of glory is the place?'

'Best try Cornhill, Nelly,' advised Mit philosophically. 'Might as well start there.'

Three hours later found them both tired and dispirited after they had combed the warren of alleys in the parish of Cornhill. They could find no house beneath a sign resembling a nodding cow and there were few to ask the way.

'Not but what those we see back off like *we've* got the sickness,' complained Mit, easing her foot in its shoe. 'If I tramp many more streets I'll be as broiled as the meat in this basket.' She looked down at the muslin-covered basket crammed with provisions which she held.

Nell mopped her brow and gazed down the street, shaking her head in wonder. 'It's so *quiet*,' she said. 'Funny how you don't notice till there's no noise, how noisy it must have been. Nobody calling out "Four for sixpence" or "Old shoes for brooms"; no 'prentices—nothing! 'Tis as if all London's become like Alsatia, sort of eerie and—'

'Nelly,' whispered Mit. 'D'you see that man over there?' She gestured at a slouching figure leaning against the boarded-over window of a shop opposite and regarding them out of a pair of cold grey eyes.

'Come on, Mit, let's move on,' murmured Nell. 'I mislike the look in yonder gentleman's oglers.' Mit hitched the basket up and followed her down the street, but both of them heard the footsteps treading behind. Nell quickened her pace; so did he. 'I'll warrant there are several anglers like him in the city. Think of all the empty houses people have fled. Lord! It must be like a dream to the fencing cullies.'

'The answer to a patricio's prayer,' agreed Mit gloomily. Suddenly she dug Nell in the ribs. ' 'E's gorn, Nelly!'

Glancing round, they both saw the empty alley. 'Thank God for that,' murmured Nell. 'The last thing I needed was a gull dabbler to sort out.' They walked along peering up at the stained and weathered signs that hung motionless above. 'Dancing women, prancing unicorns, crowns and roses—but no goddammed nodding cow,' she said irritably. She ducked her head under a low archway that spanned the alley beside a richly decorated house with fine pargetting carved and painted. A single toll of a bell sounded out above their heads, and Nell sighed, 'Enough to give you the jerks, isn't it, Mit?'

'That's the bell of St. Michael Archangel, Nelly. It's famous in Cornhill parish. Time was that was reckoned the first peel in all London—ten bells strung in a row. It used to sound like music in the sky, they say. There's a foundling hospital behind the church and any infant left on the church doorstep is given the name Cornhill. It's—Oh!' She looked terrified and her hand went up to her mouth.

Nell whipped around. There, lounging under the gabling, stood the man with the cold grey eyes, looking mockingly at them as they stood open-mouthed.

'Arternoon,' he remarked.

'What were you doing following us?' flared Nell. 'I suppose now the city's empty of men you think you've a chance with a woman who wouldn't mind a tumble with a dancing bear as the city's so bereft of gallants. Well, you're no gallant—you're no more than an ounce of ratsbane!'

Mit tugged at her arm frenziedly. 'Nelly, look!' Above them, creaking slightly in the wind, hung a gilded sign painted with the device of a dun-coloured cow under a crescent moon. 'The Nodding Cow,' breathed Nell. As their eyes travelled downward, she felt her heart stop and then thud suddenly. Before her gaze was writ the legend now common to all the city. A huge clumsy cross, daubed in bull's blood, spread its tentacles across the door, and beneath it the fatal cry: *Lord have mercy upon us.*

' 'Tis the plague.' The man with grey eyes nodded. 'It's spread into Cornhill for a week or more now. This my reg'lar beat—see!'

'Beat?'

'Aye. I'm appointed by my Lord Mayor and the City Council to patrol all this street and round the corner to make sure them what's shut up stays shut up. You wouldn't believe it, but the pest 'ouses are full up to the brim now. The only way to stop the infection is to shut up all them what's in an infected house, and leave 'em for forty days. 'Course, I shoves some food through to 'em onct in a while. That and the dousing.' He gestured to a wooden bucket standing by his side on the cobbles which Nell and Mit had not noticed. 'I bin to the conduit to get the water,' he explained, and his eyes, which before had seemed sinister, now merely seemed bovine to the two of them. 'You has to put vinegar in and throw it all over the street.'

Nell spoke urgently. 'D'you know who's shut up in there?'

'Well now'—he scratched his head— 'there's so many of 'em. I reckon there was a vintner and a couple o' goldsmiths and their wives—they're dead now, cart came for 'em last night— and a Scottish merchant, if I remember aright. Don't know if 'e's still alive.'

Nell took the basket from Mit. 'You go back to the Cock and Pye and wait for me there.'

'You're not going in!' protested Mit, horrified. 'You can't. It's infected, Nelly, you can't!'

Nell calmly placed her hand over Mit's mouth. 'I've got to go in. It's Master Duncan and he might be dying. I *must* go in, don't you see, Mit? You go on back to the Cock and Pye; no sense both of us getting infected. I'll have all I need for a week in here.' Her hand patted the basket. She turned to the guard. 'I want to go in,' she said.

He gaped. 'You can't do that—there's no rule that says—'

Nell took the knob of the door in one hand and put her weight against it. It gave, and as it opened, the seal of black tape put there by the order of the Lord Mayor broke and hung down, severed.

'You'll get me a hemp halter, you will!' gabbled the guard.

Nell ignored him and turned to Mit. 'Wait a week, and if I'm not back, go on without me. Go to Rose—she might be hard, but she'll see you all right. Goodbye, Mit.'

As the door swung away they could see a gaping black void behind. Before Mit could stop her, Nell had slipped inside and the door closed.

'She's as mad as springtime—I'll cry flounders if she ain't!' exploded the guard.

As her eyes became accustomed to the light that filtered through the cracks of the wooden shutters, Nell saw a staircase stretching up before her. She climbed up, carrying the basket, and found a narrow passage with four doors set in it. With heart thumping uncomfortably, she opened the first door. The room was empty. Keeping her cloak up before her mouth, she trod softly along and made to open the second door. A choked cry suddenly assaulted her ears. It seemed to come from behind the door at the end of the passage. She froze as the cry rose to a shriek, then ended in a moan that finally died away. The house became utterly still, and Nell's footsteps sounded hollow on the boards as she quietly edged herself forward and flung the door open.

Before her was a large bedchamber furnished richly in black bog oak. The light entering through the slats over the window showed up the dull richness of maroon velvet hangings and the ornate gilding on the carved chimney piece. The room was in total disarray: clothes laying in piles on the floor; soiled linen was draped over the back of one chair and trailed across the room. As Nell's eyes wandered to the great bed against the wall, she saw with dismay a table on its side, surrounded by many pieces of broken pottery strewn around. A privy stood in one corner surrounded by flies.

Then she heard the steady plip-plip of dripping liquid and saw that it came from a jug of blue-painted galleyware that lay on its side, the claret which it had contained still dripping to form a purple stain on the floor. A man's hand lay slackly curved about a wineglass behind it. He lay back in the great bed, his hair, grey and tousled, sticking to a brow wet with the heat of fever. His eyes, sunken in their sockets, were clouded and blank as they focused on Nell, who moved slowly into the chamber. She came up to the bed and stopped.

He felt a cool hand on his brow; he heard a voice exclaim fiercely, 'You stubborn, stupid, blood-cussed old fool!'

Eight

Among other stories one was very passionate methought, of a complaint brought against a man in the towne for taking a child from London from an infected house. Alderman Hooker told us it was the child of a very able citizen in Gracious Street, a saddler, who had buried all the rest of his children of the plague, and himself and wife now being shut up and in despair of escaping, did desire only to save the life of this little child . . .

—*The Diary of Samuel Pepys
September 3rd, 1665*

When Robert Duncan awoke he could tell from the glow of the candlelight by his bed that it was night. Then, turning his head on the pillow, he saw her crouched before the fireplace, heating something in an iron saucepan on the fire. He moistened his cracked lips and uttered one word: 'Nell.'

She turned and came swiftly over to him. Her hair was bound close to her head in a snood and she smiled at him, showing a row of perfect little white teeth. 'I see you're awake, Master Duncan,' she said.

Duncan looked bemused; his voice was weak and there was

a beading of moisture on his brow. 'I thought I saw ye afore and then I thought it was a dream. When I woke up a second ago I was sure you'd be gone, but here ye are. Am I still dreaming, or what?'

She squeezed out a cloth from a bowl and sponged his forehead. 'Rest, Rob. You've caught the sickness but I doubt not we'll pull you through it.'

One of his hands pulled free and gestured vaguely around. 'You've changed the look o' this room, hinnie.'

The golden candlelight bathed the bedchamber in a gentle light which revealed the gleam of gilding on polished wood, a newly swept floor with no trace of debris and the savoury aroma of broth simmering on the hob. The atmosphere was ordered and quiet. Duncan lay back on the pillows, panting, while Nell moved back to spoon the broth into a wooden bowl. 'I'll clean this muck hole out properly tomorrow,' she said over her shoulder. 'By rights it'd be better for a pulvill of sulphur and vinegar, but I doubt that would see me off as well as the plague.'

This sally drew a chuckle from Duncan, but it turned into a racking cough which shook his whole body. He lay wheezing while she held him till the spasm had passed. 'Why did you come, lassie?' he gasped. 'When I went to a' that trouble to get ye out o' London, for why did ye come back, in heaven's name?'

'I had a mind to see the sights,' replied Nell soothingly and lifted him up to take some broth.

Duncan managed a few spoonfuls and then shook his head. 'Enough for now,' he murmured. There was a pause while he lay resting. After a while he spoke. 'They're a' dead, you know, a' the lot o' them. We all came here to escape the plague and we a' ended by being shut up together to die of it. Ah mind there must be a corpse next door. I'd taken the sickness myself when he died and I couldna' lift him out to the cart when it came. That's when I fell and caused a' the damage.' He found her eyes upon him and smiled a little. 'I'm a gae fool—I heard ye say so when I dreamt o' you first, and you're right.'

She shook her head silently and patted his hand.

'I'd urge ye to go, Nelly, but I know you're a stubborn wench, as stubborn as a mule, and you'd never listen. In truth I've no energy to argue. I'm more glad to see you, my dear, than a host o' ships returning wi' full cargoes. Haply I'll . . .' He suddenly arched in pain and remained rigid for a moment, sweat pouring from him, his mouth working as he sought to repress the cry that leapt to his lips, and then he subsided again, muttering 'My armpit . . . swelling.'

Nell ripped open his shirt to find the skin under Duncan's arm stretched taut over a hard knotty lump that glistened slightly and felt solid to the touch. As she pressed gently on it Duncan groaned. 'Leave it, lassie, dinna' fash. For the love o' God.' Carefully she soaked the cloth and folded it into a pad which she placed over the buboe. Straightening, she saw that Robert Duncan had fallen asleep.

As she surveyed him lying there, Nell felt a feeling of panic well up in her. She was alone in a city of the dead and dying. Duncan relied on her utterly, and yet she had no knowledge at all of the plague or of how to treat it. She knew Duncan was gravely ill but could not help him. Some words Bab Knipp had told her months before came to mind: 'The crisis comes when the buboe bursts. When that happens, they either get better speedily or die speedily. It settles it one way or the other. If they get no buboe, it's curtains.' She remembered the jibe of Charles Hart: 'You can do no good. He is as good as dead.'

Sighing, Nell went over to the window, and through the gaps in the shutters, looked out over the gloomy streets on this her second night in the cursed metropolis. Hart was right, of course, she thought. She could not cure Duncan of the plague. Again in the distance her ears caught the rattle of wheels, the dong of the bell and the distant cry: 'Bring out your dead . . . Bring out your dead . . . !" Behind her, Nell could hear the peaceful sound of Duncan's breathing in the quiet chamber. She knew she was not sorry that she had come.

All through the next day Duncan lay tossing and fevered, thrashing about on the bed and moaning, and for a time he did not appear to know her. More than once Nell caught the sound of the name 'Hamish' bubble to his lips and die away, and she remembered this was the name of Duncan's son, who had died of a dog's bite so many years before. Towards evening he regained consciousness but was too ill to take food or drink, and was bent anew with coughing until he slid off into sleep. His pallor was ghastly and his breath now came in short painful gasps. The next night Nell went to bed as usual but left a candle burning. She was woken at two in the morning by a harsh and terrible cry that ripped across the room.

Waking in a panic, she saw Duncan trying vainly to get out of bed. As she ran forward to catch him he collapsed across the bed and she had to lift him back onto the pillows, grunting and muttering. Nell saw the stains running across the bed linen and down his nightgown. The buboe had burst.

Frantically she cleaned up the worst of the mess and tried to stanch the dark trickle of blood that ran sluggishly from the hollow in his armpit; Duncan lay motionless, barely breathing. Nell went over to the bucket to wash out the cloths. His words came quiet but clear to her from the bed: 'The old man said doom was coming, and he was in the right of it. He got kicked in the gutter for his pains but he saw what was coming for this city . . . and for me.'

'What man, Rob?' Nell asked gently, picking up a flask of brandy.

'Och, just a man in the Cock and Pye a while back, lassie. They said he was mad, but it's us who were the mad ones, I'm thinking.'

Nell went over to him and sat on the bed, stroking his hand. 'Nay, Rob, we'll have you sitting in the pit of Drury Lane again and I'll throw you a flower when I come on at the end, like I . . .' Her voice cracked, and she sought unsuccessfully for her handkerchief and blew her nose fiercely.

'Lassie, lassie . . .' he said, gently stroking her wet cheek with his finger. 'Dinna fret. Life's been a sore burden to me this many a year and I'll no' repine the leaving of it. What is there left to me? I have no wife to care, no children whose fortunes need my helping hand. That was all taken from me years ago. I'll no' fight taking the swan's path.' He lay back for a time, breathing heavily. 'For all its wealth my life's borne naught but windle straws and sandy laverocks. 'Tis little enough I've made apart frae money. But money has its uses—' His voice was cut off by a sudden horrid rattling at the back of his throat. Nell put the flask to his cracked lips and poured a little brandy between them. As the fiery liquid reached him, he choked and then coughed to a standstill.

'You must rest, Rob,' she said urgently. 'Try and sleep for a while.'

His eyes under the stern bushy brows softened as they looked at her. 'Sage counsel, Nelly, but it comes too late for me, I'm thinking. You're a guid stout lassie so . . . so ye are.' He gasped at Nell, 'When I am gone, go to Master Sim Whitelife. He . . . he looks after my money for me. Take him this ring . . .' He fumbled at his hand and drew off a heavy gold signet. 'Give him this and tell him I am dead. He lives at the sign of the Dolphin in Goldsmith's Row. Take the bunch of keys you will find under the pillow and . . . and . . .'

Duncan tried to sit up, but was suddenly racked with a paroxysm of coughing that brought up a great gout of blood onto the pillow. Nell wiped his mouth gently and tried to push him back on the bed, but he shook his head wearily and took hold of her wrist. 'No, no time . . . must listen. Take ring and keys to Whitelife, tell him you are my adopted daughter. Want you to go to Whitelife . . . must . . .' His eyes took on a staring glazed look as Nell, horrified, looked down. His grasp on her wrist slackened and his head fell back. For a second or two there came again the rattling in the back of his throat— and then, abruptly, it stopped.

'Can I give you a bottle or two of Streatham spring water, William?' asked Mr. Pepys of his friend Alderman Hooker as they strolled up Fish Street hill. ' 'Twill not cure aught but 'tis monstrous comforting to have about one.'

'Let me offer *you* some roll tobacco, Sam,' returned Alderman Hooker. 'You can carry it about with you and chew it at leisure.'

Mr. Pepys thanked him. Alderman Hooker strode ahead past the old Fishmarket and the Fishmonger's Hall, followed by his friend, very point de vice in sky-blue silk trimmed with gold buttons and gold lacing at the cuffs. Despite the empty streets and the silence, both men appeared to be in high spirits. Mr. Pepys, indeed, gave a stone a thwack with his elegant cane while he told Hooker of the recent wedding of Lord Sandwich's daughter Jemima to Sir George Carteret's son.

'Never have I seen a boy so shy, I give you my word,' he declared. 'He had no idea how to behave with ladies, what compliments to pay. He hardly dared to talk to her, and as for taking her hand . . .' An eloquent shrug finished the sentence. 'I had to take him on one side; my Lady Jem was blushing for him as much as for herself!'

'I warrant they were less shy after their wedding night, when you had flung the slipper and left them to't!'

'Aye.' Mr. Pepys smiled. 'There was a sudden *change*. I think Master Carteret got organ-ised.' Both of them laughed heartily.

' 'Tis little enough we have to be merry about, to be sure,' complained Alderman Hooker. 'The plague affects us all.'

Mr. Pepys nodded. 'I heard but last week that Old Will and his family who sold ale for years at the door of Westminster Hall were all dead in a day of the pestilence.'

Alderman Hooker sighed, but he would have been astonished could he have divined the train of Mr. Pepys's thoughts. They swung on the pivot of Westminster Hall indeed, but less on Old Will than on the Swan tavern in Palace Yard and in particular on the ripe body of Sarah the tavern wench there. Mr. Pepys grinned to himself and swaggered a little as he remembered how he had taken Sarah to Tothill Fields and what had happened later in a tavern room upstairs. A sigh escaped his lips, which honest William Hooker took for one of sympathy for the victims of the sickness. A good fellow, Sam Pepys, he thought to himself.

As they made their way up to the thoroughfare of Gracious Street, Sam thought of his life since he had sent his wife for safety to the house of his friend Master Sheldon at Woolwich.

There had not only been Sarah, but Mary of the Harp and Ball tavern near Charing Cross—his eyes brightened as he remembered her lying expectantly beneath him in the chamber he had hired at Hampstead. Life had its compensations, he supposed. Sarah, Mary and eager Mrs. Bagwell, wife to one of his captains. She knew how best to please her husband's employer—leaving the light in her window at Deptford to guide Mr. Pepys safe into port while her husband was away.

Of course he missed Lizbet, he told himself. Hadn't he gone to the trouble of visiting her more than once at Woolwich; hadn't he presented her with that diamond ring worth at least £10 but three weeks past?

'How are *you* with your wife away, Sam, you rogue?' enquired Alderman Hooker jovially.

'Eh? Oh, tolerable, William, tolerable. Pressure of work leaves little time, you know.' Mr. Pepys's eyes glanced uneasily away.

'Don't work too hard, Sam. Lord knows what the Navy Board would do without you,' Hooker advised.

Mr. Pepys smiled and bowed slightly. 'I mean to keep my health, certainly.'

Alderman Hooker stopped at the top of Fish Street hill and looked down the deserted curving length of Gracious Street beneath the shelter of its tiles and gabling. 'Odsbud!' he exclaimed. 'Where's all the traffic gone—the coal carts, the hackneys and the coaches? Gracious Street's usually crammed to bursting. I remember when I took coach at the Mitre, I was a full hour reaching the highway!'

'As well ask where all the traders are or where all the ships are, unloading their cargoes at Billingsgate? We've whipped the Dutch, William, but the plague has stopped our trade just as surely.'

Alderman Hooker tutted irritably as they walked down Gracious Street. 'I only hope our fleet finds the remainder of the Dutch. God grant they find them and destroy them!' said Pepys passionately. 'At least we can lift our heads a trifle then and feel the wind in our faces. We sink Dutchmen after Dutchmen, but still they are not destroyed.'

'I think 'tis because the devil shits Dutchmen,' Alderman Hooker agreed gloomily.

They had only proceeded halfway down Gracious Street when Mr. Pepys's ears were assailed by the noises of a loud and impassioned dispute that echoed in the otherwise deserted thoroughfare. He espied a small knot of people gathered in front of a house which had the sign of a saddler—a high saddle with two stirrups suspended above what was obviously the shop—jutting out into the street. As Mr. Pepys watched, he saw to his surprise the small body of a little boy, entirely naked, being thrust at one moment out of the window at the front of the house and being as firmly pushed back the next. The child was crying and was surrounded by four gesticulating men who appeared not to notice either Mr. Pepys or Alderman Hooker, so intent was their concentration on the dispute in hand.

Alderman Hooker looked back to see why his friend had stopped, and saw the argument too. 'Come on, Sam,' he advised. ' 'Tis naught but a brawl!'

But at that instant Mr. Pepys saw the white-faced spectre of a woman lean from the casement and exclaim in tear-ridden accents, 'Pray, *pray* take my child! Let *us* die, but take him, for the love of God! Oh, *please*!'

With a feeling that perhaps he might regret his interest later, Mr. Pepys, followed by a dubious Alderman Hooker, strolled over to the group by the window. They greeted him with a wary respect, for it was obvious to all that both the strangers were gentlemen, and one, from the cut of his jib and his silks and walking cane, could be a man of substance. Mr. Pepys found at least one tugged forelock and one doffed hat as he enquired politely the reason for the disturbance.

A barrage of voices broke about his ears. The pale woman in the house burst into sobs and the little boy set up a sympathetic wail that led Mr. Pepys to tap loudly on the lintel with his cane to restore order. 'One at a time,' he said briefly. 'You speak!'

The individual thus addressed was a greasy, stocky man with a belligerent, jutting lower lip and a muted form of patois that made elucidation difficult. 'They wanna let the kid out—see, guv'nor. Can't be done! Rules is rules!' Having delivered himself of this information, he sank back into a blessed relief of chewing silence.

Mr. Pepys turned in exasperation to the man leaning out of the window with one arm clasped about the boy. His face was thin and drawn, there were deep shadows under his eyes and his smooth white hair framed an expression of utter weariness. Mr. Pepys felt interest stir in him. Then, as he asked the saddler, for such he obviously was, to inform him what was going on, he saw the message of death scrawled on the door. Instinctively he started back, putting up one hand to cover his mouth, his eyes darting up in horrified fashion to the man standing patiently within the confines of the shop.

The man's face seemed to whiten as he saw Mr. Pepys's expression and he replied in a calm voice, 'You divine aright, sir. My wife and family are shut up for the statutory period of forty days by order of the Mayor until we are free from infection or until we are dead. My youngest daughter took the sickness first . . .' He swallowed and looked directly at Mr. Pepys. 'A week past I had three daughters and two sons. Now I have only one little son, Toby here.' He laid a hand gently on the boy's shoulder. 'My wife and I are content to wait here for death, should the Lord send it. We desire only to save the life of our child. He has committed no crime—how can he hurt anyone? Anyone can see he does not carry the sickness—'He turned the boy's limbs for Sam to see. 'My wife has bathed him in vinegar and burnt all his clothes, so there is no danger of infection. My good friend here, Master Burton, has offered to take the boy. Sir'—his eyes pleaded with Mr. Pepys—'can you not order the guard and this gentleman here to allow us to save our son?'

Mr. Pepys turned back to the monosyllabic individual who was obviously the guard and felt in his pocket for a guinea. But he was forestalled by a bustling little man who pushed himself forward and sniffed that he was Master Ignatius Proudie, member of the honourable guild of Grocers and member of the Common Council of the city. '. . . And I know when I see the law being broken,' he finished fussily. 'I know not who you are, sir, but I know the order laid on us all by the Lord Mayor and aldermen with the full agreement of the Common Council!'

'I am Master Pepys, Clerk of the Acts to his Majesty's Navy,' said Sam with some hauteur, 'and this is Alderman Hooker.' He gestured to William Hooker, who bowed stiffly.

'Then,' said Master Proudie eagerly, 'you must support me in this, sir. This man and his family are bound to their homes for the statutory period by the force of law. To seek to evade this law, as you must know, is an offence punishable by death!'

' 'Tis likely death will visit this poor man in any case, sirrah,' retorted Alderman Hooker irritably. He wished Sam had never stopped to investigate. He was in a damnable position—his heart urged that the boy be released; his position as alderman required him to uphold the obnoxious Master Proudie.

'I never sought to evade the law, sir!' protested the saddler. 'As God is my witness, nobody who is infected ever left this house.'

'You have broken the law in this instance, fellow,' sneered Master Proudie. 'You have broken the law and you must pay for it.'

'Oh, go and wash your tongue in chicken's droppings!' came a crushing retort. Master Proudie found himself being regarded by a dazzlingly beautiful girl with plentiful tawny hair caught up in a snood. She carried a basket on one hip and her cloak was flung negligently over one slim shoulder. She stood in the street, watching them all, her bosom rising and falling in seething anger. 'The law's barbaric and ought to be changed, and as for you, sir'—she gave Master Proudie a withering look which made him feel acutely uncomfortable—'you'd do better to crawl back into the rathole from where I have no doubt you came.'

Master Proudie endeavoured to assert himself. He began to protest shrilly.

'You button your lip, prick'louse,' she said. 'Or I'll find ways to button it.' Her basket swung easily in one capable hand.

Master Proudie was silent.

Alderman Hooker looked at her in open admiration, but the play-going Mr. Pepys stepped forward, stammering. 'It—it *is* you, isn't it?' he said, an expression of dawning recognition lighting up his face. 'Mistress Gwynne! What in the name of God is the leading actress of the Theatre Royal doing here?'

She smiled at him as one old friend to another. 'A private matter that is closed now by the grave, sir. What is causing all this pother?'

Mr. Pepys told her the unhappy tale of the saddler, and she knitted her brows as he unfolded the details of the family's plight.

' 'Tis the law,' began Master Proudie unwisely, but a flash from a pair of fine eyes reduced him to silence.

'It seems that the child must stay where he is until death or time releases him,' finished Mr. Pepys bleakly.

Alderman Hooker, even more impressed by the intelligence that the beautiful girl appeared to be none other than a famous actress and a friend of Mr. Pepys to boot, now found himself subjected to a swift examination.

'*Is* this the law, sir?' she challenged him. 'Are the healthy to be shut up with the sick and dying?'

Hooker looked uncomfortable beneath the twin gazes bent upon him by Nell and the ubiquitous Master Proudie. 'I have to state that that is indeed the law,' he said heavily, 'unless . . .'

'Yes?' said Nell eagerly.

'Unless it could be proved that the boy does not carry the sickness. Haply a doctor . . .'

'I could fetch one,' interjected Master Burton, the saddler's friend, who had hitherto remained silent.

'Nonsense!' interrupted Proudie scornfully. 'No doctor could so pronounce, and it would be impossible to find one, what's more!'

Suddenly, standing with his back to Master Proudie, Alderman Hooker and Nell saw Mr. Pepys close one eye in a profound wink. Then he cleared his throat and said impressively, 'This is a matter which must be properly investigated. I really cannot stand in the street wrangling like a trader!' He turned to Master Proudie. 'I shall mention this matter when I call on his Grace the Duke of Albemarle this evening. We will see what he has to say about a law that spreads infection and increases the number of dead in this city!'

Master Proudie gaped at him, obviously awed by the mention of the Duke's name. 'It shall be reported upon to the Lord Mayor and the city aldermen,' added Hooker in support.

'I demand to be present when this is discussed!' bleated Master Proudie in a last vain protest.

'There is not the slightest chance you will be present,' said Mr. Pepys coldly. 'Unless of course you are an intimate acquaintance of his Grace?' The question, smoothly put, reduced Master Proudie to incoherent mumblings. Having surveyed him for a moment, Mr. Pepys turned a magnificent silk shoulder upon him. When Master Proudie did not move, he glanced back and raised his brows in surprise. 'We must not keep you, sir,' he said inexorably. 'I believe you must have some pressing business to attend to.'

Encountering three pairs of hostile eyes, Master Proudie took his leave. As he made a move to go, Nell gave a quick jerk with her basket and Master Proudie jumped before tottering off as fast as his spindly legs could carry him. Nell giggled. 'What a scurvy little mongrel zealot of a man!' she sniffed.

Having disposed of Master Proudie, Mr. Pepys returned to the business in hand. He fished in his pocket and found a guinea, which he tossed in his hand. 'What a horrific task you are undertaking,' he said amiably to the guard. 'I dare say these streets are like an oven to patrol! Let me soothe your parched throat. I saw there was an alehouse in Fish Street still open as we came here.'

A guinea landed in the astonished guard's hand, and with much forelock-tugging and bowing he shuffled off down the street.

'Now,' said Mr. Pepys triumphantly, 'we can proceed to business.' He turned to the bewildered saddler. 'Friend, I fear we cannot allow you to hand your son over to Master Burton at this time. It would create gossip involving myself and Alderman Hooker, and your son would be pursued and taken away from Master Burton and brought back here. You yourself might well end on the gibbet at Tyburn for your pains. No'—he tapped one tooth—'we must be careful and spirit him away beyond Master Proudie's snooping nose *and* the sickness. Where do you live, sir?' he asked Master Burton.

'At Greenwich, sir.'

'Then I think we may save your son,' Mr. Pepys said to the saddler. 'Tonight you must be ready to hand him over to someone I shall send. He will take him from the city and care for him safely until the plague is over.'

'Sir, I thank you, but'—the saddler's eyes were calm—'we live in uncertain times. I may well be dead before the week is out. What then?'

'I give you my word,' promised Mr. Pepys, 'your child will be looked after. We shall take your son safe away tonight. Tomorrow or whenever you are asked, you will say your son disobeyed you and left the house to go to Master Burton's. When they find he is not there, you will not be blamed. It will be assumed he took ill of the sickness and died before he reached his destination.'

Mr. Pepys found his arm being shaken by Nell. 'Let *me* come for him,' she urged. 'I am to leave London tonight and I can take him with me.' She looked at the saddler. 'Will you entrust your son to a vizard harpy from Drury Lane?'

Tears stood in his eyes. 'Aye, mistress—and God bless the pair of you!'

'We must leave, Sam,' urged Hooker. 'The guard will be back, and it will seem suspicious if we linger and the boy's disappearance is soon discovered.'

Mr. Pepys nodded and whispered tersely to Nell, 'The guard will be here tonight. You must remove the child without him seeing. That done, do not attempt to take him out of London openly, in case his escape is quickly noted. Take him to London Bridge and find there a spare barge.' He had a twinkle in his eye. 'As Clerk of the Acts to his Majesty's Navy, I can at least lay my hands on a barge when necessary!'

It was one full hour later that Nell trod up the narrow stairs and flung open the door of her bedchamber. Mit was darning a stocking by the fire. When the door latch lifted she looked up in alarm. But when she saw who stood on the threshold she gave one shriek and threw her darning to the ground. 'Nelly, you 'ole doxey you!' With which obscure greeting she seized her young mistress by the shoulders and whirled her around the room.

The moon was high in the sky, dappling the russet roofs with smears of shadow, when the guard ambling down Gracious Street stopped in the middle of a swig of 'plague water.' A drip of the aromatic-flavoured brandy trickled down his jowl when he saw who was approaching in the light of his lantern.

It was a dusky-haired girl with a shawl wrapped around her against the chill of the night air. She looked up as she drew close to him and flashed him a smile and a wink. ' 'Evenin', soldier!' she said cheerily. To the guard's mind, somewhat dulled by repeated doses of 'plague water,' her manner seemed one of invitation. The appellation of 'soldier' appealed to his vanity. He threw out his chest and winked back. 'My name's Mit,' came the voice. 'Wot's yourn?'

Feeling that fate had at last taken pity on him, the guard informed her hoarsely that his name was 'Enery Budd. She drew close to him. 'What a lonely job,' she whispered, 'patrolling these dark streets on your own. You must be brave, with the sickness about an' all.' Henry Budd felt a hand rest lightly on one whiskery cheek. 'Aren't you scared, all on your own like this?'

He shook his head. 'I ain't one t' get wind up me gills,' he told her. 'No more I ain't no gilly mort neither.'

'I love strong men,' sighed Mit, putting her head on his shoulder. 'I like a man to be a man, not a simpering fop.'

There was a clatter and a muffled oath from somewhere further down. The guard turned and squinted into the darkness; it sounded like a shutter banging, he thought vaguely.

' 'Tis only the rats,' said Mit persuasively. 'They've taken over all the city.'

Master Budd hesitated, but then he felt her lips brush his grimy neck and he abandoned notions of duty.

There under the darkest shadow of the bridge it lay, the mist rising from the water festooning the bows with a cold clinging vapour. The ripple and eddy of the flow of the river caught at the rope which was looped around one of the tall piers of the great bridge which soared above, gaunt and seemingly deserted under the night sky.

Hurrying down to the Old Swan Stairs came three muffled shapes, which detached from one another when they reached the platform at the bottom. One shape pulled at the rope, and the long, low barge came drifting in to lie by the platform.

An urgent whisper sounded oddly loud in the stillness and echoed under the chamber of the arch. 'Get in and lie flat along the boards!' There was a ripple, and the boat rocked madly as two figures settled in the bottom of the barge and lay obediently down. There came a squeaked protest: 'S'truth, I've split me petticoat on an oar!'

'Sssh!'

Nell carefully stepped into the barge and took the canvas sheet that was neatly rolled at one end. Carefully she unfolded it, stretching it over the top of the barge until it reached the two crouched people at one end. She took two little hands in hers. 'All right, Toby?' she asked. From the shadow she saw a head nod, and an uneven voice just short of tears murmured, 'All right, Mrs. Nell.'

'Good lad. Don't start on the waterworks or you'll have Mit at it, and that'll swamp the boat!' A weak protest answered her. She drew the canvas over their heads and looped rope over it, leaving just one corner free. Then she stood up and looked at it.

To all intents and purposes it appeared that the barge was deserted, possibly a coal or timber carrier that had come upstream from Queenhithe. Beneath the night sky it lay low in the water, no more than a shadow moving past in the Thames with the tide. Nell leant over and cut the rope which held it,

and the current of the river took the boat in its grasp. She
crept under the canvas and lay there looking up at the stars
while the swift-running Thames took the barge out into mid-
stream and floated it past the tall shuttered warehouses of
Billingsgate wharf.

A solitary sentry standing on the ramparts of St. Thomas's
Tower fancied he saw something pass beneath in the moonlight. Yet as he shaded his eyes with his hand he decided that
it must have been a trick of the light. The river kept its secret
as the barge bubbled its way past the Tower and down to
Richmond.

Part Two
Charles the Second

*Much more her growing virtue did sustain,
While dear Charles Hart and Buckhurst sued in vain.
In vain they sued, curs'd be the envious tongue
That her undoubted chastity would wrong.*

*Panegyric on Nell Gwynne
Anon.*

One

*The King lived with his ministers
as he did with his mistresses; he used them,
but he was not in love with them.*

A Character of Charles the Second
—*George Savile, Marquess of Halifax*

Queen Catherine of Braganza was crying in her apartments at Whitehall Palace. As in everything she did she was discreet in her grief. No one could see her; she had locked the door of her bedchamber and dismissed her ladies before she gave way to her private misery. And as she cried, the words beat fiercely in her brain: 'Barren . . . barren . . . a barren wife . . . a barren Queen . . . a barren lover.' It throbbed like a pulse in her head. She saw again the look of startled surprise on the face of Lady Silvis and the look of embarrassment on that of the Countess of Suffolk, but it was too late. Catherine had heard the words clearly as she rounded the corner of the Privy Garden: 'His Majesty is wedded to a blotted piece of alabaster. She is barren in money, barren in looks and barren in her seed. As well look for a great belly in a rock as in her!'

Too late she had heard the rustle of the Queen's gown

against the leaves. The words had hit home even as Lady Silvis turned, her thin face crimsoning in horror to see the pale, set figure of her royal mistress standing before her. Catherine's dignity, as ever, had not failed her. Not by the veriest flicker of an eyelash did she betray her feelings, but calmly passed the low-curtseying ladies and went on to her apartments. Once there, her control had evaporated and she had only just been able to dismiss her ladies before her emotions forced themselves to the surface. It was in vain to tell herself that Lady Silvis—a busy cruel-tongued beldame if ever there was one—was notorious for her ill-humour. There were too many others at Court, Catherine knew, who shared her sentiments. She saw again the sneer on the face of my Lady Castlemaine, the scorn in Buckingham's lazy eyes and the contempt in the looks cast at her by people like Lord Bristol and Bab May as she walked down the Stone Gallery.

The summer sunlight streamed through the diamond panes of her room overlooking the Thames, sending green watery patterns gliding over her smooth olive skin. But Catherine buried her face in the silken pillows of her great bed and looked instead into the depths of her heart. Her very posture showed the defeat of a woman who had accepted humiliation and drunk deep of a cup of life that was to her as bitter as gall. For once the mask of the Queen had dropped and Catherine had allowed herself a momentary relaxation from the schooled impassivity that had been drilled into her from childhood.

Now, alone in her chamber, she was no longer Catherine the Queen but a fragile and lonely child who was aware of too many failings. She had failed to gain her husband's love, she told herself; she had failed to give him an heir; and she was only too well aware of the hostility all around her. She felt alone in this great rambling Palace of Whitehall.

She had tried so hard to win him. She had studied to please him, learning English for several hours a day, adopting the revealing costumes of the English ladies, painting her face and forgetting all her upbringing and maidenly modesty to join in the ribaldry at Court. She had fought to hide her chagrin at his affection for Castlemaine and carefully learnt a lightness of wit to charm him and cheer him in his moments of melancholy. And yet, all was in vain. True, Castlemaine was in decline; her greed and her tantrums had driven Charles from her bed and left Barbara's appetites to be satisfied by that pimp of hers, Harry Jermyn. But Catherine still had enemies at Court, and they were legion. Buckingham; Bristol, with his prying nose and scurrilous tongue . . . Already there had been plots to dispose of her.

First there had been an attempt to prove Charles's bastard son, the Duke of Monmouth, legitimate, which would have undermined the position of the Queen. Then Castlemaine had tried to force Charles to divorce her and marry his fruitful mistress instead by spreading the tale that the King's marriage was invalid and should be formally annulled. Only Charles had stood between her and disgrace, and she even smiled a little as she remembered how—one winter evening, six months before—he had turned on the plotters and their lies and come to her to promise his devotion. All the Court had been shown the King's affection for the Queen. It was a love upon which she knew she could depend, but it served at the same time to make her misery worse. For she was barren, and a barren Queen made mockery of a royal marriage which was formed for the begetting of children to inherit a throne.

Her isolation was accentuated by the fact that her solitary ally at Court, Lord Clarendon, was as much in decline as Castlemaine. Beleaguered and falling from favour, his influence was but a shadow of what it had been. Wherever she looked, Catherine saw danger and dislike.

She needed so much to be loved, this foreigner in the land of the English. When the plague had come she had sold her jewels and given virtually all the resources of her slender privy purse to relieve the sufferings of the poor and needy of London. The iron cold of an English winter had frozen the plague in its tracks in London, but though spring had brought a thaw to the city, it had not thawed the English dislike of this Queen. They took her money, she thought, but they did not love her, these English. They hated all foreigners and the

Catholics worst of all. She heard the stony silence that greeted her coach when she went into the city or sat in a box at the play. And privately she wept in her chamber.

If she could give England an heir, perhaps they would love her, she thought desperately, and back into her mind came the sharp clear tones of Lady Silvis: '. . . barren as a rock . . . a barren wife . . . a *barren* Queen.' The New Year had brought another miscarriage, and Catherine despaired of giving Charles, who had sired so many bastards, a legitimate heir to his throne. Neither the purgative draughts of the royal doctors nor the cure of the waters at Tunbridge Wells had made her quicken with child. She yearned for a great belly to bring her close to Charles and assure herself of her usefulness to him as a wife. But her hopes were slim.

A firm knock on her door interrupted her despondency. Catherine roused herself and sat up on the bed. 'Quienes?' she called. 'Who is zere, plees?'

'It is only I, your Majesty—Lady Suffolk. I would not disturb you, but the Earl of Rochester is here and desires to see your Majesty. Shall I send him away?'

'Momente!' Catherine blew her nose and dabbed at her cheeks with a kerchief, and then slid off the bed to stand in her chamber with the quiet dignity well known to Whitehall. 'Tell him he may enter.'

The double gilded doors opened to admit a gentleman airily clad in pink brocade, a golden periwig surmounting the whole. He was a beautiful youth, with a smooth skin like a girl's and a pair of eyes of the most cornflower-blue. John Wilmot, Earl of Rochester, was but nineteen years old. And yet the cynical gleam in those clear blue eyes spoke already of an experience far beyond his years. Already the young Rochester had lain in the arms of Monsieur le Duc d'Orleans at Versailles and then left the vices of Sodom to travel across Europe and taste the natural delights of the flesh. He had returned to scandalise Whitehall by his irreverent wit, which did not spare even the King in its scurrilous barbs. Charles had stigmatised him 'a very wicked boy,' and so he had proved.

And yet he had courage, as Catherine well knew. He had

begged his way out of imprisonment in the Tower to go to sea to fight the Dutch aboard the *Royal Catherine*, and the Queen remembered Charles's amazed approval at his gallantry at the siege of Bergen in August '65. Now a Gentleman of the King's Bedchamber, he was as strange and unaccountable as the rest of his countrymen, Catherine decided. She looked critically at the top of his golden frizzed periwig as he bowed low. She was slightly surprised that he should come to see her. 'Milor'?' she asked gently. 'Do you bring some message from the King?'

Rochester's eyes slid over her in a questioning fashion. 'One overhears many things at Court, madam, and this has—ah—formed the reason for my presence.'

Catherine stiffened. Had the news of Lady Silvis's insult already spread through the galleries and brought this indolent young man to mock her? Her voice was frigid. 'Indeed, milor'. I t'ink it ees possible sometimes to hear too much.'

But if Rochester were intended to be abashed, he did not show it. On the contrary, he smiled, showing small even teeth, and shook his head reassuringly. 'I am not the page of the Countess of Castlemaine, your Majesty, nor do I spend my time running after intrigue. When inclination takes me, I might *make* scandal, but that is my affair. Behold me here rather in the guise of tutor.'

'Tutor?'

Rochester bowed. 'Talk has drifted my way via my Lady Sears—aided, I might add, by liberal potations of hypocras two nights past at Mistress Stuart's card party—that your Majesty finds royal—ah—protocol irksome and would learn more of our ways.'

Catherine shrugged warily. 'I believe I have said I find the English race hard to understand, but I fail . . .'

'Ah, we are "barbare," all the world knows it, with our ale of mud and our greasy puddings. We are famous throughout Europe for our habits. Yet I heard of more than your Majesty's puzzlements. It seems your Majesty would copy the King and has a mind to venture out into the city—ah—incognito?'

'But I have never . . .'

'Even Maids of Honour will gossip in their cups, madam. I

beg you will rest assured only I heard such a dangerous whisper, and 'tis locked within me. I wonder, however, is such a whisper true?'

Catherine looked at him as he gazed lazily down at her, swinging a small hand mirror from a riband between his fingers. Why should she be looked down upon by smooth, assured men such as this; regarded with faint boredom as being dull beyond bearing, incapable of either intrigue or any behaviour out of the ordinary? What mattered it that an indiscretion had brought such a fleeting, momentarily expressed sentiment to the ears of such a fop as my Lord Rochester, one of the most debauched rakes at Court? She saw the light of mischief in his eye. He expected her to hastily disclaim any such indecorous wish, and he would tap back to the Stone Gallery on those high-heeled shoes of his to tell Buckingham and Ossary and the rest of the Queen's outraged modesty. She was expected to do naught but huddle over her stitchery and take a sip of metheglyn for her health's sake. An overwhelming desire took hold of Catherine to behave out of character and to shock this young nobleman standing so languidly before her.

'The wine spoke true in thees case, my Lor' Rochester. I have it in mind to mix with those people I have only ever seen through a coach window and whose heads I have gazed upon from a box at the theatre. I have long desired to hear them talk as they might do when the Queen is not present.'

'A novelty, madam, but one fraught with danger withal, I might venture to say. Which is why you see me here.' He winked. 'I am a rake beyond reclaim, madam. All the Court talks of my debauchery. Who, then, is better qualified to show your Majesty a London you have never seen—but I, who know even the rats in the gutter by name?'

'*You*, my Lor' Rochester?'

'Who better, madam? I will show you that which is not usually vouchsafed to queens, and return you, none the worse for such an adventure, to your chamber before midnight. After all, who could see through such a disguise as I might devise?'

'A disguise?' Catherine's eyes gleamed as she considered the possibilities of such a plan as Rochester suggested. She had never done anything like it in her life. What would her old duenna, the Duchess of Penalva, say? Catherine had just one lingering worry. Was there more danger in this than met the eye? Was it yet another plot to disgrace her, hatched by Buckingham? Yet as she looked at Rochester's delicate features, she felt a curious certainty that this time there was no plot. Rochester's eyes held amusement and nothing more.

'Well, your Majesty?'

'I t'ink my 'usband is right, my Lor' Rochester. You are ver' wicked boy,' she scolded. 'And I shall be delighted to accept your invitation.'

'Such weather makes one thing of last summer at Greenwich, does it not, Dicky?' Bab Knipp commented to Mr. Pepys as they sat in a tiny box at the Moorfields puppet theatre.

Sam Pepys was enduring the most uncomfortable afternoon, and his embarrassment was clear from the way he constantly tugged at the lace jabot round his neck and tapped his walking cane nervously on the sill of the box. He coughed at this arch reminder, blushed and murmured something inaudible in reply. Upon his other side sat the taut, upright figures of his wife and her prim maid Mercer. As he shifted on the bench they all occupied, waiting for the play to begin, Sam recognized the glint in Mistress Pepys's eyes. She shut her fan with a sharp click and her voice had an edge to it when she spoke. 'Ah yes, your "petit vacances," Samooel. No doubt'—she turned to Bab—'you too needed a rest after a season on the boards at the Lane, madame. They say the life of an actress is most *exigeant*. The King's Servants, after all, are paid to serve 'is Majesty's pleasure.'

Mr. Pepys realised the folly of his idea of an afternoon's entertainment. He had his wife on one side and a fair lady friend on the other, and Sir William Penn sitting behind watching the proceedings, Sam thought suspiciously, with more than a little amusement at his discomfiture. Both he and Penn had for once sunk their differences and left their offices for an afternoon's sport. Mr. Pepys began to wish he had never come, and a sharp taste in his mouth told him that the galantine of eels he had consumed but an hour earlier at the Three Cranes had returned on him.

'I think the curtain is about to go up,' he said, making an effort at conversation, and encountered a blazing look from his wife that silenced him in his tracks. Still he persevered. 'Does the show start at once, my dear, or is there a farce?'

'I do not know. It is you who have brought *us*, not the other way about.'

Mr. Pepys sighed. He had known Bab Knipp for close on a year. They had first met when Sam's Navy office had moved out of plague-ridden London the previous summer to the more healthy atmosphere of Greenwich. He and several of his cronies had been delighted to find at Mistress Pierce's lodgings the presence of Mrs. Knipp, Beck Marshall and a few of the actresses from the King's House at Drury Lane. The gay charm of little Mrs. Knipp, with her laughing blue eyes and fairy curls, had whiled away many a long summer evening agreeably, and he had been glad at the time to pursue the relationship to a point behind the bed curtains of her chamber. Now he saw there were troubles along with this delicious acquaintance. It was one thing to spend a cosy soirée with his friend Lord Brouncker and Captain Cocke and Mrs. Knipp and her friends singing to a gittern and playing cards into the small hours. It was another thing to maintain such a friendship under the eye of his wife. For Mistress Pepys knew her husband only too well.

Mrs. Knipp, he thought irritably, seemed to take a roguish delight in goading his Lizbet's suspicions to glaring certainty. A trip for them all to see the Polichinello puppets had seemed a harmless enough diversion, but Sam Pepys saw he had underestimated the subtety of women.

Sir William Penn's voice broke in on his thoughts. 'I rather think there will be a song or some such thing to begin with.'

'Oh!' cried Bab Knipp. 'You should have your own song printed, Dicky. Do you not remember how you wrote it last summer and we all sang it—you, my Lord Brouncker and

Mistress Pierce and me? How did it go now?' She hummed gently to herself and then burst into song:

> 'Beauty retire; thou dost my pity move,
> Believe my pity, and then trust my love ...'

'Yes, yes,' said Mr. Pepys testily.

Bab Knipp gave a demure smile and lowered her lashes over twinkling eyes. 'I think you have forgot the words, Dicky.'

There came a cool, dry question from Mr. Pepys's other side. 'Il parait que tu as un autre nom, Samooel. Qu'est ce que this "Dicky"? *That* I do not understand.' Her tone implied that there was a good deal else that Mistress Pepys had no difficulty in understanding.

Mrs. Knipp smiled. 'Oh, that is just our little sport, madame. "Rien du tout mais fort amusant," as *you* might say. 'Twas a game we played last summer. I would sing a little ballad by name of "Barbary Allen," and Sam—that is, Mr. Pepys— would reply by singing "Dapper Dicky o' London Town." We penned little notes to each other and I signed myself "Barbary Allen" and he "Dapper Dicky." A pretty game, do you not think?'

'Many games are pretty to play, madame. It is losing them that is not so pretty, I think.'

'It was all a long time ago, Mrs. Knipp,' interrupted Sam tersely. Bab Knipp's blue eyes widened but she said nothing, though a dimple quivered in one smooth cheek.

Mistress Pepys's eyes blazed with an ill-concealed anger. 'I expect you are quite used to such "pretty games" in the tiring rooms at the Theatre Royal, madame. We have all heard of such, I am sure.'

'Men are but men,' replied Mrs. Knipp equably. 'A title and a fine name makes them no different from others of their kind. Some are amusing, most are whoreson rogues, God knows. I dare swear the King himself is but a man when all is said and done.'

'More than a man, if tales tell true.' Sir William Penn chuckled. 'They say little Miss Davis at the Duke's Theatre is still keeping his Majesty a close attender of the play. I had thought that Mrs. Gwynne of the Theatre Royal might take his fancy a twelvemonth past, but I see it came to naught.'

'London has suffered the plague,' countered Mrs. Knipp. 'The theatres have been closed ever since. Even now the City Council refuses to allow the Theatre Royal to open, for fear of infection. We actresses have found times are hard. Ann Marshall was reduced to selling her tawdries on 'Change and Lizzie Weaver has married into taffeta. Nell has naught but her wits to live on now she and Master Hart have parted. Our pay's over six months in arrears and I doubt not we shall be a theatre of rags and spangles when we face the pit vizards again.' Bab Knipp shrugged. 'Thanks be to God that the company has survived intact. Master Killigrew is petitioning the King at this moment for the Theatre Royal to reopen, now that the pestilence is past.'

'And so London may see Mrs. Nell Gwynne upon the boards once more,' said Sam a shade too eagerly.

His wife turned and looked him up and down with a scornful look. 'I think per'aps you are in danger, mon cher.'

'Of what, Lizbet?'

Mrs. Pepys smoothed the folds in her gredaline petticoat. 'Of making too many appointments in your mind that your body may not be able to keep. Mercer, my gloves, if you please!'

There was a slop of water onto the floorboards of the chamber as Mistress Nelly Gwynne shifted in her position and extended both slim legs over the edge of the wooden tub that served her for a bath. The soft brown rain water lapped around her, rippling playfully around her breasts. The gentle haze of steam that rose from the water made her hair cling to her forehead in curling tendrils and her skin glowed pink and fresh as she lay back, gently sluicing the water over her shoulders. 'Mit,' she called lazily. 'Where's that bleeding towel?'

Mit's head under a mobcap poked itself around the door. 'At your service, m'lady. If you sit in that steam much longer, you'll come out looking like a scabbed sheep! I've told you taking baths is bad for you—weakening it is, as everyone knows. Once a year's enough for anyone. Still'—with a sniff—'if you've got to be nifty as a parrot, I s'pose I'll 'ave ter go and fetch you one out of the dower chest. 'Ang on.'

'Ill-affected bawd!' shouted Nell after her and settled back with a sigh in the tub. She snorted at the ironic title Mit had given her—a faint hope indeed! A good thing, she thought, that Mit had no notion how different things might have been —but for the plague and Master Whitelife. She could still remember staring at the smashed-up front of the shop in Goldsmith's Row, looted like so many, its owner dead and despatched on the clanger cart, his coffers emptied and stripped clean as the bones on carrion. Ah, well . . . She rubbed one arm absently as visions of wealth were abruptly dissipated. What you never had, she supposed, you never missed. The face of Robert Duncan on his pillow came into her mind, but she thrust it resolutely away. What was past was past.

Now only that small leather bag of groats that hung from the bedpost behind her stood between them and penury. For she had not only Mit to keep, but that young limb of Satan, Toby Phelps, who would eat a horse and then chew its bones, as Mit had told him disgustedly. Yet she would not have it otherwise; Toby was a lad of much wit and a deal of skill in music, and he regarded Nell in the light of a goddess, following her about adoringly. She smiled a little, humming gently, as she massaged one shoulder.

They had never seen Toby's parents again, and when she and Mit had brought him back to London in December they had found the leather-seller's shop in much the same state as Master Whitelife's. So Nell had taken him in. Now she wondered distractedly how she was to keep them all. Mit hadn't been paid since God knew when! It was a joke between them. When she asked Mit the last time she had been paid, Mit would pretend to consider and then say, 'Last week, madam,' with a respectful curtsey. It had in reality been a string of weeks. In vain had the remnants of the King's Servants demanded their arrears of pay from the Lord Chamberlain. There had been but one niggardly payment in January and then nothing for one . . . two . . . three months. Master Killigrew had promised them when the theatre closed that none of them should come to want, but the promise looked a vain one. It had driven some of them to the direst straits; Nell knew for a fact that Beck Marshall had fallen back on the alternative profession of the actress to keep the wolf from the door.

There was a click behind her of a latch on the door and Nell heaved herself up with her hands grasping the edge of the tub. 'Come and give us a scratch,' she said idly.

'Would that not be a trifle indecorous, mistress?' said a voice.

Startled, Nell whirled around to see a tall, dark blue-eyed gentleman looking at her in amusement. She put up her hands to cover her nakedness. My Lord Buckhurst, clad in a rich flowered tabby vest with sleeves of silver lace and holding a gold-tipped malacca cane, strolled into the chamber with a broad grin on his face. Nell watched him as he walked slowly around her, cocking his head first to one side and then to the other while she sat stiffly in the warm water. 'Have you seen your fill, my lord?' she asked icily.

His eyebrows rose in exaggerated surprise. 'I but wondered which area required scratching,' he explained. ' 'Tis a vast change to be looking down on you rather than up at you from the pit at the Theatre Royal.'

'You have a good memory, my lord. 'Tis at least nine months since you must have done so.'

'You too have a good memory, my dear, if you remember who I am, but perhaps mine is the better.' His eyes travelled over her with overt interest. 'I remember one night at a bawdy house in Lewkenor's Lane two years past and the shimmer of a girl's hair in front of a candle flame and her head on my shoulder.'

He saw her eyes twinkle. 'Is this how you begin all your jill-flirts, my lord?' she enquired with interest. 'What happens next? Ah, I know, I have eyes like stars, skin like alabaster and my beauty casts you into torment.'

Buckhurst rubbed his nose, nonplussed, while Nell lay back in the bath and called, 'Come on, Mit, or I'll be as wrinkled as a crab apple.' Back into the bedchamber came her tire woman, who stopped short when she saw my Lord Buckhurst. Her expression was hardly welcoming. 'Come to deliver a bucket of Thames water, 'as 'e?'

'That is no way to speak to a peer of the realm,' Nell informed her. Mit held up a protective towel and Nell stepped from the tub. 'In very truth, my Lord Buckhurst has not yet said what brings him here.' She looked at him questioningly.

'This may sound hard to believe, Mrs. Gwynne, but I was under the impression you were Master Nicholas Windle the apothecary.'

'Who in God's name is he?'

'He's that pimply herbalist that keeps rooms round the corner at the Golden Goat in Maypole Alley,' Mit asserted, bending to empty the bath with a wooden jug. ' 'E supplies love philtres and such-like to the Court. They say my Lady Castlemaine goes to 'im reg'lar.'

'Do I so closely resemble him, my lord?' Nell asked.

'Nay,' disclaimed Buckhurst hastily. ' 'Tis but that I was given the wrong direction . . .' His voice trailed off and he stood watching while Nell sat on the bed and crossed one leg over another to draw on a knitthread stocking. The towel fell away to reveal all the fine length of one white thigh that swept down to the neatest-turned ankle my Lord Buckhurst had ever seen. He let out an audible sigh. 'How long will it be until we may see those legs tread the boards once more, Mrs. Gwynne?'

She chuckled, tying her garter. 'Not till Doomsday, belike, if the Lord Chamberlain has his way, for fear the theatre might breed the plague anew. At least not until the winter comes again, Master Killigrew believes.'

' 'Tis too long,' Buckhurst said warmly. 'Far, far too long, by God.' He picked up her other stocking and bent on one knee, taking one foot in his.

'May I be vouchsafed an earlier glimpse than a pit full of 'prentices, Mrs. Gwynne?'

She looked at him straightly. He really was far more handsome than any man had a right to be, she thought. He was tall, with wide shoulders, and had a pair of the bluest eyes she had ever seen and a complexion to turn many a girl green with envy. His own black hair, worn long, curled in loose ringlets, which brushed her bare leg as he leant forward to draw up her stocking. As his hands came up past her knee, his voice was soft and persuasive. 'You have eyes like stars, skin like alabaster and your beauty slays me. And may I send my town coach to the Cock and Pye this evening, Mistress Gwynne?'

She gave a gurgle of laughter. 'You can dress it up how you like, you cozening rogue, but I make no doubt your mind's as filthy as the Fleet ditch and you've a tongue to match it when you choose.'

Lord Buckhurst opened his mouth in protest, but before he could reply the door slammed open and in came a small tow-headed boy with a grubby face and a torn jerkin who walked up to the startled Lord Buckhurst and poured a small stream of copper coins into Nell's lap. 'That's for you, Mrs. Nelly,' he said proudly. 'I *earned* it!'

Nell looked sternly at the five-year-old urchin standing beside Lord Buckhurst. 'How did you earn it, Toby?' she demanded. 'You've not been on the frater lay, have you?'

Toby blew out aggrieved cheeks and raised himself to his full height of three feet six inches. 'No, I have not!' he protested. 'I went down to the Fleet Bridge where the cockle sellers stand and I sang to the gentlemen. I sang "To all you ladies now at land," Mrs. Nelly—you know, like we sing together.' He nodded at the coins in her lap. 'They threw me groats and *one* threw a shilling. Then some pompous alderman came up and told me I was begging and that I'd best be off or the constable would take me off to the Bridewell. A right bit of whoreson puff-paste he was,' he added reminiscently.

'Toby!' scolded Nell sharply.

Toby stood on one leg in embarrassment. 'Well, but he was! And anyway, that's what *you* called my Lord Falmouth two nights back in the taproom, 'cos I *heard* you!'

Nell had the grace to blush, while Lord Buckhurst threw back his head and boomed with laughter. 'A sprightly bantam indeed!' he commented ironically, and squatted down on his haunches so his face was level with Toby's. 'So you've been singing "To all you ladies now at land," have you, my master?'

Toby nodded shyly.

'This is my Lord Buckhurst, Toby,' Nell told him. 'Make your bow. It was he who first wrote "To all you ladies now at land." '

Toby's face was comical in its dismay. With eyes round as saucers he looked at Lord Buckhurst as though he were an angel dropped from heaven.

Buckhurst chuckled and lifted him up, placing him on his knee. 'You sing it to me, Toby, like you sang it down on the Fleet Bridge just now,' he said encouragingly. At first Toby looked down shyly and would not answer, but then he risked a peep at my lord, who gave him a wink and a squeeze.

'Go on, Toby,' urged Nell.

In a clear high treble the boy began to sing:

>'To all you ladies now at land
>We men at sea indite;
>But first would have you understand
>How hard it is to write;
>The Muses now and Neptune too;
>We must implore to write to you—
>With a fa, la, la, la la, . . .'

On the last line Toby paused, and all at once both Nell and Buckhurst broke in. His rich baritone quite swamped Toby's voice and blended with Nell's light, sweet voice in a pleasing contrast. The song ended.

'Bravely done, sir.' Buckhurst clapped, and fishing in his capacious embroidered coat pocket, produced a guinea, which he pressed into one grimy paw.

Toby looked at it and his mouth formed a soundless O. Suddenly his skinny arms locked around Buckhurst's neck and he kissed him. Then in a flash, his face crimson with embarrassment, he scrambled from Buckhurst's knee, ran out of the chamber and clattered down the stairs.

My Lord Buckhurst got to his feet, reached over and picked up a long shift of Holland linen with balloon sleeves, and looked down at Nell, holding it out. 'Well, Mistress Gwynne,' he asked, 'wilt go with a piece of whoreson puff-paste tonight?'

Her eyes danced. 'With a good heart, my lord.'

'Odsdeath, I'd rather have young Toby's name than that! Can you not call me Charles?'

'I have already been connected with one named Charles,' she told him dubiously. 'You will have to be my Charles the Second.'

Lord Buckhurst made her a profound leg. 'Madam, I am truly honoured.'

The moon that hung like a blood orange above the broken spire of Old St. Paul's sent a fitful ray of light down the winding length of King Street to play across the oak-framed timbered front of a small leaning house on the corner of Axe Yard. Through the open casement of an upper window it stretched across two twined figures in the bed and up the wall, highlighting the musty embroidery of an ancient arras of tapestry. The stiff characters, etched in a faded hunting scene of years gone by, gazed with calm expressions, oblivious of passion beneath.

Moll Davis lay with her head cushioned on the black-matted chest of King Charles the Second, who absently stroked the chestnut tresses of his mistress. Perhaps, he decided, the emptiness he felt was only because he was tired. It had, after all, been a gruelling twelve months through which he had just passed. The Dutch war dragged on and England had been faced with appalling odds. All the might of France had been flung in the gage by his golden cousin Louis, who, with characteristically unscrupulous diplomacy, sent the well-equipped forces of the lilies to aid the stubborn barques of the Dutch butterboxes.

All through the summer at Whitehall they had heard the dull boom of the guns as Albemarle had fought De Ruyter to a standstill in the Channel, and at the same time nigh broken

England's fleet, which limped home in sorry state. What desperate days England had seen! The country, weakened by the plague, had seen the actual danger of invasion and struggled feverishly to build and equip a new fleet while the trained bands of Kent and Sussex polished rusty pikes to repel the French. Even now the fleet was once more at sea in search of De Ruyter. Only God knew the outcome! Charles made up his mind to ride to Greenwich on the morrow and find out what news had been received.

At home the plague had well-nigh brought trade to a halt and Charles knew the state of the royal exchequer was naught but a mountain of debts. 'As bad as my damned days in exile,' said the King aloud in the darkness. Moll Davis flung one arm in her sleep across his face. 'No, no,' he chided gently, 'don't you attack me too, child.'

Moll slumbered on while Charles regarded her in amusement. She was at least one respite from the troubles that even assailed him in his Palace of Whitehall. His mind swung back to the ever-present problem of Catherine's barrenness; the New Year had brought another miscarriage and he doubted whether she could ever give him an heir—he, who only had to look at a woman to get her with child! Charles grimaced at the irony of an unkind fate. Only James's children, two girls, were left in the new generation to inherit the throne of the Stuarts. His thoughts slid over to consider his natural son, the Duke of Monmouth. A skittish gallant, thought his father approvingly. What a pity that he had begotten him of Lucy Walter and not the Queen.

The King lay back, breathing deeply. Surely no monarch was ever subjected to such problems as he had to endure! His senses reeled, battered under the onslaughts thrown against them. Even Charles's resilience and good humour had its limits. At least he had resisted one onslaught on his peace of mind: Barbara had been dismissed from the Court and had left in disgrace, screaming imprecations against him to all who would listen. Her day of power was over; he had endured her tantrums and her greed for long enough—and her beauty was fading. Yet the corridors at Whitehall seemed empty without her flamboyant, brazen personality. Who could fill a gap vacated by one who, if demanding, had known how to satisfy his body? The pursuit of Frances Stuart was an enjoyable pastime but its progress was halted by that lady's implacable virtue. A singular quality which made the pursuit the sweeter, or so the King had thought until recently, when a faint resentment had begun to creep in. He was, after all, the King and he had started to wonder whether Frances was really so worth pursuing. She was perhaps merely a habit, as Barbara had been; as his marriage itself was. As ever, Charles shifted in embarrassment as he thought of the Queen. She was the glass of metheglyn to a man who needed deep draughts of life-giving rich claret; sweet enough and fair to look upon, but unexciting. Yet he knew how she loved him.

Charles looked down at the tip-tilted nose of Moll Davis, her green eyes shut tight in sleep, the long lashes lying thick on her smooth damask cheeks. What dreams of avarice did her pretty little head hold? he thought to himself with a slight smile. Five yards of gimp lace and a roll of mulberry velvet cheered this little waif from the streets as much as a string of manors had ever cheered Barbara.

The little waif yawned and snuggled up into his shoulder, where Charles obligingly made room for her. ' 'Ere, Charlie,' she murmured in his ear. 'You know those pearls wot you give me?' The King grunted absent assent. 'I wore 'em s'arternoon in the Shift at the Duke's and it knocked 'em inter gutters.'

'I'm glad you like them, m'dear.'

Moll stretched up and kissed him. 'You 'aven't arf got a whiskery cheek, Charlie,' she told him with interest.

Charles rumbled good-naturedly, 'No one will ever accuse *you* of Court flattery, Moll.'

But Miss Davis was anxious to return to her earlier theme. 'I put 'em on for re'earsal s'arternoon, 'cos Sir William reckons we'll be allowed to open by the City Council come a sennight, and anyway, they was all there—the other actresses, I mean—and I jest gets 'em out all casual-like and sticks 'em round me stretcher.'

'Stretcher?' said Charles blankly. 'Oh . . . I see.'

'Aye, well, you should 'ave seen 'em gawping. Like a row of dabchicks at the Fair, all eyes an' teeth. An' ol' Gutsey...'

'Who?'

'Peg Dawes—you know, the scrawny 'un wiv the elbows and the freckles. We allus calls 'er Gutsey 'cos of her welter. Anyway, she looks at me like I'd jest crawled out of an 'ole in the ground, and guess wot she says?'

Charles opened his eyes and shook his head. 'I don't know, tell me.'

'She says, "Bin to St. Martin's, I see, Mistress Davis," sharp as flint. "This ain't no brass and glass from no St. Martin's, Mistress Dawes," I says, prissy as a Puritan, "nor I don't blame you for thinking so, for I dare say you ain't ever seen aught else!" 'Ere, Charlie...' Moll rolled over and tickled the bluish cleft in his swarthy chin. 'She don't b'lieve that you give me the gawdies at all! Nah, if you was to give me some earrin's ter match that'd stick 'er one in the lugs, wouldn't it... eh?'

Charles flicked at her little nose. 'My exchequer is entirely to let, Moll. I give you my word.'

Mrs. Davis chuckled. 'Ah—give over, Charlie, you know that's just an old jaw-me-down an' all.' She slid away from him and out of the bed. 'You're as bad as a merchant on 'Change,' she said, pouring out a mug of ale. 'You don't allow no credit!'

Charles looked at her naked form, which the moonlight caressed, revealing the line of her white thighs and the firm roundness of her tight little buttocks. Fine legs, thought the King, and a head as empty as a coal scuttle. He leaned on one elbow, watching her. 'How would you like to change lodgings, Moll?' he asked speculatively. 'Perhaps to some chambers in Suffolk Street. Chiffinch tells me he has a lease going spare.'

Unashamed, Mrs. Davis turned to face him, her eyes gleaming with excitement. 'Really, Charlie, you ain't selling me boskey wine?' She came back eagerly towards him. ' 'Ere, can I 'ave a coach an' all?'

Charles's voice was soft. 'Is it not a small price to give a King a release from care?'

Mrs. Davis climbed back into the bed and snuggled up to

him with a sigh of content. 'I think you're a right teeth-biter, Charlie, straight up I do!'

The King's hand came down over her breast and she felt his breath as he leaned over her. 'Can we deal on credit tonight, m'dear?' he whispered, and she giggled.

Two

None ever had so strange an art
His passion to convey
Into a list'ning virgin's heart
And steal her soul away.

—Sir George Etherege

Acquaintance with Charles, Lord Buckhurst, was, for Nell, a unique and exciting experience. The balmy summer days passed like the light froth on the new French champagne all London was drinking. Buckhurst was a man who loved pleasure, and to be with him was at once to be caught up in a whirlpool of gaiety. Nell drank it in without a care for the future. Despite her reluctance, Buckhurst was a master of seduction and knew just how to turn indecisive longing into a river of desire that flowed and ran at the touch of his fingertips.

Twice he called for her, and Mit heard her return in the early hours just before the pink dawn rose over the city's rooftops; the third time she did not return at all. Neither ever spoke of love, for neither was in love, yet they were happy for all that and for Nell a new phase in her life began.

It was something new for her to see a coach drawn by six horses elegantly caparisoned stop in the stuffy little alley outside the Cock and Pye tavern to await her convenience of an evening. She loved the way Buckhurst continued to treat her as though she were a 'grande dame' of the Court. He took her to the ladies' tailors in Paternoster Row to buy her shifts of the finest linen, petticoats of Colbertine lace, stockings of clinging silk and lace-edged gloves to set off her fragile wrists. His taste was impeccable: he took her to the New Exchange in the Strand, there to make her try on hats of a most ravishing design, with huge floppy brims and curling ostrich feathers, and she had a hilarious time with him trying them all in turn.

She was carried off to Unthanke's, the Court dressmaker, where Buckhurst had her measured for a gown of silver brocade, a stiff narrow dress that clung to her hips, with a low-cut bodice sewn with pearls and fine lace cuffs. She remonstrated with him on this occasion, telling him that she had no need of such finery and never went anywhere where she could wear it. He took her chin in one hand and kissed her lightly on the nose. 'You will do as you are told, you stubborn child, and you will be seen as befits you.' He seemed to take delight in squandering money on her and decking her like a duchess.

Nell had her hair styled by Monsieur Rochfort with loose curls 'à negligence' and a 'crêve coeur'—those two small ringlets curling naughtily at the nape of the neck that the ladies of the Court affected. Thus accoutred, Buckhurst took her in his wicker chariot to the ring in Hide Park of an afternoon to see the monde and show herself. She gurgled with laughter to watch the ladies in their coaches roll stately past, some recognising Buckhurst, inclining their heads in greeting and she nodding back gravely. They did not recognise her, she knew, or she would not have been acknowledged by any of them. Yet with a modest lace whisk covering her bosom, who could think she was not a lady, but Nelly Gwynne of the Theatre Royal?

Buckhurst grinned at her and she winked back before bowing to the Countess of Suffolk on the way by. She found Buckhurst's company easy and congenial; his wit was sharp and his kindness real. One afternoon in the park he nudged her and said, 'Watch exhaustion pass by,' and they both saw a large, heavily gilded coach pass along the avenue, inside which could be clearly seen the snoring figure of my Lady Castlemaine. Buckhurst looked sadly at the sagging chin below the open mouth before the coach went on its way, and murmured, 'Can it be that *that* once drove a king to frenzy? To be a king's mistress is like the falling of snow: it glares brilliantly in the sun's favour but fades away to nothing. The shafts of time have caught her untimely methinks. Poor Barbara. And you know, Nelly Gwynne, even in her heyday she was never as beautiful as you are today.'

Nell tossed her tawny head and laughed lightly, but she told herself that Buckhurst was noted for his flattery even while she hoped that in this case he meant the words. For a second her mind turned to the tall, harsh-featured figure who had bowed before her so courteously in a stuffy chamber overlooking the Thames. But she forced herself instead to think of her rakish, handsome lover and told herself she had let her wits go a-begging.

Certainly they made a handsome pair. When Buckhurst called to take her out with him to Mulberry Gardens she caught a glimpse of them both in her new French mirror and gasped at the sight.

'What is it, Nelly?' he quizzed her. 'Didst see a ghost?'

She shook her head. 'Look at us, Charles . . .' Their reflection stared back at them in the candlelit chamber: Buckhurst, darkly handsome in a sky-blue satin doublet and sash, with ruby hose and white lacing topped by an ornate black chedreux peruque; Nell, small, pale and dainty, clad simply in saffron satin and seed pearls, her auburn hair coaxed to fall in a curl on one white shoulder. 'I think we are both quite beautiful, don't you?' she said, studying the reflection quite seriously. He caught her to him in a tight embrace and she felt her lips melt into his. 'You must be the most gorgeous thing this city has spawned for a century and more,' he told her as his mouth wandered to her neck and down to her breasts. She felt the fire leaping up inside her and her knees seemed to collapse. He drew her over to the bed and pushed her back on the pillows. His love-making seemed to pluck at the fibres of her being in a way her flesh could not resist.

She felt his body heavy on hers, she felt him inside her as he moved urgently to his fruition, but she did not feel that he reached her or claimed her in any way. There was none of that delicious oblivion she had known before. It was as though a part of her remained detached and apart from him; strangely inviolate, it watched while her body moved and arched towards its climax.

And yet they were happy, these two who took delight in each other's shafts of ribaldry and in each other's union behind the bed curtains at night. For Buckhurst it was the simple honest satisfaction of a physical appetite; for her, a warm, loving gift of gratitude to a man who was good to her and who made her content, surrounding her with warmth and luxury.

Yet she remained Nelly Gwynne of the King's House. She refused to move out of the Cock and Pye in Drury Lane to chambers which Buckhurst offered her in a new mansion of elegant gilding and fine pargetting in St. James's Street. She would not let him set her up as Rose had been set up in lodgings under a gentleman's protection. She was Nelly Gwynne of the King's House and she would make her own life. He laughed, shrugged, chucked her under the chin and let her have her own way.

Of course, Nell's lodgings took on a somewhat different appearance. Hempen sheets were changed for silk, for my lord could not be expected to sleep like a farrier; spoons of horn became silver and heavy damask curtains soon enclosed the bed to seal the draughts from disturbing them.

Buckhurst soon discovered that she was no ordinary tumble fodder. He took great pleasure in her quick brain and great common sense, and it persuaded him to take her into the company of his friends, whose names she already knew and whose persons she had oft rejected in the Women's Shift in an afternoon or turned away disconsolate from the Cock and Pye. He took her out one evening to sup at Chatelin's, the new French eating house at Covent Garden, for an elegant ragout of eels, to while away the time over brimming glasses of ruby malmsey and raisins in the glittering company of his Grace of Buckingham, Lord Rochester and Sir Charles Sedley. Her manners charmed Buckingham, but it was on Sedley that the girl from Lewkenor's Lane made an impression in every sense of the word.

Sir Charles Sedley—rubicund and blessed with a searing cast of wit—had been vaguely offended that Buckhurst had brought his whore with him. He supposed in his half-drunk state that she had been asked along to lend colour to their drinking activities. With a low mocking bow he greeted her and his voice, still clear though his brain was not, welcomed her in dulcet sarcasm: 'What a pretty flower to delight us, Buckhurst! I congratulate you! Such gay and fragile petals to blossom from the sawdust boards of Drury Lane.' He lifted one of her hands to his lips. 'Haply such flowers are ripe for plucking.' She felt his other hand touch her waist and moved back sharply. 'Do your petals close when exposed to the light, sweetheart?' he asked with a slight sneer on his lips.

Buckhurst flushed angrily, but Nell was used to worse than he. She curtseyed even as her eyes flashed at his words and her voice was easy and conversational. 'Your compliments overwhelm me. But'—she looked him up and down in his full glory of rich emerald slashed satin and heavy gold lacing, and paused—'I cannot compare with the dazzle of your own magnificence, sir. You, after all, are a gentleman. It reminds one, doth it not, of the words of Sir Walter Raleigh: "Say to the Court, it glows and shines—like rotten wood." May I have a glass of hypocras, Charles?'

Buckingham's lazy eyes glinted with appreciation from behind his wineglass, while Sedley gazed at her, startled, and then suddenly burst out laughing. 'I misnamed you, madam,' he told her. 'You are no flower, but a thistle belike.'

'Then beware my prickles, sir,' she advised him coolly, and shedding her miniver-edged cloak with its pointed bird's-eye hood, sat down, shaking out the folds of her gown placidly.

Rochester turned to Buckhurst. 'We meet tonight by way of celebration, Buck—or haply you have not heard?'

Buckhurst's eyebrows rose questioningly. 'Heard what?'

'Why, man'—Buckingham thumped the table with a fat fist—'the best news ever! A messenger had just arrived at Whitehall this evening with it. 'Tis the Dutch—we've beat them to flinders, boy! That scurvy whoreson rogue Rob Holmes went over to Dutchland cool as you please with a thousand men and set light to their whole damned fleet. Not only that, but he set fire to a brace of towns and came back home with enough loot even to settle young Rochester's debts!'

Rochester raised his glass in mock salute and drained it at a draught. 'A notable achievement, certainly.'

'What a nation of young Ajaxes we are breeding, to be sure,' said Sedley. Always in his voice there was a tinge of irony. 'I do hope you are not going to have a recurrence of your unfortunate malady of last year, Rochester, and gird up your loins, or whatever it is that one does when one decides to volunteer.'

'Why not, Charles?' asked Rochester.

'M'dear soul, if *you* go I shall be reduced to quarrelling with Buckingham, and 'tis a fate not to be wished on anyone! I blame it all on women, 'pon m'soul I do.'

'Blame what, sir?' Nell was puzzled.

'Martial vigour, manly strength, gaiety and martyrdom, madam. All that sort of thing. Men do but try, poor creatures, to live up to women's ideal of them. Take my advice and eschew women. I *always* have—recommend it to anyone.'

'Nonsense, Charles,' protested Buckhurst. 'You're not only married, but you've begotten a daughter to boot!'

A faint look of bewilderment crossed Sir Charles Sedley's features. 'Really? I have no recollection of it. It must have been a momentary aberration.' He searched in his pockets and then swore softly. 'Pox take it, where's my apoplectick snuff? I'm sure I brought it. It disagrees with me vastly, but Doctor Arbuthnot told me I was to go nowhere without it. Ah, I remember, I gave it to Jules for safekeeping. Jules! Jules!' A little man with a face rather like a frog ran up and stood bowing and scraping before his master. 'Jules, give me my snuff,' commanded Sedley.

'Your snuff, milor'?'

Sedley grimaced. 'Keep your distance, if you please. I swear you stink like a garlick! Where is my snuff? I gave it to you to look after.'

Frantically the unfortunate Jules patted his pockets, but produced no snuff.

Sedley's fingers drummed on the table. 'Well? Well?'

'I think, milor', I 'ave—'

'If you have lost it, Jules, you may as well cast yourself off London Bridge,' advised Sedley unemotionally.

'Ah no, milor', never! I would not lose—I mean I have not lost it, milor'! It—it must be at milor's lodging. If milor' will excuse—'

'Milor' will wait precisely fifteen minutes, and if you are not back by then, you may as well not return at all,' retorted Sedley. 'Be off with you! And do not stop'—he caught the sleeve of the agitated little valet—'even to pray!'

Jules fled, and Sedley leant back, stretching out a hand with long white fingers and faint blue veins to the dish of raisins that sat on the table between them. 'One can't even dismiss one's valet now,' he complained. 'Now we're fighting the French, the supply of lackeys has totally disappeared. I find I am a positive casualty of war!'

Buckingham directed a look of unholy amusement at Nell, and shyly and to her surprise, she found herself smiling back.

As the malmsey flowed, the talk of these elegant, gorgeous gentlemen turned naturally to gossip of the Court and its doings. Buckingham guffawed over the sight of his King dining in public state in the Banqueting Hall. 'As I live, 'tis as good as a play! There's old Berkshire, who must be eighty-five if he's a day but still insists on performing his duties as Lord in Waiting, talking to himself and doddering around like a Bedlamite. 'Tis enough to make one heave! He turned up last time in a coat I'd not give to a lackey and cuffs fairly stiff with grease, and shook so much he put more claret on the King's breeches than in his cup. He'll never give up while he can stand and Charles can never bring himself to turn him off. He knows well enough now to wear only his oldest clothes when he dines, but Lord, to watch his face while old Berkshire pours half a ragout of eels down his waistcoat to follow the claret is a sight indeed!'

'We've little else to amuse us,' agreed Rochester moodily. 'I wonder sometimes if this damned war will ever end. God send the Dutch to perdition! The world would be best served if the sea rose and drowned them all. Pack of greasy merchants. I saw them on the Tour; their heads were full of trade and naught else.'

'My dear Wilmot, barbarity is not a perquisite of the Dutch alone. We live in a world of barbarians. The Scots are as bad. Look at that bull-necked pike drawer Lauderdale!' Sedley complained. 'He told the Queen at her musical evening a week past he'd as lief hear a cat mew as any viol in the world, and that to hear a lute positively made him want to spew. Pretty talk, I swear!'

'Aye. They say he refused an invitation to Clarendon House as he'd have to sit listening to what he called "sawbones" all night long.' Buckhurst laughed. 'Even my Lord Chancellor could not persuade him to go, so I'm told.'

The mention of Clarendon's name to Buckingham was like a red rag to a bull. His colour rose alarmingly as he set down his glass with a thump. 'Lord Chancellor!' he snorted. 'His Majesty does not need that—that clerk, that jumped-up lawyer, to run the country for him. He prates at us all like a preacher and builds himself up like a Prince of the Blood! Ever since that fat daughter of his became Duchess of York he has thought himself without compare.' Buckingham's eyes had a fevered look as his acrimony bubbled over. 'All the world knows it was his idea to sell Dunkirk back to the French, and then he has the damned gall to build that palace of his before our very eyes with the money he made from its sale! As well rely on a leech for counsel! His Majesty has people enough to help him rule the realm. Why does he not turn to the lords, to his natural advisers?'

'To you, in short, your Grace' came a quiet interpolation at his left.

Buckingham stopped short, and the fevered look died away

as he became aware of what he had said. 'Aye, haply,' he said shortly and drained his glass at a draught. He shot a searching look at Nell and his expression was one of grudging amusement. 'Methinks little of rumour or gossip would escape your pretty ears, Mistress Gwynne.'

'I come from the gutter, sir,' she explained. 'And all the world knows the gutter hears rumour first.'

'One does not encounter creatures as pretty as you in the gutter, my child,' returned Buckingham smoothly.

She smiled, showing her little even teeth. 'Almost, your Grace'—and her voice was soft as she sipped—'I might suspect your Grace of commonplace flattery.'

Buckhurst gave a bark of laughter. 'A thistle indeed, George, I give you my word!'

Privately Buckingham wondered how it was that Mistress Nelly Gwynne had not yet been summoned by Will Chiffinch to a night's assignation upriver at Whitehall, and he was about to ask her in his bluff way if she had royal ambitions when the panting, almost gibbering little shape of Jules appeared, thrust a small box of snuff into Sedley's surprised hands and backed away, bowing like a pendulum, his face puce and perspiring.

'Poor little rogue!' exclaimed Nell compassionately. 'He looks as if he fair burst his breeches to get here. I hope 'tis worth his efforts. May I try some, sir?'

'By all means.' Sedley flicked open the lid with practised ease and offered her a pinch of speckled greyish powder.

Nell took a pinch between finger and thumb and inexpertly sniffed. The result was a paroxysm of coughing that sent Rochester into fits of mirth and Buckhurst to plying her with hypocras and patting her on the back at the same time.

Sedley regarded her reproachfully. 'I did *say* it was apoplectick snuff, Mistress Gwynne.'

'Aye.' She sniffed, red in the face, with eyes pouring water. 'But not that it *caused* apoplexy, sir.'

'A veritable producer of passion,' commented Rochester, picking up the delicate French enamelled box. 'I must give some to the King. It has seemed to me that of late he has shown the need of a philtre.'

'Too true,' agreed Buckingham. 'But there, what would you? He has naught but that sallow bag of bones to slake his lust upon. Now my poor Barbara has fallen from grace, the King's view is restricted to Mrs. Davis's legs and the unattainable Mrs. Stuart. Neither give enough for old Rowley. I swear he stalks the Stone Gallery like a bloodhound these days, with that damned long stride of his, pacing up and down.'

'I must say, he looks rather restless.' Rochester nodded. 'Rather as if he searched for something—God knows what! There can be few aspects of the passions of Aretin that his Sacred Majesty has not encountered!'

'I think he is unhappy.'

They all turned to look at Nell. At once she coloured and shrugged. 'From . . . from what you were saying, he sounds most unhappy.'

There was a short silence. Buckingham's eyes, shrewd and perceptive behind the laziness, settled upon her speculatively. 'I think you are right, madam.'

Shortly after, Nell and Buckhurst rose to leave. Nell kissed Buckingham and Rochester on the cheek, as was the custom, but when it came to Sir Charles Sedley, she sank down in a deep billowing curtsey, extending one hand for him to kiss. 'Adieu, *milor*,' she said, her eyes twinkling. Sedley took her fingers and brushed them with his lips. 'I wonder no one has yet thought of poisoning you,' he said conversationally. 'Adieu, Mistress Gwynne.' She saw the suspicion of a smile is his eyes.

But in the hackney on the way back to the Cock and Pye and later in bed, clasped in Buckhurst's arms, Nell found, despite herself, that her thoughts drifted back to the swarthy man who had seemed so drawn and tired in his bedchamber overlooking the Thames. She told herself fiercely how hopeless it was. She was nothing but a night's pleasure to him. How many other women had Chiffinch greeted at that landing stage and shown up those back stairs? He was the King, he looked upon her as he did Moll Davis, Lizzie Weaver and any other actress—they were just tumble fodder, tumble and tawdry. 'Jill flirts and whores,' she murmured, and Buckhurst grunted. 'What did you say, Nelly?'

'Nothing, Charles.'

August cast its procession of long golden days in agreeable ease, with none of the shadows of the plague of the year before. Twice more Buckhurst took her out with Buckingham, and she found that despite his arrogance, there was a certain strength and intelligence behind the pose of the fop, and indeed, a certain outrageous wit that somehow endeared him to her.

Buckhurst arranged a party on the river and took Nell and Mit with Rose and Bab Knipp and a group of friends for the day to take the air at Putney. They drifted back downriver in the cool of the evening while Buckhurst took a theorbo lute and sang to Nell in the prow of the barge, where the others were tactful enough to leave them alone. Nell was won over completely by his kindness and easy charm. Later she curled up on the bed in her chamber while he sat Toby on his knee and placed the boy's fingers on the strings so that they could both serenade her. Toby glowed with pride and pleasure.

She had no worries. Buckhurst supplied her with ample funds, and though the theatre showed no signs of opening, she never feared to come to want. Twice a week she went with the rest of the company to the empty King's House to rehearse under the watchful eye of Master Lacy and sometimes Killigrew himself, but her time on the boards—now over a year away—seemed a lifetime's distant. Insensibly, though she herself was not aware of it, she was slipping into the ways of her sister Rose.

Meanwhile the time flew by, from lazy mornings in bed to long evenings lit by the sparkle of candlelight on jewels and Venice glassware. For one week neither she nor Buckhurst arrived back at the chamber in the Cock and Pye until Mit could hear the pot boy below stirring to take down the shutters of the tavern and pour out the pots of the morning's small ale.

On the last night of August, a hot summer's night, Nell lay in her chamber in Buckhurst's arms, listening to the watchman making his round. 'Past two of the clock and a rare fine night!' he shouted, and she heard the muffled dong of his bell as she fell asleep snuggled up to her lover.

But she awoke later in the early hours and was conscious of a sense of unease. It seemed to Nell that the heat was oppressive. There was not a sound outside either of man or beast; the silence lay over the sleeping London streets like an ominous pall. It was as though life had departed the city. She suddenly felt the need of human contact and put out her hand to the darkness of the far side of the bed where her lover lay. 'Charles,' she whispered, 'are you awake?'

He stirred and yawned deeply. 'Aye, what is't, sweeting?' he murmured.

'Bab came to see me this afternoon—Mrs. Knipp, you know, one of the company at the theatre. She brought Master Kynaston with her and we broached a vessel of tent. I said we would see them tomorrow at the Tabard over Southwark side, where we go to celebrate Master Lacy's birthday.'

'Ods my life. Do you wake me to tell me that, Nelly?' he groaned. 'Devil take you! And in this case, howsoever, it can't be done, sweetheart. I must leave London tomorrow.'

'Charles, no!'

He glanced at her sleepily. 'I have to go and see my bailiffs down at Knole in Kent. I'll be gone but a few days. Why the outrage, Mrs. Gwynne? Can you not go alone?'

'Yes, but . . .'

Startled, he saw the bright glint of tears on her cheek. 'Sweeting, what is it? We'll be parted but for a few days. You don't want to come down to Kent with me, surely?'

'No, I don't know. I have a feeling that if you go, something dreadful will happen. Don't leave me, Charles.' She saw him smile, and his hand stretched out to grasp hers. 'Why, what is this? Methinks you ate too much of the pigeon pie at supper or haply we run about too much. This is just the megrims. I'll tell Mit to call on Master Arbuthnot tomorrow and get you some oil of mithridate or I shall have you looking quite hagged, love.' He bent over and kissed her and then lay back on the pillows, satisfied that he had calmed a mere irritation of nerves.

Nell heard his breathing deepen into the rise and fall of slumber, but she lay awake, sleepless, looking through the window. Was it, she wondered, just her fancy that the sky around the rooftops of Maypole Alley seemed to glow an iridescent fiery red?

Buckhurst left at dawn to journey into Kent, creeping from the bed where Nell lay in a sleep of exhaustion. She awoke late, hours after he had gone, and pressed puzzled hands to her eyes as she saw the crumpled empty pillow at her side.

The sunlight streamed through the diamond windowpanes, lighting up the rich blues and greens of the wall tapestry and the sombre burnishing of oak floorboards. From the street below came the cry 'A tormentor for your fleas! Trap your vermin, ladies all!' from the street pedlar and all the noise and bustle customary in narrow Drury Lane.

Her fears of the dark hours seemed naught but sick fancies and she flung back the coverlet with a brisk motion. 'Mit?' she called. 'Look out my pattens and smock-sleeved gown, will you? I've a month's mind to pack a few things for Ma and take 'em to her this morning. That'll rouse 'er from 'er snoring, I make no doubt!'

It was a busy day for Nell, packing a venison pasty and some of Mit's preserves into a basket, which she covered with a snowy linen napkin, and then, leaving Mit to watch over 'that young limb of Satan' Toby Phelps, setting off to visit her mother. The plague had killed all the Fletchers who had not moved out of the city with Madam Gwynne, and after the pestilence was over, Nell's mother had remained in the village of Chelsea, living in a cottage Nell found and rented for her. She well knew, as she set off, what a task of cleaning awaited her at her journey's end. It was a fine day. Nell took a wherry upstream to Vauxhall and hailed a hackney coach to convey her to Chelsea village.

The dusk was falling as the boatman rowed her back up the Thames against the tide, and Nell lolled, tired, under the awning at the back of the skiff. She felt disinclined to change and venture out carousing in Southwark, but she knew John Lacy would be disappointed if she failed to show and toast a loving cup with him. A day spent rooting her mother from the alehouse, followed by several hours on her knees in a sackcloth apron scrubbing, left her with no desire but to sip one of Mit's sack possets and fall asleep in bed. Resolutely she banished such halcyon visions.

Four hours later found her, bathed, seductively perfumed and clad in a becoming gown of lavender silk, being carried in a chair across London Bridge.

Tom Killigrew hailed her with great delight and hugged her till she gasped. Then he turned and introduced her to a quiet shy-looking damsel with ash-blond hair who smiled uncertainly. 'This, my dear, is a new addition to the Theatre Royal—Mistress Anne Quin. I have wooed her away from Lincoln's Inn Fields and the clutches of Sir William Davenant. She has acted with Harry Harris for the past two years and I doubt not will cause ecstasies in tragedy. I must say, I have been quite unscrupulous in tempting her away.'

Anne Quin blushed and stammered as Killigrew pinched her chin. He smiled at Nell. 'You must look to have your nose quite put out of joint, Mistress Gwynne, and I must look to have a friend the less.'

Nell twinkled at him sunnily. 'Ods my life, sir, I hope I am better-spirited than that. Mistress Quin, I bid you heartily welcome. Attend to Master Killigrew and ignore Master Lacy's tantrums and I swear you'll do famously!'

There was an outraged boom behind her. 'Less of your St. Giles sauce, Nelly Gwynne, or you'll feel my hand on your backside. And here was I thinking you had come to do me honour!'

She turned and saw the huge towering figure of John Lacy frowning at her. 'Happy birthday, Master Lacy. 'Tis good to see you indeed!' She stretched up and planted a kiss on his mouth. 'As though I meant a word!' she cooed.

'Aye, I know your smooth tongue, you beauty,' he retorted, straightening his periwig, but he gave her a hug to equal Killigrew's. 'Indeed, 'twould not have been my birthday without you here to celebrate it.'

Killigrew gave a glass of claret to Nell and one to Anne Quin. 'Here, Master Lacy, you see my foundation for the new opening of the Theatre Royal. On one side my actress for comedy'—he bowed to Nell—'on the other, my new actress for tragedy.' He bowed to Anne. They drank a solemn toast.

'Do you mean you expect the theatre soon to open, sir?' enquired Nell eagerly.

Killigrew looked mysterious. 'As to that, my dear, I have an announcement to make later this evening. Come, child, I wish to introduce you to the rest of the company of the King's House.' He offered his arm to Anne and they strolled over for Killigrew to introduce her to Edward Kynaston.

Lacy whispered in Nell's ear. 'If you would like to see a vinegar bottle on legs, my dear, look over yonder.'

Nell followed his eye and saw Lizzie Weaver gazing at Anne Quin over the rim of her wineglass with an expression of malevolent hatred. 'Methinks the Weaver is less pleased at our friend's arrival than you, Nelly. Her memory is short. Two years ago, when she looked to enter the Fleet prison for debt and Weaver disowned the child she was carrying, she was grateful for any help we could give her and whined like a rusty gate. But now . . . odsfish, the woman's impossible! She's been so damned top-lofty since she married that silversmith of hers that we expected her to send in her parts any day. In fact, she told us that we must not hope for her to continue acting for long,' Lacy declared. 'Yet because we get an actress who can knock her into flinders, she takes a pet and will barely be civil to the poor little soul.'

'Mistress Quin seems very . . . quiet,' commented Nell doubtfully.

'Aye, so I thought myself on first meeting, and you'd not turn your chair round to look at her. But see her on stage, my dear, as Killigrew and I have, and she'd strike you dumb. 'Tis as if a spirit enters into her—her eyes flash, I swear she grows six inches in height. But there, you wait to judge for yourself.'

Nell nodded slowly. 'I see what you mean. Oh, I nearly forgot . . .' She fished in her bodice and triumphantly produced a small box with an elegant grisaille lid. She presented it to Lacy. 'A keepsake for your birthday, sir. 'Tis snuff of a new sort, called apoplectick snuff. Sir Charles Sedley's own sort from Barcarol's. They say it does wonders for those of a choleric temperament!'

Lacy snorted with laughter. 'You don't change, m'girl, 'pon my soul, you don't. Impudence! Impertinence!' He turned the box this way and that, the light catching the delicacy of the working on the lid and flashing on an amethyst set in the patterning. 'As to the snuff, I resent the inference, Mistress Gwynne, but the box is quite exquisite and I thank you.'

She curtseyed. 'My pleasure, sir.'

A hand waved frantically from the other side of the room at Nell. She smiled at Lacy. 'Excuse me, sir, I think I am stayed for.'

A flushed and excited Bab Knipp awaited her. 'Nelly, dear heart, I am with child to tell you! Such news! You'll be on the boards within the month. Mr. Pepys has heard that the City Council debated the matter yester e'en and decided they could allow the theatres to reopen again. Rumour hath it that my Lord Mayor has been as timorous as a sheep over the whole business but was overridden withal. My Lord! To think we'll see the pit filled once more!'

'I think Master Killigrew may have something to say later.' Nell nodded. 'Did you say 'twas Mr. *Pepys* told you the news?'

'Aye. He went to see his Grace of Albemarle a day or two back and picked it up from some lackey or other.'

'What's the connexion, Bab?' asked Nell, looking at her friend with interest. 'Do you have a tendre for Mr. Pepys?'

'Oh, as to that'—Bab shrugged—'we but find pleasure in each other's company. He's a gentleman and they're rare on the ground these days.'

'Aye.' Nell thought with quick sympathy of a small, feminine little lady with a French accent and weighed up in her mind whether to brave Bab's tongue by remonstrating with her. But before she could do so she found herself looking into the cool, haughty features of Charles Hart.

She found a blush spreading and a feeling of hot embarrassment coming over her, as it had been with Charles Hart ever since they had parted in acrimony near a twelvemonth before. When she had come back to London in December from Rochester, where she, Mit and Toby had taken refuge after escape from the capital, she had found most of the company dispersed still. It was only in January that the first rehearsals began and Nell found herself once more on a stage with Charles Hart. He had bowed, she had curtseyed, and that had been that. The strange thing was that their acting together was quite unaffected—she found she could act torrid love scenes with him quite as she had used to. The difference was that when they left the stage they parted without a word, and she had never done more than exchange the barest civilities with him since. But every time she met him she coloured up despite herself and Hart seemed equally ill-at-ease. To Nell's annoyance, Bab Knipp glided away with a nod to Hart and they were left alone.

'I hear the theatre may well open again,' he said slowly.

'Aye, I gather so,' she answered politely.

'So we shall face the crowds together once more.'

'It would seem so.'

Hart took a deep breath. 'Nelly, must we go on like this? I swear I do not wish it! I know all has been over between us for a year and naught can take us back in time. But can we not forget the bitterness? If I could unsay words I know I said in anger—oh, hang it, Nelly, if I can't get you to speak to me, I shall be reduced to paying addresses to Lizzie Weaver! Have pity!'

Behind the lightness of tone Nell discerned a look of guilt in those haughty eyes. She chuckled. 'Major Mohun is before you, Charles, and he seems not to enjoy the experience!' They gazed over to where the elegant major was seen vainly trying to strangle a yawn while Mrs. Weaver's mouth opened and shut and opened and shut. 'Do you think that moustache of hers is in emulation of the King? Or is she preparing for a new career of a singular sort?'

Hart grinned. 'I trust not, Mistress Gwynne, or I shall be out of a job.'

The banging of a pewter mug on a table caused the babble of talk to die down. Tom Killigrew climbed on a stool to address the company. 'My dear ladies and gentlemen. After the trials through which we have all passed, I have the most pleasurable of duties tonight. I have to tell you that the City Council has acceded at last to my repeated petitions and has agreed that the Theatre Royal may reopen at the earliest opportunity. I gather that heretofore the objections of his Grace the Archbishop of Canterbury on the one hand and the fears of my Lord Mayor on the other have thwarted us, but no longer do they have their way. We shall begin rehearsals immediately.'

A burst of cheering interrupted him and he held up his hand for silence. John Lacy handed him up a glass of wine, which Killigrew raised in the air. 'I give you,' he shouted, 'happy birthday to Master Lacy, welcome to Mistress Quin, and all hail to the new Theatre Royal!'

Charles Hart grabbed two glasses from a passing tray and put one in Nell's hands. 'I have a better toast,' he said, smiling. 'To better times, Nelly.'

She smiled back at him and clinked glasses. 'To better times, Charles.'

It was only just before midnight when two sleepy chairmen trailing behind a yawning link boy bore Nell back across London Bridge. The sway of the chair was lulling her off to sleep as she leant back against the squabs, dreamily savouring the thought that soon she would be facing an audience once more: the ogling gentlemen in the galleries; the swearing watermen and 'prentices in the pit; the vizard pretties with their satin cloaks and black masks. She would savour the smell of sawdust, sweat and paint that went to make up the world of the theatre. A jumble of thoughts seethed through her brain. It was so long since she had acted on the stage, would she still draw the crowds? More important, could she still act at all? Horrid doubts assailed her. 'Don't be a fool!' she told herself firmly. 'If you've done it once, you'll do it again.' Suddenly she found herself wondering if the King would come back to the Theatre Royal once again. Before the plague he had neglected them, but time had passed by. Would he now come and grace first showing? She felt a twinge of guilt. Was it not, after all, her fault that the King came no more and that the Court neglected the Theatre Royal?

Distracted, she gazed out the window of the chair. They were just passing Nonsuch House on the narrow Bridge Road. One of the curious sights of London, it was an old building brought over from Holland and put together with wooden pegs, like a child's toy. Nell glanced at it idly as they passed by and then saw a knot of struggling figures beneath its timbered gabling. Snatches of abuse drifted over the night air. 'Papist . . . stinking rotten Papist!' . . . 'French whore . . . Catholic bitch!'

Nell's eyes narrowed. As the chair drew up near them, the light cast by a lamp suspended from the anchor beam disclosed three 'prentice boys holding a small cowering girl between them. She appeared to be one of the tray sellers who habitually stood at the foot of the Fleet Bridge selling gingerbread or cockles. Her tray lay tossed on the cobbles, its contents—indeterminate in the dark—strewn all around. The abuse redoubled: 'Frenchy cow! Papist devil's spawn!'

One of the youths grabbed at the girl's shoulder and her dress ripped back, showing one shoulder and exposing a breast. Nell heard her gasp. 'Pliss, sir . . . Pliss . . .'

'Pliss . . . pliss.' The voices mocked her accent. 'Come on, lads, let's strip the little doxey and then chuck 'er in the Thames! Haply she'll swim back to France then!'

'No!' screamed the girl and backed against the oak beams. As her face looked up, anguished, terrified, Nell caught a glimpse of her white features. 'God's bones!' she gasped in horror. She flung open the door of the chair, and jumping on to the cobbles, ran across to the struggling group. 'Take your filthy paws off her!' she screamed. 'You whoreson knaves, you let her alone!'

Three

Which is the basest creature, man or beast?
Birds feed on birds, beasts on each other prey,
But savage man alone does man betray.

—*My Lord of Rochester*

Two of the apprentices holding the girl fell back uncertainly at Nell's sharp command, but the third kept a tight grip on her elbow. Their victim's tense little face amply illumined in a pool of light verified Nell's worst fears. Although the girl was dressed in a short skirt of coarse brown serge, with cloth stockings and a pair of pattens on her feet, her blouse torn on the shoulder and her hair in a tangle, her face was one that Nell had seen many times, looking down from the royal box in the theatre. The cowering tray seller was no Fleet Bridge whore, but Catherine, Queen of England.

Though terror lurked in a pair of luminous dark eyes, Catherine shot Nell a look of wordless warning, guessing that she had been recognised. How she came to be dressed in such garb or, more incredibly, how she came to be found alone on London Bridge at midnight were questions which seethed in Nell's mind, only to be instantly dismissed. These were things which could be gone into later. Now she needed to get the Queen out of the hands of a group of louts who clearly saw her as possible bed sport. They looked at Nell with a mixture of suspicion and admiration, but Nell did not detect any recognition in their young faces. Desperately she hoped none of them had ever been to the Theatre Royal, and adopted what she hoped was a reasonable accent. 'Duw! Bronwen! So 'tis you indeed! And where've you been, you wicked girl? There's Master Cledwyn having the whole city searched and Ianto combing the streets this very minute. There's thoughtless you are!'

The 'prentice boys looked at her blankly while Catherine goggled, mystified, at Nell. She glanced at the 'prentices quickly, trying to sum them up. One lad of about eighteen was quite obviously a candlemaker's apprentice, judging from the wax-encrusted apron that he wore; she guessed he came from one of the tallow-makers' shops in Thames Street over the river. He looked to be a nervous, somewhat dim-witted youth, and as he glanced from Nell to Catherine and back again, his eyes held more apprehension than aggression. His companion, dressed in hempen homespun, had a sharp freckled countenance which put her in mind of a ferret; a bully, she decided, but a weak one withal. The main obstacle, she saw instantly, was a tall, stocky bull-necked youth who held the Queen's frail arm in a tight grip with one huge fist. He eyed Nell truculently. Only guile of a singular kind, she thought, would avail her here.

Hastily she continued her reproaches. 'Combing the streets Master Cledwyn was at dawn and poor old Mrs. Llewelyn saying you'd be found dead floating in with the tide. What are you doing here at this time o' night—and what are *you* doing, you lump of dead mutton?' she said belligerently to the stocky youth.

'What you on abaht?' he retorted derisively. 'This yere's a Frenchy wench.'

'That's Bronwen Hughes,' Nell asserted firmly. 'She came to us but two days back—to Master Cledwyn's, that is, in Featherbed Lane. She came as lady's maid to Mistress Cledwyn, but the mistress took a pet when she did sommat or other and threw a handbrush at her. The silly child got a fit of the waterworks, packed a bag in the night and made off all incontinent.'

'Garn,' snorted the stocky youth. 'You can go tell *that* to the conduit well. Think I'm a lackwit or sommat? It's all bite biscuit or I'm not Tom Lugsley.'

'You please yourself.' Nell shrugged. 'But he's a rich wool merchant is Master Cledwyn and an alderman of the City Council, and when he finds out you attacked and molested one of his household—'

'She's no serving maid, she's a Frenchy Papist. You listen to her talk,' argued Tom Lugsley, yet with a note of doubt in his voice.

Nell gave a crow of laughter and scorn that made Tom Lugsley feel at least six inches smaller. 'Our Bronwen . . . a Frenchie lass? My Lord, she's *Welsh*, you sapskull; she's only just come from Wales and in her village they don't speak English hardly. She's only been brought to London by Master Cledwyn two days ago. What d'you expect, you loopworm?'

The candlemaker's apprentice looked down at his feet. 'Come on, Tom,' he mumbled, '. . . city alderman, we'll be in great trouble haply.' His thin companion glanced at Nell and shook his head, but said nothing. Tom Lugsley made a last attempt to assert himself. 'Well, if she's *Welsh*,' he said belligerently, 'why doesn't she *say* something in Welsh, then?'

There was a dead silence. Catherine's mouth opened and shut twice, but no sound issued forth. 'Come on, Bronwen,' said Nell hastily. 'Say something.' Feverishly she tried to help her. 'Glan wizbeth ist glan flar blier?'

Catherine's eyes widened in horror. She coughed. 'Ziz glas vill gan trod glottle,' she said unsteadily. 'Fan ottle tolder.' Her chin tilted up and she looked at Nell with a glint in her eye. 'Sled fan glan doler willer glamswiderglister!' she said clearly.

'There you are!' cried Nell triumphantly. ' 'Tis Welsh she is; she's no more French than you or I. Poor little wretch, you've near frightened the life out of her.' She smiled at the trembling Catherine. 'You come with me, love, we'll have you home now. A posset and bed is what you need. And as for you, you weak-chinned whoresons'—she sniffed at the discomfited assailants of the Queen—'you'd best be off home and hope Master Cledwyn don't have you clapped in the Bridewell.'

Nell placed her hand on Catherine's arm. For a moment Tom Lugsley's grip remained firm, but as he encountered a pair of eyes flashing hazel fire, he stepped back reluctantly. Nell took the Queen by one hand and led her back to where the chair men stood waiting.

Catherine turned to Nell, her eyes large, liquid and doelike, bright with relief. 'Thank you so much. I do not know what I should have—Digo! Thank you for coming to help me. Dios mio, I was so scared.'

'Your Maj—'

'Hsst!' she said, glancing over at the chairmen. 'Can you not see what would happen if you . . .'

Nell nodded and was quiet.

'You recognised me, mistress, but I know you too! I remember you back a twelvemonth. You were Master Killigrew's new discovery at the Theatre Royal. Mistress . . . er . . .'

'Gwynne,' supplied Nell helpfully.

'Ah, so. Ger—wynne,' said Catherine, nodding. 'You I remember well.'

' 'Tis a matter to be thankful, madam, that none of those knaves knew either me or you—or that there was no Master Cledwyn, for *that* matter.'

Catherine giggled. 'I did not understand at all, you know,' she confided. 'De nada! And then I saw what you meant. All those people—are any of them real?' Nell shook her head, laughing. 'Not one!' Catherine laughed with her, but then her face grew serious. She glanced at Nell shamefacedly. 'You must wonder what I am doing here—like this.'

' 'Tis your own business, madam, and not mine, God knows.'

'You I should like to tell, Mistress Ger—wynne. I t'ink you have a right to know and per-r-haps you would understand. I came out tonight to see how people live—*really* live. I only see them through a coach window and I wanted so much just to be with them for once, to see why they don't like me, to see if I could *make* them like me. I was stupid, I know—'

'Surely,' Nell interrupted her, 'you did not come out alone just like this?'

'No, no. I came with milor' Rochester. We had good time at first. We went to Spring Gardens and took a wherry down to Vauxhall and, oh, many places—but then we came back to the bridge and I wanted to go in the Bear here and milor' Rochester he took me in. But then he—er—drank a lot and there was a brawl and I came out and then those boys—'

'You didn't come out like that with Lord *Rochester*!' exclaimed Nell incredulously. 'Lord, ma'am! As well ask a blind man for direction. He always was a soak bucket, as all London knows. I dare say he's back at the Bear under a table by now. Unless they've called in the Watch.'

'I t'ink so,' said Catherine gravely, but her eyes twinkled as she caught the gleam of humour in Nell's.

'You must return to the palace at once, madam,' Nell told her. 'Take my chair, I can easily get another. And you must get home before your absence is discovered at Whitehall and his Majesty sends out a whole regiment to search for you.'

Catherine allowed Nell to lead her over to the chair and she got in before the chairmen hoisted the straps on their shoulders once more. 'Please convey this wench to Whitehall,' Nell said, putting a coin in the nearest hand. 'Her mistress will be wondering where she is.'

Catherine's head poked out of the window. 'Mistress Ger—wynne,' she stammered, 'I can never t'ank you. If ever there is anything I can do for *you* . . .'

'Pish,' said Nell lightly, 'I think 'tis best if we both of us pretend tonight never happened. I for one shall make a point of forgetting it.'

Catherine leant out and planted a kiss on Nell's cheek. 'T'ank you,' she said softly.

Nell smiled and banged the side of the chair, then raised her voice. 'What Mistress Cledwyn will say to *you* when you get back, I tremble to think!' she shouted. She felt sure it was not her imagination that she heard an answering muffled choke of laughter before the chair swayed off into the darkness.

At the same time that Nell was clinking glasses with Charles Hart, a vulgar squabble was rending the air in a shop halfway down Pudding Lane towards Thames Street. Thomas Farryner, the King's baker, was huddled over his ovens in the backhouse preparing his loaves for the morrow. Mistress Nan Farryner was known to all the neighbourhood as a scold, her tongue was notorious throughout East Chepe, and on this occasion her unfortunate spouse had been foolhardy enough to arouse his lady's ire. She stood, arms akimbo, in the doorway of the low little parlour just behind the bakehouse, shrilly denouncing her husband's morals, his general demeanour of living and his amorous propensities. Doggedly he continued to grease his tins with pig's lard while the words fell about his ears like grapeshot.

'Out at the alehouse morning, noon and night. I wonder you don't *sleep* there! 'Tis like being married to a gin bottle, *and* I know why you go, you cockroach. If you think that brassy young hussy of a tavern wench is going to look at your whiskery phiz, you're far and out, my lord, and so I promise you! Leaving me here to scratch things together; all day spent in that bakehouse turning out quartern loaves till my hands are like pudding bags and my face looks like a pumpkin—and for what? For you to use the money to souse yourself at the Rose and Crown till dawn!'

Nan Farryner was one of that breed who was seemingly able to continue a stream of words without ever pausing for breath. That this was largely responsible for her husband's frequent disappearance to the alehouse never occurred to her. When he forbore to answer, she redoubled her attack.

'How d'ye think I manage, you wenching coxcomb? There's just me to do everything *and* look after Betsey, who's never there when you want her, and that Job Cantwell, who's three parts asleep most of the time. A journeyman he calls 'imself. My stars! *I'd* send 'im on a journey if I had my way—to the Fleet prison, by God I would!'

Thomas Farryner unwisely sighed.

'King's baker you call yourself? King's baker? That's the fondest diddly I've heard in an age. 'Tis me that bakes the King's loaves, me that bakes them, packs them and sees 'em off to Whitehall of a morning while you're still snoring in your cock loft! And I might've known how it would be. My mother warned me. "Don't you take that 'un, Nan," she said. "He's a maundering rogue if ever I saw one and he'll come to grief, you mark my words!" I should've listened then!'

'For the love of God,' murmured her husband irritably. 'Leave it, Nan.'

'Aye, leave it—leave it, that's all you ever say. All you ever *do*, come to that.' She watched moodily while Thomas stacked the loaf tins on the table, and moved aside grudgingly as he brought the tins through into the bakehouse, filled them with dough and bent to arrange the loaves in rows on the iron shelves of the huge oven. His very silence grated upon his wife's nerves and drove her to the last extremes of provocation. 'All on my own,' she repeated harshly. 'Aye, and I know why. You're not even man enough to father any brats to be of use!'

Thomas Farryner stood up and turned around. His wife saw that his face was dead-white and a muscle twitched convulsively at the side of his temple. In one hand he held the heavy long-handled iron loaf ladle that was used for stacking the tins in the oven. The look on his face was at that moment terrifying and Nan Farryner stepped back as he advanced on her. 'Jesus...' she gasped.

'If you say one more word,' said her husband, his voice low and menacing, 'I swear by God I'll brain you with this, and God help me, I'll go to the gallows at Tyburn with a happy heart!'

Nan Farryner gazed at him transfixed. She made a small, strange choking sound in her throat and then backed away, her eyes fixed on him. Suddenly she gave a high scream and turned and ran back into the parlour, slamming the door.

He threw the ladle into one corner of the bakehouse and stood looking down, breathing heavily. Then with a sudden oath he stormed out of the room and slammed the door onto the street with such force that the whole house shook. Thomas Farryner had forgotten, in his temper at his wife's words, to shut the door of the great bake-oven. The force of the slam was just enough to dislodge one of the glowing coals inside.

With a hiss it rolled out of the grate and fell to the floor, where it lay smouldering. There was some straw packing lying quite nearby.

It was the much-abused Job Cantwell who was woken first at two o'clock in the morning by smoke filling his little chamber over the bakehouse. He opened his eyes, coughing and spluttering, to see tendrils of it, thick and heavy, seeping through the ill-fitting floorboards. He heard an ominous crackling coming from below.

'My Lor'!' he gasped and with frantic haste thrust his long skinny legs into his breeches. 'My Lor'!' he said again as the smell of burning timber reached him. He flung open the door and clattered up the stairs to the main landing, shouting at the top of his voice, 'Master . . . mistress . . . Lord save us, the shop's afire! Master! Wake up!'

Nan Farryner, wrapped in a coverlet, appeared at the top of the stairs and looked at him bemusedly. Job stabbed at the air with one outstretched finger and goggled up at her. ' 'Tis the bakehouse, mistress! 'Tis afire. The master . . .' Nan glanced, bewildered, down the stairs and saw the leaden cloud drifting up the stairwell. There was a rumble and a crash and the crackling noise was redoubled. 'That be the parlour,' said Job in terror. 'We'll all be burned where we stand!'

Nan Farryner for all her faults was no weakling. Her commands were crisp. 'Stop gibbering and go wake Betsey in the garret. I'll go wake the master. Don't on any account go down the stairs till I come back.'

Ten minutes later Thomas Farryner, his eyes heavy with sleep and a stumble in his step, staggered down the stairs, followed by his tight-lipped wife, his journeyman and a sobbing maidservant.

'For God's sake, Betsey, button your lip,' snapped Mistress Farryner, 'or I'll give ye something you *will* cry about!'

They reached the bottom of the stairs, where a door led into the passageway. But a horrible shock awaited them. As Thomas Farryner opened the door a gust of hot air hit them, and they staggered back before a roar of flame and belching clouds of black smoke. ' 'Tis no good!' shouted Mistress Farryner, 'We'll have to climb out on the roof. There's no way out below. Back up the stairs and shut that door!' she screamed to her husband. But it was too late. The onrushing flames engulfed the doorway and licked greedily at the lintels and staircase. 'Back up the stairs!' repeated Mistress Farryner. 'We'll have to climb out on the roof through Betsey's garret window.'

The timber of the stairway was dry and the flames seemed almost to follow them as they desperately staggered up the stairs. Smoke was everywhere, dragging on the lungs and filling the eyes with water. Panting, they arrived inside the tiny garret at the top of the house. Mistress Farryner pushed open the small skylight in the roof. They all stood for a moment looking up at the night sky while the cool air was sucked in gratefully. 'You first, Betsey,' said Nan Farryner briskly. 'I'll hoist you through.'

The girl backed away with her fist stuffed to her mouth. 'No, mistress, I daren't. I can't climb out there.'

'You can't go down, girl, so you'll *have* to,' cried Mistress Farryner, exasperated. 'Come now, give me your hand.' An acrid haze began to fill the garret and they heard a crash as the staircase disintegrated in a mass of burning timbers. 'There's no time!' shrieked Mistress Farryner. 'Come, Betsey, *give me your hand*.' The girl still shook her head violently and her mistress hesitated but a moment longer. She saw a horrid flickering cast shadows on the wall of the dark garret and smoke begin to pour in choking clouds under the door.

With a whimper Job Cantwell scrabbled at the skylight and pulled himself through onto the tiles. Tucking up her skirts, Nan Farryner followed, and together they heaved through the wheezing bulk of the King's baker of Pudding Lane. 'Betsey!' screamed Mistress Farryner, peering down through the skylight into the smoke. 'Betsey, for the love o' God—' There was only a dreadful crash of burning timber for answer as a leaping wall of fire reached up at her, and she started back, slithering down to the eaves. Slipping and swaying, the Farryners stumbled from their burning home onto the stable roof of the Old Star Inn, which lay next door and stretched the length of Pudding Lane and round the corner to Fish Street Hill.

Aroused by the shouts and screams, the ostlers of the inn ran out and gaped at the flames now pouring from the Farryners' house. Willing hands put ladders up to the fugitives and they climbed safely to the ground. But their home was doomed. As Job Cantwell's foot finally touched the courtyard the main beam of the Farryners' roof collapsed, sending a cloud of sparks and bits of burning wood high into the night air. Even as the screaming people rushed from their rooms in the inn, the wind took these lethal missiles and carried them to alight on the tinder-dry thatched roof of the galleried courtyard of the inn. Within seconds a ribbon of flame spread along the roof. Panic-stricken people fled hither and thither. The ostlers desperately tried to pull down the burning thatch with long poles, but the flames curved under the gabling to the wooden galleries that lay beneath and the stables crammed with dry straw.

A pile of hay heaped in the stableyard burst into flames, which then caught the timbered front of the stables. The screams of terrified horses and the sounds of their kicking hooves only ceased as men dashed in, wrapped cloths around their heads and brought them out in snorting, plunging terror.

Thomas Farryner gazed bleakly at the burning pile of timbers which had been his home while his wife sobbed noisily beside him. Already the fire had made a gap in the houses of Pudding Lane and fiercely burning sparks and bits of timber alighted on the houses nearby. The wind was fresh and blew the debris westward to the twisting close-packed mass of houses that wound down Pudding Lane past Fish Street Hill to Thames Street and the river itself.

There were shouts and calls behind the Farryners as efforts were made in vain to save the Old Star Inn. Job Cantwell heard Nan Farryner mutter to her husband in a queer blank voice, 'She's dead, isn't she—Betsey. She's dead. My Lord! Dead—like that, in the flames! Christ help her, it's horrible.' She broke down in a paroxysm of grief. Thomas Farryner put his arm clumsily about her and strode on grimly. Job looked at the frightening sight of the Old Star Inn all ablaze, the fire leaping up the walls. The light of the flames gave his face a macabre look as he murmured, 'And she be not the last, I reckon.'

Four

The King was in the City on horseback from early morning ... Laying regal dignity aside the King ... himself took a share in the work, handling spade and bucket and inspiring the courtiers about him to do the same. Bespattered with mud and dirt, his laced costume dripping with water, his hot face blackened with the universal fire dust, but himself alert and tireless ...

—*The Diary of John Evelyn
September, 1666*

Samuel Pepys was fast asleep when his favourite maid Jane came banging on the door of his bedchamber. 'Wake up, sir, wake up. There's a great fire in the city!' Grumbling, Sam saw her standing in the doorway, her nightcap askew and a candle held in one hand. Below her nightgown her ankles and dainty little feet showed slim and white, and Samuel was gazing at them interestedly when he realised what Jane was saying with such agitation.

'I wouldn't never 'ave seen it, sir,' she continued breathlessly, 'but me and Mercer was up late tonight, sir, as you well knows, preparing the syllabub and dowsets for your party on the morrow, and the glow of it fair shone through the window like a branch of candles. Do come and look, sir. 'Tis a great fire, to be sure—I've never seen aught like it!'

Mistress Pepys's pretty head surmounted by an elegant nightcap stirred on the pillow beside him. 'What is it, Samooel?' She yawned. 'Did Jane say there is a *fire?*'

'Not here, my love,' Mr. Pepys reassured her. 'It seems there is some fire or other in the city. Though why I should be woken at this hour . . .' He slipped on his nightgown, grumbling, and went over to the bedroom window, shading his eyes with his hand to see better. Away in the midst of the dark pile of houses to the westward a glow of light appeared to flicker and leap, and Sam could dimly make out a spiral of smoke ascending above it. ' 'Tis way and far off, Jane,' he said, shrugging. 'Looks to me as though it's to the backside o' Mark Lane, if no further. 'Tis far enough off, at any rate, not to worry. Ods my life, you know as well as I that there are always fires of some sort breaking out in the city. Don't fret, my dear, go to bed.' If his wife had not been wide awake he would have been tempted to plant a kiss on Jane's upturned anxious face. As it was he patted her shoulder, and she left the room while Sam padded back across the chamber and fell into bed again. His wife was already asleep once more. ' 'Twill be out by morning, I doubt not,' he murmured to himself drowsily, closing his eyes.

Mr. Pepys was quite mistaken. As he was just arranging a new periwig in tasteful curls about his shoulders next morning and admiring the contrast of chestnut locks on lemon brocade, Jane once more broke in on him unceremoniously. 'Really, Jane!' he protested. 'This will not do. How many times must your mistress tell you not to enter without knocking?'

But Jane bobbed only the sketchiest of curtseys before gabbling off her news. ' 'Tis the fire, sir. 'Tis worse. Master Hatchard says that over three hundred houses have been burned a'ready and 'tis now burning all down Fish Street and looks to reach the bridge before long!'

Mr. Pepys once more peered out of the window. He could not see too clearly, for a cloud now hung over all, obscuring his vision. But the amount of smoke disturbed him. 'Fetch my sword, Jane,' he called over his shoulder. 'I must be off at once—I think to the Tower first, to see how far it has spread.' Suddenly it seemed to Mr. Pepys that the fire might not just die of its own accord.

An hour later he stood on the parapet of the White Tower, looking down across London. A disturbing sight met his eyes. Flames leaping higher than the huddled houses wrought havoc amongst the dry timbers and plaster of which the city was chiefly constructed. A wall of orange fire seemed to be moving westward. Already it was but a short distance from the bridge and a fresh wind was moving it inexorably into the packed cluster of streets and alleys that ran down to the waterfront. Down by the river it had seized, like a bird of prey, on the warehouses of Thames Street. They were packed with canvas, oil, timber, wax and tar, which sent up a pother of black fumes to drift on as herald of the fate to come. It seemed to the horrified Mr. Pepys that most of that part of London around Thames Street was bathed in a flood of liquid flames.

'God's death,' he muttered. 'Old Mitchell's house at the Old Swan has gone by the bridge and that's the Fishmongers' Hall afire over yonder, an' I mistake not . . .' Above the housetops his eyes caught the sight of the spire of St. Magnus Church wreathed in flames.

He ran back down the stone steps and hailed a waterman at Tower Stairs. 'Will you take me upriver, my bully?' he asked, jerking his head to where the ominous cloud of smoke was moving across the Thames from the houses backing onto the river. 'Aye, marry, will I?' snorted the waterman and spat on the ground. Mr. Pepys was not discomposed. He tossed a gold coin into the air and watched the man's eyes gleam. 'Aye, marry, will you?' he asked again softly.

King Charles the Second was dining informally in his Closet at Whitehall with his brother of York when a distraught Mr. Pepys was ushered into the royal presence by a bowing lackey. Charles looked up as he came in. 'Ah—Pepys?' he said questioningly. 'I gather you have news for us of a conflagrationary nature?' His tone was light, bored even; his hand fondled a spaniel that lay sprawled on his lap. But his dark eyes looked shrewdly at the Clerk of the Acts for his Majesty's Navy. 'It seems,' he remarked genially, 'that you have been fire-fighting already.'

Certainly Mr. Pepys was not as 'point de vice' as he had been when he had left Seething Lane; his lemon brocade coat was covered with smuts and a light feathering of grey ash disfigured his periwig as he made a leg to the royal brothers. 'Sire, your Royal Highness, I came hot foot to see your Majesty, for the fire is worse than I had ever thought, and if 'tis not stopped soon, I fear it may destroy the whole city.'

'Go on, Mr. Pepys,' said Charles.

'I persuaded a waterman to take me from the Tower through the area the fire is ravaging, and 'tis horrifying, your Majesty! The heat is enough to stifle you and the flames rage as high as two houses placed one atop the other all along the waterfront, even reaching out over the river. Thames Street is near consumed and the fire hath taken hold up towards Cheapside and down to the Three Cranes a'ready. The bridge itself is threatened. No one is doing anything to combat the fire, everyone is too busy trying to save their goods and their lives. 'Tis like hell's inferno, your Majesty! There are poor people staying in their houses till the very flames lick the rafters, and then running into boats to escape being fried to cinders. The very pigeons hover about the rooftops till their wings are burned and then plummet to the ground dead. The chaos is indescribable. What with the crackle of the flames, the screams of women and the splash as overloaded wherries tip their contents into the water—you'd think the French had landed and the Dutch with them!' Mr. Pepys mopped his brow. 'Nothing is being *done*, Sire. The wind is mighty high and driving into the city. After the drought, everything is dry as tinder and nothing will stop the fire until a gap is made which the flames cannot bridge. If I might suggest, your Majesty could command that houses are pulled down in the fire's path . . .'

Charles stood up, pushing the spaniel down, and his voice was terse and commanding. All his air of languor was suddenly gone. 'Mr. Pepys, I thank you for coming here and I take your advice. Pray go and seek out Sir Thomas Bludworth and tell him on my orders to spare no houses in the fight against the fire. I will draft as many soldiers as can be found to join a line of bucket fighters to stem the blaze. You'—he snapped his fingers at the lackey—'pray go and find his Grace of Albemarle and bid him attend me here with all speed. On your way out tell Chiffinch to send a page to Sir Thomas Harvey and Sir William Penn with a like message. James . . .'

'My liege?'

'How many sailors can you spare me?'

'At least one hundred I should say, your Majesty. Am I right, Mr. Pepys?'

Sam nodded. Charles tapped impatiently on the table. 'We must gather as many fire fighters as possible and stop the people panicking. Mr. Pepys, tell my Lord Mayor when you find him that the city's churches are to be thrown open for the refuge of those poor wretches who have lost their all in the flames and order him to organise some rudimentary relief. James, tell the naval stores to release blankets and ship's biscuits and any other available foodstuffs so that it may be distributed to the needy.' Mr. Pepys watched, amazed, as the King, whom he had often written off mentally as an amiable farradiddle, now strode up and down calmly issuing commands like a seasoned general ordering his troops into battle. At the end of a string of instructions the King stopped and looked at Sam from under hooded lids. He held out his hand, and as Mr. Pepys bent to kiss it he heard Charles's level voice. 'I do give you hearty thanks for your detailed news, Mr. Pepys, and I assure you I am very sensible of our debt to you this day.'

There was a warm flush of happy embarrassment about Mr. Pepys's neck and ears as he hurried off to do the King's bidding.

And yet, for all Charles's efforts, little was done to stem the tide of the fire that day. Even when Mr. Pepys had pushed his way through a chaos of frightened people, waggons, handcarts and horses around St. Paul's and run my Lord Mayor to earth in Canning Street, he found nothing but disappointment. Sir Thomas Bludworth, plump, pink and indecisive, mopped his fat jowls with a lavendered kerchief and moaned at Mr. Pepys for all the world, Sam thought, like a fainting woman. When he heard the King's orders he shook his head feebly. 'Lord! what can I do? I am spent; people will not obey me. I have been pulling down houses, but the fire overtakes us faster than we can do it.' He blinked watery eyes at Sam and coughed miserably.

Mr. Pepys looked at him in disgust. He well knew why my Lord Mayor was reluctant to pull down houses. It was one thing to demolish hovels in Cheapside but another to blow up the mansion of a rich merchant in Lombard Street who might fall in wrath on Sir Thomas and demand compensation. When he mentioned gunpowder, the Mayor looked horrified. 'Nay, sir,' he gasped. 'There is no need surely—why, 'twould carve huge lumps out of the city. I am sure it will burn itself out without *that*!'

Charles came to view the fire for himself that afternoon. He went quite informally with his brother James and Mr. Pepys by barge to the city and had himself brought to Queenhithe as near as he could get to the flames. All three stood watching the billowing curls of smoke that stretched along the waterfront and blew in gusts under the piers of the great bridge itself. The river was crammed with boats of all kinds filled with teetering piles of furniture which spilled into the water around them. Everyone was too busy saving their belongings to recognise the identity of the tall man in the plain black suit who stood frowning in the prow of the barge.

'Charles,' burst out the Duke of York, 'all the city will be consumed ere the day is up!'

The King did not move his head. 'Not quite, brother, but 'tis bad enough for all that. I warrant the fire will be stretching clear from Billingsgate to Puddle Dock come dusk and will spread further if that infernal wind keeps up.' He turned to Sam. 'And do you say my Lord Mayor refuses to use gunpowder?'

Sam nodded. The King ground his hands together in rage. 'God's death! I have offered aid to those damned aldermen of the Common Council and they refuse it. Tell me they can manage alone! I see now how they *manage*.'

The stench of charred timber drifted out across the river and with it a certain sickly smell that was vaguely unpleasant. Charles watched the scurrying desperate efforts of his people to escape with their lives and goods, and as he watched, a small skiff drew up to the Old Swan Stairs and was almost immediately overrun by terrified people who ignored the loud protests of the watermen. It suddenly capsized, throwing shouting, swearing people into the water. Charles ordered his barge over to pick the casualties out of the river. As the oars dipped to his command he swung round and his brother saw an unusual light of rage in his eye. 'I know well my Lord Mayor and the aldermen prize the liberties of their city and resent royal interference, but damn it, if the Crown's jurisdiction continues to stop at Temple Bar, they'll lose their city and all their moneybags to boot! Waterman, turn around. We must return to Whitehall, James, and organise this. You must take command; I will tell the Privy Council—'

' 'Ere!' said a voice from the quay above. 'Where d'ye think *you're* going wi' that empty barge? There's crowds of us needs an 'and 'ere, and my wife and kids looking to get the clothes singed orf their backs with the fire at the end o' Black Raven Alley. You might be a flash cove, but ye can give us a bit o' room, surely!'

'Fellow,' shouted James wrathfully up to a workman on the wharf. 'You do not—'

'Nay, James,' said Charles quietly. 'You are very right, friend, I forgot myself. Waterman, turn back and pick up those people.'

The boat sculled slowly back and the King held out an oar into the water for frightened hands to cling to, and then he and Mr. Pepys and the Duke of York hauled dripping men and women into the bottom of the barge, where they lay gasping like wet fish. The King ordered the barge up to the wharf and handed down his erstwhile accuser together with wife and three children. Then the prow of the flat barge turned in the water and they rowed upstream towards Whitehall.

Charles tried vainly to hail a man on horseback as they passed Allhallows Stairs. 'Brown—Sir Richard—tell them to pull the damned houses *down* and not just run like rabbits!' The man on horseback turned and looked across the plethora of boats and then shook his head and rode on along Thames Street. 'Odsfish, James,' murmured the frustrated King. 'The sooner I get some fire fighting organised and then get back into the city m'self, the better!'

The barge was halted for a moment as the press of boats in the water grew so dense that they knocked against each other and a man could have stepped from boat to boat from one side of the river to the other. James peered over to see what was holding them up, and then shouted in surprise, 'They're emptying Worcester House! There's a flock of lighters taking Clarendon's goods. Look, they're passing them from the windows up there.'

The people in the barge looked up to see chests, chairs, tables and even lengths of curtaining being handed down to the river by an army of busy lackeys. Charles snorted with mirth as he saw a glitter of heavy gold plate. 'Now tell me your father-in-law ain't lined his pockets, James.'

All the rest of that day Charles was busy, closeted with his Privy Council and drafting measures to fight the fire. He had London divided into sections around the fire and put each one under a man he could trust to organise resistance. Each section was allocated sailors, soldiers, constables and such equipment as could be found. The whole was put under the command of the Duke of York, and Charles had letters sent to the Lords Lieutenants of the Home Counties to send in their militia and fire-fighting equipment. A tactful, soothing missive was despatched to Sir Thomas Bludworth telling him that the King had taken over the fight against the fire. The London-trained bands were called out.

It was past one in the morning before Charles let his tired Council go and strolled up the stairs to his Closet. He threw open the casement and leant his shoulder against the frame, breathing in the night air. The windowpanes caught the harsh flicker of the flames that rose above London. Against the night sky the fire took on its most horrific aspect, spanning an arch of bloody colour for a mile over the doomed city. Behind St. Paul's the sky was as light as day, lit with a macabre dancing orange light streaked with black smoke drifting in on the wind. Charles shook his head wearily. 'Zoun's,' he murmured. 'Pray God, I am in time.'

Soon after dawn the King was up and on horseback. With his brother of York at one shoulder and the calm figure of the old Duke of Ormonde at the other, they rode under the Holbein Gate and down Whitehall to Charing Cross. They threaded their way through the debris of abandoned furniture and carts and other relics of headlong flight, until Charles took them over the Fleet Bridge and up the winding path of Ludgate hill. As they drew nearer to St. Paul's the air grew hotter and a cloud of heavy ash settled about them, getting in their nostrils and making them want to sneeze.

Charles skirted the perimeter of Old St. Paul's. Its stone superstructure was surrounded by scaffolding, for major repairs were being done to the great church. The King eyed the timbers around the tower uneasily and then briefly ordered James, Duke of York, to have them removed, for, as he told his brother, 'There is no knowing yet how far the fire may penetrate.'

They were stopped as they rounded Amen Corner and turned into Paternoster Row by a scurrying pack of 'prentice boys, all loaded high with lurching piles of their masters' books, running down Paul's Alley into St. Paul's churchyard through the old lych gate. 'They're lodging them in the crypt,' explained James. ' 'Tis expected to be safe even if the fire *does* reach here.'

'I pray they may be right,' said Charles briefly. Digging his heels into his horse and leaving Old St. Paul's, he led them eastward down Ludgate hill and into the heart of Cheapside. They coughed as the thick smoke tore at the lungs and obliterated virtually all trace of the sun now riding high in the sky above them. Yet as they rode on towards the Poultry the wind blew a gap in the smoke for a second and a sight as lamentable as Samuel Pepys had described was laid open to sight.

From where Charles sat on his horse, he could see that all the houses right down to the river were one mass of flames. Tower Street was but a heap of smoking ruins and Allhallows Stairs, where he had hailed Sir Richard Brown, was obscured from view by the leaping destruction which rose into the sky. Charles saw the fire creeping towards them in a long arc on a front a mile wide. He spurred his horse onward into the denseness of the smoke down the Poultry, until he reached the point where he could actually see the timbered front of a merchant's counting house in Threadneedle Street burning and the flames dancing in devil's ribands like snakes along the roof gables to reach the next house in line. As he looked up, the tall marbled splendour of the Royal Exchange stood before him, flames gutting its frontage and wrapping about the building like a winding sheet in the embrace of death. As the King glanced to the right, he could see all the length of Lombard Street in similar condition. Tugging at his lace neckcloth and coughing, he backed his uneasy horse and cantered back down the Poultry through a fighting mass of people.

A woman pushing in the opposite direction pressed past the King's horse, crying like one demented, 'Dickon! Dickon! Where are you, my Dickon? Oh God . . .' Charles caught a glimpse of her round pale face. For a second he saw it: a face of anguish with the most desolate, hopeless expression he had ever seen. She ran back into the smoke, still screaming out for her child, and was swallowed up by it. Fear-maddened people jostled the King, pushing by in terror, carrying bundles of clothes and what they had been able to save. All around was the noise of the crackling burning houses, the cries and shouts of the citizens amidst the black pall of tossing smoke. Charles pressed on grimly with his brother and Ormonde behind, until he came to the corner of the Poultry by the ornate carved steepled façade of the Mercers' Hall. Turning his horse, he straddled the cobbled street and rose in his saddle, one hand upraised. 'Good people, hold! Hold, I say!' he shouted.

One or two faces looked up at him bemusedly, and then a soot-encrusted sailor recognised the features of the man on the black horse. ' 'Tis the King hisself!' he bawled. ' 'Tis the King!'

'Help is coming,' continued Charles at the top of his voice. 'We must fight the fire, not just flee from it! Sailors, fire fighters—all are being gathered with haste and will be directed here as soon as may be. But you—you too must help. Women and children must be allowed free passage, but all able-bodied men must stay and form a water chain to fight the blaze.' His eyes swept over them curtly, and reluctantly their onward pushing stopped at his horse's pawing hooves. Charles gestured behind him to the squat well of the great conduit of Cheapside. 'Yonder is water a' plenty. A line of buckets must be formed from there to the fire itself.' He pointed a finger suddenly downward. 'You, fellow, let your wife take your child and go. You stay, and find me as many buckets and bowls from the houses hereabouts as you can garner.' The man put a hand to his forelock, looked in awe at the King and then turned and ran off down the street.

The moving crowd was for the moment stationary, held by the eye of the King as he sat his horse. But Charles knew that to hold their panic in check, instant action was necessary. 'James, go and find Berkeley down at his station at the Cordwainers' Hall in Distaff Lane and tell him I want as many of his drafted sailors as he can spare.' James nodded and galloped off. 'And now,' continued the King amiably, 'to work!'

To the amazement of the panicked citizens, he swung his leg off his horse, jumping to the cobbles, and then proceeded to strip off a coat of rich velvet and silver lacing and an elegant waistcoat, and roll up his sleeves. The scene was almost comic, Ormonde thought—they fell back a pace as the King jumped down and looked at him in mesmerised astonishment, their mouths open, as if he had stripped to the buff. Charles's eyes twinkled up at him as he took off his wig and threw it down just as the man he had directed ran up with a brace of buckets. 'Thank you, my fine friend. Now, I am keeping this one—who will take the other?' There was a shuffle of feet and then a stout alehouse keeper strode forward. 'I will, your Honour!'

Charles tossed him the leather bucket and then tossed a guinea after it. 'That for your trouble. Now follow me . . .' Down the street he strolled and they fell back before him. And as he went his finger jabbed first at one and then at another. Ormonde heard his voice, deep and jovial: 'Surely you can manage a brace of buckets, a great ox like you . . . Wilt come and save another being fried to cinders, friend? . . . What about you, sir—fine hot weather for a day's exercise?'.

They were unable to withstand the humorous but penetrating look of those dark eyes under straight brows, and fell in awkwardly behind him. There was one minor crisis. As they reached the conduit a hurrying stocky man shot around the corner of Ironmongers' Lane and cannoned into Charles. 'Hold, friend!' The King's hand gripped his shoulder. 'Stay with us and fight the flames.' The man twisted, terrified and panting. 'Pox take you, let me go! 'Tis hopeless. All Cornhill is afire—nothing can stop it. 'Tis every man for 'isself. Get outta my way, curse you!' He aimed a blow at the King's face, which Charles neatly sidestepped. A second later Charles's fist took him under the chin, lifting him from the ground with a hefty crack, and he dropped unconscious. 'Now—' The King turned. 'Are any more of you of a like mind?' One or two heads looked down guiltily, but none moved. There came a cry from behind him: 'Your Majesty—this yere shop's a ship's chandler's! There be enough buckets to dredge the Thames!'

A succession of leather buckets passed through a broken shutter, and just as the last one was taken, there came a tramp of feet. Down from Cheapside appeared the Duke of York—behind him, on foot, was a troop of brawny sailors who dragged with them a pair of carts on which were mounted hand squirts and lengths of coiled hose. Charles sighed with relief. 'A gift from heaven . . .' Within minutes the two hand squirts were rolled up to beneath the tall gabling of the

Mercers' Hall just as the first sparks carried by the wind and smoke from the inferno of Threadneedle Street alighted on the tiles above. Charles strode to the end of the line, dipped his bucket in the conduit well and passed it along. The front of the Mercers' Hall was drenched with water until pools ran down the timbers and over the cobbles.

But it was nonetheless doomed—its timbers were tarred and painted and the wood was dry as hay. The flames creeping along the gabling from behind were higher than the feeble hand squirts could reach to quench them and the water directed upwards fell back harmlessly to the ground. No sooner had they licked inside one upper window frame than the entire timber façade was on fire and the sweating bucket carriers were forced back by the heat, one hand up to protect their faces, while they threw a bucket on the spreading flames in vain hopes of dousing them.

There was a sudden warning creak, and Charles looked up to see the surface of roof tiles buckle and flap like a blanket. 'Back!' he shouted desperately. 'Back, I say!' Even as the fire fighters turned tail, there came a terrific crash and the steeple of the Mercers' Hall tottered for a moment and then fell, crumpling as it went, smashing through the tiles of the roof and sending them spinning in splinters on the cobbles all around. The roof gave first at one end and then the other, to subside eventually in a gout of smoke with timbers falling inwards while the flames leapt up. The pavements began to glow with heat and Charles could feel the scorching through the soles of his shoes as they fought on, falling back before the flames while smouldering bits of wood and flotsam dropped on their heads and shoulders.

The wind seemed to laugh at their efforts: at times, almost gusting a gale, it drove the fire towards them, fanning the heat up into their faces and driving the smoke with it until their eyes watered and their lungs racked inside their bodies. Crowds continued to stream past them. From time to time they heard sinister news of the progress of the fire. A man on a stout cob rode past as they toiled, shouting, 'The flames have got as far as Baynard's Castle—they say there's been explosions down on Broken Wharfe and many killed.'

'You said the fire would have reached Puddle Dock come evening, Charles,' gasped the Duke of York as he threw yet another bucket on the flames. 'If this wind keeps up, 'twill carry the fire clean to Whitehall. There is nothing to stop it leaping the Fleet and burning the Bridewell right down to Whitefriars.'

'We *must* make a gap the fire cannot bridge,' said the King flatly. 'Houses must be pulled down with grappling hooks even if my Lord Mayor will not hear of gunpowder.'

Reports of the fire were followed by vociferous rumour and stories of catastrophe. A plump merchant with hat and wig askew galloped up Soper Lane from the direction of the river, with a tale to curdle the blood in the veins. ' 'Tis the cursed Papists! The French and the Dutch have invaded and are even now entering the city. 'Twas they started the fire and made it spread. Look to your lives . . .' He galloped on, still shouting. James, Duke of York, shrugged, grimaced at his brother and bent again to fill his bucket. But the merchant's tale was greeted with cries of alarm and renewed panic welled up. The line of bucket fighters wavered and must have broken but for the example set by the King, who told them shortly not to believe in rumour and urged them back into the fray before they had time to think again. From palm to palm they laboured on, with sweat pouring off them, and always in front, pushing forward, the terrible glow and crackle. Fire and more fire . . .

They could not save the Poultry. Back and back they retreated, until the great conduit itself was enveloped and they could no longer use it. They were forced then to extend the chain of buckets back round the corner into Bread Street, while before their eyes the huge wall of lambent flames engulfed Bow Church almost within minutes. Inexorably the fire was pushing through Cheapside and there seemed to be nothing they could do to stop it. As the flames raged higher the heat became too intense to bear and too dangerous to approach. Above their heads there were cracks like small explosions as the slates on the roofs sundered and fell with a rasping noise and splintered on the cobbles. More than one man passing a bucket was knocked unconscious by falling debris. The dockyard sailors fought valiantly, but after several hours they began to tire. Charles ordered grappling hooks to be brought, and teams of workmen strained at the houses to bring them down before the fire could reach them, trying to create a gap it could not jump.

Time after time a house was demolished in an eruption of dust and cinders, only for the exhausted men to see the fire leap the gap and sweep on unappeased. It seemed as though nothing would ever stop it.

Charles looked up wearily. He could see that the narrow timbered streets had become tunnels for the flames, that the wind made them enormous blast furnaces which devoured these veins in the body of the capital and sucked at its life blood. It was as though the fire had gathered a personality of its own: huge, dominant and devouring, it squatted on the dying city like a malignant spider consuming its prey.

Suddenly, above the roar of the flames and the cries of the fleeing crowds, he heard a sobbing high scream and glanced upwards to see a serving wench pressed in terror against an open casement on an upper floor of the Mermaid tavern. Already the lower floor was in flames and the outside staircase which had led to the upper storey hung in charred ruins. The actual sill on which the girl leant was itself smouldering. Charles could barely make her out, so dense was the smoke.

Even as he ran over to the burning tavern a small cart laden with furniture detached itself from the press of traffic and came to rest beneath the window. A female figure with a shawl over her head stood with her back to Charles. Her hands were outstretched, and though Charles could not hear her, she was obviously imploring the girl to jump. But the girl only drew back, sobbing and shaking her head. Charles jumped lightly onto the cart. The woman in the shawl pushed a chest towards him hurriedly: 'Haply you could stand on this.'

He climbed up, and his hands were just level with the window. Gusts of smoke poured out as he wrenched the other casement open. Coaxed by his calm, persuasive voice, the young girl inside leant out, put her hands thankfully in his strong grip and slipped down in his arms. As the woman below held out her hands to take the girl, Charles saw the shawl slip back, revealing a surprising sight. He was looking into the startled face of Nell Gwynne.

For her part Nell found herself confronted by a very tall man in a torn shirt, his face darkened by soot and sweat. On one cheek was a large purple bruise and encrusted dirt reached up above his eyebrows. A merry smile played about his mouth. 'Well met, indeed, Mistress Gwynne.' Her eyes widened incredulously as she recognised his voice, and then she smiled back. 'What in the name of Hades do you here?' demanded the King. His eyes flickered over a cart packed tight with things—gilded chairs, the dismantled pieces of what looked like a bed, a row of copper-bound chests and a pair of virginalls slotted on one end at the rear. She made a quick gesture 'A—a friend was out of town and I knew he would not wish for all his things to be burnt, so I took a cart and went to—'

'My Lord Buckhurst's lodgings in Lombard Street. What an infernal out-of-the-way place to live!' Charles finished for her. '*And* I warrant his lackeys only loaded up this cart after you'd calmed their fears with your honeyed tongue.'

She snorted, throwing back her mass of hair in a way Charles remembered from their last meeting. 'Maw worms! I'd almost to grab their coat skirts to keep 'em long enough to load Buck's movables. More a taste of pepper than honey, I promise you!'

He gave a shout of laughter. 'Poor wretches! The flames licking around the doorposts of Lombard Street and your tongue to boot. What did they fear most, I wonder—it seems it must have been your tongue.'

'They'd never worked harder, I make no doubt, for all they wriggled like ferrets in a sack.' She chuckled impishly.

A gust of wind blew smoke up between them, and with a sudden eruption the upper story of the Mermaid tavern became a rearing, solid wall of fire. The girl Charles had saved tugged desperately at his arm and turned a stricken face up at him. 'Sir, there's old Mistress Bellows. She's still in there. She can't walk, see—' Charles took one look and then climbed back onto the chest. A voice stopped him. 'One moment.' He found a shawl pressed into his hands. 'Here, take this. Wrap it round your head and shoulders . . .'

The King muffled his face and vaulted up to the blazing sill, swinging his long legs over. The smoke filled the window and he instantly disappeared from view. After only a couple of seconds, from within the depths of the tavern there came a sudden eruption and sparks flew out of the casement and fled up into the air. Nell jumped, and she felt a shock go through her. Her heart thudded so heavily that she felt faint and she found herself whispering, the words tumbling out unbidden and frantic, 'Please don't let him die. Dear God, please don't let him die . . .' The time seemed interminable, but it was in reality only a minute before Charles reappeared, coughing heavily and carrying over one shoulder the unconscious form of an old woman. He handed her out, then climbed out after her. 'Drive on, Nelly,' he shouted loudly. 'Drive on—*now*!'

Nell flicked the nervous horse, and as the cart jerked off there came a second thunderous noise behind them and the front wall of the house fell in with a roar of flames and clouds of plaster dust. Charles slumped beside her, gulping in the air, his chest heaving. The frightened serving wench held the old woman in her arms and cried silently. The rescued woman lay inert, breathing stertorously, her face sunken and grey. Nell did not stop the cart until it reached Old Change Alley, well away from the raging inferno, and then she threw down the reins. Before Charles's startled eyes she pulled back her skirt, displaying slender legs up to the thigh, and fumbled amongst her petticoats. The King's eyebrows rose but he said nothing, and finally Nell gave a whistle of triumph and drew out a small flask. She took a deep swig from it, sighed, gave the top a wipe with her hand and passed it to an amused Charles. 'Gut rot,' she told him. 'Have a swallow—you must need it.' Charles drank deep and then, with a sigh, rested his head on his hands, but she jumped down and went to the rear of the cart. 'Could you give me a hand, your Majesty?'

A pained expression crossed his features. 'Odsfish, what for?'

'To throw this curst instrument of Buck's into the gutter.

That poor old soul needs a bed in the back here and there'll be room once we heave it out.'

He blinked at the bulk of it. 'A singularly inappropriate instrument for Buckhurst to own, if I may say so,' he remarked. 'For *Buckhurst*—a pair of *virginalls*?'

Nell's eyes danced. 'Then the sooner 'tis gone, the better.'

'You're a slave driver, Mistress Gwynne,' the King told her, climbing down from the cart. Between them they lugged the object out and dropped it, with a discordant noise of protest, over the side. Charles's eyes twinkled as he watched Nell's small arms heave away, amused at the resolute expression on her face. 'Nelly—'

But he was interrupted by the anxious figure of the Duke of York on horseback emerging through the smoke on the corner of Fryday Street. 'Charles!' he cried in relief and cantered up to them. 'I'm glad I found you, brother. Charles, we must *blow* these houses *up*! 'Tis not enough to pour water on them and pull them down by hand. Pox take the Common Council —there is no other way to save the houses left standing.'

'In a moment, James.' Charles threw the words over his shoulder, but remained looking at Nell. 'Mistress Gwynne . . .' He stretched out his hand and one finger lightly brushed her cheek. She heard his voice, low and soft: 'This time in his fishing, methinks Buckhurst has caught a pearl beyond pricing.' His lazy smile lit up his harsh features. Before she could reply he was gone, walking off back into the smoke with his easy long stride and without a backward look.

For the next hour Charles and James rode up and down the perimeter of the fire, organising the lines of bucket carriers and the teams of sailors armed with grappling hooks. Down as far as Baynard's Castle on the riverfront Charles rode, and from the naval storehouses at Queenhithe—in imminent danger from the flames—he commandeered kegs of gunpowder, which were carried on the shoulders of the sailors up to Blackfriars near the Fleet, where Charles hoped to stem the tide. But as he came through the smoke up Ludgate hill a shout assailed his ears: ' 'Tis Old St. Paul's! 'Tis afire! God save us, 'tis Old St. Paul's!'

Charles urged his horse to a gallop. But even before he reached Ludgate Street he could see that it was too late—the church was a holocaust. From the tall Gothic windows of its grey stone tower, rearing up against the smoky sky, flames belched forth in clouds. The choir could scarce be seen for the blaze that lapped over it and reached out to the transepts. Like a mighty titan, wreathed in smoke, ravaged mortally from one pinnacled end to the other, St. Paul's was dying.

Ormonde met him breathlessly. 'There's nothing we can do, Sire. The flames crept down Paternoster Row and sparks landed on the scaffolding behind. No one saw that the church was on fire until too late.'

Charles inched his horse forward, but he could get no nearer than the churchyard. The heat was so fearful, none could approach; it sent back the fire fighters with singed hair, coughing helplessly. Charles sat motionless, watching, while the great cathedral that had sat on Ludgate hill looking down on the grey Thames for over six hundred years was changed to a gutted skeleton of calcined stones and rubble.

'Pity the poor booksellers,' Ormonde heard Charles murmur.

'Sire?'

'They stored their books in the crypt of St. Paul's to keep them safe. I misdoubt whether any will escape.'

Ormonde shook his head wearily. 'The heat is such that the very lead on the roof hath melted and runs down the aisle into Creed Lane in a hissing torrent. For all the world as if an ale cask were broken.'

The fire continued to spread westward at a tremendous rate. Dusk found the King still on his feet, deploying hand squirts and buckets down the length of Fleet Street from the conduit there. The fire was halted for a time by the gap of the Fleet ditch, as it was by the gap in the houses on the bridge which saved Southwark from its advance over the river. But there was no dependence on its remaining on the right side of the Fleet; fate seemed to set its face against London. The wind which had blown all day continued and did not die, but threw the fire towards them like some voracious monster. The sun stared above the smoke like a great crimson orb in a streaked sunset, and Charles felt himself on the point of exhaustion. He turned to take yet another bucket of water to add to the number standing ready to greet the flames should they cross the Fleet Bridge, when he stopped in amazement at the sight which came into view.

It was a gentleman. Down the street he came, idly swinging his cane and fanning himself with a kerchief, followed by a valet carrying a valise. He did not look either to right or left, though the crackle of flames and the crash of falling timbers was all about him, but strolled languidly on, dabbing at his brow and suppressing a yawn. As he came abreast of Charles he stopped and looked intently into his sooty and begrimed face, and the King saw his blue eyes blink in astonishment. Then he flicked out his whalebone skirts just as though he were at a presentation ball in the Stone Gallery and made a profound leg. 'Your Majesty,' he said in tones of deep respect.

'My Lord Fox . . .' said Charles blankly. 'What finds you *here*, my lord?'

Perfection Fox looked resigned. 'I am searching for a chair, Sire. Do you know, there are *none* to be had? I swear I have walked a mile searching, if I have walked a yard. But so it is always. I was expected a clear two hours past for dinner with my Lady Bellasis, but I dare say she has *quite* given me up. Isn't it damned hot? I dare swear I shall develop a megrim. Ods my life . . .' His eyes travelled over his sovereign's stained person. 'Your Majesty has had a trying day?' he asked politely.

'One might say so,' replied Charles with heavy sarcasm.

Lord Fox shook his head sagely. 'I know how you must feel, Sire. I recall when I removed to London from Leicestershire in the spring the trouble it caused—you have no notion! I was laid up for close on a sennight.' He bowed once more ceremonially and strolled off, seemingly unconcerned as to why he should find the King in shirt and breeches passing leather buckets along a life line of sweating, exhausted men.

The King watched him go with a twitch of his lips. A second later a team of sailors drafted from the Deptford dockyard succeeded, after a good strain, in pulling down one of the houses in the fire's path. It was demolished in a crash of lathe and plaster and a huge piece of timber descended with a dull thud, narrowly missing my Lord Fox's luxuriant periwig and coming to rest in a cloud of dust at his feet. He winced as it hit the ground and eyed its solid bulk as he took a pinch of snuff. 'Dear me,' he said.

Charles saw him continue in his path, carefully stepping over the obstacle and followed still by his almost gibbering valet. The team of sailors watched him, open-mouthed. 'Is he Bedlam bait or what?' asked one. Charles suddenly gave vent to a huge boom of laughter. Tears rolled down his face as he shook with mirth. 'Odsfish,' he moaned. 'No one would ever believe me!'

His jocular mood did not last, however. The day was virtually done and the King felt he had accomplished nothing. The last straw came with a roar and an explosion from down by the waterfront, and the news that arrived shortly after was that the naval storehouses on the wharf at Queenhithe had blown up when the fire had reached the store of gunpowder there.

'God's bones!' exclaimed Charles passionately to his brother. 'I *told* them to shift it out *hours* ago!'

James, Duke of York, looked gloomily down the burning length of Fleet Street. The fire had leapt the Fleet ditch, and as he peered into the flames, the dark timbering was silhouetted against the devastation. The black clouds moving slowly between a sullen sky and ravaged earth testified to the last rites offered up as the angel of death with calescent wings passed over London. Then James gasped. Charles felt him grip his elbow suddenly. 'Charles, look!' The Duke of York's head was cocked as he stood motionless. 'The wind, Charles—the wind has dropped, brother! 'Tis dropped!'

For a second the King gazed silently at him. His subjects were then treated to the unusual sight of their sovereign and the Duke of York jumping up and down and shouting like two excited schoolboys.

Five

London was, but is no more.

*—The Diary of John Evelyn
September, 1666*

Sir Thomas Bludworth and a group of flustered aldermen craved audience of the King soon after dawn next morning. The Lord Mayor wrung his hands and rolled his eyes above pendulous cheeks as he poured forth his tale of woe. 'Your Majesty, we come to throw ourselves upon your Majesty's protection. We know not what to do—the fire is out of control, it has got as far as the Inner Temple. All Fleet Street, the Old Bailey, Warwick Lane and Newgate all—all lies in ashes!'

The King looked at him sardonically. 'I offered my royal protection two days past. I seem to remember you received it differently then!'

The Lord Mayor's reply was inaudible and the aldermen looked sheepish. Seeing their discomfiture, Charles relented. 'Come, come, 'tis not as bad as all that. I rather think we may see the fire checked before long. I have posted soldiers at the city gates to ensure that the people may escape the city as soon as possible and camps are ready at Islington and Highgate to receive them. There was pandemonium yesterday, what with carts jamming, horses and fighting people, so I'm told. You may rest assured all possible is being done for your distressed citizens.'

The news appeared to afford the mayor little joy. ' 'Tis not that, your Majesty. The fire still spreads—St. Paul's, Guildhall, Christ Church, the Royal Exchange . . . Where next, I ask myself?'

The King's eyes glowed cynically and his voice was soft. 'Why, even to your own fine new mansion now a-building in the Strand, I doubt not. You have reason for worry indeed, my Lord Mayor!'

My Lord Mayor's jaw dropped and his eyes goggled. 'No, no, your Majesty, I protest—I was not thinking—'

'No, no, of course not,' said Charles soothingly. 'Merely my little jest. But indeed I believe the worst is over. I have sent out teams of sailors armed with kegs enough of gunpowder to create such gaps as will stop any fire, however large. I think if they are placed aright, we may save Somerset House and *all* the Strand.' He clapped Sir Thomas Bludworth on the shoulder. 'Why, man, I do not want to see Whitehall in ashes any more than you do *your* home! Now the wind has dropped, I think a goodly touch of fuse to powder in the right places . . .'

'But—but 'twill wreak havoc and destroy numerous houses,' wailed the mayor.

Charles lost a little of his tact. 'They'll be destroyed anyway, you fool, if we don't use powder—*by the fire*—and a whole lot more besides!'

The mayor sighed unhappily but did not reply.

' 'Tis the spread towards Tower Street that worries me,' continued the King inexorably. 'Our magazines of powder lie in the White Tower and we can't move them in time. If the fire gets there, there will be such an explosion as will demolish the bridge, all the houses round about and blow boats out of the water like so much matchwood.'

Bludworth turned to the King and his face took on a sickly pallor as the import of Charles's words hit home. 'Your Majesty,' he whispered, 'your Majesty must do as you think best.'

Coming hastily down the Stone Gallery some twenty minutes later, the Duke of York was too late to see the departure of the Lord Mayor and his broken Council, but found Charles instead, locked in animated discussion with a slender white-haired man with an intelligent fine-cut face and gentle cast of countenance.

'God knows, Master Evelyn, 'tis little enough. They lack clothes, medicines, cooking implements, bedding—all the most basic necessities of life. I have issued a Royal Proclamation to have provisions brought in from the country. The hospital for the wounded we had established at Smithfield is crammed to bursting—' He broke off, seeing his brother. 'What's to do, James? Have you prepared the powder-keg battalions? We have got them ready this time,' he told Evelyn. 'If we can make gaps enough, I hope we may save the city. Now I must away to the Tower to see that we don't blow ourselves all to kingdom come. Please tell your people that I hope to come and see them out at Moorfields in a day or so, and if there is anything I can do to organise your food supplies, or if you need more canvas or anything, you must let me know.'

Evelyn bowed. As he left he glanced back at the King, and James saw a look of surprised awe on the man's face. 'You've made an ally there, Charles,' he said.

'No, just astonished him a trifle,' said Charles easily. 'He thinks I'm a fribble—told me so once, come to think of it. He's a bit of a proser our Master Evelyn, but there'—he winked at James—'no doubt he's right. What a pair we are, aren't we? I'm looked upon as a dissolute good-for-nothing, and here's you, the most notorious Papist at Court, helping to put the fire *out*! Don't you know that 'twas the Papists who *started* it?'

James shook his head in exasperation. 'Why is it that when people have genuine troubles enough, they fabricate false ones? All my lackeys are sure that the French and Dutch have invaded—my man even told me that the Dutch had burned Rochester and were expected in London any time. Do you know that poor little French valet of Sedley's was near lynched yesterday? He was carrying some tennis balls in a box down King Street and they fell on him, screaming they were fireballs to set light to Whitehall. If Brouncker hadn't been going past, they'd have strung up the poor little monkey. I wish I knew who started these stories.'

Charles steered him towards the stables. 'My dear brother,' he said lightly, 'they fly—on the winds of rumour.'

All through the day London shook to the booming as placid gangs of sailors set off powder kegs that tore rents in the houses of Tower Street and the Temple and intensified the terror of citizens, who had begun to fear that the end of the world was nigh. But the action saved the city. For the rest of the day the fire burned and Samuel Pepys saw it reach the foot of Seething Lane. But it got no further. Londoners awoke the next morning to find their city strangely silent, though a heavy cloud hung over all.

But it was a ravaged London which remained under a leaden sky. Charles felt himself to be passing through some strange desert as he rode through the city to visit the homeless in Moorfields. The ruined houses were smoking, sultry heaps of rubble out of which charred timbers stuck like so many crosses. People were out picking over the remains, trying to root out something from the mountains of rubbish, moving quietly across a grey, dismal desert of ash, betwixt flakes of vast stones strewn in doleful fragments. All the landmarks of the city—the Exchange, Guildhall, the Halls of the Livery Companies, monuments, statues—all were gone. A stench of tar, wood and burned flesh hung in the nostrils. James saw the tears in the King's eyes when they reached the camp of refugees in Moorfields. Above two hundred thousand people had been made homeless, and now wandered up and down the narrow gaps between the makeshift tents erected on the King's orders. They looked dulled and shaken at the tragedy that in such short time had taken from them their homes, possessions and even the lives of their families.

The King's activities in the fire had not gone unnoticed. As he was recognised, people dropped what they were doing and came running forward to touch his horse, clutch at his legs and throng about the royal party. Awkwardly he waved, held down his hand to be kissed, bowed in the saddle and acknowledged their welcome. James saw him bend to shake hands with a stout goodwife with a muddy baby in her arms. 'God bless your Majesty!' she called cheerfully. James was close to his brother and saw again the trace of tears running down Charles's face as he looked down at her. The lines of cynicism were nowhere to be seen as he dug in his pocket and pressed a clink of gold into her hand. 'God bless you, my people . . . God bless you . . .' he repeated, riding slowly through them, scattering a veritable storm of guineas.

One man only appeared not to share their affection. Clad in sober black, with a plain white neckerchief about a thin grubby neck, he waited till the King was abreast of him, and then called, in a penetrating voice, 'Doom be upon you, O King of corruption! 'Tis your lusts and debauchery that hath brought this city to fall under the Lord's wrath. This city of Sodom hath fallen even as Sodom fell! Yea, the profanity of you and yours hath cursed us with the curse of Nineveh!'

'Profanity my arse!' shouted a bulky coalheaver threateningly. 'If 'tweren't for the Black Boy, you'd not 'ave no city left at all, for it was burning down like a bonfire afore he came and sorted it out. *And* he weren't afraid to pick up a bucket or two hisself, 'cos I *saw* him wi' me own blinkers.'

'Aye,' said a voice from behind him, and there was a concurring murmur all around.

'*And* you'd not 'ave no shelter, no food, nor no blankets and such, if 'is Majesty ain't released 'em free o' charge!'

The man sniffed, sensed the mood of the crowd and was silenced.

' 'Twas the Papists started the fire!' shrieked a woman. ' 'Twas the French—Papists—set the city on fire on purpose, they did. They'm want to burn us all like in ould bloody Mary's time! 'Ang 'em, I say. 'Ang the lot on 'em. Devil's spawn!' A roar of agreement greeted this speech and a cluster of shaken fists and chorus of oaths.

Charles held up his hand, and the roar gradually subsided. He gazed about him at the desperate, frightened faces and his voice was firm and carrying. 'My people, dear people, I am your King and you have greeted me this day despite your troubles and your miseries in a way I shall never forget. Do not despair. All is now in ruins, but it will not long remain so. London will be rebuilt. Houses will stand where they stood before. A new London will rise on the ashes of the old. We will rebuild your city, on that you have our royal word, and it will be a city of which you will be proud. It takes more than this to break the stomachs of Englishmen.'

A frenzied cheer answered him, but the King held up his hand again. 'We have grievous troubles indeed, but no good can come of rumour and lies. The calamity which has beset us was sent by God—not the French, nor the Dutch, nor the Papists. I have myself had inquiries set afoot and I have found *no trace of proof* of such plots.' He paused for the words to sink in, and then continued, 'We will need all our strength and all our courage to face the future. As your King, I ask you—do not brood on invisible enemies and imaginary plots, rather, join with me to build again. I fought with you to save our city and wept with you as it burned. I shall need your aid if London is to live again. I appeal to you, the people. What is your answer to me, the King?'

There was a silence. Then from the back, surging towards the royal party, came a wave of cheers and calls which rose up and up. Hats were flung in the air, a girl came running forward and slid a rose into the King's topboot. 'God bless your Majesty . . .' The shouts echoed all around him.

'You have your answer, my liege,' said the Duke of York with a smile.

Charles looked down at the sea of faces, but his eyes appeared to look beyond them to something distant as he murmured, 'I see that the King must look to the people to find the solace he needs.'

Six

Lord! What a grievous thing it is for a she-citizen to be forced to have children by her own husband.

—*John Dryden*

'Why *not*, Nelly?' exploded Lord Buckhurst in exasperation. 'In the name of flesh, give me one good reason why not?' He looked, frowning, across the chamber above the Cock and Pye.

Nell continued to sponge at the Colbertine lace edging on a petticoat quite composedly and did not even turn her head to answer. 'I am an actress, Charles, as I told you before. My life is on the boards, earning my own bread, not stuck in some cosy nest at Lincoln's Inn Fields living under your protection —though I thank you kindly for the offer. Take yourself to m' sister Rose and I doubt not that you'll be accepted. I won't do it.'

'Anyone would think I was asking you to leave the cloister,' he argued, 'rather than the stage. What can make you wish to stay? I've told you—I'll give you £100 a year and a house rent-free if you'll but send in your parts. Lord knows it's more than you get now. What sort of a reputation do you think actresses have that you've got such a calling for 't? I'll tell you what image you Cyprians have got: "Into the pit already you are come, 'tis but a step more to our tiring room." That's how the world sees you, make no mistake! And what future have you but to grow fat and forty like Kate Corey, the butt of every crude comedy line Dryden can shake out, and an object of mirth for the giggling gallants in Fop's Corner!'

'Pox take you, Charles,' Nell replied with knit brows, as if he had not spoken. 'You're in my light and this must be ready to wear for tomorrow's performance. I don't know why you've brought this up. We've only been open for four months and already you want me to retire. We might all be a collection of Doll Commons, as you make out, but I'll not serve Tom Killigrew such a Dutch turn as that. Tomorrow we've got our new production's first showing and—'

'God's bones, Nelly, you don't have to leave this instant. But soon, sweetheart, soon, if you love me. Look at the life you have now; at the life any of you actresses have, for that matter. I've seen 'em come and I've seen 'em go. There was Elizabeth Farley, king's whore, duke's whore, and then anyone's whore. She was last heard of in a bawdy house in Whetstone's Park and all her beauty gone. And then there was poor Nan Child —*got* with child and died of it but two months since. Lord, Nelly! 'Twas only a month past Beck Marshall was ruffled down an alley by those mousers set on by Sir Hugh Middleton when she wouldn't lay with him—cankered toad that he is!'

'Beck Marshall's a fire ship and a night walker, as all the Company knows, and she deserves all she gets,' retorted Nell tartly. 'I'm not tired yet of the odour of candle grease, Charles, and that's all there is to it. I know that what you say is true— Master Lacy always says an actor is but half a gentleman, for he has all the appearance and none o' the substance—but what would you? If I give up the stage, what would happen to me?'

He took her hands and drew her up close to him. 'You'd come to me, Nelly, and I'd treat you like a queen.' His mouth came down to her neck, but she drew back. Her eyes fixed on his and her voice was soft and even. 'For how long, Charles— three months? Six? You'd tire of me, my heart, and I should tire of you belike and I'd be left on the streets with a bastard for company.'

Buckhurst flushed. 'Never in this world, Nelly. I'd keep you safe and—'

'Moonshine, Charles! If you think I'll believe that sort of pie in the sky, you've a poor notion of me indeed! I'll give *you* an example to beware of. I've no mind to turn out like Hester Davenport—tumbled by my Lord Oxford, deceived into a sham marriage and now lodging in a garret at Seven Dials, calling herself a countess without a bean to live on. No, no'— she placed two fingers over the protesting lips of her lover—'I know you'd never treat me like that snake Oxford, but haply you'd wish you'd never made the offer you've just made. And that I couldn't bear. Odsbud, m'lord, let's go on as we are.'

Buckhurst bent to kiss her and then sprang back with an oath. 'S'blood, Nelly, what have you got on that sponge? It stinks like Bedlam!'

'Salt and dog's urine,' she said mildly. ' 'Tis the only thing to remove stains.'

'Faugh!' Buckhurst shuddered. 'I hope they don't smell you from the pit or you'll get pelted.'

She smiled and did not seem unduly worried. Buckhurst watched while she carefully spread the lace flounce in front of the fire, and then asked very casually, 'There's no one else is there, Nell?'

'What?' All at once she was in his arms, laughing, her tumbled tawny tresses against his cheek. 'Foolish, foolish Charles,' she chided, 'I'm not so devious. The devil fly away with your suspicions.'

He felt her breath in his ear. 'There's a clear two hours before we need to meet Sedley. Shall we consummate a new understanding?' She unlaced her stomacher carefully and took his hand, sliding it over her. Her skin was satin-smooth and warm to the touch. He could feel her heart beating fast as his fingers gently eased back her shift. 'Make the most of it, my lord,' she advised him. 'As you said, 'twill not be long before I'm naught but a shrew of copper lace and corsetting.'

That same evening in the Rose tavern in Russell Street, just around the corner from Drury Lane, Tom Killigrew and John

Lacy toasted each other's success with brimming tankards of lambswool clinked over a repast of ling and herring pie and a venison pasty. For the first time in months Killigrew's brow was free of the lines that had fretted it ever since the fire had destroyed the city and the substance of his customers. Lacy saw the old glint back in his eye as he outlined his plans for the future.

' 'Tis necessary to find new playwrights as well as new actors,' Killigrew declared eagerly. 'You know how we have generally relied on trusted favourites—Shakespeare's tragedies, Beaumont and Fletcher. And Master Dryden is a pearl above price, of course, but I look for new directions for the Theatre Royal to expand. I must say, I scarcely thought I should be so optimistic a few months back, for the audiences have been but half the size of what we were used to before the fire. Now I verily believe we've turned the corner at last.'

'It would certainly seem so,' agreed Lacy.

Killigrew gave a belch of pleasure. 'Davenant can't compete at all. I own the Duke's Theatre has had its triumphs in the past with those offerings of Etherege, like *Love in a Tub*. But now I've hired those Italian fiddlers and Mistress Yates, who sings in the Italian manner better than any woman living, thanks to Signor Baptista's coaching, Davenant's company is no better than a bear garden in comparison.'

'Mistress Yates has the garniture of a queen certainly, but I wonder if she perhaps displays too—ah—ample a portion of her person, especially in her low corsage. Did you know Etherege slid into the pit yester e'en when she was singing on the stage and delivered a shaft which sadly deflated her?'

Killigrew's eyebrows rose in interest. 'What did he say?'

Lacy snorted with mirth. 'He sat in the pit gnawing his cane—you know how he does—and then suddenly he bawled at the poor jade in the midst of her singing, "Is that flesh for sale?" pointing his stick at her breasts for all the world as if he were at Billingsgate market. "No, sir," says she, blushing the while and dropping her fan. "Then, madam," retorts Etherege, "if you won't sell, I'll thank ye to shut up shop!" '

They both shouted with laughter and Killigrew dabbed at

his eyes and called for more ale. But he shook his head ruefully. ' 'Tis an acid tongue, but more truth than fiction. Odsblood, what else has the theatre come to? Naught but a crowd of booing 'prentice boys, with here and there a languid gallant curling his flaxen wig and paying more attention to his China orange and the vizard masks than to the play. It's something I would change, John, if I could.'

'Why change what is successful?' asked Lacy, perplexed. 'Have you not just said 'tis the wink of a Cyprian or two on stage that draws the crowds? Where'd the Theatre Royal be, in God's name, without Bab and Nelly and Beck Marshall?'

'Nay, nay, I'd not do without 'em, I'd do *more* for them! God's bones, John, I'm tired of being worried whether my best actress isn't going to get clinkered down some back alley each night. Twice now Beck's been tousled and forced to petition Whitehall for protection, and I notice that new little jill flirt Betty Hall's getting the attention of that lecher Philip Howard. He's casting his eye upon her to make her his mistress if I'm not mistook, and he's as profligate a rogue as my son Harry, saving his name! 'Tis the way the city looks at the theatre and the actors I've a mind to change. Body o' me! We're surely due more respect than the cock pit next door in the Lane, pox take it!'

Lacy sighed. 'It's ever been thus. An actor is a King's Servant in name but he has less to live on than many a menial in a noble house. That's why we all live around the Lane, though it's as shady an area as Alsatia if you like.'

'A plaguey, dissolute neighbourhood you mean, and that's exactly what I was saying. 'Tis a fine place for the King's Theatre, I swear; naught but ale houses and bawdy houses, and such people to rub shoulders with as Moll Cutpurse—and how *that* woman's escaped Tyburn so long, I'll never know, incidentally, for she's committed enough crimes to hang her five times over! And then there was that den of hell cats with their terrorising and their blackmail till the constable took 'em off at Michaelmas.'

Lacy nodded and quoted:

'Did you ever hear the like?
Did you ever hear the fame?
Of the five women barbers
Who lived in Drury Lane?'

'A good song of yours, Tom. A pity I'm living round the corner in Cradle Alley. I miss a lot, I fancy.'

'Aye, aye,' said Killigrew irritably, 'but it's no matter for jesting, nonetheless. I've a mind to a new theatre, Lacy.'

'Man, you've only had the one you've got scarce four years, and lucky to have it still after the fire, I might add.'

But Killigrew did not hear him. An intent, dreamy look came into his eyes. 'If you'd seen the plans Doctor Wren has for the new city, as I have, Lacy, you'd understand. I've stood at his Majesty's shoulder in the Privy Chamber and watched while Wren unfurled his scrolls and . . . Lacy, you should see. He's going to build a fine new piazza at St. James's and it will be surrounded by lofty mansions for the Court. What a place for a theatre, John. Only think of it!'

'And only think of the money it would cost,' advised Lacy prosaically. 'As it is, we've beat the spots off the Duke's Company, for all the allure of Moll Davis and her dancing. The Theatre Royal has never been more popular. We've Charles Hart, Kynaston and Mohun; we've Nelly Gwynne and we've Anne Quin—why, I'm even coaching Beck Marshall to step in as tragic understudy. Man, there's no stone been left unturned.'

Killigrew appeared to chew over Lacy's words. 'Aye,' he admitted, 'there's something in what you say. Who've they got at the Duke's to match my Nell—that horse-faced Jane Long or that drunken slut Madge Norris? Neither can touch Nelly or Bab Knipp either, for that matter. I venture to think *her* dancing is better even than that of Moll Davis, and both she and Nelly were made for breeches parts.'

'Mrs. Gwynne will have all the city at her feet after tomorrow, Tom,' commented Lacy firmly, taking a bumbard jug of lambswool from a fat serving wench. 'She had 'em at her feet in *The Humorous Lieutenant*, but this time she's better than she's ever been. The child's made for comedy and Dryden has written the play especially with her in mind.'

'*Secret Love*,' pondered Killigrew thoughtfully. 'I wonder if there's a message to that title, Lacy. Do you know the King called Dryden especially to Court a month past and made a point of suggesting that as a title for this new play? On my oath, I heard him.'

Lacy stopped midway through pouring out a tankard. 'My Lord Buckhurst might not be best pleased,' he said.

'He's not worthy of her,' declared Killigrew roundly. 'If Moll Davis is good enough to be the King's whore, then so is Nelly. At least Nelly don't put on airs. The numbers of actresses now who give out they're daughters of decayed knights who lost their all in the wars must be legion.'

'Aye—Mrs. Davis will have it now she's a royal filly that she's the daughter of the Earl of Berkshire, though all know a blacksmith sired her.'

Killigrew looked pensive. 'There's a mystery here if I'm not mistook,' he said. 'Ever since the Theatre Royal opened again four months back, his Majesty has been a more attentive patron of the play than ever before. He comes to the theatre at least once a week and often more. I wonder . . .'

'Gossip does not speak of Mistress Davis falling from favour,' pointed out Lacy. 'And Nell gives no hint of wanting a royal lover, bless her.'

'But the King still comes to the play,' retorted Killigrew. 'And who else should he come to see?' He leant back in his chair, and taking out his snuff, inhaled noisily.

'I have a feeling,' he said, idly flicking at the lid of his snuffbox, 'that when his Majesty looks down from the royal box tomorrow into that warm hollow of Mistress Gwynne's bodice, he may well forget he is the King and feel—yet again —the frailties of a man.'

'What a pity,' commented Lacy with deceptive sweetness. 'Just when you were wanting to raise the tone of the theatre, Tom.'

. . .

The Earl of Rochester hiccoughed suddenly as he passed the sundial in the Privy Garden at Whitehall late that night. As he leant rather heavily on Sir Charles Sedley, that nobleman was hard put to it to retain his own balance but appeared to bear his burden no malice. 'God bless you, Wilmot,' he murmured amiably. 'Etherege, is it not monstrous agreeable to look upon Rochester's fair features once again, now that we no longer have Buckingham to charm away our megrims and Harry Savile's laid up with the great pox?'

'Enrapturing,' agreed George Etherege. ' 'Tis something indeed to know that one's company is enough to charm a man from his nuptial bed. Two months without a sight of you at Whitehall, Wilmot—almost one had begun to think you had turned respectable. The lady's charm must be considerable, but then, so must yours. How many men, after all, can abduct a wench as you did and then a year later woo her to such effect that she disdains all comers, including poor Hinchingbroke, and gives her vast fortune and herself to you?'

'Miss Malet is a merchant's daughter with discernment.' Rochester shrugged. 'She gains a title, which she craves, and also my person with it—a rare acquisition, you will acknowledge—and in return she brings me a not inconsiderable dowry. The exchange is fair. I have performed my conjugal duties in all obedience at Adderbury, but there comes a time when duty . . . palls.' He changed the subject swiftly. 'What a' God's name is this damned coil about Buckingham's absconding to escape the royal wrath? Last thing I heard was he'd had some back-biting with Dorchester. Is that the cause of all this pother?'

Etherege seemed amused. 'The first of a veritable catalogue of crimes, Wilmot. What a viper's brood the Villiers are, to be sure! Dorchester was stupid enough to question Bucks in the Lords one morning when he'd had no sleep the night before, and his Grace took off the old newt's hat, plucked his periwig from his head, stamped on it, and then rammed the hat over his pate.'

Rochester tittered. 'Dear me! How very choleric of him. But surely *that* hasn't driven him into hiding?'

'No, no, they both went to the Tower for a bit to cool their heels, but Bucks was no sooner out than he was intriguing again—this time against Clarendon, of course. And the King discovered the plot, included forgery and a deal of much else. Lord! There was such a howl set up, with the chancellor and York, his son-in-law, crying out for Buck's blood and the King was near as angry himself.'

'Never could resist intrigue.' Sedley shook his head. 'The stuff of life to him—as well ask him to give up brandy or tumbling tavern wenches . . .'

'Rowley sent him back to the Tower,' explained Etherege, 'or rather, he ordered his arrest. But *someone*—it couldn't have been his cousin Barbara, of course!—warned him in time and he beat off quick, Lord knows where.'

'Until the royal anger cools. I see.' Rochester grinned. 'It will. Charles can't live without Buckingham for long any more than Bucks can live without meddling in plots and scandal.'

They passed under the Lord Chamberlain's gateway and trod, somewhat unsteadily, across the cobbled square to where the lights blazing from the tall windows of the Banqueting Hall and the sounds of music told them the ball given in honour of the Venetian ambassador was yet continuing. A bowing lackey took the gentlemen's swords and Etherege's cloak and watched while Sedley aided Rochester up the broad curving marble stairway.

'B' our Lady . . .' the lackey murmured, watching Rochester. 'Everyone else goes orf for a recover in the country. Don't look as if it's done *'im* much good!'

The sight revealed when the double doors were flung open and their names announced was spectacular. All down the center of the painted ceiling above their heads crystal chandeliers flared so that it was as light as day. The walls were draped in damask worked with rich embroidery. Against a background of crimson and gold and gilded scrollwork two long rows of gentlemen and ladies moved in fast measure. The room was a whirl of satin colour and the sparkle of precious stones. On a raised dais beneath a crimson canopy at the end of the long hall glimpses could be caught of the two thrones, on one of which the Queen sat alone, striking in black and white lace with diamonds in a blaze at throat and wrist.

'Nothing's changed, I see,' said Rochester. 'I thought when I left with the smell of burned timber in my nose that the King had declared a retrenchment. We were all to live on small ale and crusts, as I remember.'

'We did, veritably, for a time,' Sedley told him. 'Didn't you know? All the Court was forbidden to wear its old finery and we were given a penitential Court uniform. Quite liked it, m' self—long white underskirts of satin and black Persian vests—but it didn't catch. Charles said that when we all lined up we looked like a brood of magpies, and Fox declared that if he was expected to look as if he was at his own funeral, he may as well put a pistol to his head and complete the effect. So our era of self-denial ended. Good thing really. We heard later that Louis had put his lackeys into the outfit as a retort!'

Rochester smiled. As the two rows of dancers parted, couples tripped down the centre, led by the King himself clasping my Lady Castlemaine in his arms. 'The lady still endures. I see . . .'

'The Villiers tenacity,' commented Sedley. 'One wonders if she'll ever totally lose her hold over him.'

'She's sworn she'll die a duchess,' sighed Etherege. 'And I'll lay odds she does.'

'I see Buck's whore is present, even if *he* is absent . . .' Rochester nodded to a comely girl, with braided golden coils above shining dark eyes, dancing in the embrace of Harry Killigrew. 'I wonder—is old Shrewsbury really as unaware as he pretends that he's been cuckolded by Buckingham this year and more? They say his innocent-looking young Countess is insatiate for Buck's embraces and makes little secret of it.'

'Shrewsbury believes what he wants to believe.' Sedley shrugged. 'Anna Maria is no barque of frailty, for all her loveliness, and scandal follows her like dogs follow a butcher. All the Court knows 'twas she who was the cause of that duel betwixt young Jermyn and Howard, and now she's flirting with Killigrew till he's no more head than a moon-mad sheep. I foresee trouble when Buckingham returns to Whitehall.'

Rochester's eyebrows raised. 'Such scrambling for favours! Haply'—his eyes followed her whirling figure—'I'll join the queue.'

'You'll wish you hadn't,' sighed Sedley. 'She's the sort takes pleasure in rousing a man to a frenzy, and then leaves him disconsolate. It's all a game to her.'

Rochester's clear blue eyes held a hint of mischief. 'Perhaps in this case 'twill be *she* who is left disconsolate.' He went forward up the length of the Banqueting Hall, followed by his cronies to the dais where now sat Charles and Catherine together. Rochester swept out his coat and made an impeccable leg to the throne. There was no hint of any unsteadiness in his poise or his balance.

Charles greeted him indulgently. 'Ah, my lord Earl! We rejoice to see you amongst us again. I trust you have brought your new countess with you.'

'Alas no, Sire.' Rochester made a gesture of regret. 'She cannot travel at the moment. She is—ah—in an indelicate state of health.' His lazy gaze held a message part mockery, part pride.

Charles grinned. 'Quick work, Rochester—even for you. But we look forward to seeing her ere long.'

Catherine leant towards him. 'May I offer my congratulations, milor' Rochester,' she said in her soft voice. There was no hint of malice in Catherine's manner, either for the nature of such news of a fecundity denied to her or towards Rochester himself. Rather, as she looked at him Rochester could see how her lashes veiled the quiet laughter in her eyes, and he smiled back at her. 'Thank you, your Majesty,' he murmured.

Sedley and Etherege made their bows, and shortly afterwards the King led the Queen down from the dais into the dance. The three gentlemen sat down at the side of the ballroom, watching the dancers idly.

'Where's la belle Stuart?' asked Rochester. 'I don't see her here tonight. Is she ill?'

'She cannot attend tonight; she says she has the headache.' Sedley sneered. 'But haply 'tis an assignation elsewhere keeps her absent.'

'Ah, 'tis a story indeed, as we have to tell you, Wilmot.' Etherege chuckled. 'A tale of love spurned and secret doings. You remember, after the fire was put out Charles went into a frenzy of wooing to gain the Stuart. Such a stream of jewels—I warrant Castlemaine's teeth could be heard grinding in fury the length of the galleries. But as ever she rejected the royal advances, whether from virgin modesty, calculating cunning or plain stupidity is a matter for individual judgement. Such singularity of restraint at Whitehall was, however, bound to bring its reward. I happen to know that at one point, in desperation, Charles offered to make her a duchess if she would become maitresse en titre—*that* would have cast Castlemaine into a spasm!—but the silly minx refused him.'

'Poor Barbara.' Sedley sighed. 'She only befriended Frances Stuart to get her claws in the Queen, and then when it looked as though Charles were indeed thinking in terms of marrying her, she realised what she'd done. If the King *did* divorce the Queen and marry Frances, who then littered like a brood mare, it would mean the final end of my Lady Castlemaine at Whitehall!'

'Such a turnaround you never saw.' Etherege giggled. 'She stopped speaking to poor Frances, who couldn't understand *what* was going on, and then, dim-witted as ever, the Stuart played right into Castlemaine's hands by falling in love at long last.'

'Falling in love?' asked Rochester, startled. 'Who with, in God's name?'

'His Grace of Richmond no less.'

'That drunken oaf? He loves his bottle more than he'll ever love any woman!'

Etherege looked politely incredulous. 'La belle Stuart ever was a ninny, as we are all agreed, but I am bound to own that in this case her affections have appeared to lead Richmond back to a path of sobriety as yet maintained. Unfortunately, Frances took to having cosy suppers in her chamber with him and Barbara's spies got wind of it. She, of course, told the King one evening that far from being modest, Frances was a slut and a liar and was being tumbled by Richmond every night of the week. Charles stormed along to her apartments and found them together—with Frances a little déshabillé—playing cat's cradle!'

Sedley shook with silent laughter and then, dabbing his eyes, continued the story. 'When Charles burst in, Richmond was so appalled he lost his head and jumped out of the window and then Frances had the vapours and . . . oh, 'twas famous, I give you my word!'

'What happened?' Rochester asked, intrigued.

'Oh well . . .' Sedley shook his head. 'She protested her innocence of course, but Charles left her in a temper and Richmond was banished the Court—that was a week past. Frances asked the Queen in floods if she could enter a convent, and Charles has been as mournful as a Puritan ever since! But he's still as keen on her as ever, or at least he *seems* it.'

'Seems it?'

'Pox take him, I don't know. 'Tis just that there's so little to interest a man in the Stuart—couldn't ever understand why she was so courted at the best of times. It's almost been as though he's pursued her for want of anyone better in a way.'

'Who knows the mind of the King?' commented Etherege lightly. 'As well take to alchemy.'

Across the ballroom, gesticulating violently, arm in arm with Charles himself, came a short dumpy man with a huge periwig and a coat encrusted with gold lacing. With a look of relief the King beheld the three gallants and steered his voluble guest of honour towards them. Charles introduced them suavely, commenting with his low rumbling laugh, 'His Excellency tells me he is somewhat perplexed at our English manners.'

The ambassador's eyes rose to the heavens in an attitude of dismay. 'Ebben! Your country it—it is beautiful, but wherever I go I am pointed at like—like a man who is mad, and as soon as I open my mouth they scream at me that I am a Papist! Every scagnozzo in the street follows behind me shouting abuse. It is a country like I have never heard of—scherza coi fanti e lascia stare i santi. The very watermen on your river accuse me of coming to plot against them and ask if the King plans of an alliance with the Pope!'

'Our humour is as earthy as a Besseleigh turnip and Derby

ale, sir,' Rochester told him. 'I might say—gia sono impenitenti tutti quanti! But you will grow used to us, the longer you stay.'

'Odsfish!' boomed Charles. 'You should hear what I have to suffer, Mister Ambassador. My Parliament lectures me as though I were a schoolboy and keeps me short of money like one, and people like that damned rogue Coventry don't scruple to upbraid me for extravagance when the fancy takes 'em. My lackeys haven't been paid since Cromwell died and my sailors are in a state of starving mutiny. I'm kept poor as a parson, I give you my word. I had a monkey from Sedley here two days since and another from poor Churchill one coranto ago. I can't feed m' household, let alone run the state.'

The ambassador shook his periwigged head in wonderment. The King turned to Rochester in resignation. 'God knows how they think the government should be maintained. The Dutch fleet is allowed more than thrice what we are given for our entire naval establishment. No account is taken of the debts which swallow most of what is granted. But if I ask for more, they fall on me like a pack of wolves and accuse me of spending it on Barbara and debauchery.'

'Yet,' said Rochester whimsically, 'I am persuaded, Sire, the nation's sufferings cannot be, as once supposed, a punishment of God for our sins. It could not be, unless the Divine hand faltered, a punishment of heavenly origin that London was consumed by the fire.'

'How so certain, my lord?'

Rochester's eyes opened wide in surprise. 'But, your Majesty, was not Whitehall left standing?'

The King gave a shout of laughter and punched Rochester affectionately on the shoulder. 'Ye rogue. It's good to have you back, Wilmot.'

Nobody noticed the page in crimson and gold livery who darted through the press of people until he came up to the King, plucking nervously at the royal sleeve. 'S—Sire . . .'

Charles turned and looked down at the agitated boy. 'What is it? Mistress Stuart? Is she ill?'

The page shook his head. 'N-no, your Majesty. I went with

your message, Sire, just as you said, b-but Mistress Stuart is not . . .'

'Well, lad, well?'

The page's face crimsoned. 'She—she's not there, Sire. Her chamber is empty. Her maid had not seen her either. But she had a letter, Sire, addressed to you.'

There was a silence as Charles ripped open the paper and read its contents. The Venetian ambassador saw the blood drain from the King's face and his features set in harsh, almost murderous, lines. 'I'll have his life for this.' He breathed heavily, gazing down at the letter, which he suddenly crushed between his fingers in a single convulsive movement.

'Eloped—eloped, by God!'

Seven

And, Gallants, though you are but seldom good,
Yet to us women most of all you shou'd.
No sooner comes a beauty here in play,
But strait your coach and six takes her away...

—George Porter

The applause was deafening. The 'prentice boys stood on the matted benches in the pit and cheered and clapped until both throats and palms were sore. Flowers floated down onto the stage from the galleries above. High up in one of the boxes Tom Killigrew looked down at the small elfin figure in frilled shirt and breeches who stood alone on the apron in front of the proscenium arch, and his eyes were moist—an unusual thing for him. 'If only Rob could ha' lived to see this,' he murmured. 'He'd have cried like a woman.'

To Nell it seemed as though the very rafters reverberated with an acclaim even the Theatre Royal had surely never heard before. She was both frightened and exhilarated by it; half of her wished to run away and hide from the clamour, at the same time as she stood lapped by the warmth and admiration and almost swooning with the shouts dinning in her ears.

Could this all be for her—Nelly Gwynne from the Coalyard? Was it really she that they called for again and again while she moved forward to make her bow? She did not thank them, it was too much to thank them, but the smile on her lips and the tears in her eyes were enough for them and they redoubled their cheers.

She stepped back and looked into the wings, calling out Charles Hart to come and share this moment of triumph. And as she did so her eyes travelled up for a second to the royal box to the right of the stage. He was looking at her; she knew he would be. He gazed down with a smouldering look in his black eyes. And what did those moody eyes send as their message? Was it anger, was it love? Every time she came on the stage she was conscious of it, and him, though she appeared not to notice. Week after week—how long had it been?—he came and sat, watching her with that curious intent gaze. And uttered never a word. No message, no plea for assignation— yet his silence was as loud as if he had leant out of the box and called her name. Once she had thought he mouthed it, there in the box one cold December day, when she had played Lady Wealthy and floated forward with the laughter still about her to make her curtsey to the King. What did he want of her? But as she bowed low before him in her ruffles and her breeches, she knew and backed away, eyes downcast.

There behind him with Sedley and the rest of the Court sat Buckhurst, clapping and pleased at her success. Did she love him? Did she love the King? She didn't know, and fled off into the wings, her cheeks burning as much with uncertainty as with pleasure at the noise of voices still calling her name.

From above Charles watched her retreat, her hair curling loose down her back to the waistband of her breeches. Even Sedley had a smile on his cynical lips and James still mopped his face and snorted with laughter in that bluff way he had. Yet the King hardly noticed them, nor the pit packed with people. It was a matter between her and himself, no one else. He had almost refused to come this afternoon, with the smell of Frances's betrayal still rank in his nostrils, and now he was here, he was but tortured again with rejection. And yet ... This time it was somehow different, less futile, less ridiculous.

This was no simpering girl, coy and superficial, who played with him and took fright when the game grew too serious; this was a woman, with a woman's love and tears and wit and tenderness. He realised with some surprise that while he had watched Nell, he had not even thought of Frances—so little significance had she seemed to have. She had gone; that door was closed. But—God's death!—what was the purpose of sitting here day after day like a lovelorn farmer's boy, mute as a stone, watching for a sign, if sign there ever was to be?

He felt a spasm of anger knot inside him. How dared she toy thus with him—was he not the King? Was she not a Royal Servant? Could he not command her to come to him—aye, and reject her after if it pleased him? Charles sucked heavily on his lower lip and looked all unseeing at the empty stage.

Nell's part in *Secret Love* brought her to a pinnacle of success. Day after day the theatre was packed with crowds who cheered at her entrance and followed her every move with shrieks of mirth as she impudently cast Dryden's shafts of wit back at them liberally spiced with ad libs culled from the language of the Coalyard. Sam Pepys went half a dozen times and laughed as much each time, commenting in his diary that he had never seen a comical part done better in all the world.

But the King did not appear at the Theatre Royal again for several weeks. Afternoons found him instead at the Duke's Theatre, leaning approvingly from his box to watch the sprightly dancing of little Mrs. Davis. Moll Davis was quick to take advantage. Amiable and absent-minded as ever, Charles had neglected to provide the lodgings for her as he had promised so many months before. One day Moll greeted him on stage with a dulcimer and a song to touch the King's memory, as well as his sense of humour, singing sweetly,

> 'My lodging it is on the cold ground,
> And very hard is my fare,
> But that which troubles me most is,
> The unkindness of my dear.'

Charles took the hint. Moll removed to elegant lodgings in Suffolk Street, where she took pleasure in inviting compatriates of the Duke's Company for a dish of tay to listen to her coy allusions to the King's ardour and to display the luxury of her new surroundings.

It was a time for popularity for the Theatre Royal such as Tom Killigrew had never expected to see. Charles Hart and Nell between them drew the crowds and became accepted as the gay couple of the boards acting always together, where the sauce and wit of Mrs. Nelly brought flowers dropping onto the stage and guineas into Killigrew's pocket. So wealthy did he feel that both Nell and Anne Quin found themselves installed in brand-new dressing rooms with a privacy hitherto unknown, while Beck Marshall and lesser lights seethed with an ill-concealed envy and dislike of Nell's privileges.

But in the midst of success Nell felt a sense of disquiet, an unease that traced itself in some strange, unfathomable way to the moment she stepped onto the stage at the outset of each performance and let her eyes travel casually up to the royal box. Always of late it had been empty. She could not ask Buckhurst about the King, much as she would have liked to, and his conversation revolved less around the royal amours and more on the twin themes of Clarendon's lack of success in securing a peace with the Dutch and Buckingham's continued disappearance. What Buckhurst did tell her, however, was that Charles still languished after Frances Stuart—now the Duchess of Richmond ever since she had been married to the Duke after her night's escape from Whitehall. The King had failed to prevent the match, and now, said Buckhurst, he hankered after her.

'I thought his anger was terrible to behold and shocked all who saw it. And he swore her name was never again to be mentioned,' queried Nell mildly.

'Aye, well, it cooled as time passed,' replied Buckhurst. 'And now 'tis clear she has taken something from him, for he's as empty as a drum; the old life has gone out of him somehow . . .'

'Moll Davis tells a different tale,' commented Nell wryly.

'Bed sport merely.' Buckhurst shrugged. 'The wench is an amusement, nothing more.'

Nell glanced at him swiftly but said nothing.

'The King is almost become a respectable married man,' he continued. 'His attention to the Queen has never been more particular since they married, and since she miscarried again he has been as tender a nurse as could be wished. Why, when she fell sick in bed the other night he got up in his shirt for a basin, and when she laid up all in the sheets, he sponged her down himself before calling her ladies and then came three times from his own chamber to see how she did.' But Buckhurst shook his head. 'Duty flourishes at the expense of the old quip on his tongue. He's plaguey morose these days.'

Nell was to see for herself the next day, for when she came out onto the boards and looked up at the royal box, Charles was there, this time with Catherine on one side and his son James, Duke of Monmouth, on the other. Killigrew had warned her he was present, of course, and she felt her heart thudding as though it were her first showing when she stepped out above the pit. She found the King staring down with eyes of lead—expressionless, the mouth under the thin black moustache a hard tight line.

All through the performance it was as though his eyes bored into her very being, sapping her natural spontaneity, and the time she spent on the stage under his scrutiny seemed interminable. Certainly on this occasion she felt she gave less than her best, though the audience seemed not to notice any falling-away in her performance. In all the theatre, however, it became noticeable that the King never smiled once, but sat immobile, drumming his fingers the while on the sill of the box. When at last she made her final entrance, Nell was too nervous to do more than bow swiftly to the pit and barely sketch a bob to the royal party before backing hurriedly off the stage.

John Lacy awaited her in the wings. 'And what's wrong with *you*, Nelly Gwynne?' he demanded irritably. 'I've never seen you act worse, gel. This isn't a canvas tragedy at the fair, you know! Are you not well?'

She gratefully seized on the excuse he had given her. 'A touch of colique, Master Lacy. I've been fair doubled with gripes this past two hours and more.'

The severe expression in Lacy's eyes softened a trifle, but before he could reply they were both hailed by Thomas Killigrew, who ran up to them panting. His face looked pale, almost stricken, and he shook his head as though he could not believe what he had to say.

'What is it, in God's name?' demanded Lacy, seeing his expression.

' 'Tis the King,' said Killigrew, bewildered. 'I was up in the box at the end of the play and went to offer my hopes that he had enjoyed the play, and he cut me dead like a whiplash.'

'Whatever for?'

' 'Tis the play,' answered Killigrew unhappily. 'He—he says that the play mocks the institution of marriage, which is a sacred one.'

'*What!*' Lacy's voice was incredulous.

'Aye, and he looked me straight in the eye when he said it.' Killigrew moaned. 'He said it was offensive to the Queen and asked if I didn't agree parts of the dialogue smacked of profanity—*profanity*, I swear to you! Did you ever hear the like from Old Rowley? He with Sedley one side and Harry Savile the other!'

'I don't believe it.'

'I promise you, Lacy. And then he strode down the steps, followed by the lot of 'em, calling over his shoulder that he'd have more to say anon. No compliments, no jests, as you'd expect normally. He was into his coach before I could say another word.' Killigrew sighed. 'I shouldn't wonder if we'll be closed down before he's done,' he finished gloomily.

'Nonsense,' said Nell bracingly. 'I warrant he had but a touch of the colique or something and felt out of sorts.'

'Like you belike, Nelly,' suggested Lacy softly. 'It must be the humours in the air, I doubt not! A new plague of infection seems to be preparing.'

She felt her cheeks crimson under his penetrating scrutiny, and making an excuse, hurried back to her dressing room, where she shut the door and sat trembling, her mind in a whirl. What was this? she asked herself agitatedly. Was he trying to force her into his bed? Was this to be his way of enticing her—to persecute the theatre until she gave in for all their sakes? Nell shook herself mentally and told herself she was becoming hysterical: he had but to look at her and she believed he was half out of his mind with love for her. More likely it was sheer boredom or pique at Frances Stuart's elopement, if the gossip ran true, Nell told herself firmly. But her fingers still nervously plaited the ruffles on her shirt as the image of a tall black-visaged gentleman rose before her.

Royal disfavour came posthaste to Tom Killigrew the following day in the form of a missive from the Lord Chamberlain, accompanied by the constable with commands of another sort that made Killigrew clutch at the desk in his office in surprise and amazement. 'Arrest . . . ?' he muttered weakly. 'B—but who . . . why . . . ?'

The constable cleared his throat in a pompous fashion. 'His Majesty has expressed himself to be displeased at the nature of the entertainment at present offered by the King's Players at the Theatre Royal, and in particular by certain members of the company who have used the stage to make mock of the Court and sundry figures in public life.'

Nell was learning her lines for her new part in a fresh comedy *All Mistaken* when Bab Knipp burst into her dressing room, big with news. 'Nelly,' she cried 'they're closing down the Theatre Royal!'

Nell slewed around in her seat. 'What?'

'Aye,' agreed Bab. 'And that's not all. The warrant's out for the arrest of Kate Corey and John Lacy too.'

'That's impossible! What can they have done? John is the King's favourite player—his Majesty's said so times beyond numbering.'

Bab shook her pretty head. ' 'Tis true, sweetheart, for all that. The constable said his Majesty was offended at the mimickry Kate displayed on the boards yesterday. You know how she loves to take the jump out of that fat old cow Lady Harvey. Apparently she's complained to the King, and this is his answer.'

'He's never bothered before,' retorted Nell hotly. 'Since when has the King attended to the vapourings of a blow bladder like Lady Harvey, pox take him? And you still haven't said what Master Lacy has done to put all Whitehall into pisspots!'

'Gagging, so Master Killigrew said.' Bab shrugged. 'They say the King was angry at Lacy's abuse of the Court in *Change of Crowns* last week, but little enough was said then. I don't know any more except that his case is the same as Kate's and they've been committed to the porter's lodge at Whitehall for a period of his Majesty's pleasure. Haply Ned Howard has complained to the King about Lacy's assault on him. Their last quarrel—'

'Was over a month past,' retorted Nell. 'And what man would complain to the King that he'd had ale thrown over him?'

Bab looked at her, eyes bright with anger. 'But what other reason could the King possibly have for closing us down, sweetheart?' she asked innocently.

Nell shot a suspicious look at her but said nothing.

'How long will we be shut this time, I wonder?' Bab continued wearily. 'Will it be a week or a month afore the King's heart has a great thaw? I shall be reduced to sips of boskey wine and borrowing groats like Joe Haines before we're done, I dare swear. 'Tis all taffeta living for you, Nelly—you've my Lord Buckhurst to fall back on. What about us poor doxies— we've only the boards or the piazza strut. Odsbud ...'

'I know, Bab, I know.' Nell looked at her reflection in the looking glass hanging over the table. 'God damn you, Charles.'

Why she should thus suddenly abuse my Lord Buckhurst, Mistress Knipp had no notion.

Indeed, Buckhurst took the fact of the theatre's closure to renew his pressure on Nell to give up the boards and live under his protection. She promised to think about it and smiled upon him, but in reality she felt she might be *forced* eventually to accept his offer. If she remained at the theatre, all the company would suffer and she could not easily earn her own living at any other trade. Nell smiled to think of herself bent demurely over needlework as a sempstress at a Paternoster Row ladies' tailors, but something still prevented her from accepting Buckhurst's suggestion. She loved the theatre; she felt it in the deepest fibres of her being. It was her life—no one, she decided, who had ever stood on the apron stage with the sounds of their cheers in her ears could ever give it up. The strain began to tell; she began to look peaked and thin.

Nell's sister Rose had no time for such mawkish freaks. 'Lord, Nelly!' she exclaimed pettishly one afternoon when she dropped in to see her at the Cock and Pye. 'You need the leach to bang your head against the wall! Moping around here like a slattern jade when he's offered you his love *and* a pension.' Rose's tone implied quite clearly that the latter was of prime importance. 'He's smitten, Nelly,' she insisted. 'I've seen the signs, and *I* ought to know by now.'

Nell began to wish she had not been so indiscreet as to tell Rose of Buckhurst's proposition. She shrugged wearily. 'I know 'tis a handsome offer and I'm fond of Buck, God bless him, but—'

'But *what?*' Rose was amazed and scornful. 'Anyone'd think you were an earl's heiress the way you talk. Look at me . . .' Rose brushed the enormous feather on her modish hat. She was dressed, as usual, in clothes of an obvious ostentation, with her hair curled and perfumed; all results, as Nell knew, of her recent association with a city alderman of advanced years but an eager eye. 'I have to live with old potbelly to pay for this lot'—she dismissed him witheringly—'and 'ere's you bleating about the likes of my Lord Buckhurst.' She winked. 'I'd pay *you* for a night with *'im* and I don't mind who knows it. Nelly, you sapskull, you'd be a fool to refuse 'im!'

On reflection Nell felt that there was more than a seed of truth in what Rose said. It seemed that before her eyes there lingered two separate images, both gentlemen of a dark, compelling aura, who demanded something from her she did not want to give. If she did not succumb to the command in the royal eye of one, she must hand in her parts and obey the insistent persuasions of the other. She was on the point of giving in to Buckhurst when the King suddenly and inexplicably relented and Killigrew was told the Theatre Royal might reopen after a closure of only four weeks. John Lacy, as irrepressible as ever, was to take the lead with Nell in a new comedy, *All Mistaken.*

They had to rehearse the play even as they continued to perform in *Secret Love.* Nell was too busy to think about anything but learning her lines and practising her dancing steps, before staggering home to the Cock and Pye in the lengthening cool of a spring evening. But her anger against the King had not lessened, and she felt that a little gentle mimickry of his other foray into the world of actresses might show him the gulf that now lay between her and the man who had tried to force her into his bed.

The King's charm of manner was nothing lessened. He told Killigrew benignly that he had a mind to see his new comedy and would attend first showing. If he had yearned for amusement, he was not disappointed. Mrs. Nelly, with a defiant toss of her red-gold head, stared firmly in every direction but that of the royal box and proceeded to evoke waves of mirth from the pit with her comic expressions of horror and her defensive gestures as she was pursued across the stage by two lovers—one thin, played by Charles Hart, and the other, outrageously padded out to fatness, played by John Lacy. She and Lacy sat on the stage together while Nell patted his vast stomach with one hand and turned a face of mock awe to the audience, saying, 'What a *lump* of love have I in my arms!' The audience loved it and the King seemed as heartily amused as his subjects.

But it was at the end of the performance that she aroused a veritable storm of laughter, when she appeared with a dulcimer in one hand and in the shirt and breeches habitually worn by Moll Davis, and perched impudently on the apron, unlacing her shirt below the point of decency and singing in a high, affected cooing voice:

   'My lodging upon the cold ground is,
   And wunnerful 'ard is my fare,

But that which troubles me more is
The *fatness* of my dear.
Yet still I cry, "Oh, melt, Love,
Oh, I prithee, *melt* apa-a-ce;
For thou art the man I long for,
If 'twere not for thy grease!" '

The cheering rose to a crescendo, flowers rained onto the stage; and when she leant forward deliberately, one was tossed neatly into her bodice, where it lodged saucily between her breasts. Suddenly she raised her eyes and looked up at the royal box from under her thick lashes. The look she received brought almost a gasp from her: it was a look she would never forget. Such love was expressed in those sardonic eyes, such an open affection on those harsh features, that at last she knew what he wanted from her. There could be no pretence or disguise any more. It was as though he were willing her to come to him. Abruptly she stood up, bowed briefly to the audience, blowing a couple of kisses at the pit gallants, and then walked off the boards, running blindly back to her dressing room.

But she was not allowed to change out of her costume. Bab Knipp came banging on her door. 'Nelly, you've got to come. The King wishes to congratulate you and Master Hart in the royal box. *Hurry*, sweetheart!' Quickly Nell checked her reflection in the mirror, carefully patted her curls into shape and then hurried out and down the narrow passageway to the stage.

Two minutes later she and Charles Hart trod up the elegant staircase that led to the curtained archway of the royal box. Nell felt her heart thudding uncomfortably as she heard a woman's voice raised in arguement. 'Surely, as Buckingham has thrown himself upon your royal mercy, your Majesty will extend forgiveness for offences which, after all, cannot but be described as slight . . .'

A deep voice replied, 'Your meddling cousin George will not hurt reflecting on the fruits of his meddling in the Tower for a spell, Barbara, and the less you badger me on the subject, the sooner, I assure you, I may be prevailed upon to release him. I don't, incidentally, look upon the casting of horoscopes to find out when I'm going to die as a *slight* offence, I might add. It happens to rank as high treason.'

Hart stood to one side and a lackey pulled back the drapery, announcing them in a flat monotone. There was a sudden silence. Nell went forward two steps and sank into a deep curtsey. A voice above her said genially, 'Rise, Mistress Gwynne.'

She lifted her head, to find Charles lounging at his ease in the centre of a knot of courtiers, including Buckhurst himself at the King's shoulder and Lady Castlemaine sitting haughtily with her arm linked in that of the young Duke of Monmouth. The Queen was at her husband's side, smiling broadly. But Nell scarcely noticed any of them. *He* was there before her, his eyes still with that expression in them which, curiously, made her throat constrict and made her irrationally want to burst into tears. Suddenly she realised he was talking. 'Such a performance, I swear my sides will ache for a week, my dear,' he was saying lightly. 'And Jimmy had a seizure, did you not, m' boy?' James of Monmouth grinned, looking Nell over with appreciation.

'You are ver' clever actress, Mistress Gwynne,' Nell heard the Queen's soft voice say, and she smiled slightly, dipping another curtsey. 'You are gracious, your Majesty.'

Catherine took a pretty pendant of sapphire from about her neck and beckoned Nell to her. 'This is in nature of an ap-p-preciation, child,' she said softly, and Nell saw one of her eyes just flicker with the suggestion of a blink. 'Such acting is indeed a gift from heaven.' Nell murmured her thanks, and the Queen smiled once more.

'It is to be hoped,' Charles continued slyly, 'that no member of the *Duke's* Company was here today to relay reports of mimickry, Mistress Gwynne.'

'An imitation bordering on flattery, Sire,' Nell said demurely, and Charles rumbled good-naturedly, 'You also have a presence that is commanding, Master Hart,' he said. 'I must have you address Parliament for me one day. My Lady Castlemaine says I mumble my speeches like a parrot.'

The courtiers tittered obediently. But then Charles stood up and Nell saw the quick glance he threw at her. 'I have been drawn here with a promise,' he said. 'Though I have been to the Theatre Royal many times since it opened, never have I seen what lies behind the stage, as most of my gentlemen have. Your Master Killigrew promised me a conducted tour, if I wished it. Now, who would take me?' He paused for a moment and then moved forward, placing Nell's hand firmly on his arm. 'Who better,' he said pleasantly, 'than the leading actress of the theatre to show me the theatre?'

Nell saw Castlemaine's eyes narrow suddenly and a gentleman behind the King gave Nell a wink quite openly. Charles took her under the archway. 'Now, m'dear,' he said loudly, 'let me tread in rogue's footsteps and show me this Women's Shift, where, they tell me, boys become men and the most beautiful ladies in London are to be found.' Irresistibly she felt herself being drawn down the steps on the King's arm and the curtains fell to behind them. Soon they were out of earshot of the box full of courtiers.

' 'Tis long time indeed since I have seen you, Mistress Gwynne,' said the King slowly.

'You are the King, Sire, and I am but an actress. Our paths do not cross.'

'I could have done with your company these last months, Nelly. Whitehall has been like a wasp's nest and your wit would have sent many an hour winging away. There's more laughter in your little finger than a week's supper parties.'

'Thank you, Sire.' Her tone was polite.

They were in the passage that led behind the stage up to the dressing rooms. It was deserted. Abruptly Charles's hand closed on her arm and turned her about so that she faced him. 'What is it that you want, Nelly?' he demanded, and there was now suddenly no more lightness in his voice at all.

'What, Sire?' She faltered. 'I don't understand—'

'Devil take you, Nelly Gwynne, don't play off those die-away court airs on me! You know I want you; you've known these three months and more. What do you want of me, what have I got to do? I'm half out of my mind wanting you. Me—the King. I'm not the King with you, Nelly, I'm Charles Stuart and I want you.' She felt his hands grip her shoulders cruelly and his eyes wandered from her face and down to her breasts. 'I want you,' he repeated in a thick voice taut with passion. 'God's death, am I so repulsive? Don't you care for me at all?'

Her eyes filled with tears and she put her hand up before her face in a helpless gesture. 'I—I don't know. What have we in common? My Lord Buckhurst . . . the Queen . . .'

He took her hands and held them fiercely. 'I love you. I love you so much I can't believe it. I come to the theatre and 'tis like being on the rack. I stay away and fret like a woman in labour. You make me feel like a fifteen-year-old again, did you know that?'

'You cannot force me into your bed, Sire. What will you do next? Arrest all of us and keep us in Newgate until I give in to you?' She heard herself fighting against him.

'Force you? What the devil d' you mean?'

Her voice suddenly flared into anger. 'Aye, I've known you wanted me. I know you expected me to come to you, and when I didn't, you put on the pressure, didn't you, Sire? Poor John Lacy had to spend a month in prison with Kate to bring me to my senses. Is this your love?'

'No,' he said angrily. 'Of course it isn't. Is that how you think of me—someone who thinks to buy people and force them to do his will? I *had* to close the theatre. The French ambassador was insulted by Lacy the last time he was here, and this time he arrived, his royal master made it clear that he hoped it wouldn't be repeated. You don't know it, but I'm in the midst of some particular negotiations that mustn't—on *any* account—be jeopardised. I desperately need French gold and I had to sacrifice the theatre just so long as the embassy was here. As soon as it left, I told Killigrew the Theatre Royal could reopen. Don't you believe me? I love you, Nelly. Pox take Buckhurst and the theatre too.'

Still she fought on, longing to be beaten. 'You have loved before,' she heard herself say.

His grip tightened. 'Aye, and I may well again. What of

that? Do you think love is exclusive? I tell you I love you. Whatever happens, I love you now, and whoever *else* I love, I promise I will always love you, always protect you, always honour you until the day I die.' His voice was very low and the words seemed wrung from him. 'I need you, Nelly. By God, I need you.'

She heard him and her mind reeled before the depth of sincerity in his words. But as she opened her mouth vainly to explain the tangled nature of her own feelings, she was prevented by the clear footsteps of two men sounding in the passage, and Charles Hart accompanied by Tom Killigrew came into view around the corner. The King quietly took his hands from Nell's shoulders and turned unhurriedly to greet them. 'Mistress Gwynne tells me if I enter the Women's Shift now, I shall put your ladies to the blush,' he said amiably.

Killigrew smiled and bowed. 'I fear so, Sire.'

'Ah well, I must come another day and look around your tiring rooms in a respectable fashion before the performance.' The King turned to Nell. 'A most interesting discourse, Mistress Gwynne,' he said. 'I never learnt so much of the Theatre Royal before in one day.' She curtseyed silently and Charles bowed before sauntering back along the passage, ushered by a polite Killigrew to whose conversation he appeared to be listening with every attention.

Buckhurst found Nell sitting in her dressing room when he strolled in a few minutes later. He came up behind her, and bending, kissed the top of her head. 'A veritable triumph indeed, my sweet,' he congratulated her. 'But I would that I could persuade you to leave in glory and let the theatre mourn your passing.' His hands caressed her shoulders, and she quivered slightly but said nothing. 'Here is summer almost upon us, and Sedley tells me of a house offered for lease at Epsom which he promised I could have if I wanted. I could take it, Nell, and we could all go and stay there away from the stink of the city. We could have Sedley and Etherege and Bab down to stay and make merry all summer long. Come with me, Nelly . . .'

She did not move or answer him. Buckhurst's hands came

away and he brushed past her, slumping into a chair, digging his hands in his coat pockets. 'I've never asked you for anything, Nelly, but I wish you loved me a little more,' he said ruefully.

'Charles, I . . . I do love you,' she said hesitantly.

'Then come with me to Epsom,' he said instantly.

'But I can't just throw up my acting like Lizzie Weaver does when she has a fit of the vapours,' she insisted. 'The last six months have been worrying enough for all the company and—'

'Nelly, for the love of God . . .' He came over to her and took her hands, squatting down so that his face was on a level with hers. 'You owe me nothing, sweetheart, but the time has come to decide, I think.' It had happened just as she had known it must. How ironic, she thought, that Buckhurst, all unsuspecting, should press her like this minutes after the King had poured forth a royal passion. There was no alternative, no room for shilly-shallying any more. His blue eyes looked deep into hers and a lilt of amusement touched the corners of his lips. 'I need you, Nelly,' he said softly.

She had to go with him, she saw that—she could not decide between them and there was only one way to find out. As she looked into his eyes, Nell knew she could not bring herself to say all was over between them. She was deeply fond of Buckhurst; he had been unforgettably kind to her and generous to a fault, helping her over the hard times and giving her days of light and laughter and nights of expert love. She leant towards him and his lips brushed hers, and then his hands came up either side of her face and he pressed hot violent kisses upon her.

Thomas Killigrew was sitting in his office that evening doing his accounts, alone in all the theatre, apart from the solitary old crone in the pit cleaning out the rubbish and pieces of orange peel from under the benches. He could hear her broom distantly banging against the hollow planks of the stage above the scratch of his quill, and then all at once the door of his office opened and he thought he had stepped back in time.

She had not changed much. She was cleaner and better dressed, but she still looked the same frightened child who had come so long ago to this same office to demand aid for her imprisoned sister. Her face looked as white as it had then but her voice was steady, though Tom Killigrew heard it with total disbelief.

'Master Killigrew,' she said clearly, 'I've come to hand in my parts. I'm leaving the Theatre Royal.'

A week later Samuel Pepys wrote sorrowfully in his dairy: 'My Lord Buckhurst hath got Nell away from the King's House and gives her £100 a year, so as she hath sent her parts to the house, and will act no more.'

Eight

*God's pampered people whom,
Debauched with ease
No King could govern,
Nor no God could please.*

—*John Dryden*

A crowd of courtiers waited outside the velvet curtains covering the entrance to the royal apartments at one end of the Stone Gallery in the Palace of Whitehall. Harry Savile edged as close as he could to the curtains, but not one sound issued from the Council Chamber in which the King was closeted with the Earl of Clarendon, Chancellor of England. There was an expectant hush amongst those waiting outside, a silence pregnant with tension.

Next to a window, in casual attitude, one hand toying with his lace neckband, stood a portly man with a majestic, self-conscious air of dignity. He wore a black patch on the bridge of his nose—proof to the world of my Lord Arlington's valour, as it covered a wound received in the late wars fighting for his martyred King. His expression was impassive, even bored. But a nervous tic afflicted the facial muscles of his companion, a thin frail gentleman who seemed dwarfed by the enormous flaxen periwig which he wore. His voice was shrill and irritated as he whispered to Arlington, 'How much longer must we wait? The King has been with him now for two hours or more...'

'You distress yourself unnecessarily, my dear Ashley,' soothed Arlington. 'Revenge was always the sweeter for waiting. I confess I am pleased to find you so *anxious* to witness our Chancellor's downfall.'

Ashley glanced sideways at him for a second but said nothing, though there was a momentary flash of dislike in his cold green eyes. Both of them knew that Lord Ashley had been a loud supporter and friend of Clarendon until he had seen that the Chancellor's fall was imminent—and had judiciously forgotten his friendship. It had taken some dexterity and a deal of careful humility for Ashley to join the group of gentlemen who had been meeting for months at Lady Castlemaine's supper parties secretly plotting Clarendon's downfall. Now he stood with Lord Arlington, waiting to hear of the Chancellor's disgrace, and Arlington derived a certain delight in watching Ashley glower when his loyalty was thus delicately held in question.

'The old dotard is doomed,' Arlington continued in smug accents. ' 'Tis merely a matter of either rendering up the Great Seal to the King at once, or having it wrested from him when the Commons impeach him. Nothing can save him now.'

For all the air of languor in these richly dressed perfumed gentlemen, the atmosphere in the gallery was the same as the final scene in a hunt—all were greedily waiting for the kill. Gossip was quick to travel in Whitehall; it was said that it ran through the palace faster than the wind. But many could not wait to hear at first hand whether their destiny henceforth was to move upward to power, fame and riches, or to be dragged down in the Chancellor's headlong fall.

Only the King's favour had kept Clarendon in power so long. He was hated by them all: by the Cavaliers whose fortunes he had failed to repair at the Restoration; by the Catholics and Dissenters he had outlawed in his Clarendon Code; by those ladies like Castlemaine whom he had loftily refused to court and openly condemned; and by those younger men who wished to be rid of him and seize power for themselves. Now the King whom he had hectored and lectured for so long had at last grown tired of him.

The velvet curtains parted. Through the half-open door Arlington heard the old man's last querulous protest: '. . . to betray a faithful servant of yourself and the Crown for the past thirty years . . .' The tall figure of the King, sombre in black slashed silk and goat's hair, stood rigid on the threshold of the Council Chamber, his back to them, and his deep voice was cold. 'I but seek to save you from a disgrace which is now inevitable, my lord. Secretary Morrice will call upon you for the Great Seal anon.' Then, turning, he strode past them, lips tightly clenched, seemingly unaware of the way they fell back guiltily before him, and disappeared with his long stride down the staircase to the Privy Garden. Two spaniels followed excitedly after him.

' 'Tis just as Coventry predicted,' said Ashley in satisfaction. 'From that exit I deduce that we shall no longer find his Majesty's Council waiting at Clarendon's mansion, while he lies gouty on a couch telling us all what to do as if we were schoolboys.' His eyes flickered back to the Council Chamber. 'With Southampton dead and Clarendon gone, the field is . . . open . . . to talent.'

'It was entirely inevitable,' replied Arlington. 'How could a Chancellor survive who was responsible for the fleet being laid up and who left us naked and undefended, so the Dutch could sail up the Medway in open display? God's death, I even find myself agreeing with Buckingham, loth though I am to admit it. We have sustained the grossest defeat in a century. We have seen Sheerness taken, our ships burned and our flagship towed back to Holland. We have been forced to make peace in as humbling a treaty as I have ever seen, for if we had not, the Dutch could have sailed clear up to London Bridge itself! Our Chancellor has much to answer for indeed.'

'Did you hear, the mob broke his windows last night and m' lackey tells me someone had hung a placard on his gate:

'Three sights in England to be seen:
Dunkirk, Tangier and a barren Queen.'

They know who's to blame for England's disgrace. God, how they hate him!'

'No more than we, my dear Ashley. They are just a trifle more . . . voluble.'

'Cast off the old bastard, has he?' said a jovial voice. 'They'll have him now. He'll lose his offices, his place at Court and his freedom too, if they can take it. Pox take him, I say. I'd have his privities to boot, if I had *my* way.'

A look of faint disgust crossed my Lord Arlington's features as the huge, stocky Duke of Lauderdale lounged up to them, grinning. 'Thrown him out before Parliament does, I assume. Good thing York's ill of the smallpox. I feared he'd persuade the King to keep his father-in-law in office.'

Ashley's smile was mirthless. 'I hardly think even the King's royal brother could have aided the Chancellor at this time, your Grace. The hounds are in full cry. Buckingham has been released from the Tower and my Lady Castlemaine has planned his downfall assiduously this year and more. Marry, even Rochester's been provoked to pen verses on our Chancellor's ruinous policies. He is as doomed as a cutpurse in Newgate.'

There was a creak as one of the double doors opened, and a sudden silence fell. The Earl of Clarendon stood looking around at them haughtily, encountering a variety of stares, some openly hostile, others betraying ill-concealed delight. Clarendon's pale gooseberry eyes swept coldly over them, and then, placing his hat on his head, he walked through them and passed slowly down the Stone Gallery, a defeated man. As he came to the staircase at the end he was surprised by the sudden appearance of the Duke of Buckingham coming up. For a moment they stared at each other, deadly enemies for so long. Then Buckingham doffed his hat in greeting. 'Good day, my lord,' he drawled insolently. 'I see you are . . . going down and I am going up.' The implication of the statement was obvious.

'Do not climb too fast, your Grace,' said Clarendon drily. 'I would not have you fall.'

Buckingham smiled a little. 'Though I may have a slip or two, my family are renowned for their surefootedness, I thank you, my lord.' He stood to one side politely, and after a tiny pause—under Buckingham's gaze—Clarendon descended the staircase and walked out to the Privy Garden.

The news had already gone before him. As he walked across the lawns he was conscious of the eyes of many following him and he heard an audible giggle or two. And then a voice came clearly from above him: 'I give you good day, Chancellor.'

Lady Castlemaine stood on her balcony looking down at him. She was still in a state of undress, her nightgown of lace pulled lightly about her and her hair flowing free down her back. There was an open look of triumph on her face as she leant over the balcony. 'Perhaps I should rather say adieu, my lord,' she said softly. 'I feel somehow that we will never meet again.'

Clarendon met her eyes calmly. 'Well then, I but go today and you tomorrow, madame.'

Barbara's face paled and she turned angrily away without another word. All at once her victory seemed hollow, for the words had more than a grain of truth. Together they had ruled in power and magnificently ignored each other. Now his day was done. And what of her? Without beauty—and the power and wealth that beauty brought—life would be nothing but tedious existence. Barbara stared at her reflection in her gilt mirror, noting the fine lines now obvious at the corners of her eyes and the sagging flesh of her throat, and felt the weight of time breathing down her back. What could the future hold for her?

She and Charles were tired of one another; their passion had burnt itself out and he rarely sought her bed these days. She knew now he would never divorce the Queen to marry her, as she had once dreamed in her days of glory. For the first time Barbara found herself regretting her many flagrant infidelities with Chesterfield, Harry Jermyn and Jacob Hall. By her promiscuity, she realised too late, she had forfeited the one thing that could have maintained her in power. Without the love and protection of Charles, she would be nothing but a jaded whore of ill notoriety, left neglected in the Court she had once dominated by her beauty and imperious temper. There would be no mercy for her from her many enemies in Whitehall. With a sudden hysterical sob Barbara picked up a silver-backed hairbrush and smashed it into the glass, shattering it into fragments. Alone in her chamber, my Lady Castlemaine began to see the years of weary decline ahead even as below on the Privy Stairs the Earl of Clarendon stepped into his barge to float off to his own disgrace and exile.

Strolling in St. James's Park that afternoon, Charles sardonically recognised the dawning of a new era in his reign. With Clarendon gone, there were only too many ready to step into the gap created by his going; only too many anxious to seize the wand of office prised so recently from the Chancellor's unwilling fingers. Charles was resolved that never again would one man hold power in the realm as Clarendon had done; he and he alone would be King in his kingdom.

Yet he would need men to help him. Not men he could trust—Charles had long since ceased to trust any man—but men of ability, with some wit, if possible; men he could understand and thus control. Dispassionately he flicked through the possibilities. His black eyes gleamed appreciatively as his thoughts immediately turned to Buckingham. Of all his cronies, Charles had least illusions about this acquaintance since childhood days. He knew Buckingham to be vain, selfish and utterly unprincipled; but Buckingham had great intelligence beneath his laziness and Charles knew him too well to consider his intrigues dangerous. Perhaps on this occasion, he mused, it might be possible to use *him* for a change. Arlington, of course, he could certainly employ; the man was too inordinately ambitious to dare to be disloyal and he had coveted the treasurership ever since old Southampton had died. Odsfish, Charles thought shrewdly, let him wait for it and he'll serve me well enough while he's waiting.

The King took some crusts from his pocket and threw them to a brood of wild fowl in the reeds bordering the lake, watching thoughtfully while they squawked and scrambled noisily for them. How like them we are, he thought, fighting and struggling for the impossible goal and treading on each other to do it. One bird in particular took his eye. Solitary and knowing, it stood quietly watching while its brethren fought for the bread, and then, as one bird tried to break free with a large lump, it was stopped by a peck from behind and turned to defend itself. No sooner did the crust drop than the solitary bird picked it up and finished it in one gulp. It regarded the King out of one beady eye.

'Aye, my friend,' said Charles, 'we have your sort too.' Looking at the bird's thin flat head, Charles was suddenly reminded irresistibly of Lord Ashley. The expression, blank and impossible to read, was identical. A dangerous man and one with a thirst for power which was formidable, Charles judged. He had a growing influence in Parliament, which could prove dangerous to the Crown if his thirst could not be satisfied. To dupe him would be dangerous, and yet to exclude him from government would be more so. With his Puritan past, the King decided, Ashley would be a good cover for what he was planning.

Limping across the grass towards him came one of the sights of London which drew crowds to gaze in wonder. It was a Balearian crane brought from far-off Astrakhan and presented to the King by the Russian ambassador. The bird had fallen soon after its arrival in the park and broken its leg, but the park gardener, who was an old soldier, had neatly amputated it and then replaced it with a jointed leg made of wood upon which the crane walked as well as ever. Charles was especially fond of it and greeted it with a piece of bread held in his palm, and with a gentle finger stroked its smooth feathers. 'You are like me, I fear, sweetheart,' he told her. 'You are half what you were and I am half what I would be.'

Charles recalled the look of astonishment on the face of the Venetian ambassador when he had told him of the Crown's poverty and helplessness, and his mouth set in determined lines. It had been a humiliating year for him. Things had to change—on that he had made up his mind. He was no longer prepared to be a puppet. What sort of a king was it, he thought resentfully, who only had one neckband to his name because his lackeys had taken the rest in lieu of wages still unpaid? His Parliament kept him chronically short of cash and that was the root of the trouble. Charles sighed as he remembered the descriptions his sister Minette had sent him of the glittering Court of his cousin Louis and of the beautiful château he was building outside Paris at Versailles. Louis was a king indeed. He was not trammelled with Parliaments and a shortage of money. And Louis was extremely rich.

Sir Thomas Clifford, a Roman Catholic nobleman of much cunning, was already urging the King to let Louis pay him handsomely to guarantee English neutrality when the Grand Monarque launched his French armies against the Dutch. England could remain at peace while Charles let French gold flow into his coffers. It would certainly be a change from going a-begging to Parliament, thought Charles, and he remembered Clifford's sly words: 'After all, Sire, you might as well be a slave to one man as to five hundred.'

Charles saw no reason to feel a pang at aiding Louis to destroy the Dutch. They had burned Chatham, attacked the Medway towns and humiliated him. It would, to the King's mind, be nothing but poetic justice if they received some of the same medicine.

But he had to go carefully. He knew his people hated the French and he could not depend on their continuing to hate the Dutch. Many English saw the Dutch in some way as brothers of the faith, Protestant comrades in the war against Papistry. Many even now were urging the King to form an alliance with the Dutch against France. Yes, he would have to go very carefully. His thoughts returned to his new Council. The solution was to proceed along two paths at once, one to lull suspicion while in secret he pursued his policy of friendship with Louis. Minette would help him, indeed she had already offered to do so. But he needed help at home too.

There were people at Court who shared his feelings and desires: Clifford was one, Arundel was another, and Arlington was known to have deep Catholic sympathies although he had never openly declared himself a Papist. With their help on his Council he could form a treaty with Louis that would give him the money he needed. With Ashley as a front, together with Buckingham, who despite his dissolute way of life had declared himself a convinced Protestant, he could face the world in all directions, appear to favour none and be amenable to all. Charles smiled grimly as he pictured these moves.

'I'll send William Temple to Holland and proclaim my intention of signing a Dutch treaty with that fox De Witt,' he told the Balearian crane. 'That'll fool Ashley and Buckingham. Odsfish, I'll even let George draft the treaty. That will puff him up like a turkey cock. And meanwhile . . .'

Meanwhile he would write to Minette and tell her he desired a French alliance.

There was a broad grin on the face of the King as he strolled back down one of the flower-fringed avenues to Whitehall. It would be a grand design, he told himself, but if it succeeded, he would be King as he had never been since his Restoration.

That evening Buckingham begged Charles suavely to attend a small supper party in the apartments of my Lord Arlington on the corner of the Privy Garden. This alone made Charles smile to himself, since Arlington and Buckingham had been on the coldest of terms in the past. Now, it seemed, a common purpose had suddenly bound them together, and what it was, Charles could guess.

In the event, the King found Arlington's candlelit apartments filled almost to bursting late that night with most of the members of the royal household and their hangers-on. The atmosphere was scarcely short of a celebration. Nodding genially in response to the deep curtsey of the Countess of Suffolk, the hatchet-faced Lady Silvis and several others, he made his way over to greet my lord and his lady, reflecting, as he bent to kiss her fingers—to her embarrassed delight—that as she was also Dutch, her husband's inclusion in his Council would further aid his attempt at deception and please the Protestant members of the Parliament. His eyes wandered around the room while she thanked him garrulously for thus honouring them, noting the usual company to be seen at Whitehall. Harry Jermyn was playing sice-ace at a table in the corner with George Etherege, Rochester and fat Harry Savile. Charles's quick eye soon espied the beautiful Countess of Shrewsbury deep in conversation with her brother Lord Brudenell in the opposite corner of the room. When she caught his eye upon her she blushed, hiding coquettishly behind her fan. Charles grinned.

Mingled amongst the glittering throng he discerned all the people who had long plotted for the downfall of Clarendon; slouched in a gilt chair staring resentfully over at Brudenell was Buckingham, together with Bristol, whose malicious talebearing Charles had often had to stem with a royal snub. Bab May, erstwhile Keeper of his Privy Purse and a toady of Castlemaine's, was bent over Buckingham, whispering earnestly into his ear. Buckingham began to reply, but suddenly saw the King looking at him and abruptly stopped. Charles lifted his hat in polite greeting and then became aware that Lady Arlington was talking to him. He complimented her on the success of her soirée.

'Yes, is it not vun big crush, your Machesty.' She simpered gratefully. 'I hardly hoped to think it could be so big a draw.'

'Haply Whitehall feels a desire to celebrate,' observed her husband pointedly.

'Aye?' Charles was as easy as ever. 'It would certainly seem so. But then, when is Whitehall aught else?' He presently excused himself and wandered over to where Rochester's dice were clicking between that nobleman's palms. As he did so he was conscious of Buckingham's gaze following him covertly, and then, with a stab of surprise, he saw Barbara seated in a window embrasure, looking unexpectedly demure while she watched him carefully over the rim of her wineglass. Charles smiled again.

Rochester greeted him in merry fashion and the King sat down, asking if he could join the game, since, he told Rochester, ' 'Tis the only chance I have now of keeping the Crown solvent.'

Rochester grinned. 'A desperate policy indeed, Sire. As God's anointed, you would surely do better to throw yourself upon the mercy of Providence.'

'Or get the Countess of Castlemaine to do it for you,' urged Harry Savile helpfully. 'Of course, there are those who say that she turned Papist just so that she wouldn't have to sit in that damned draughty chapel of a winter's morning but'—he paused as Charles's rich laugh interrupted him—'I am persuaded *that* is just a remark prompted by ill nature.'

'No doubt, Master Savile, but I believe you have lost a five guinea to Wilmot.'

Rochester swilled some claret around in his glass meditatively. 'God really does have a fond diddly in mankind, I fear,' he observed. 'After all, no one has ever actually come back from the dead to tell us 'tis all an illusion. I remember the night before we fought the Dutch at Bergen on board the *Revenge*, I made a pact with Philip Wyndham that if either of us died, one would come back to tell the other of any afterlife and what it was like. But though the poor gentleman had his belly took off by a cannonball the next day, he never appeared to me in any guise and probably never will.'

'A frightening spectre should he appear *without* his belly, Wilmot,' Etherege sapiently pointed out. 'He was hardly well-favoured at the best of times. And can one, I wonder, wear a periwig in heaven?'

Charles shook his head in mirth. 'I fear you are all damned gentlemen. You and Buckhurst and Sedley and that young devil Harry Killigrew are all of a case.' He threw two dice. 'Ods my life, the devil's in the bones again . . .' He watched while a shining pile of guineas was scooped up by Etherege. 'Where are they all tonight?' he asked idly. 'All the rest of my court of cuckolds appears to be here.'

'Buckhurst's down at Epsom with his whore,' Rochester informed him. 'And Sedley's gone to join them for a sennight. Buck's got Nelly Gwynne of the King's House to throw up her parts and make merry down there with him till they tire one of the other. Sedley's just been freed of the great pox with Mrs. Fourcard's mercury baths and says he needs a repairing lease.'

'First the pleasure, then the pain, but still a man but sins again,' sighed Etherege. 'Have you heard of that petition supposedly signed by all the whores of London and addressed to Castlemaine?'

But Charles scarcely heard him. He stared unseeing at the dice rolling across the table until a voice from behind begged obsequiously, 'Might I have the honour of a private word with your Majesty?' It was Buckingham.

The King roused himself. 'What . . . eh? Odsfish, is it you, George? What can I do for you?'

Buckingham seemed a trifle uncertain of himself. Looking at him, Charles knew exactly what he was thinking. Buckingham had but lately been released from the Tower and had been under grave suspicions of treason; and he no doubt wondered if he had regained sufficient credit with the King to be able to angle for power now that Clarendon had gone. On the one hand, he dared not be premature; on the other, he could not let opportunity slip by. Charles saw the twin feelings of prudence and ambition battling within him—as usual, ambition had won.

To the surprised Buckingham, Charles was affable, even friendly. 'What is on your mind, George?' he said.

'Could I have a *private* word, Sire?'

Charles allowed himself to be drawn away from Rochester and his cronies, and Buckingham ushered him courteously into an anteroom nearby, curtained off from the main apartment. Impassively Charles waited to hear what approach Buckingham would use to gain what he wanted.

Buckingham cleared his throat. 'I have not had a chance, Sire, since your gracious mercy released me from confinement to thank you in person for your clemency and to express my regrets at our previous—ah—estrangement.'

'Think nothing of it, George—and rather thank Barbara. 'Twas her pestering got you out of prison. But I think you have more to say to me than that.'

'What? Oh, I must confess . . .' Buckingham endeavoured to summon up a rueful smile. 'I *did* have something particular I wished to say to your Majesty.'

'I rather thought you might. Well?'

'My recent sojourn in the Tower gave me time to think,' Buckingham began. 'My family have long served the Crown and I have not perhaps done as much as I might. I thought that if you released me of your royal mercy, I might make some form of recompense, might atone for past errors with some ... *service*.'

Charles's lazy eyes watched him. 'Service? Oh—an ambassadorship or something of that nature you were visualising, I suppose.' He saw the exasperation leap into Buckingham's face and saw it as instantly repressed.

Buckingham shook his head slowly. 'I had hoped that I might find employment nearer to home. Of course, in the past my Lord Clarendon has opposed my sincere desire to serve your Majesty, but I am only too willing to—ah—do what I can in any way your Majesty might think fit.' He watched Charles carefully, hoping that his words would not be taken too literally.

The King appeared to ponder. 'Yes,' he said at last. 'It has seemed to me of late that some of the criticisms levelled at Clarendon by you in the past have proved to have some foundation. Perhaps you should have been heeded more. I have not really had time to think about it, but of course I must form a new Council—one which is made up of men upon whose loyalty I can depend.' He looked at Buckingham. 'You are right, George. I should turn to the families that have always supported the Crown. That is a sure base for good government. This needs thinking on ...'

Buckingham felt his palms become suddenly clammy. He moistened his lips and his voice was just a bit unsteady. 'Does your Majesty mean to honour me with a place on your Council?' he asked, and his acquaintances would have been amazed at the meekness of his tone.

But Charles appeared to notice nothing strange. He nodded ruminatively. 'It might well be I should, George. 'Tis time I looked to the Cavalier families, haply to help the Crown recover its old glory. Clarendon neglected them for too long. Come and see me tomorrow, George—it needs further discussion.'

Breathless with delight, Buckingham bowed deep and then

backed out respectfully. Charles heard him hurry away; back, he had no doubt, to report to his friends that their wildest dreams looked like coming true. 'You may indeed be of service to me, George,' he murmured. 'More than you might think.'

As Buckingham came out of the anteroom he saw Clifford and Ashley together enter Bennet's apartments. The one was a fanatical Catholic, the other a calculating Protestant. Hitherto they had hardly spoken, and yet they now were arm in arm. Buckingham hurried anxiously up to them. The vultures had gathered. Who, Charles wondered, could he really trust amongst this concourse of devious self-interested butterflies? There was a sudden crash by one of the tall windows and a shrill voice cried, 'God's death, you cheesecurd—if I don't claw you into blushes for this!'

All eyes turned as my Lady Castlemaine jumped up with a scream. A decanter of claret had spilt down her smooth satin gown. A small table lay up-ended on the ground.

Charles began to guffaw as he saw a huge bulky figure on its knees trying with one massive hand and a kerchief to sponge the stains off the delicate material, while Barbara's strident voice spat abuse at him and she tore the gown from his grasp with a petulant oath. Lauderdale, of course! Brutal, villainous old Lauderdale, who had as much finesse as a pig loose in a tailor's shop, who was quite ruthless and not overclever, and who was, Charles knew, quite devoted personally to him as he had been to his father. Lauderdale had no pretensions. Charles chuckled as he remembered Doctor Tenison's icy rebuke to Lauderdale during the sermon the previous Sunday in the Chapel Royal: 'My lord, my lord, you snore so loud you will wake the King!' A man after his own heart. And a sheet anchor for his government.

But as he looked at Barbara storming away at his unfortunate minister, his mind suddenly recalled Rochester's airy words: 'Buckhurst's down at Epsom with his whore . . .' Was that what Nell really was; had he not endowed a pretty face with virtue in the manner of a lad of fifteen summers? He had told her that was what she had made him. Despite his declaration, she had ignored him, had indeed spurned him, and taken the whore's path with Buckhurst down to Epsom like the rest of her kind. He shrugged. After all, what else had he learnt to expect from women ever since the day Mary Wyndham had taken his virginity and his innocence with it one unforgettable May day twenty-two years ago?

Mistress Wyndham's face, not surprisingly, Charles found difficult even to picture after the passage of so many years. But as he strolled back to join Rochester, the fair vision of the face of Mistress Nelly Gwynne came sharply into his brain and irritatingly insisted on lingering there, so that the King lost quite a hundred guineas in the next half hour, though he appeared hardly to notice.

Part Three

Charles the Third

Permit me, Sir, to help you to a whore:
Kiss her but once, you'll ne'er want Cleveland more.
She'll fit you to a Hair, all wit, all fire—
And Impudent to your own Heart's desire
And more than this, Sir, you'll save money by her.
She's Buckhurst's whore at present, but you know—
When sovereign wants a whore, the subject must forego.

Sir George Etherege

One

Love is a god, to which all hearts must bow.

—*My Lord Orrery*

The King's Head tavern was the largest building in the High Street of Epsom, a pretty little town, nestling in a fold of the downs, and in the summer months much resorted to for its waters by gouty merchants, creaking dowagers and exhausted gallants alike. Leaning up against the ivy-covered gabling of the tavern was a small bow-fronted cottage with tendrils of honeysuckle about its trellis porch. There was a breathtaking view across the valley, which was admired one balmy August morning by Lord Buckhurst as he sluiced warm water from a copper bowl over his face and shoulders.

Nell lay in bed watching him sleepily. He was wearing nothing but a pair of breeches as he carried out his ablutions, blowing noisily through his fingers as he wiped the drops out of his eyes. Her eyes travelled down the length of his back from wide shoulders to slim waist, watching the muscles move supple beneath the skin. She felt the familiar stab of desire course through her and she knelt forward on the bed and stroked her hand slowly down his spine.

'Days o' my breath, Nelly,' protested Buckhurst. 'Would you wring me dry as a dish clout? Today's the first day I've been up afore noon, and you know we've got to be ready by eleven for this damned expedition of Sedley's.'

'A visit to look at some ancient mosaics?' Nell yawned. 'I don't understand why Sir Charles should wish to see some pile of Roman relics. He's never been interested in looking at old ruins before.'

Buckhurst smiled a trifle secretly as he pulled on his shirt. 'No, but haply there is something else to see on the way.'

Nell's eyes narrowed in suspicion. 'You're a pandarly rascal, Charles,' she said tartly. 'What else is there to see?'

Buckhurst burst out laughing. ' 'Tis for Sedley to say, not me,' he declared, and Nell could not get him to tell her any more.

That Sir Charles Sedley should be even capable of setting one foot before the other, Nell found hard to credit. The amount of liquor the gentleman consumed made her mind boggle. Last night before she had tottered to bed, leaving Sedley and Buckhurst together, she had seen him finish two bottles of claret and a handsome amount of brandy without scarcely seeming to turn a hair. It occurred to Nell that since he arrived a week before, she had hardly seen Buckhurst, for he had lingered late over the dice with his friend and come stumbling to bed only to wake at noon to kiss her out of her ill humour and ride off after a mug of ale to go hare coursing on the downs or shooting with Sedley. Life in the country, surprisingly, appeared to suit them both.

Sedley was an amusing if irreverent companion, Nell was forced to admit, recalling his conversation the night before. 'After *one* bottle and *before* the second,' she observed, 'he must be the wittiest man in England.'

Buckhurst shook out his ruffles. 'You've not heard Rochester in his cups, m'dear. I've seen him hold the King spellbound when he's reeling like a tapster. Though I'll admit Sedley's tongue sharpens as it loosens.'

'But what a plaguey lonely life to lead,' Nell said meditatively. ' 'Tis a pity he and his wife cannot agree.'

Buckhurst snorted. 'Thus the mind of a woman! Sedley's

happy enough. You forget 'tis just not fashionable for man and wife to dote upon each other any more.'

'But he never speaks of his wife—ever. One might think she was dead.'

Buckhurst paused in the middle of tying his cravat. 'Actually, Nelly, not everyone knows this, but poor old Sedley has the devil of a life with her. Don't be deceived by that bored air of his. My Lady Sedley, I'm afraid, is as mad as a March hare. They say she thinks she's a queen, and Charles, together with all the lackeys, have to address her as "your Majesty" or she throws a fit and anything else near to hand as well. I don't know the details, but Etherege says she holds the purse strings, so poor old Sedley has to knuckle under or face the consequences.'

'No wonder he spends all his time taking gut rot in the Rose tavern of an evening, with fulsamic fops like Gerard and his ilk.' Nell nodded understandingly. 'I suppose sluicing your troubles away is as good a way as any.'

A moment later there came a knock on the door, followed almost immediately by Sir Charles Sedley himself, who entered the chamber looking as spruce and elegant as ever in green ferrandin with matching ribands. He greeted them benignly. 'As I live, 'tis a perfect morning!'

Nell groaned, lying back with her eyes closed. Sir Charles Sedley looked hurt. 'I vow, Mistress Gwynne,' he complained, 'you make me feel as unwelcome as a looking glass after the smallpox.'

'Nell ain't so used to Nantes brandy as you, Charles,' explained Buckhurst.

'Odsbud,' mourned Sedley, 'I begin positively to feel a pariah. 'Twas bad enough two nights back being dragged out to dine at Berkely's with Lady Warwick and being stared out of countenance all evening, as though any moment I was liable to sprout horns and leap over the table to ravish her. No'—he turned to Nell as she protested, giggling—'I give you my word. For all she was seventy if she was a day and such a damned *odd*-looking woman. No teeth at all and had a habit of sitting with her mouth open, looking for all the world like an oyster at low tide.' He paused. 'My God, you're not going to put *on* that waistcoat, Buckhurst. 'Pon my soul, man, give it to your lackey, I beg you. One of Master Pym's worst confections, clearly. I cannot entertain the thought of looking at that shade of green satin all day long in the confines of a coach. I should turn bilious before we'd gone a mile.'

Buckhurst laughed, shrugged, and took it off. Nell regarded Sedley with some amusement. '*Where* exactly are we going, sir?' she asked pointedly.

'To the ruins of the villa I told you of,' he said blandly. 'Mosaics have been uncovered there, I am told, of a singular magnificence. They say 'tis a sight not to be missed. A well-preserved example of a design which is supposed to be dated from the time of Diocletian—'

'Where after that?' Nell inquired suspiciously.

'To a pretty dinner I've bespoken at the White Hart at Richmond of calvered salmon and a carp in black sauce and enough baked meats to feed an army.'

'And where after that?' Nell pursued ruthlessly.

There was a silence. Sedley took out his snuffbox and took a pinch. 'As to that, Mistress Gwynne, the time is our own. I collect I *did* hear that there's to be a cock fight at a little farm near—'

'*Now* I see!' she said triumphantly. 'Just as I suspected. All this flummery is just a cover to drag me off to a cock fight. Faugh! How you men can sit watching a bird claw the life out of another and derive pleasure from it, I just don't understand. Rose took me once—two half-starved birds with wicked great spurs on their feet tearing lumps out of each other while great men sat watching gloating over the blood flowing.'

Buckhurst had the grace to look abashed. 'If you don't want to come, Nelly . . .'

She saw him looking guilty, and shook her head. 'You look just like a little boy who's had his top taken from him, Charles. I'll come—provided I can stop in the coach while you watch the feathers fly.'

. . .

The day passed agreeably enough, though much as Nell had expected; the look at the mosaics was cursory in the extreme and the time spent over the meal at the White Hart curtailed so that none of the cock fight was in danger of being missed. She found herself, by the time the calvered salmon was just an aromatic memory in the nostrils, sitting alone in Buckhurst's coach waiting for the cock fight to end. It was taking place in a barn in the middle of a farmer's ploughed field. Only two other coaches waited with her and both were empty. The afternoon was sultry and close.

As she watched the swoop of a bee onto a solitary gilly flower that had by some strange means managed to sprout in the hedgerow, Nell found herself feeling a little aggrieved at the way things were developing. Her idyll, held out so promisingly by Buckhurst, in which they alone would love the summer away seemed to have become insensibly a long roistering of Buckhurst and his cronies in which she was included to dispense wit by day and love by night. They had had Rochester and Etherege to stay, now they had Sedley. Was she not, she asked herself, a trifle in the way? Nell had tried to repress such thoughts; she was not his wife to hold him, she told herself, she could not expect him to devote himself entirely to her; he was never anything but kind and generous. But still a little voice inside her seemed to say with monotonous regularity, 'He may love you in his way, but he is not in love with you.'

Nell knew the nature of men as well as her sister Rose did. They were not by nature monogamous and it was not something she had been brought up to expect. It was not suspicion of infidelity that troubled her, nor evidence of hidden cruelties or meanness. Something told her that she should not have left the theatre; she recalled Thomas Killigrew's cold adieus after he had paid her the money owing to her and bowed her formally out of his office. Was it for this that she had abandoned the theatre? There was something missing, something she had always known but tried not to notice. A burst of loud cheering came from the barn and interrupted her thoughts—a kill, no doubt. She shook her head as she stared down at her hand adorned with a fine opal ring given her only the week before by Buckhurst. 'You're becoming a sour belch of a wench, Nelly Gwynne,' she told herself wryly. 'He's as good a man as ever drew breath.'

A horrible suspicion did lurk at the back of Nell's mind. Was she in fact becoming a drag already on Buckhurst's carefree existence? He would never say so, he was far too good-natured to tell her—but was he not happier with his cronies, his dice, his roistering and his wenching without the constant tie of a girl who could give him nothing but brats and extra trouble to bedevil his easy way of life? This was all nonsense, she told herself fiercely; she should drink less at night and think less about herself. To indulge in these sick imaginings was nothing short of folly. How had things changed? Did they not delight in each other as much as they ever had? Was he not as expert a lover as ever? She dismissed her unworthy doubts from her mind. But she knew she had not banished them.

It was on the way back to Epsom that evening that Nell first felt inexplicably cold. Her body seemed to shiver and shake and she heard her teeth chattering. Nell felt quite suddenly that the draught coming through the coach window had made her head thud uncomfortably and her throat became dry. She snuggled up to Buckhurst, who asked her anxiously what ailed her as he saw the flush of fever on her cheeks and the brightness of her eyes. Nothing, she told him—it was just the chill of the night air, and she tried to rouse herself to some hectoring banter with Sedley. It was to little avail. By the time Buckhurst's coach drew up in the High Street at Epsom, Nell had to be carried half fainting into the house and put to bed while Sedley knocked up the local doctor.

Nell opened her eyes to find a kindly small gentleman leaning over her as he placed a cool hand on her brow. He turned back to Buckhurst. 'The lady has contracted a marsh ague—'tis something like the sweating sickness but not, thankfully, so serious. I have a dozen others in like condition at the moment. 'Tis only to be expected, with Mars entering the House of Virgo as 'tis at present. I will leave unicorn's horn to reduce the fever and an extract of woodlice stewed in spirits of wine to prevent the phlegm settling on the chest. If your lordship has any further need of me, you have only to call.' He bowed to Nell and Buckhurst and left, promising to return in the morning.

Sedley came in with a glass in his hand and looked scornfully at the medicaments that the doctor had left. 'If you wish to give her that Shoreditch dirt, you can,' he said disdainfully. 'Mere quackery, but harmless. What I have here is worth more than the lot of it.' He sat on the side of the bed and raised Nell gently with his other arm, presenting for her inspection a clear liquid in the glass.

'What—what is it?' she mumbled.

'That, my dear, is the King's Drops—a royal medicine distilled by the King himself and given to me by him some time ago. I never travel without it. They say it cured the Queen when she was like to die, and it will, I have no doubt, cure you. Drink.'

After she had drained the bitter potion Sedley laid her back down again in the bed, and Nell was left alone. Buckhurst had drawn the bed curtains, so she lay in a musty close atmosphere, and as she drifted off to sleep Sedley's words echoed in her mind: 'King's Drops . . . royal drops . . .' She murmured the words as her eyes closed. The heat beneath the bedclothes grew more intense; she fancied she saw the flames in front of her once more, and a familiar figure was leaving her, climbing into the fire from which there could be no return. The smoke filled her nostrils. She wanted to call him, tell him to come back, but she could not shout, no sound came out . . . He was tall, tall and dark. She could not miss him when he reappeared, but he did not reappear—there was only smoke and flame and then the thunder of crashing timbers. 'Charles!' she wanted to cry. 'Please God, Charles!'

Her breathing was scant and hurried, her forehead wet as the darkness returned. And then he was close to her again— she saw the thin black moustache on the swarthy face. 'I am no king with you, Nelly Gwynne . . . I am Charles Stuart and I want you . . . want you . . . want you . . .' She sobbed desperately into the pillow. 'Charles, Charles . . .'

The scene changed. She was Nelly Gwynne of Drury Lane, she was on the stage at the Theatre Royal and the shouts of the audience were in her ears; she looked up to see him leaning out over the royal box with his hands towards her, and she ran over to him, sobbing, but she was prevented. The further across the stage she ran, the further away he became; she could not reach him. And then they loomed up before her. Buckhurst with grief-stricken eyes: 'You told me you loved me, Nelly. Would you leave me now just because he is the King . . . ?' 'No, no!' And then the small, hurt figure of the Queen: 'I thought you were my friend, but now you take my husband from me.' And as she blundered hopelessly on, the haughty eyes of Lady Castlemaine swept over her and the voice like drops of silver water: 'What makes you think you're fit for the King? You're just a whore from the gutter . . . a common little whore.' With a start she woke up, her eyes wide open and her face wet with tears. 'Charles,' she murmured brokenly. 'Charles . . .'

By morning Nell's fever had lessened but the ague had left her weak and listless. Buckhurst did his best to cheer her, spending hours in her room and amusing her as ever with his quips and gay absurdities. He had Nell's chamber festooned with flowers so that it smelt fragrant as a meadow. Sedley amazed her with his kindness and thoughtfulness. Regularly he came into her chamber bearing a steaming glass of metheglyn brewed with honey and herbs, and begged her to drink it at once as he really couldn't bear the smell of it. She laughed, obeyed him, and by the end of the week was well enough to leave her bed for short periods and lie on a couch to play cards with the both of them.

It was while she was up, leaning against the window sill two nights later, that she saw what she had always known she would see one day. Her chamber looked down directly onto the courtyard of the King's Head tavern and through into the taproom, which had a large window overlooking the High Street. A lantern hung on the lintel spread a pool of light over the table inside. On one seat lounged Buckhurst, on another lounged Sedley. Buckhurst had a serving wench on his knee and she giggling while Buckhurst playfully unlaced her stomacher so that her breasts burst free from their confinement. Sedley dipped his finger in his tankard and then carelessly flung drops down her cleavage. At first Nell's eyes blazed—so much for his concern! And then a smile began to hover about her lips and she suddenly found herself helplessly laughing—great gusts of mirth that left her with eyes streaming as she realised the significance of her discovery. She had found the worst; she knew he did not love her and it left her not aghast but blessedly relieved. Dear Charles—he wasn't in love with her at all! What a blessed relief it all was!

That night she met him standing outside the door to her chamber. He was surprised; they had not lain together since her illness. She smiled at him, moved up to him and twined her arms around his neck. That night was a night Buckhurst thought he would never forget. He had always found her exciting, but on this occasion she seemed to break through every experience he had ever known before—her hands dominated him, her lips claimed him, her body responded to his; they clung together in an ecstasy that pushed Buckhurst to the brink of reality and over it to a world of shadow on which he floated out to delicious oblivion. He stirred lazily just after dawn as he felt cool lips touch his, and then, as he opened his eyes, he saw.

She was dressed with cloak wrapped around her and beside her were two bulging valises. She was smiling tenderly and her hand stroked his cheek. He caught the words as she leant over him to plant the kiss on his forehead.

'Dear Charles—I won't ever forget you.'

Thomas Killigrew was undergoing one of his periodic loud laments for the old days before women had been allowed on the London stage. This was a favourite theme from time to time when the ladies of the company had upset him in some way, and the actors at the Theatre Royal—Lacy, Mohun, Kynaston and Hart—were all too familiar with the sentiments then expressed. He was, he told them, when he arrived one morning to watch rehearsal, a man sore beset.

'First we are closed down by order of the King. Then, no sooner are we opened than that jill flirt Nelly goes off to be gentleman's whore, and no sooner do I train a new comedienne to take her place than disaster strikes again!'

'God's wrath—what calamity is it now?' asked Lacy with a pained expression.

'Betty Hall,' sighed Killigrew in a hollow tone. 'She's five months gone with Philip Howard's bastard brat. I should have seen it coming—God knows, we've had it before.'

Charles Hart was disgusted. 'The girl's been a slut ever since she joined us. Gossip hath it she's been joining the coursers on the pick-up outside the New Exchange. She'll be lucky if she can get Howard to own it, for the brat could be anyone's—aye, I warrant if her bolster could talk, it would tell a fine tale!'

Lacy tore his wig off his head with an oath. 'It took me eight weeks of labour and cajolery to turn that simpering little bawd into some semblance of an actress, and even then she wasn't a candle to Nelly. And all the time she must have known she had a great belly. I thought she was getting plump.'

'She'll soon be fat as a malamucca melon,' moaned Killigrew.

Mohun's intelligent eyes showed a trace of amusement. 'Surely, er, that will make it rather difficult when we revive *The Indian Emperor* next week. She was to have had Nell's old part of Cydaria, "a maiden of the Court of Montezuma." A trifle difficult surely, when her stomach reaches half across the stage.'

Edward Kynaston chuckled. 'You'll have to hold a fan in front of her.'

''Tis a hopeless position,' Killigrew declared. 'It either means employing that old sow Lizzie Weaver, who's quite unsuitable, or trying to train a hireling by next week.'

'If only Nell hadn't walked out.' Lacy shook his head. 'Betty Hall was never a good substitute as comedienne. Nell could sing better than all the silk knitters of Cock Lane and she had as clean a pair of heels as Moll Davis for dancing. What am I supposed to do now—teach Kate Corey to coranto?'

'Nelly's gone and there's an end on't. I wouldn't *have* her back even if she begged me, malapert slut that she was . . .' Killigrew muttered petulantly.

Lacy threw him a quick look of doubt but said nothing. Charles Hart tapped his cane thoughtfully against a bench. 'I have a feeling that she'll come back,' he said.

'Little use now!' retorted Killigrew frostily.

The rehearsal went badly. Tom Killigrew was in an irritable temper and found fault with virtually everything he saw. After trying out Anne Marshall, Beck's sister, in Betty Hall's roles and declaring her to be colourless as almond milk and dismissing a new little hireling called Peg Hughes as a mere Doll Common, Killigrew decided, as it was nearly noon, to cut his losses and seek refuge in a glass of tent at the Crown tavern with Charles Hart.

They were strolling out under the archway into Little Russell Street when Killigrew recognised the slim figure waiting by the ticket office. His eyebrows raised. 'Really, Hart,' he commented ironically, 'your omniscience is quite astounding. One might almost suppose you had a sibyl for a nurse.' Charles Hart said nothing. He was looking open-mouthed at the uncertain figure of Nelly Gwynne. She smiled tremulously at Killigrew and then looked down, embarrassed; she made no move towards him.

'The return of the prodigal son, or should I rather say *daughter*,' Killigrew remarked drily. He saw the expression in her eyes as the shaft hit home, and relented slightly. 'Well, mistress, what business have *you* any more at the Theatre Royal?'

'Might I see you, Sir? I know you have every right to refuse me, but I would take it as a kindness if you would.'

Killigrew's face remained quite impassive. 'Very well,' he said shortly. 'Come with me. Charles, I will be with you in just ten minutes . . .' Turning, he strode back through the theatre without looking to see if she was following him.

Nell soon found herself in the familiar surroundings of Killigrew's office being regarded by a pair of gimlet eyes. 'Well, Mistress Gwynne?' he asked coldly.

'I have come to ask you to take me back into the company, sir.' Her voice trembled slightly.

Killigrew's eyebrows rose once more in faint hauteur. 'Really, Mistress Gwynne? I fail to follow such tangled volatility of spirit. Two months ago you told me you *had* to go and had to leave there and then—indeed, you were quite definite upon the point as I remember. Yet now you calmly say you wish to rejoin us. Unfortunately, I cannot run the Theatre Royal upon such whims. We have managed very well without you, I must tell you, and I make no doubt that we shall continue hereafter without your aid.' He had conducted such interviews before, and now he waited for the expected burst of tears and vows of eternal obedience that usually followed such dismissals. It was what he wanted and what he usually got. But as always with Nelly Gwynne he found himself surprised.

She stood coolly erect, and when she spoke her voice had lost all tendency to tremble. 'It is your right, Master Killigrew, to appoint and dismiss within the company. I am sorry that I have caused such trouble to the theatre and yourself. Thank you for your past help. I will trouble you no further.'

Killigrew heard her in some dismay. He needed her desperately; he was under no illusions as to who amongst the company had drawn the crowds in the past and would do in the future. What would happen, he suddenly thought, if she went and offered herself to the Duke's? Why, Davenant would snaffle her in a flea's elbow! Besides, he didn't want to lose her—he had always had a soft spot for Nelly Gwynne. Though she had made him angry by leaving, he had felt at the time that there was some hidden reason for her sudden decision. He hadn't really *intended* to put her off, just to frighten her a little and— Hang it, thought Killigrew, how could he get her to stay without looking a flamster?

'Nelly—'

She turned and looked at him straightly from under those dark, fine brows.

'Come and sit down, child. Smooth my band if I spoke too

sharply. Come and have a brandy . . .' He pulled a bottle and two glasses clumsily from a drawer. His voice held a grudging warmth. 'Devil take you, you hussy, I've missed you sorely. And John Lacy's been sinking into a decline this month past.'

She smiled suddenly at him and came to sit down, remarking, ' 'Twould be no matter to wonder at had he utterly cast me off.'

'Hmph,' said Killigrew. 'You chose your time to return well, my girl. Betty Hall has got a great belly and she's too sick to be of any use in comedy for some time to come. Next week we're reviving *The Indian Emperor* and she was to have taken your old role, but now you're back you can take Cydaria again.' He looked at his watch. 'Pox take it—is that the time? I can't stop here jawing; I've got to discuss the arrangements for refurbishing the Men's Shift with Hart and then we've got the King and York coming this afternoon, so I must be back to see all's ready to receive them and—'

'Please, Master Killigrew!' Nell was conscious of her heart thumping suddenly in a most uncomfortable fashion and she had a feeling of hot embarrassment as she interrupted him. He looked up in some surprise as her words poured out. 'I know I have no right to ask anything of you and I dare swear you're convinced that I'm a black-souled bawd—indeed, you have every right to think so, for I've been in such a state I've scarce known what I was doing or why these last weeks—but please grant me this one favour. Let me appear this afternoon on the boards. I don't want a *part* precisely, but I must *appear*. Please, if you have any feeling at all for me, let me appear this afternoon.'

Killigrew looked blankly at her. Nell's eyes were bright and she threw him a look of appeal he was unable to resist. 'Very well,' he said after a pause. 'I think we may well be able to help, Nelly—on one condition.'

'What is it, sir?' she gasped.

There was just a hint of the old warmth in his voice. 'That you don't have the vapours in my office. 'Tis a thing I can't abide.'

. . .

The Duke of Buckingham glowered down at Beck Marshall from his seat in the royal box and meditated anew on the inconstancy of women. All his love, or at least as much of it as Buckingham could spare from self-adoration, he had bestowed on the beautiful Anna Maria, and yet she had spurned him or at least tried to tease him by indulging in a ridiculous flirtation with Harry Killigrew. Buckingham's fingers drummed irritably on his chair arm. To prefer that young popinjay to him—a nobody, son of the King's jester, who owned this flea pit of a theatre! To Harry Savile and my Lord Rochester, who sat either side of Buckingham, it was obvious that his Grace was in a foul mood indeed.

His choleric thoughts were interrupted by a rumble of laughter from the King, who sat on the other side of Rochester and who now rose and doffed his hat at Beck, who collapsed in respectful curtsey before him. He took a carnation from his buttonhole and tossed it onto the boards and winked at Beck as she gaily stuck it in her curly hair. Then she made a final bob to the audience and ran off.

'She has an excellent tongue,' said Buckingham. 'I would she had as excellent a complexion,' he added scathingly.

The King looked surprised. 'Nonsense, George—as wholesome a little barque of frailty as ever I saw. You're plaguey distempered this afternoon.'

'George,' complained Rochester sweetly, 'has no one ever told you that you have a particular knack of spoiling company?'

'How so?' grunted Buckingham.

'By coming into it, my dear soul—'tis enough.'

Buckingham shot a look of fury at Rochester, but Harry Savile diplomatically took his attention in another direction. 'Another entertainment, I see . . .'

There was a sudden shocked silence, and then from the pit there came a wave of cheers that spread back across the whole theatre as a solitary figure carrying a guitar walked onto the boards and curtseyed silently. Shouts came in discordant greeting, together with whistles and stamping: 'Nelly!' . . . 'God save you, Nell.' . . . ' 'Tis good to see you, Nell . . .' She smiled at them all and waved, blowing kisses out into the pit, and then walked calmly and slowly over to the corner of the stage just below the royal box. Deliberately she sat facing the King and the Duke of York, who was at his side, though she did not raise her eyes up to theirs. Her head was bowed, almost it seemed in submission, as her fingers ran over the strings and her voice raised clear above the press of rabble in the pit:

'Here's a health unto his Majesty
With a fa la la la la la la
Conversion to his enemies
With a fa la la la la la la.

And to him that will not pledge this health
I wish him neither wit nor wealth
Nor yet a *rope*—to hang him*self*
With a fa la la la la la la la la la
With a fa la la la la la la . . .'

As her hand strummed the last chord she paused and gazed up at Charles. Her eyes held a promise that made him feel suddenly weak; she looked at him for a second lingeringly and then she turned away to address the audience. 'I'm going to sing this again, and as we've got a royal visitor, all you woollen-witted pilchards can sing an' all!' A mixture of jeers and cheers greeted this admonition, but as she began to sing again, there was an answering chorus which gradually swelled to a crescendo.

The King stood up in the royal box, smiling while all the theatre sang a loyal wish for his continued well-being. Charles hardly heard the words—he was conscious of a feeling of wild elation such as he had not felt for many cynical years, a certainty that had hitherto eluded him but which he thought he had glimpsed in two hazel eyes. And then Buckingham's drawling voice broke in, disintegrating the spell. 'I see Buckhurst's cast off his whore and now she's aiming at higher things,' he observed. 'Odsbud, I warrant you'll find every Cyprian now dreams of treading Moll Davis's path.'

The King stood stock-still as the words penetrated into his brain. Cast off by Buckhurst—was that why she smiled thus at him? She had left the stage and gone off with him, and now Buckhurst had cast her off, so she came back and smiled up, waiting for a new bed to lie in. He ceased to question it—a whole lifetime of lying women, fawning courtiers and past betrayals told him it was true. A bitter smile twisted his lips, and Buckingham heard the King murmur, 'Know a woman by any name, beneath the skirts they're all the same.' He turned abruptly from the box and looked at Buckingham. 'Sometimes, George, I wonder *why*—exactly *why*—I bear with you at all . . .' Buckingham's mouth dropped open at the violence in the King's voice. Those dark eyes blazed at him and then the lids veiled them from his sight.

Rose Gwynne found it hard to credit what Mit told her. She put down a bumbard of Bide's ale with a hearty thump on the table and her voice was hoarse with incredulity. 'I'll cry flounders if ever I heard aught like it! You mean to tell me *she* left *him*—threw away money, a cosy nest and as handsome a gallant as you'd meet if you walked from the Strand to Pimlico? She must have run mad—an April fool in August!'

Mit sighed. 'I don't know no details. Nelly ain't said and I don't like to ask, but 'tis all over betwixt 'em for certain. Toby's fair upset. 'E keeps asking when "Uncle Buck" is coming back, poor little toad.'

But Rose was less interested in Toby's disappointment. She couldn't seem to get her sister's improvidence out of her mind and went over it again and again. 'She could have been as rich as a thrice-laid bawd if she'd wanted. I know she's always been nifty, but this beats all. Has she anyone else who's tipped 'er the cork?' Rose groped blindly for sense in seeming nonsense.

Mit shook her head. 'Not that I know of. No one's been round since she got back—two weeks since now it is—and I note she don't go round to Master Lacy's like she used to. Seems they're still all ratsbane over her handing in her parts to go off like she did.'

'When I think . . .' snorted Rose after a deep draught of ale. ' 'Ere's me saddled to a pocket tipstave with a moth-eaten periwig and five ells of bastard scarlet—and a mouse yoked to a peascod would carry *his* fortune—and my own sister turns down an offer like that. It's—damn my lugs—it's not natural!'

It was at one o'clock in the afternoons that the King habitually dined in the Banqueting Hall at Whitehall. This was a chamber of lofty splendour, different in both style and size from the huddle of smelly, untidy two-storied buildings that, sprawling along the river front, made up the rest of the palace.

Here in royal dignity and before the public eye the King and Queen dined every day in solitary state at a table set on a dais before a wall of gorgeous tapestry worked with cloth-of-gold. Above in the gallery a gawping crowd stood to watch the King eat. Charles disliked the ceremony and would have discarded it if he could, but protocol insisted on the custom, and easy as ever, he submitted to it.

Thus, promptly at five minutes before the hour, two royal heralds clad in scarlet cloaks with facings of silver lace advanced to the centre of the chamber and blew a resounding blast on long golden trumpets. Then the King, with the Queen leaning on his arm, entered the Banqueting Hall and walked up to the dais, nodding to either side in acknowledgement.

Catherine took her seat at one end of the table, with Lady Suffolk behind her on one side and a row of ladies-in-waiting on the other. She smiled shyly at her husband, and the harsh features in his dark face softened as he winked at her. Despite the magnificence of Charles's dress, the beautiful ordered black curls of his periwig against black satin and heavy lacing in old gold, Catherine thought he looked tired and told him so. He disclaimed it. 'Merely a Council meeting followed by a game of pell mell with Albemarle, m'dear. I think the Council meeting tired me most.'

The page-in-waiting offered the King a large sturgeon and lamprey pie on one knee and Charles regarded it with distaste.

A strange pungent odour arose from it which made him wrinkle his nose. 'No matter how much sauce or pickle is added to sturgeon, it turns off in the summer quicker than candles,' he remarked. 'I advise you to let it pass, m'dear. I certainly shall.' He turned to pick out a morsel from a dish of quails and then saw who was holding the dish. 'Odsfish—save you, Buckhurst. I forgot 'twas you in attendance this month. We've not seen much of you lately.'

Buckhurst bowed. 'I am glad to be back, Sire.'

Charles smiled. 'I'm monstrous glad 'tis you and not old Berkshire. I've got m' new Rhinegraves on today'—he indicated his short petticoat breeches—'and 'twould be a shame to ruin them on first wearing.'

Buckhurst went on one knee to proffer the boeuf à la mode. Charles eyed the grease floating on cold gravy. 'Monsieur de Gramont always said I'm served my dinner on bended knee by way of apology for such plaguey poor vittals, and I'm inclined to think he's right. Put it down there, man. I hear you were at that ball of Purbeck's last night. Buckingham tells me the ladies there wore masks but not much else.'

Buckhurst offered a bowl of water and a napkin for the King to rinse his fingers. 'An exaggeration, Sire. Only half of them wore masks.'

Charles gave a bark of laughter. He reached out and took a peach from a bowl on the table. 'I hope the air at Epsom agreed with you. Sedley swears he feels ten years younger.' His tone was quite casual. 'I gather you have tired of the delicious Nelly Gwynne, who is now back at the King's House.'

'No, Sire.'

'Eh . . . ?' Charles looked up at him swiftly. 'I thought that you had cast her off.'

Buckhurst shook his head. 'Mistress Gwynne and I no longer keep company, but I fear 'twas the other way about. She left *me*. Cast me off with a kiss and a smile.'

'Why?' His tone was suddenly curt.

Buckhurst blinked, wondering why the King should suddenly be interested in the 'affaires' of his gentlemen. 'Why, I—er—I'm not sure. I *had* thought she had fallen in love with someone else unknown to me. In fact, now I recall it, she said she left me because I did not really need her and she was going to someone who did. Lord knows who—I gather she's not took up with anyone yet.'

There was a long silence, and then Buckhurst heard the King mutter, 'God's bones, what a fool . . . what a damned fool . . .' There was another pause. Buckhurst saw the King's peach lay uneaten before him. Suddenly Charles looked up at the page-in-waiting standing opposite. 'You—what's your name?'

The boy addressed, a willowy youth with spots, stammered, 'V-Villiers, your Majesty, Edward V-Villiers. I . . . I am cousin to my Lady Castlemaine and have only been at Court a week.'

Charles looked him up and down speculatively. 'Have you indeed? Well, Master Villiers, I think I have a job for you.'

Nell soon found that if Tom Killigrew's reception had been one of Biblical forgiveness, that charitable sentiment was not universally held by the rest of the company. John Lacy was as kind as always, for he had a fondness for her; so indeed was Charles Hart, and Bab Knipp was as open-hearted as ever, but Nell knew she had broken one of the most sacred rules of the theatre—she had put her personal life before that of the company. There were those who resented her return; relations between Beck Marshall and Nell had never been cordial and now Beck made her hatred clear. She had been given larger parts during Nell's absence and had nurtured dreams of becoming the leading comedienne of the Theatre Royal. Now in an instant those dreams were shattered and Beck's brain dwelt on revenge.

Her complaints were loud in the Women's Shift. ' 'Tis nothing short of favouritism,' she declared. ' 'Ere's me and Betty Boutel every bit as good as Anne Quin and that slut Nelly, but Madam Fantail only 'as to show 'er nose back again and it's "thank you, Mrs. Marshall" and you're thrown on the streets in naught but your sey petticoat.'

Beck's resentment began to manifest itself in more than

words. Pinpricks of rudeness that Nell could ignore were followed by sudden 'accidents' happening to her costumes and make-up. Twice Nell found her gown had been spattered with mud only minutes before a performance, and once she found a glutinous pool of make-up awaiting her on the stool in her dressing room. Gossip, she knew, followed her down the passage when she left the Women's Shift—all the company believed that my Lord Buckhurst had tired of her and cast her off within weeks of her leaving the stage. Beck sniggered over such a sad ending to 'Madam Fantail's' ambitions and Orange Moll relayed the scandal to those interested amongst the lounging gallants in the fops' corner.

There came no summons from the King, and Nell was conscious of an empty ache inside her, which she did her best to ignore as she flung herself back into the hard work of the theatre. Life was rather lonely. Apart from one quick visit from Rose, who told her in sharp accents that she was 'daft as turnips,' life became a simple matter of bed and work and supper alone with Mit and Toby Phelps.

It was inevitable, of course, that matters between Nell and Beck Marshall must come to a head, for Beck's resentment had become almost obsessional and she was determined on destroying Nell's standing in the company. She waited until the company was due to present a new comedy called *Philaster*, in which—to Beck's chagrin—Nell had been given the chief comedy role, a breeches part, and then she positioned herself in the wings just before Nell's first entrance. As her rival moved forward to enter, Beck craftily put a foot before and a hand behind and pushed so that Mistress Gwynne's first appearance on the boards was with a lurch that landed her flat on her back.

Beck began to giggle hysterically, but Nell's reaction was unexpected. She got to her feet and made as if to retreat off the stage, but instead, moving backwards, she whirled around and dragged Beck by one arm into the centre of the stage under the scrutiny of the entire theatre. Holding her thin arm in a tight grip and before the amazed gaze of Edward Kynaston, she addressed the audience:

'I'd like you all to meet the angleworm that just made me enter on my arse rather than my feet. This'—she shook the offending Beck—'is Mrs. Marshall. You've probably seen her before. She's a bit of a bawd, is Mrs. Marshall, but she's made up her mind that she should be the toast of the Theatre Royal. So far she's ruined two of my best costumes and thrown all my paint around my dressing room to make 'er point.' Nell turned a steely look on the shuffling Beck. 'I think 'tis time that I made a point or two.'

She took hold of the mobcap Beck was wearing, pulled it down over her nose, then in a quick deft movement she turned the girl around and pushed her off the stage with a well-aimed knee in the bottom. Beck sprawled on the boards as Nell had done, and then hurried off, her face crimson—whether from rage or mortification it was impossible to tell.

Later when Nell came off the stage and paused for a word with Bab Knipp in the Women's Shift she found her erstwhile victim waiting for her in the doorway of the tiring room. Beck started when she saw her and moved menacingly forward. Nell looked her up and down. 'If you lay one finger on me, Beck, I swear to God you'll carry the bruises for a week—aye, and scratches too. I have nails as well, you know.'

Beck paused.

'It was your own fault and you know it,' Nell added levelly.

Beck sneered. 'You think you know all the answers, don't you? You only 'ave to come back and you think we should go on our knees and the town conduit should piss claret.' She eyed Nell for a moment, meditating assault, but then decided against it and shrugged contemptuously before slouching off to a stool in the corner of the dressing room.

Bab Knipp, who had watched them with a twinkle in her eye, greeted Nell equably and asked her how the new comedy had been received.

'Well enough, but odsbud, I'm getting tired of these breeches parts.' She chuckled. 'I swear half the men in the pit take me for a man!'

'Then I make no doubt the other half could tell 'em otherwise . . .' came the retort from the corner.

Bab raised her eyes in exasperation to the heavens, and Nell whipped around with a flash of anger. 'Did you say something, Beck?' she asked in a dangerously quiet voice.

'Aye.' Beck turned to the other actresses. 'To hear 'er talk, you'd think she was a countess or sommat. S'life! She strips faster than a snake hoping for a new skin—Charles Hart, my Lord Buckhurst, and all Covent Garden as well, I'll warrant. A pander and a bawd she is, and no mistake! She don't *know* who her father was; her sister's a whore and 'er mother was a whore and so's she!'

Nell threw a stool out of the way and advanced on her enemy threateningly. 'You—you tell me I'm a whore? You who can be debauched by a cup of ale and naught else. God's bones! You're a termagant strumpet—pure whorewood in the grain, you slut. I've only ever been but one man's mistress, even if I *was* brought up in a bawdy house to serve strong waters to the gentlemen, while you're happily mistress to three or four at a time, though a Presbyter's praying daughter!'

Nell was so incensed, and the other ladies of the company of the King's House so intent on watching the confrontation, that no one noticed the arrival of a solitary gentleman until, after two unavailing repetitions, they all became aware of a stuttering voice asking, 'C-can you direct me to M-Mistress Nelly Gwynne?' He saw a girl with a rippling mass of hair and a look of fire in her eyes turn and throw him an irritable glance, and then all at once her eyes softened and she said, 'That is me, sir.'

Nell found herself looking into a pair of sad brown eyes with an expression much like an anxious spaniel's. She noticed that he was somewhat younger than most of the gentlemen usually seen in the Women's Shift and he blushed fierily as he bowed before her. 'M-my name,' he informed her, 'is M-Master Edward Villiers.'

Nell looked, puzzled, at him. 'Have you come to arrange an assignation, sir?' she asked gently.

'No! N-no. That is, have you somewhere m-more private where we can talk, madam?'

Mystified but slightly intrigued, Nell took her visitor along the narrow passage to her tiny dressing room. She shut the door and offered him a stool, upon which he perched uncomfortably. When she enquired his business, the answer astonished her more than ever. In a stammer so pronounced as to be almost unintelligible, the unfortunate Edward Villiers gasped out, 'I w-wondered if y-y-you could c-come to the theatre w-with me t-tomorrow afternoon—t-t-to the Duke's Theatre, I mean, w-with me, and then p-perhaps afterwards we c-could go for supper t-to— Let me perish—where was it?' His face contorted with the effort to remember.

'The Bear tavern or the Three Cranes?' hazarded Nell helpfully.

'No, it was definitely— Ah, I have it! 'Tis the Half Moon tavern in Covent Garden.'

'You wish me to go with *you* . . .' Nell faltered.

Again a blush rose in the gentleman's cheeks. 'Aye. I—I have long admired you, Mistress Gwynne, and I would c-count it an honour if you w-would give me your company . . .'

His voice trailed off into mumbles. Nell considered him shrewdly. He had obviously only just come to London, and she cast a swift look at his clothes and came to the conclusion that he was not overplump in the pocket. He said that he had long admired her and yet he had not even known what she looked like. And yet—as she gave a second glance at him sitting unhappily on his stool—she felt no sinister design could possibly be in his mind. He had obviously checked the playbill, for she was indeed free the next day. A strange curiosity made her desire to find out more.

Edward Villiers, who had begun to eye the door with a dawning wish to bolt for it, was startled when she bobbed a demure curtsey and with a charming smile told him she would be delighted.

The next day—appropriately costumed in a green petticoat of flowered satin with black and white gimp lace and a hat with an enormous ostrich feather perched at a rakish angle—she sallied forth to meet the blushing Master Villiers. They travelled together in a hackney coach to the Duke's Theatre, which stood in Portugal Row at Lincoln's Inn Fields. Nell was amused to see how poor Master Villiers was careful not to press close to her in the coach and how he stammered dreadfully when assisting her to alight at their journey's end. No risk here, she told herself ruefully, of returning home tousled and tumbled—and a little smile hovered about her lips as she remembered my Lord Buckhurst's behaviour in a hackney on more than one occasion.

Politely Villiers ushered her through the entrance of the Duke's Theatre. Then she found, to her surprise, that he was ushering her up the steps that led to the boxes above the stage—the most expensive seats in the theatre. Touched, she plucked at his sleeve and whispered, ' 'Tis very kind, but you know, we'd see just as well in the pit and the cost of a box is fair ruinous.'

Feverishly he disclaimed that it was an expense, and eventually, to save his composure, Nell agreed to accept one of the velvet-covered seats in a private box. To reach it she had to climb an ornate short staircase of gilded wood. As she went up, the pit filled with the usual press of people and a girl walked below selling Portugal oranges. There was a curtain at the top of the steps over the entrance to the box, and she pulled it back.

A pair of dark eyes looked merrily at her; a deep voice exclaimed, 'Cry you mercy for such a long track of dark deceit, Mistress Gwynne.' She looked up at a familiar tall figure, gasped and sank into a deep curtsey. It was the King.

Two

One clasp, one hug, one eager glance was more,
Than worlds of pearl, or heaps of golden ore.
—Sir Charles Sedley

Behind Charles stood the Duke of York, who winked broadly at Nell as she came slowly and dazedly into the box. She saw that they were quite alone and both were dressed incognito; neither the Garter sash nor the George was evident to proclaim the fact that the King was present and the box was a small one at the side, overlooking the stage and out of the vision of most of the pit below. A rueful smile lit up his face as he saw her dismay. 'I beg pardon for our deception, Mistress Gwynne, but to tell true, I had doubts whether you would come if I told you the truth.'

The Duke of York saw the sparkle of amusement in her eyes as she curtseyed, and she threw a saucy glance at the King. 'Aye, I vow and swear I'm ruined. All London knows if the King looks at you in public, you're undone in more ways than one when he gets you in private.'

York's eyes twinkled. Charles seemed unperturbed at this suggestion. 'You've been listening to gossip, Mistress Gwynne. I have heard, however, that Buckingham declares if I'm not the father of my people, at least I must be of a good few of 'em.'

They both laughed, and she sat down on a seat at the front of the box. Edward Villiers hovered uncertainly at her elbow. He seemed sadly embarrassed, and Nell at once took pity on him, patting the seat beside her invitingly. 'Do not go, Master Villiers. Come and sit by me—'Twas *you*, after all, I came to spend the afternoon with.' She turned to Charles. 'Your Majesty has been well served. Such was the gallantry and mysterious allusion of this young man, that I had to come to find out exactly what was going on.'

A bawling hearty voice from the pit floated upward. 'Well, pickle my kidneys in a pisspot, if it ain't that pocket whore from the King's House, Nelly Gwynne! Come ter see some real acting, 'ave you, ducks?'

Nell looked down, grinning, to see one of the lady comediennes of Davenant's company—a fat woman with at least three chins. Leaning over the rail, Nell's voice carried clear across the benches: 'You button your lip, Annie Gibbs, you twice-a-week trull. Why don't you stand up and let six people sit down?'

James, Duke of York, blinked at this minatory speech and Charles smiled his lazy smile as he watched her. 'Might I say how ravishing you are looking, Mistress Gwynne?'

She shook her head sadly. 'I would I could return the compliment, Sire, but truly I cannot. Not in that doublet!'

'Eh?' Charles regarded the green homespun in puzzlement. 'What's wrong with it?'

'*That*,' Nell informed him, 'is *exactly* the shade that turns Sir Charles Sedley bilious. He can't abide it at any cost.'

'I'm so sorry,' he apologised. 'I must remember to avoid it in future. Sir Charles does have unexceptionable taste, I well know.'

Nell attempted some consolation. 'He's not always right, but in this case . . . Well, when you've got tallowy skin it *does* make you look like coffin meat,' she declared consideringly.

'Quite right, Charles,' agreed the Duke of York. 'Thought so m'self when you put it on, but I didn't like to say.'

It was to be borne in upon the King that afternoon that he had a somewhat unusual guest to entertain. Not that she was in any way difficult—she followed the play with polite interest and commented suitably upon any topic of light conversation which he introduced. To all outward respects, in looks and behaviour, she appeared to be a lady of fashion much like any other—this much had Killigrew's training made of her. Yet it was nevertheless evident that underneath lurked a current of frankness wholly unlike any he had met before.

The star turn at the Duke's Theatre was, of course, Moll Davis, who was yet acting though she now lived under the King's protection. Mrs. Davis did not notice that her royal lover was present in a side box when she ran onto the stage in the interval to delight the audience with her dancing. Many eyes in the pit watched her as she began to dance a jig, a roguish dimple in each cheek as she winked at more than one male in the audience.

Nell watched her critically. 'She's a perfect dancer,' she told Charles. 'You can tell the way one movement flows into another. She has a lightness of touch and a grace I could never equal. Of course, she's not got knock-knees like me, but God knows, she has a sense of rhythm few are born with.'

Charles saw no calculated desire to please in Nell's face; her voice was entirely unforced and the comment rang true. With a slight smile on his lips, he thought it unlikely that the talented Mrs. Davis would have been so charitable to a rival. It occurred to the King that the lightness of touch of the adorable Mrs. Davis also included her mental capacity, a lightness palpably not shared by her rival at the King's House.

Neither did the King's guest mince her words. As his eyes raptly followed Moll's slender legs in tight breeches across the stage twirling in a baccarole, he failed to hear Nelly Gwynne's next remark, though she patiently repeated it twice. Then he heard a dry voice in his ear: 'Don't you think, Sire, that one whore in an afternoon is enough for you?' The King looked around to see two hazel eyes regarding him in a straight enquiring fashion. 'You didn't hear me before,' she explained.

'I think my attention wandered a trifle,' he excused himself.

'And your eyes with it,' she added helpfully. 'If you were sitting next to Annie Gibbs down there, she'd tell you you looked like a tomcat in heat. I, of course, would *never* be so rude.'

Edward Villiers goggled at Nell in horror, but the King's reaction was not one of outrage. He threw back his head with a roar of laughter. 'I see you have not changed, Mistress Gwynne.'

Abruptly her face grew pale, and then when she spoke, the words came out so softly that only he could hear them. 'Oh yes I have, Charles.'

He heard the blood dinning in his ears as he placed one hand over hers—a gesture noted by the Duke of York—but his voice too was audible to her alone. 'Do you know, I have waited close on three years to hear you say that?'

Her hand returned his pressure and she coloured delightfully. It was all the King could do not to gather her into his arms there and then.

As they came down the steps after the play was over, Nell heard someone calling her name. 'Nelly! 'Ere, Nelly!'

She looked down, peering into the pit, and then a smile lit up her whole face and she waved to a bent old man pushing his way through the crowd. Charles and the Duke of York watched while she flung herself upon a tattered figure with one leg and a crutch, who, it appeared, was not only a beggar but a friend of some sort. When Nell gestured to Charles and his brother, the King saw the old man shake his head for a moment and throw them a dubious glance, but Nell took him firmly by one arm and brought him over. 'This is a friend of mine,' she said. 'His name's Hobey.'

Charles bowed without a flicker of surprise, as though meeting such people was an everyday experience. ' 'Tis an honour, sir,' he said. 'I am—ah—Master William Jackson and this is—er—my brother.' The Duke of York was less resilient and regarded Hobey's raiment with a fixed stare. 'Just so,' he murmured.

But the beggar had scarcely time to reply, before Nell was at him. 'Where've you been?' she demanded sharply. 'Mit's not seen you for more than a month, and I can see you've not had a good meal in all that time.'

The beggar looked uncomfortable. 'I bin busy, Nelly—couldn't come. Just . . . busy.'

Her eyes narrowed. 'You've not been tooling again, have you?'

'No, I ain't—nor ruffling neither, though I could 'ave done.' He turned on a hurt expression. 'I don't mind admitting I ain't 'ad a grind for two days, Nelly, straight up I ain't, and there's no mort could 'elp it if 'e turned to the tooling trade when the rumblings got to 'is guts.'

'You're a pandarly rogue you are,' she told him roundly. 'We're just off to a tavern for a bite, and I suppose you'd better come.' She turned round to Charles. 'That's all right, isn't it . . . Master Jackson?'

It occurred to the King that whether it was or not, there was little he could do. 'Quite all right, Mistress Gwynne,' he said gravely.

Half an hour later an odd assorted party sat around a table in the Half Moon tavern while a somewhat affronted-looking innkeeper placed a hog's harslet in front of Hobey. While he ate Charles sipped at burnt wine and watched him. 'Would I be right in thinking you're an old soldier?' he asked presently.

Hobey took a pull at his ale tankard, sighed and wiped his mouth on his sleeve. 'Aye, your honour, thass right. I lost this'—he tapped his leg—'with a Frenchie cannonball close on forty year ago.' He belched in satisfaction. 'Now, the present Duke o' Buckingham—well, it were 'is dad that we went with, aye, and I can tell you the ships were rotting at the seams . . .' Hobey continued the story Nell had heard many times before.

Charles listened intently, his dark eyes alight with interest. He looked at Hobey's rags and his crutch propped against the table. 'And what do you do now?' he asked gently.

'I don't do nothing—leastways, there's nothing much I can do. No one will give a man with one leg work while there's two-legged 'uns to do it better. If it 'adn't been for Nelly, I don't mind admitting, I'd 'ave stuck me peg in the wall before now when winter arrived, for that's when the flux takes 'em off—and no mistake. Still I manage. There's always jobs, even if they're not the sort *you're* like to 'ave heard of, with respect, sir—no more'n any 'ave who live around Alsatia.'

'You live at Whitefriars in the sanctuary?' Even the King had heard of the area south of Fleet Street backing onto the Thames, where the constable dared not go and where decaying mansions let off in filthy and insanitary lodgings were the homes of London's criminals and where its worst dens of vice were to be found.

Hobey looked wary, but decided a friend of Nell's could be trusted. 'Sometimes, sir, sometimes not. I go there when I've got sommat for the fences, but there's all sorts in Alsatia; all them what's on the kinchen lay and the toolers and the dippers take what they've got and then there's the shofulmen and the screever morts o' course . . .'

'Of course,' said Charles, bewildered.

'Mind you, there's snoozers a' plenty living outside in the Strand or King Street even, though that's more for the breefers or the huffs and the ivory turners. They pretend they're respectable, but—'

Nell sniffed at her glass. 'Boskey wine,' she said suspiciously. 'I thought it was. They always try it on when it's mulled. You taste, Hobey.'

The beggar sipped, rolled the liquor around his mouth and then spat it out. 'Turnip ale,' he said disgustedly.

'What in heaven's name is boskey wine?' asked the Duke of York.

' 'Tis a fake claret,' Nell explained. 'They doctor it up out of cider re-fermented with turnips and serve it up when they think you've got bosky enough not to notice. You'd be surprised how much purl and mulled wine is made up of turnips.'

'Ah, there's many a secret hidden in a bowl of Bishop puch,' asseverated Hobey. 'Now, old Ma Ross, Nelly, she could mix it so's you'd never know. She was a rum cully o' vinegar she was.'

'Who's Ma Ross?' asked Charles politely.

'Oh, she used to run the bawdy house I worked in till the plague took her off,' Nell explained.

Under probings from Charles and liberal pourings of boskey wine, Hobey began to instruct the surprised King in the doings of a world he had never known existed. He learned that not only was wine faked, but jewelry and gold too. Hobey told him of a certain gentleman who made a rich living selling nitre gold trinkets in the Exchange—'gold' made by boiling iron in vinegar and nitre—and who was a specialist in St. Martin's glass, cleverly faked precious stones made out of tawdry and base metal. He heard of the screevers who could forge any document he could want and the shofulmen whose coins could not be told from the real thing.

It appeared that there were endless ways of making a criminal living. 'There's the Abram men who pretend they're mad, and when people stop to watch their fits their friend in the crowd picks their pockets; and the clapperdogeons who use children and— Oh, you could go on forever,' said Nell.

'They'll even marry you in Alsatia,' Hobey added. 'You find a patricio—that's usually an unfrocked priest like—and he'll marry you over the corpse of a dead 'orse. A cow'd do, but it should be a horse by rights. You shake 'ands with your lady mort and then you're hitched proper as if 'twas in a church.'

'A lot simpler,' agreed the King, his eyes twinkling.

'Mind you, Master Jackson,' Hobey added to Charles, 'it's no joke with Tyburn and the toppin' cove 'anging over you every day, and if you get stretched, who'll feed your kids, eh?'

Nell nodded. 'Like sitting in a pew in thin breeches. They can never rest comfortable, poor devils.'

Having finished his meal, Hobey took his crutch and stood up. 'I've got to go, Nelly.' Charles noticed that though Nell looked at him reprovingly, she did not ask him why. The beggar shuffled off, leaving the King in a reflective mood. 'Where were you born, Mistress Gwynne?' he asked.

Nell told him, and then one question followed another. Charles was a shrewd interrogator, and though his manner was urbane, he extracted all the information he desired about the background and early life of Mistress Nelly Gwynne. She made no attempt to cover anything up or to pretend that she was other than she was, he noticed, and she told her tale without a trace of self-pity but merely in a factual way, as though it concerned someone else other than herself.

In describing the scum of London with whom she had been brought up, she managed indeed to draw shouts of laughter from both the King and the Duke of York, especially when she spiritedly described how she had been trapped behind a dresser in a chamber at Lewkenor's Lane and for the first time had watched, open-mouthed, two people making love. The actress in her enabled her to bring to life the furtive 'prentices and the soldiers and the petty criminals and the roistering gallants she had seen.

Charles and his brother learnt about a part of London they had never visited and only dimly heard of through people like Buckingham and Buckhurst. The King was shrewd enough to see, behind Mistress Gwynne's graphic descriptions of Madam Ross and the bawdy house at Lewkenor's Lane, a poignancy and fear which she did not mention. The Duke of York, an intelligent man, was frankly horrified. 'What a terrible life you have had, child!' he exclaimed impulsively.

She looked surprised. 'Not at all. I was sometimes hungry, but I survived. Far better than being born the daughter of a nobleman and taught to do nothing but stitch and sit simpering behind a fan like a bride with bad teeth.'

Charles regarded her steadily as he sipped at his wine. 'I suppose problems are just what you are used to,' he observed. 'To you and Rose a good meal and a warm bed was riches and no food for the day was poverty. To me riches is a full exchequer, and poverty the necessity to call Parliament to grant me money when my coffers run dry.'

'As they do after Barbara asks you to pay her gaming debts,' added the Duke of York.

Charles sighed. 'That woman alone could bankrupt me. She's a shrew like to a devil—swore she'd slit her children's throats and her own did I not pay a cool five thousand yesterday, and in one of her tempers I verily believe she might. You know, Barbara apart, James, ever since old Southampton died

I've been short. 'Tis always the same—every time you find someone useful, they either turn crooked or die on you. Damned annoying, Southampton's going like that, just when I needed him most.'

A soothing hand poured out a new glass of wine. 'Very inconsiderate, but I dare say he didn't mean it,' Nell said consolingly. He saw she was looking at him with an attempt at innocence, and he pinched her chin. 'I begin to see you are a unique antidote to royal melancholia, Nelly Gwynne.'

The candles crept gradually down in their sockets, and the Duke of York tactfully endeavoured to engage a somnolent Master Villiers in a discussion of hunting, while Charles and Nell sat together sipping at their wine and looking at each other, saying very little. Under the table Charles mischievously stretched out his hand and slid it along one satin-covered leg, and then one of his fingers caught on an obstruction. There was a faint ping, and he looked up, startled, as Nell gasped and then began to giggle.

For a few seconds he watched perplexedly while she shook her head and flapped her hands, and then she gurgled breathlessly, 'Pox take you, you've just snapped my garter, your Majesty.' He felt her hand come down, fumbling. 'Devil take you for a fingering rogue,' came the soft whisper. 'If you're not careful you'll wake up Master Villiers.'

She saw him laughing at her and then, putting one hand in his pocket, he drew out a length of black velvet with a flashing brilliant set in the middle. 'I took this off before I came to the theatre this afternoon.' The candlelight showed the winking of a priceless diamond. 'The most excellent and noble Order of the Garter,' said the King. She felt a hand deftly push up her petticoat, and then he cushioned her foot in his lap while he straightened her stocking and placed the garter around her leg above the knee. His touch was sure and it was swiftly tied. Nell watched him above the table while his hands were busy beneath. 'I have a feeling,' she remarked suspiciously, 'that you've done this before.'

'Ssh,' said the King, 'you'll wake Master Villiers.' He gave her thigh a pat and then replaced her petticoat.

'Well, I hope it keeps my stocking up till I get home, that's all,' she said severely.

Charles's eyes danced. 'Indeed yes, Mistress Gwynne. 'Twould be a tragedy should you lose your stocking in the dark. To say nothing of my—er—garter.'

This drew a reluctant smile. 'You've too much charm, that's your trouble,' she reproved him.

The King looked hurt. 'Can I not sweeten you a little with sugar loaves?'

'Not me.' She regarded him frankly with her expressive hazel eyes, then her hand reached across the table and gripped his reassuringly. 'In truth, Charles, there is no need.'

The Duke of York interrupted their intimacy. 'Charles,' he whispered, leaning across the now-sleeping Master Villiers, 'brother, do you realise we're the last ones here?'

With a grin the King glanced around the empty tavern. The innkeeper was hovering by the door of the taproom, obviously waiting for them to go.

'We'd best be off,' urged the Duke. 'Your people will be falling asleep waiting for you.'

'Not they!' snorted the King. 'You remember I was foolhardy enough last month to appoint Rochester as a Gentleman of the Bedchamber. This week has been his first on duty. First night he turned up pickled, tripped over one of m' spaniels and had to be carried out by m' lackeys; second night he didn't turn up at all; and last night he brought Etherege and Sedley with him with a pair of dice and we were up playing dubblets till dawn, so I scarce got any sleep to mention! Damned fatiguing fellow Rochester, for all his wit, and his pockets are always worse to let than mine, so when he loses you don't get a groat out of him.'

The King's brother was none too keen on Rochester or any other intimate of Buckingham. 'Rochester has tastes beyond his means,' he said austerely. 'He loves wine, women and wealth, in that order. The first aids the second, but alas, saps the third.'

'Erhum!' The King heard a cough at his elbow and found the innkeeper standing awkwardly before him. 'The bill, my masters . . .' he said politely, putting a billet of folded paper on the table between them.

The King and the Duke of York looked at it blankly and then at each other. Charles picked it up and whistled ruefully as he scratched his nose. 'A ten guinea, Jamie—as near to a shade.' He dug first in one capacious pocket and then in another, but brought his hands out empty. 'I haven't a penny groat, brother. Have you?'

The innkeeper sighed and tapped his foot on the floor.

The Duke ferreted amongst his pockets and shook his head. 'Not a bean, Charles.'

The King became conscious of an amused pair of eyes looking at them both, and then a guinea and a small pile of groats were placed on the table. 'That,' Nell informed them, 'is all I can muster, I'm afraid . . .'

The innkeeper looked from one to the other of them and folded his arms belligerently. 'I ain't a' movin' from 'ere till I gets me clinkers,' he announced, and it was notable that his tone was far less respectful than before. Neither the King nor his royal brother was dressed as a gentleman of means, and it was evident that mine host suspected they might well disappear without paying their shot should he turn his back for more than a second. On the faces of both the King and his heir presumptive were expressions of ludicrous dismay.

'Odsfish,' gurgled Mistress Gwynne, looking from one to the other, 'this must be the poorest company that ever I was in before at a tavern!' She glanced across the table and began to gurgle even more. 'There's nothing else for it'—she nudged Charles in the ribs and whispered with wicked clarity—'you'll have to wake up Master Villiers!'

The King was forced to admit there was no alternative, and the Duke of York shook the slumbering Master Villiers into wakefulness. 'I'm so sorry,' apologised the Duke shamefacedly, 'but I'm afraid we seem to have come out without any money. I wonder—er—have you . . . ?'

Under the twinkling gaze of Mistress Gwynne and the

threatening look of the innkeeper, the unfortunate Master Villiers found his pockets being efficiently turned out by his Royal Highness until a further nine guineas was added to the pile on the table.

Nell gathered them up and presented them to their creditor. 'And lucky you are to get them,' she told him. 'Turnip tops is what you're selling, sirrah, and you'll not get me to believe different.'

The landlord confessed himself at some length to be outraged at such a suggestion and his accent was suddenly painfully refined. 'Never would I so demean myself,' he declared. 'H'if you 'ad any taste for wine at all, you would know that *that* was the finest Gascoigne Bordeaux!'

'Pisspots!' said Mistress Gwynne crushingly.

Five minutes later found them all outside the Half Moon tavern, the King's arm firmly tucked in Nell's.

'I wonder if we can procure a hackney at the Maypole at this hour?' pondered the Duke of York aloud.

'I—I have n-no more money, your R-royal Highness,' declared Master Villiers anxiously, obviously fearing that his pockets were again to be rifled.

The King's lips twitched. 'You may rest easy, Master Villiers. You can pay when you get back to Whitehall. I shall not in any case be coming with you, as I intend to escort Mistress Gwynne to her lodgings.'

The Duke of York raised his brows slightly but did not seem unduly surprised. There was a deal of comprehension in his eyes as he remarked lightly, 'I will see you later, then, Charles.'

The King bade farewell to the both of them, with a whispered echo from his fair charge, and then he drew her irresistibly away down the deserted length of Swan Street.

The air was cold and Charles drew up the hood of her cloak, his hand hovering for a second close to her cheek before it dropped away. Her voice when it came from the muffled depths took him by surprise. 'Sire, there was no need to use Master Villiers so. If you had asked me, I should have come.'

Charles looked embarrassed. 'I could not risk it.'

'Risk?'

'I well remember,' he said with a soft laugh, 'what you said last time we met, my dear, on the subject of the arrogance of kings, and 'twas obvious you thought me no exception.'

She threw back her hood, and the King saw that her eyes burned like fire in her pale face. He felt her nails dig urgently into his sleeve. 'Charles, I scarce knew *what* I was saying! Lord! Surely you could see . . . I was as demented as a woman in labour. There was Buckhurst to consider and'—she swallowed—'and if I believed what you said, and I *did* really— And oh, if only you had beat me down instead of letting me argue myself into misery! Don't you understand, pox take you? I *had* to persuade myself you were ruthless and . . . and arrogant and all those other things because I was so scared of my feelings for you. I think I have loved you from the time I fainted in your bedchamber and I was so abominably rude and you were so kind but—but what was I to think? I couldn't believe that you really wanted *me*. You forget—you are the King, the *King*! What could you want with such as me? I was bed sport, a whore from the theatre like those others Chiffinch shows up the back stairs that the gossips of London's bawdy houses whisper of. I loved you—oh, so much—and if you had taken me and then tired of me, I think I should have died of it!'

She saw him blench, and he stopped. Then slowly Charles turned her to face him, and bringing his hands up to either side of her face, with gentle movements he pushed back her hair, damp with the night mist, and she could feel the trembling in his fingers. She saw the pain in his eyes and he looked at her directly. 'I loved you from the first time I saw you,' he said simply. 'But it was not until I met you that night in my bedchamber at Whitehall that I realised how totally unique you were. My dearest, you could not know it at the time, but you gave your Sovereign an enchanting surprise.'

'I seem to remember I was uncommon rude, Charles.'

He snorted reminiscently and she saw the twinkle in his eye. 'Aye, and what a refreshing change it was after the sycophancy and treacle that normally meets me in the Stone Gallery of a morning—honeyed words with naught behind but self-interest and an eye to self-advancement.' He chuckled retrospectively as she walked beside him, his arm tight around her. '*You* weren't seeking to ingratiate yourself—not you! You told me quite clearly what you felt about a king who thought he could buy a woman with tawdries. I doubt whether my regal state impressed you. I have distinct memories of being told what to do with the—er—paraphernalia of royalty!'

'Don't, Charles! I was unspeakably rude and you weren't—*aren't*—that sort of a man. I talked out of pure ignorance. I instantly assumed you were something that you were not—*could* not be—*ever!*'

'I once told my brother women belonged in two categories—either of looks or intelligence, but *never* both.' He glanced down at her ironically. 'I had not made *your* acquaintance then, of course. You raked me down famously!'

'It hardly seems a good reason to fall in love . . .' said Nell, rather surprised.

'But you were quite right, my dear,' he told her, smiling faintly. 'I had been surrounded for so long by lies and deceit that I had forgotten truth could exist, and I had grown weary of searching. It was so much easier to pretend my particular brand of self-pity was a stoical acceptance of reality than to still believe in people, as you do. I—a king—found a girl from the gutter who had had to struggle for everything since she was born had more integrity than I had. A singular discovery!'

She groped for the right words. 'I—I felt you could not ever *want* me for more than a moment's pleasure. You are the King, and I—'

'You are utterly adorable,' said Charles. The next instant she was in his arms, being kissed with such ardour that she felt sure he had crushed all the breath out of her. 'Nelly . . .' he breathed thickly. 'My own . . . at last . . . my own sweet love.' The embrace endured for some time, until indeed the dong of a bell behind them, a lifted lantern and a sibilant 'Gor' s'truth!' from the watchman recalled them to their surroundings. Charles grinned down at her. 'Do you know, I have wanted to do that all evening,' he whispered as he let her go and the watchman shuffled past, muttering.

She smiled up into his softened face; the harsh lines running down from the corners of his nostrils had gone and his sallow features seemed to glow with a new-found youth. 'I knew I couldn't live without you,' she said slowly. 'I knew when you dived into that flaming furnace of a house and I thought I'd never see you again. Oh, Charles . . .' She buried her face in his waistcoat and then looked up, smiling mistily. She stood at least a foot short of his shoulder. 'I shall have to wear stilts whenever I want to kiss you, you know,' she observed, wrinkling her little nose resignedly. 'Lord! You're a positive maypole of a man, Charles.'

'A black man over six feet tall, they said, when they searched for me after Worcester,' he agreed, slipping her arm in his as they strolled down Cradle Alley. 'You must have been smitten indeed, my love, if you fell for me when you saw me during the fire. I must have looked like a fiend out of hell or something worse, I swear. If your friend Hobey had been with you, he'd have warned you off me in straight terms: a rum mort, if not clear gallows meat!'

'Oh, worse! He'd have said you were a ruffler and a reeler to boot.'

'Regarding your friend Hobey's revelations this evening, I have a question to ask, Mistress Gwynne.'

'Yes?' She turned and looked curiously up at him. 'What is it, Charles?'

She saw his dark eyes glowing and felt his hand close strongly over hers under her cloak. 'Mistress Gwynne, as one—er—snoozer to another, tell me, will you be my lady mort?'

She pulled her hand out from under her cloak with his still gripped around it, and lifted them to press a kiss gently onto his fingers. 'Yes, Charles'—the words came low but clear—'yes, Charles, I will.' But then the mischief in her, never far behind, came once more to the fore. 'There's something we must do, however, before we can consider this settled,' she added seriously.

'Oh—what's that?'

He saw her teeth gleam suddenly as she exploded in a peal of laughter. 'We—we must find someone at this time o' night with a dead horse we can borrow!'

The King's deep laughter echoed in the alley, mingling

with hers while they clutched one another in helpless mirth. The moon slid out from behind the clouds in the night sky and bathed the corner of the alley in a pool of light. Nell regarded it thoughtfully and remembered a previous occasion when she had returned home late to her lodgings in Drury Lane. ' 'Tis passing strange,' she observed ingenuously, 'but all my lovers seem to be called Charles. First there was Hart, then Buckhurst. As I have had two lovers of your name before, you will have to be my Charles the Third.'

He smiled appreciatively. 'A damned common name. I apologise for't. I, on the other hand, have never had a lover called Nell before. Nor a lover in *any* way like you, my dearest love.'

Nell seemed suddenly afflicted with a strange shyness. A few minutes later they stopped outside the Cock and Pye. Charles bent punctiliously to kiss her hand. 'I think I had best leave you here, child. Necessity calls me back to royal duty. I must at least pack my gentlemen off to bed and haply attempt to sober Rochester up. Besides, if I stay, you'll think all your *lavish* entertainment this afternoon was but a lure to debauch you after the manner of prodigal kings.'

'Sweetheart'—her eyes filled with tears—'don't go. A pox on necessity—life is made up of more than necessity. We must live, you and I, Charles, and faith, I think we cannot longer live if we are apart one from the other.' Her voice faltered. 'You told me once before I must come to you. I have come, dearest Charles. Will you not stay and be satisfied?' She stretched out one hand, gripping his wrist, and led him behind her up the steps that led to her lodgings. At the top he stopped and she heard his voice, strangely uncertain and trembling: 'Nelly—'

She turned, her hand came up briefly to touch his cheek, and she smiled a tender and loving smile even as she spoke. 'Come, Charles.'

She lit the candles in a branched candlestick that stood on the table, and as the light flared up, the King saw the homely dimensions and plain furnishings of the little bedchamber in which they stood. The soft flame lit up the contours of her face, with its smooth porcelain skin, the heady glow of the night air still upon it, and her cloak hung open to reveal the shape of her body beneath. He moved towards her, bending his face to smell the perfume of her hair, and then impulsively he pulled her to him. At once his gentleness was gone and he pressed hard lips to hers impatiently, pushing open her mouth until his tongue felt the smooth line of her teeth behind.

She stood on tiptoe and kissed him long and lingeringly. Her hands ran down his cheeks gently and then she laid two fingers over his lips and stood back, unlacing her cloak.

Within seconds she stood before him in nothing but her shift. He would have stepped forward and taken her there and then, but she shook her head and then in one movement slid the gathered linen off her smooth shoulders so that it fell in creeping wrinkles to the ground. With a quick toss she let her long tawny hair flow flame-free and it fell in tumbling ripples over her ivory arms and curled in feather tendrils about her. The candlelight filtered over her pale skin and etched an aureole of amber which shimmered above two huge eyes that burned with an inner fire. Charles moved towards her and he heard his own voice as though from a long way away: 'Sweetheart...'

Nell felt his warm breath on her flesh as his hands caressed her body, pressing slowly down the length of her spine. She trembled within his embrace, lifting her face to his in yearning. 'Charles,' she whispered. 'Charles,' and she shuddered as his hands came up over her breasts. In a dream she felt him pick her up and carry her over to the bed.

She lay quite still, her breathing fast and shallow, watching while he hurried out of his clothes. Then he was above her, his elbows imprisoning her as he whispered her name fiercely once. His huge black eyes were lit with such an expression of desire that she shivered before she slipped over the edge of consciousness.

Never before had she felt like this.

Three

*Gay were the hours, and wing'd with joy they flew,
When first the town her early beauties knew:
Courted, admir'd, and lov'd, with presents fed,
Youth in her looks and pleasure in her bed.*

—My Lord of Rochester

It was shortly after dawn in the clean bright freshness of a winter's morning that Nell awoke in the little bedchamber, and as she came to a recollection of the night before, suddenly gasped and turned to see whether it had not all been a dream. The King lay sleeping soundly, one arm flung negligently across the bed, his face turned, oblivious, in sleep towards her. As she propped herself on one elbow and regarded him tenderly, she heard the regular, unhurried pace of his breathing. Without his wig and with his hair curling in dark ringlets short about his ears, he looked at once much younger and more vulnerable. His whole body for once seemed to be in a state of relaxation and a slight smile curved his lips as though his mind dwelt on something of private amusement. His face seemed less sallow and less lined. Looking at him, Nell felt she could see the boy he had once been, and she sighed a little. The King stirred and he opened his eyes to find her looking at him and laughing. 'Give you good day, your Majesty. *Now* I'll cry flounders if ever any subject gave all to the Crown more freely than I have done.'

A smile lit his swarthy features as he stretched languorously. 'Indeed yes, m'dear, but look how long I had to wait for't since I first saw you at Whitehall.'

'The second tasting is often the finer,' she said dulcetly.

'*Not* an apt analogy, Mrs. Gwynne,' complained the King, 'I had scarce a taste before.'

She twinkled back at him. 'But the best wine improves with waiting, Sire.'

He gently twitched down the sheet and looked at her with one eyebrow quizzically raised and a slight smile on his lips. One finger ran carefully down her arm. 'In general, I don't believe in any of these old sayings . . .' He took one of her hands, and lifting it, kissed its palm. ' 'Tis indeed as you say, my dear.'

She nestled up to him, resting her head comfortably in the hollow of his shoulder. 'Well, at least now I know kings are just like other men . . .' She idly wound one of his wiry curls around her finger. 'Or perhaps *more* so in some instances.'

He shook his head. 'Not so, my dear. Kings move in a different world where common things you hardly notice are luxuries beyond their attaining. You know your Shakespeare—"Within the hollow crown that rounds the mortal temples of a king . . ."' He laughed suddenly. 'Odsfish! Do you know I have never been able to *talk* like this before—not to verbally fence, not to say one thing and mean another, not to turn off a compliment with a smile and a veiled insult with the same smile. Who can kings talk to? Not their Court, for their Court is mesmerised by the Crown and scarcely sees the man beneath. Certainly not their families; they are too close to power to be trusted. Perhaps they can only talk to each other, but such is the world in which their Crowns hold sway that *that* most of all is utterly impossible! And so I wait'—his arm came down around her, holding her close, and he nuzzled into her hair—'until I meet a girl who tells me she is from the gutter and informs me I am too drunk to be worth getting into bed with. God help me!'

She twisted in his arms and slowly kissed his chest again and again, moving her lips down his body while her hair in a weeping mass of red gold spread over him like feather down. 'You're not drunk now, Charles,' she whispered. There was a sudden scream as he moved without warning; most of the bedclothes fell onto the floor and there was a deal of disorder beneath the coverlet as limbs threshed about, and she laughingly implored him to let her go. It was in fact a good twenty minutes later that he lay breathing deeply, with Nell curled up loosely in the crook of his arm. 'Odsbud, Charles Stuart,' she murmured lazily, 'you're a tawdry silkman and nothing less. I warrant 'tis your sham address and your cozening ways makes the ladies love you.'

'They love my Crown, sweet Nell, but they don't love Charles Stuart the man. Ah me, I suppose I am an ill-favoured fellow. My mother always said so. She told me she was ashamed of me when I was born. Even my people call me the Black Boy, which is hardly complimentary.' His hand gently fondled her hair. 'I am said to be England's greatest lover, but I have never loved but once and then 'twas my own sister.' He sighed. 'I have read that the gods have always sent us disillusionment to chasten us. It shows us our frailty, how impermanent we are.'

She turned his face to hers. 'I love you,' she said steadily. 'I . . . love . . . *you*.'

His sardonic eyes gazed deeply at her. For a full minute they stared, King and girl from the back alleys, and Charles knew truth, the commodity he had despaired finding in life. 'Aye, I believe you,' he said at last and his gaze dropped away as though he were afraid of what he saw.

'I always will, you know,' she continued quietly. 'Until I die.'

There was a bang as the door of the bedchamber hurtled open, and a voice could be heard from the passage scolding: '. . . How you fall over so many times, Toby, I don't know. Now rub in that lump of fried horse dung and for lor's sake try and keep *out* of the way of coach horses in future and— Bang my lights!' Mit stood goggle-eyed and silenced in the doorway, looking at them.

From the King's point of view, he found himself being inspected by a small female, in mobcap and spotted apron and with a formidable expression, who regarded him coldly. 'Who are *you*?' she asked.

Mit was startled when the large dark gentleman instantly got out of the bed, dragging the coverlet around him, and advanced on her with a dangerous expression. 'Down on your knees!' he rapped out imperatively, and there was that in his voice and manner that somehow Mit did not dare to disobey. 'You heard me. Down, I say!' he repeated sharply, and Mit sank down uncertainly before him, her eyes wide. Suddenly there was a choked gurgle from the bed and Nell's voice broke the tension. 'Mit—er—I don't know quite how to tell you this. But this is his Majesty the King.'

Mit gazed up at the towering figure clad in the coverlet and saw his eyes twinkling down at her. Her mouth opened and closed twice. 'You—you're not, are you?' she ventured at last in a whisper.

The large gentleman smiled ruefully. 'I'm afraid I am,' he said and stretched out a capable hand to aid her to her feet. Gradually her eyes took in the contours of his face and she saw his wig tossed on the table behind.

'Bloody 'ell!' she ejaculated faintly. 'You are an' all . . .'

It was not long before London had learnt the news of the King's new relationship with Mrs. Nelly Gwynne of the King's House. From mouth to mouth, behind many a whispered hand, the gossip travelled down the winding length of Drury Lane, filtering along the Strand to the ever-ready ears of the Whitehall galleries. My Lady Castlemaine was heard to laugh gently and prophesy there would be many such and another before the month was up, she doubted not. But it was to be noted that Buckingham's spies told him Castlemaine waited in vain for a visit from the King and wept in secret fury.

In Nell's own world of the theatre the tidings were received with incredulous delight. Tom Killigrew, puffed up like a turkey cock, told Lacy grandly that now there was *nothing* in which the Theatre Royal could not boast of having bested the

Duke's. He fell to planning grandiose and lavish entertainments, secure in a new royal patronage such as he had never known before. Lacy remarked sarcastically that one might suppose 'twas Killigrew himself who had been bedded by the King! But he smiled in friendly fashion upon Mistress Gwynne and told his cronies at the Rose tavern that his Majesty had ever been noted for his good taste. When Nell appeared on the stage she was greeted with redoubled affection, and crowds packed in to see the actress who had captured the eye of the King.

As Bab Knipp sagely commented, seeing her sovereign surrounded by his Court in the royal box at the Theatre Royal, 'twas no wonder the affair was common knowledge, since his passion was writ on his face as clear as cockbroth.

Nell delighted Charles and captivated him utterly. And he continued to find her surprising. When he implored her to give up the stage and live at once under his protection, she shook her head resolutely and he saw the sparkle in her expressive hazel eyes. 'No, Charles,' she said firmly. 'I want to be your lover, not your pensioner, my darling.' She was equally adamant about accepting money from him. 'I do not need it,' she told him. 'I'm an actress, and Master Killigrew gives me plenty for my needs.' To his amazement she would accept only the odd piece of jewellery: 'Save it till I'm old and hagged and need tawdries to dress up the wrinkles.' She would laugh and kiss him even as she repulsed the trinket he had offered. In all his life Charles had never met a woman like her.

She came to see him at Whitehall, as she had done before, and the first time she found herself again on the landing stage of the Privy Stairs, she thought she caught the veriest suspicion of a wink from the discreet Master Chiffinch before he showed her up to the royal apartments. On one occasion Charles was slightly offended at the casual state in which she visited him, for Nell always came just as she was and it did not occur to her that she should dress up to see him. 'I come to see *you*,' she said, puzzled, and he watched with amusement at the way her little nose wrinkled. 'Anyway,' she finished wickedly, 'there's not much point in wearing anything special, as I never have it on for long, do I?'

Charles coughed. 'I think you'd take the common tilt boat for an eight-penny ride to Whitehall, if I let you!' he expostulated, torn between exasperation and laughter.

'And good company I should have on the way,' she retorted blithely.

Charles had to accept that she was as she was, and he had no wish to change her. Nevertheless, Nell was soon to discover that being the King's mistress was somewhat different from any other man's. Her first inkling of this came in the shape of a gilt-edged card of invitation delivered to her lodgings one morning by a small blackamoor page in a resplendent green turban. When she saw the inscription upon it Nell was startled. 'God in heaven!' she exclaimed, and Mit asked what ailed her.

' 'Tis an invitation from his Grace the Duke of Buckingham,' said Nell in a faint voice. 'He begs the honour of my company at a supper party he is giving next week at Buckingham House.'

Mit was not impressed. 'Never could stand him. Fat as a malamucca melon, 'e is,' she said witheringly. 'Great slimy toad. Fair fancies 'isself. I remember when 'e used to come to Lewkenor's Lane of a night. Do you remember, Nelly, he came that night when—'

'But what'll I wear?' Nell interrupted her distractedly. 'I suppose Charles asked him to invite me, but I've nothing fit to be seen in. Lord! Half of Whitehall will be there and there's naught but the flowered satin and *that's* got a wine stain on it and 'tis in three days' time . . .'

Mit squashed the problem simply. 'Seems to me once you've lain with the King, Duke ain't much to scratch over nohow, even if he is big enough for two. Anyway, you can get yourself fitted up at that ladies' tailor in Tower Street where Mrs. Knipp goes.'

So indeed it proved. Three nights later found Nell, demure in white taffeta, but inwardly quaking, passing through the tall double doors that gave entrance to the Duke of Buckingham's apartments while a lackey sonorously announced her name. It seemed to Nell that the lofty room was already crammed with periwigged gentlemen and half-naked ladies seductive in careless silks and velvets. The babble of noise was tremendous, and she stood uncertainly on the threshold until the rustle of silks and the withdrawing of the press of people revealed Charles, with Buckingham at his side, striding forward to greet her with the old warm smile she knew so well. Though all eyes now turned in her direction, Nell felt no fear as she curtseyed and then rose, smiling, while Charles tucked her arm in his and turned to introduce her to Buckingham, who greeted her with a bow as deep as if she were a duchess born. 'I am pleased to see you again, your Grace,' she responded politely.

Charles's brows rose. 'Again?'

Nell gave a chuckle. 'You must know, Sire, that his Grace and I are already intimate. Our acquaintance stems from my dissolute days with another Charles, your predecessor.' She turned to Buckingham. 'Incidentally, how is my Lord Buckhurst, your Grace? I haven't seen him for an age.'

'Tolerable.' Buckingham grinned. 'You must know that your parting company with him drove him to Madam Buley's for comfort, where, he says, he has been languishing in the company of ladies with no more warmth than a coven of crocodiles. But I dare swear he'll come about. Possibly 'twas a blessing in disguise.' He looked meaningfully at Charles. 'His cronies Sedley and Etherege went out on the town last night with Vaughan, and I hear they made a night of it. Two watchmen with broken heads and Vaughan was clapped in the lockup.'

Charles smiled. 'I'll warrant if Rochester and Harry Savile hadn't been in attendance on me last night, they would have joined him.'

'Undoubtedly,' agreed Buckingham in bored fashion. 'Savile has always had such a damned bad sense of timing. Who else, I ask myself, could be so ill-bred as to contract the great pox when the Dutch were at our doors.'

'Disliking so many people, as you do, George, I think I should feel honoured indeed that *I* was invited,' remarked Charles blandly.

Buckingham's lips tightened, but he forced them into a

smile, and lifting Nell's hand, bestowed a kiss upon her fingers. 'The honour is rather mine,' he drawled, 'to receive such beauty in my humble abode. I declare, madam, you are the fairest offering here tonight.'

Nell blinked. His Grace was obviously in affable mood. Charles nodded to Buckingham easily and guided Nell across the room to introduce her to various notables present at the soirée, beginning with a tall, handsome, dark gentleman in slashed purple velvet.

'This is my Lord Worcester, my Lady Southesk, my Lady Falmouth, my Lord Plymouth, my Lord Orrery, Sir Francis Clinton, my Lady Silvis, Lord Henry Howard . . .' Their names were softly intoned in her ear as she curtseyed to each one, and the list seemed endless. Nell was secretly amused to see how they reacted to her. As the King stood at her side, none could do other than betray polite compliance, but she was interested to see the emotions mirrored at the back of their eyes. The gentlemen in general gazed at her in frank admiration and she caught more than one of them in an open wink. But the ladies were decidedly less friendly. Nell was greeted with stiff curtseys and slight nods that indicated a barely concealed hostility. Regarding the resentful expression on Lady Silvis's thin acidulated countenance, Nell knew the thoughts running through that lady's mind. 'Aye, you'd love to tell me that I'm naught but a common stage strumpet, wouldn't you?' she thought as she murmured her delight at making her ladyship's acquaintance.

As the King took her away a curious exception came into Nell's mind. 'Where is the *Duchess* of Buckingham?' she asked Charles. 'I don't recall having been introduced to her. Is she here?'

Charles leant slightly towards her. 'I think it would be as well not to mention her tonight, m'dear. George and she are not upon the best of terms, largely because of that lady over there.' He nodded quickly at a strikingly beautiful girl in black velvet who was laughing and flirting seductively with her fan in the midst of a group of gentlemen in the corner. 'She is the cause of the trouble,' the King went on. ' 'Tis Anna

Maria, Countess of Shrewsbury. A flirtatious wench, but she and George are—'

'I see,' said Nell.

'All the world knows she's Buckingham's mistress save poor old Shrewsbury himself, it seems. There was some trouble last year, I seem to remember, but she managed to convince Shrewsbury 'twas all nothing but malicious gossip. I wonder how long 'twill be before he finds out; George was never noted for his adeptness at intrigue. Now let me take you over to have a word with James, Nelly. He swears he must redeem himself after his recent impecunious disgrace!'

'Aye, I meant to dun him for the guineas I lent him,' she said smilingly.

The King strolled with Nell over to the chimney piece where stood his Royal Highness the Duke of York, hovering protectively behind a slender pale lady who was seated by the fire. James was pleased to see them and nodded in friendly fashion to Nell before turning to introduce his companion. 'Might I present Mistress Arabella Churchill, Mistress Gwynne.' The two ladies kissed, as was the custom, and as she did so Nell noticed that one of the Duke's hands lay caressingly on the shoulder of Mistress Churchill.

Arabella expressed her pleasure in making Nell's acquaintance. 'I have seen you before at the theatre, of course,' she confided in a soft voice. 'I must tell you how much I enjoyed *The Humorous Lieutenant*. Ja— That is, his Royal Highness was kind enough to take me, and I could scarce breathe for laughing!'

'We found the same during rehearsals,' Nell agreed. 'Master Fletcher must have split his sides writing such stuff.'

'Odsfish,' interposed Charles, 'look who's arrived—thunder and lightning together.'

My Lady Castlemaine, magnificent in furred sapphire velvet, stood haughtily on the threshold, her hand resting on the arm of the felinely graceful Earl of Rochester, who murmured something into her ear at which she threw back her head in a burst of laughter.

'Calls himself a poet,' snorted Charles appreciatively. 'Scurrilous rogue more like. I wonder the paper don't blister and burn.'

It was not more than a few moments before Barbara saw the King and his brother and bore down upon them purposefully, with Rochester languid at her heels. When she reached the King she sank into the deepest of curtseys. 'Sire.'

Casually Charles waved her to her feet and nodded familiarly at Rochester. 'Well, at least I won't be bored tonight, Wilmot,' he commented jocularly. 'I can't promise I'll be pleased exactly, but that's another thing. Who knows,' he observed drily, 'if you stop at the second bottle we might even survive the evening without broken heads or lacerated tempers. I had better present you to Mistress Gwynne here before you disappear to the gaming tables, I suppose.' Rochester bowed, and then the King reluctantly performed the same office of introduction to Barbara.

My Lady Castlemaine coolly surveyed Nell and her brows rose a trifle; she gave the barest nod before turning to Charles. Barbara held her fan in such a way as to exclude Nell from her conversation with the King. 'Sire, such a provoking thing! I left early this evening, but all the traffic was stopped by your little friend Mrs. Davis—'

'How so?'

There was a glitter in Barbara's eye. 'The axle on her coach broke and the whole thoroughfare was held up until they could drag it out of the way into the courtyard of the Bell tavern. But the costume she had on when she climbed out of the coach! The hussy was barely dressed! 'Twas no more than a wisp of satin and hardly covered her at all and there she was waving at all the chairmen and the carriers, and then, while we were *still* waiting, she had the impudence to lift her skirt and do a jig on the cobbles, which of course amused them all vastly. 'Twas a clear hour before we could get on our way again. But there—what else can you expect from an *actress* who's used to showing herself to all and sundry on the stage? 'Tis little better than a bawdy house. I would not be seen so by any man living.'

'There must, then, be many dead men in town.'

Barbara's fan dropped with a swish and she stared furiously at Nell.

'Your la'ship will forgive my straight speech, I know, as I too am an actress and, alas, know no better.' Nell slipped easily into the childhood accents of St. Giles. 'Lor', ma'am—or your ladyship, I *should* say—there's so much to *remember* when you come into company with great ladies like yourself.' She sighed mournfully. 'You must tell me if I forget myself and start to scratch my armpits in public. I have *tried* to leave off doing it, but I keep forgetting, so do feel free to drop me the wink.'

Rochester guffawed quite audibly behind his hand, and the King's face lost its thunderous expression as Barbara flushed with anger. With the briefest sketch of a curtsey, she flounced off without another word.

'Odsbud, what a viper the lady hath become,' murmured James. 'And her beauty sadly faded too. They say she's getting desperate now—seduces her men lovers by barter and pays pages to take as spoon meat.'

Rochester was unmoved. 'She's as insatiate as the sea. Who could love such a shrew?'

'I did . . . once.' Charles looked after her with a kind of pity in his eyes. 'Poor Barbara.'

'Lord, sir, love is like the smallpox—'tis best got over while young,' declared Rochester carelessly.

'Mistress Gwynne does not agree with you,' pronounced the King. His eyes were brimful of amusement as he looked at Nell. 'She holds love is like a wine that grows the finer with waiting.' He winked at her.

'But then, a gentleman expects to sample a bottle of wine before he buys it. An interesting philosophy, Sire.' Rochester looked quizzically at Nell. 'Strange ideals to come from the boards of Drury Lane.'

'Strange cynicism to come from one so young,' Nell countered lightly. 'You talk like an old man sick of the sighings.'

'Lord! I've wind like a breeding woman,' interrupted the Duke of York. 'Perhaps we could partake of some supper now!'

The banquet was lavish. In a long apartment hung with

damask the company addressed itself to pigeons a l'estuve,
baked cheewits, tansies of eggs and walnut and nutmeg, pre-
served fruit quinces, wet and dry suckets and wafer cakes, with
any number of side dishes to choose from. Nell was hardly
able to exchange more than a word with Charles. The huge
and monopolising figure of his Grace of Buckingham arrived
at Charles's elbow and remained there. Neither Charles's detached disinterest nor Nell's growing irritation was able to
remove him. The Duke was anxious to make the most of this
opportunity of having his sovereign, as he thought, in a relaxed mood to plant a few useful seeds to bear fruit in the
future.

'It has seemed to me, Sire,' he remarked suavely, 'that perhaps the present Council is a little too large. 'Twould be best,
methinks, to make a clean sweep now that the Chancellor hath
gone. The Duke of Ormonde now—'

'—has been a loyal servant to the Crown these thirty years
and more,' Charles said, reaching across for a slice of pigeon.

'Indeed yes,' agreed Buckingham hastily. 'None could gain-
say his past services. Yet he grows old, as the Chancellor did in
his thinking. Ods my life, 'tis like a walnut sitting opposite
one in Council.'

'Cunning and wrinkles go together, my lord. I would not see
him dismissed if that be your sole objection.'

Buckingham was not to be thus easily rebuffed. 'I cannot
help feeling that there is not enough *unity* in the Council,
Sire. The Commons murmur against men like Clifford and
Arlington—Papists both!'

'I have heard whispers in the galleries, your Grace, that you
and Arlington do not—ah—agree too well. Indeed, I hear you
have told him to his face that he is—ah—"a consequential
boot licker." ' Charles appeared to be intent on carving a
capon. 'Methinks perhaps this is why there may be a lack of
unity, if indeed there is such a lack. What think you, your
Grace? Do you have aught against my Lord Arlington?'

Buckingham tapped irritably with one of the new French
forks on his plate. 'May I be frank, your Majesty?'

Charles raised his brows ironically. ' 'Twould be a refreshing change, I think. You feel perhaps that my Lord Arlington is lacking in some way.'

'He has no more breeding than a bum bailey,' declared Buckingham explosively. ' 'Tis a country gentleman up to town in his coronation breeches. A damned lawyer like Clarendon was, he turned up the other day to the Queen's Drawing Room in a jackanapes coat and silver buttons, looking for all the world like an apothecary. I would not have your Majesty served by such.'

'Who would you have my Majesty served by?' enquired the King mildly. 'I cannot see that I should turn off my ministers for their dress sense any more than their age. You warn me against Clifford, you dislike Arlington and despair of Ormonde. It seems'—the King paused reflectively—'that soon there will be naught left on the Council save yourself.'

Buckingham looked at him quickly. It was at times like this that he found himself at a loss. He did not know whether the King was mocking him or agreeing with him. Charles's expression gave him no clue. 'My whole aim is but to serve your Majesty—' he began.

'No, George,' said Charles gently. 'It would not do.'

'Your Majesty?'

The King turned and looked at him. Buckingham thought he could see a gleam of understanding in Charles's dark eyes, yet when the King spoke, his voice was quite pleasant. 'You must not overtax yourself, George. I am persuaded that in your zeal you might easily . . . overreach yourself, and then your health might so easily suffer.'

Baffled, Buckingham stared at him. Was the King giving him warning to cease his desire for supreme power?

Charles watched him shrewdly. 'You know what at this juncture you ought to do, George?' The Duke shook his head —and then, to his surprise, found a glass of canary pressed into his hand. 'Go and give this to my Lady Shrewsbury,' said the King affably. 'I noticed not a moment since, her glass is quite empty.'

There was nothing for Buckingham to do but obey. With a low laugh, Charles watched him go. 'Poor George,' he murmured, 'how *annoying* you must find me.'

Nell meanwhile, tired of Buckingham's ceaseless slandering, had withdrawn to a window seat, whence she was almost instantly joined by my Lord of Rochester, who asked her permission to sit down. Nell soon found that this lounging gallant at her side had a tongue quite as mischievous as Buckingham's. His clear blue eyes slid smoothly from one group to another, and Nell found the information he imparted in irreverent comment on the world he inhabited quite as scandalous as it was wholly intriguing. She could not resist plying him with questions. 'Who is that lady with Mistress Churchill?' she asked. 'She looked at me as if I stank worse than Shoreditch dirt.'

'Lord! That's only Lady Silvis. All Whitehall knows of her temper. I'd as soon kiss her lap dog—it has sweeter breath. She delights in trouble—tongue like a swordstick, I give you my word. She's trying to coax Arabella Churchill with canary so she will be a little indiscreet about York, if I guess aright. A nose for scandal like a bloodhound Silvis has got. Lives on spirits of hartshorn so they say, which, I suppose, accounts for her expression.'

'Is Mistress Churchill—er—?'

'Faith yes, all the Court knows that! York's amours are always common knowledge. She's hardly the first. There was Lady Southesk—that one in the hideous puce gown—and Lady Denham—her husband poisoned *her* of course. And then there was Lady Robartes and Lady Chesterfield before Arabella Churchill ever came on the field.'

'That gentleman—Lord Henry Howard, is it?—seems to be mighty struck with her, at all events.'

'Pho!' Rochester sounded amused. 'He'd never get his hand under the petticoats; he's no more gumption than a flea. Poor old Howard's only got one claim to fame. He's the brother of the premier Duke of England, and *he's* as mad as a March hare. They've got him locked in an asylum in Italy.'

Nell sipped at her wine while Rochester talked. Evryone, it seemed, was the enemy of someone else; everyone was aiming at removing someone else who stood in his way. She sighed. 'It all sounds very fraught. I think yonder old gentleman has the best idea.'

Rochester laughed as they looked at a fat old man asleep and snoring in the window seat opposite. 'Poor old Morrice. He always falls asleep. I can't think why the King keeps him on. You wouldn't think to look at him that he was one of the two principal secretaries of state, would you? And Nicholas his partner's no younger. There's too many old men at Whitehall,' declared Rochester. 'The Council's still bedevilled with old thin-thatchers like Ormonde who block everything just because it's new.' He turned his head to look at Nell. 'You know, you ought to suggest to his Majesty that he pension Ormonde off.'

Nell looked uncomprehendingly at him. 'I? I have no say at all!'

'Oh, come, Mistress Gwynne. Ladies in your position—and I use the term advisedly—always have a peculiar influence.' He became aware of a frosty glare in her eyes.

'I think not, my lord.'

Rochester giggled irritatingly. 'We all try to get our share of the royal ear, you know. Why else do you think Buckingham is giving this party? 'Tis only to cement his seat on the Council and persuade Charles he is a trustworthy successor to Clarendon. All the world knows the Villiers ambition.' He looked meaningfully at her. 'A king may well, in fact, be more amenable to a lady's soft persuasions than to a man's sound advice. The fruits of love, you know.'

'It doesn't sound much like love to me,' retorted Nell coldly. All at once she saw through his smooth suggestions. Now she knew why Buckingham had invited her this evening and why he had been so affable. 'Buckingham told you to sound me out, didn't he? You said everyone at Whitehall needs a friend or two. Haply you need Buckingham for a friend and this is how to make certain of it. Aye, I know how the mind of a slug like Buckingham works. Another royal mistress, another handhold to grope for power between the sheets of a royal bed!'

Rochester's expression did not change by so much as a flicker. 'My dear Mistress Gwynne—' he began in pained protest.

'You button your lip, you tawdry silk merchant, and listen

to me! I love Charles—do you understand? I said *love*, and that doesn't mean love only as long as I can get what I want out of him or in order to get me a coach and four. As long as Charles needs me I shall stay with him, and that's all. Devil take you—I've not even arrived at Whitehall yet and already you're trying to drag me into your dirty intrigues. I won't have anything to do with it. You tell your friend George to go and piss in the gutter!'

Rochester looked straight back at her. 'I'll tell him. But, Mistress Gwynne'—she had risen to her feet and was about to leave him—'before you go, let me give you some advice. Our Sovereign Lord the King has not the reputation for constancy; his affairs are more numerous even than York's, if more discreetly conducted. All women think they can reform a rake, and 'tis the commonest folly of female kind. How long will he love *you*, my dear? As long as he did Lucy Walter or Castlemaine? Perhaps a little longer, who knows? And then what? What when he leaves *you* as he left them? Learn a little from the rapacious Barbara, my child. Get what you can while you can, for your day of glory may not be a long one. Virtue and honesty may be admirable, but Whitehall strangles both in minutes. I should hate to see you strangled, Mistress Gwynne.'

Her expression was contemptuous. 'Where I come from, *my Lord Rochester*, you have to fight to survive. I doubt not I can as well fight here as I have elsewhere. As far as being strangled is concerned, I believe I have a strong neck.'

Her eyes pricking with angry tears, she left him and went to find Charles. She found him seated at a table in the card saloon playing sice-ace with York, the Earl of Orrery and my Lady Castlemaine.

Barbara was shuffling the cards and looking at the King pettishly. 'Honestly, Sire, you must move Annesley to other apartments further from mine. He keeps me awake at all hours with his carousing and I keep bumping into him in the corridor, where he proses on for hours talking of nothing but card games which he lost and his gout.' She took a small pile of guineas. 'You can scarce tell what he says, for his teeth have all fallen out and he stinks like the Fleet ditch.'

'I'll do what I can, Barbara. A pity Mr. Jermyn is such a light sleeper.' Charles looked weary and morose, and then became aware of Nell standing by his side. All at once his brow cleared. 'I fear your friend Hobey would not approve of this.' He smiled. 'Such dubious company. He'd warn me to watch out for—ah—*breefers*, I fancy, even if I'm not a coll precisely.'

She smiled back. 'Not to mention huffs or filers, Sire.'

He surveyed her shrewdly. 'You look in a devil of a temper, Nelly. Is aught amiss?'

She shook her head quickly. 'Nay, a slight headache. Naught else.'

He looked as if he would say more, but Barbara interrupted, cutting across them: 'Heaven forbid *I* should ever cause mischief, Sire, but really—'

'I scarcely think heavenly assistance will be necessary, m'-dear Barbara,' snapped the King. 'The very air of Whitehall breathes it.' He got up from the table and turned to Nell. 'Come, my dear, let me get you a glass of malmsey and then I think you should go home.'

Gratefully she slid her arm into his and he took her out of the card saloon, only to bump into a small wizened gentleman who bowed and then said hastily, 'Might I have a word, Sire? 'Tis an urgent matter of some importance. Let me perish if I should incommode you, but I find I have been grossly slandered.'

Nell saw the look of impatience cross the King's features, and then Charles pulled out his watch. 'Come and see me tomorrow at noon, Clifford. Whatever the slander is, 'twill have to wait until then.'

Sir Thomas Clifford drew closer. He seemed quite agitated. 'B-but, your Majesty, it has come to my notice that his Grace of Buckingham has—not to put too fine a point on it—been spreading rumours about me concerning my integrity. Let me perish if I may not clear my name in your Majesty's good opinion.'

Charles looked resigned. 'His Grace of Buckingham always has spread rumours about other people's integrity and probably always will. Both you and I, however, know better than to listen to them. I bid you good even, sir.' The King walked away quickly before Clifford could delay him further. 'A loyal servant to the Crown,' he whispered to Nell, 'But I confess at times he makes me fussy as a cat does a canary. "Let me perish" he always says, and I must admit there are times when I'm tempted.'

Nell felt an overwhelming desire to leave this room full of tensions and veiled threats. Behind each smiling face there appeared to be nothing but cynical calculation and hypocrisy; under the jewels and the scent and the finery, nothing but the law of the jungle. She said as much to Charles.

The King laughed. 'Aye, 'tis true they're nothing but walking scent bottles. Wring them out and in most cases there'd be naught left but the vapours.'

All at once the subdued level of conversation was broken by the sudden opening of the tall gilt double doors at the end of the room. A figure still in hat and cloak stood motionless upon the threshold. He was not dressed for company, wearing riding dress with boots splashed with mud and a hat from whose feather the raindrops still dripped. His eyes swept quickly over the company and came to rest upon the lovely face of my Lady Shrewsbury, who, appalled, stared at him from where she sat with the arm of the Duke of Buckingham still openly about her waist. The silence in the chamber was such that the intruder's quick breathing was quite audible to Nell's ears.

He paced into the room, tapping his riding switch against his leg, and walked straight up to where Anna Maria sat. 'My lady,' he said quite clearly, 'you will come with me.'

His wife flushed scarlet at this public humiliation and Buckingham lounged to his feet. 'I believe the lady will stay here,' he drawled insolently. 'My lackeys will show you out.'

The Earl of Shrewsbury glared at Buckingham. 'I believe I have the right to command my wife.' His hand shot out and dragged Anna Maria to her feet.

Buckingham's hand closed over the Earl's. 'You whoreson cur! Get out of my house before I kick you out!' he snarled. Deliberately he paused and then spat full in Shrewsbury's face.

Anna Maria gasped as her husband pulled himself free and raised his riding whip to slash at the Duke's face. Nell heard Shrewsbury's voice, harsh and hysterical: 'God curse you, you have no right—'

'My lord!' Charles's deep voice echoed across the room. The King walked over to where they stood and offered his arm to Lady Shrewsbury. 'Damned fatiguing, these gatherings,' he said pleasantly. 'Your ladyship must allow me to conduct you to your coach.' He glanced quellingly at the two men, and then, before the assembled company, the King strolled out of the room with the Countess upon his arm.

Having hustled an embarrassed Anna Maria into her coach, Charles returned to the supper room to find Nell waiting for him. She cocked a quizzical eyebrow. 'I see how right you were, Charles.'

He grinned. 'Right about what, my dear?'

'You said we had more in common than I thought. Pox take them, I can see no difference at all 'twixt your Court at Whitehall and my bawdy house at Lewkenor's Lane!'

Winter passed agreeably. It was not as severe as the one that had gone before and life in the capital had begun to return to normal. The blackened ground where the fire had ravaged a twelvemonth earlier was now cleared and houses sprang up once more on Ludgate hill around the ruins of Old St. Paul's. A new skyline began to emerge. Despite the injunctions of the King and Council, many little streets and alleys grew again in the same narrow winding patterns as before, but his Majesty spent many hours closeted with Dr. Wren, poring over grandiose and spectacular plans for the building of a fine new city radiating out from the hub of a new Royal Exchange, whose foundation stone the King laid himself. London was spreading westwards; from off St. James's Street, wide stately avenues were planned, with raised pavements to protect pedestrians from the splash of mud from coach wheels. Many members of Charles's Court enthusiastically planned the construction of new mansions—houses of brick, with elegant stone facings, to be built in the squares and piazzas of Wren's devising.

To Londoners it was a time of reassurance; they could see that the King's promise was being made good as London rose again from the ashes. The Guildhall, centre of the city, which had been badly damaged by the flames, was repaired and reopened, only the stains of soot on its frontage a reminder of the disaster which had occurred.

Not everyone was pleased at the character of change. My Lady Castlemaine, furious at her fall from royal favour, sought solace in gaming and astonished even the Court by winning £15000 in one night, only to lose £25000 on the next. It was as if a shadow had passed from off the face of England. Crowds flocked again to the theatre, where Mr. Pepys could be found eying the ladies from his seat in the pit and dallying after the play was over in the company of Bab Knipp, an occupation which his wife knew nothing of.

Comedy in the persons of Mistress Nelly Gwynne and Charles Hart nearly brought the house down at the Theatre Royal, where in *The Mad Couple* the two proved yet again what magic they could produce between them. Life was not without its own humour—the mother of a child whom Hart had introduced to the stage and who cried a little too realistically jumped up onto the boards before the whole audience and smacked Hart soundly on the ear before marching off in high dudgeon, to the delight of all save the afflicted actor.

The King's friends were surprised at the enduring nature of his passion for a mere actress. Apart from the Queen, whom Charles never treated with anything but kindness, he seemed to have eyes for none but Nell, and indeed often refused the invitations of Buckingham or Rochester to keep an assignation in the city with her. The Court was amazed and bewildered, though Sedley and others declared that Mistress Gwynne was as unlike Moll Davis as an oriental pearl to a dead whiting's eye.

His Grace of Buckingham was not impressed. 'A refreshing change, I grant you,' he conceded magniloquently, 'but hardly likely to last. 'Tis a fancy and nothing more. Like water after wine—good as a physick but not enough, I think, to sustain life.'

As the weeks became months, with no sign of a slackening in

the King's ardour, it seemed as though his Grace might for once be wrong. Mistress Gwynne became a regular attender at the King's supper parties, and it was seen that though she had rejected his intrigues, even the Duke could be brought to smile when she sat upon his knee and patted his stomach, telling him that his whores got more for their money than any in London. The King found her lightness of touch a refreshment on more than one occasion. It was now common knowledge that his Highness of York had embraced the faith of his intellectual wife and become a Catholic, and his passion for his new religion, constantly proselytised, soon became obvious. The King found it wearisome and worrying—he had to face the fact that unless he divorced the Queen, he was unlikely to have a legitimate heir, and the thought that James must one day occupy the throne made him fear for his dynasty. Charles doubted that Catholic-hating England would ever stand having a Papist for its monarch.

Mistress Gwynne was perplexed and aghast to hear James's views on life. He spent all one evening boring the King and herself with warnings on the peril of their souls, and as Nell told Charles crossly later, quite put her off her dinner. 'Our souls,' the Duke told her in a sepulchral voice, 'are but vessels carried in the stinking carcase which we inhabit on earth.' To his surprise, Nell burst out laughing and then dug him in the ribs with a chicken bone she was gnawing. 'You speak for yourself,' she said in outraged tones. 'I'm quite happy with mine, and anyway, I had a bath only this morning!'

James looked shocked, but the King gave a bark of laughter and patted her knee. 'Quite the loveliest carcase I've seen in years!' he agreed warmly.

Nell shook her head gravely at the Duke of York. 'You know, if you go on like this, you'll turn the wine to vinegar. Do you have to be such a dismal Jimmy?' Ever afterwards, both Nell and the King found it difficult to think of the Duke of York in any other terms, though, as Charles thought gloomily, it was hardly a laughing matter.

Try as he would, however, Charles could not persuade Nell to give up the stage and live as befitted her new station in life.

Though she was pleased to see gallants like Rochester or Sedley and have supper with the King and his cronies, what she had seen of the world of Whitehall at Buckingham's soirée had filled her with repugnance. It was not, she told Charles, her world; she was at home in the Cock and Pye, in the world of Drury Lane and the theatre, where she belonged, with people she understood. Give her Beck Marshall, Nell thought, for all her foul-mouthed ways, rather than the elegant, haughty ladies she had met who smiled and plotted your downfall at the same time.

Her absence from Court indeed occasioned remark in more than one direction. Bab Knipp told Nell of one particular interpretation when she came to borrow a costume from her just before the performance began at the Theatre Royal. 'Mrs. Pierce and I were at the Dog and Cat last night, and who should come in but Moll Davis in a company, dressed as fine as fivepence and tossing guineas about like they were feathers. When she saw us she started talking in a loud voice, Nelly, about you and his Majesty.'

'Saying what?' inquired Nell, a dangerous glint in her eye.

Bab Knipp looked a trifle embarrassed. 'She was more than a bit bosky, you understand—said the King had tried you and found your manners too low and coarse to be endured. Now he'd conceived a disgust of you and you couldn't get him to visit you. And then she went on—you know how she does—about how her father is the Earl of Berkshire and how his Majesty knows quality when he sees it.'

'Quality? Moll *Davis*?' snorted Nell.

Bab shook her head grimly. 'There's more. I turned and let her have it—told her that it was a damned lie and that you and the King were as close as you'd ever been, so she cut right in and asked why you'd never been seen next or nigh Whitehall, while she'd been more than once to dance for the King and Queen, and *other* reasons. 'Course, I knew the King hadn't seen her nearly as often as he'd used to, though she's got a pension and that house of hers, so I asked *her* when she was due to see the King herself, and she snapped that she had invited him to supper with some other gentlemen next Friday and then we'd see whether she wasn't as enticing as you are.' There was a pause. 'She kept flashing that ring that the King gave her,' added Bab morosely.

'Did she?' murmured Nell, smiling dangerously. 'I can see I shall have to do something about Mrs. Davis.'

At the same time that Nell was hearing of Moll Davis's slander, his Grace the Duke of Buckingham languidly entered a box overlooking the stage at the Duke's Theatre—that same stage where Mrs. Davis had first captured the eye of the King. Upon the Duke's arm was the Countess of Shrewsbury. From several other side boxes greetings came, and his Grace took off his hat and bowed before handing his lady companion to her seat. It was just as he was laying her cloak on the seat beside her that a voice rudely broke in on their privacy.

'All hail—all hail to his Grace and his whore.'

Buckingham swung round to see Harry Killigrew leaning against the pillar that divided their box from his. Master Killigrew's face held a particularly stupid smile and it was obvious from his unsteadiness and the strange angle of his wig that he was extremely drunk. 'Afternoon to your Grace,' repeated Killigrew with a faint giggle. 'What say you we change boxes at the interval. I've a pie wench here that's as willing to lift her petticoats as your little bawd.'

'Devil take you, sir, I'll slit your throat for this!' roared Buckingham and leapt upon the hapless younger man. He ripped Killigrew's hand away from the post and endeavoured to pitch him over the rails into the pit below. But Killigrew's very drunkenness saved him. He reeled back and collapsed at the feet of his own fair companion, who stared aghast at the bulk of the Duke of Buckingham, who had clambered over the side and now swung his legs over into Killigrew's box. Below them the pit had realised what was going on and cheered the Duke lustily as he advanced to wreak vengeance.

Killigrew staggered to his feet and wrenched his sword from its scabbard. 'I d-demand satisfaction from you, your Grace, for unwant— unwarrr— damned plaguey temper!'

Buckingham sneered. 'I hardly think you are in a state to fight. But since the challenge is yours . . .' He drew his sword in reply and the blades hissed together. Within seconds the fury of Buckingham's attack penetrated his opponent's feeble, hopeless attempts to fight and his sword passed cleanly over Killigrew's to sink into the fleshy part of his arm.

Harry Killigrew lurched backwards, dropping his sword, while a dark stain welled up between his fingers and dripped to the floor. His face paled and he goggled at Buckingham, who still stood breathing heavily. 'Pick up your sword, you foul-tongued scum!' he shouted. 'Pick it up and fight!' Killigrew took one look at the purple-faced Duke and his heart misgave him. He turned and fled, scrambling over the rails of his box into the gallery beyond.

The Duke followed, with the shouts of the audience for encouragement: 'Slit 'is guts, your Grace!' . . . 'Stick 'im like a pig!'

As he ran along the length of the gallery, Killigrew's foot caught on the corner of a bench and he sprawled headlong. Buckingham stood over him and his lip curled unpleasantly. 'You little snake, you're not worth the killing, but by God, I'll teach you to besmirch a lady's name!' The flat of his sword came down with a wallop across Killigrew's shoulders and then, with the roars of the crowd in his ears, Buckingham rained blows down upon his victim, who curled up in a vain attempt to escape them and feverishly begged the Duke to cease.

Buckingham slid his sword back in its scabbard and stirred the recumbent body with a contemptuous foot. 'God's death,' he said in disgust, 'a boy of seven could beat you with a trapstick!' With these withering words he left Killigrew and stalked back to my Lady Shrewsbury, honour satisfied.

As the herald walked onto the stage to announce the beginning of the play, it seemed to many people in the Duke's Theatre that afternoon that the best performance had already finished. With a grunt Buckingham eased himself into the seat at Anna Maria's side. Erect and pale, she stared unseeing into the pit below, her hands clutching the rail so hard that the knuckles were white.

'Lily-livered cur,' muttered the Duke. 'Ah well, that's the end of that.'

The Countess did not move her head, and the words came throbbingly from between clenched teeth: 'You're mistaken, George. This is only the beginning.'

Four

*A pox upon my nurse, she frighted me so when I was young
with stories of the devil ... She made me believe wine
was an evil spirit and fornication was like
the whore of Babylon, a fine face but a dragon
under her petticoats; and that made me have a mind
to peep under all I met since.*
—*Thomas Killigrew*

A few days later there was a rattle of coach wheels outside the Cock and Pye as an elegant town chariot drew up and a veiled lady descended. An enormous cartwheel hat with a pink feather perched upon her head, and she glittered with jewels in her hair, about her neck and festooned generally about her person. She wore a cloak of vivid pink satin edged with ermine, and when it blew back it revealed one of the new French sacque gowns in a ballooning taffeta of the same shade. The total effect of this ensemble was that of a large and extremely ornate cake. She shook back her cloak, revealing one small hand, and a gratified smile, almost a smirk, could be seen to cross her features as she looked at the large diamond ring set on her middle finger. Moll Davis was ready for visiting.

Her brows rose significantly and the smirk spread when she

saw the narrow little stairway which led up to the lodgings of Mistress Nelly Gwynne, and she delicately trod up the steps and rapped upon the door with a pink-gloved hand.

Nell greeted her affably: 'Afternoon, Moll, 'twas good of you to come.'

Mrs. Davis permitted herself a gracious smile and suffered herself to be led into Mistress Gwynne's bedchamber, where she divested herself of her cloak and patted her chestnut locks. 'I vow and swear I've been jolted to a jelly in my coach. I was only saying to my Lady Southesk a day or two past, these new wicker chariots may be all the rage but they bump you up and down till your guts turn over.' She fished in her reticule and produced a small hand mirror. 'What a frightful phiz! A moment, I beg you, Mistress Gwynne, until I have put myself a little in repair.' Her accents were noticeably different from before. Mrs. Davis had ruthlessly schooled herself to speak as befitted her new station in life, and the result was painfully precise.

If Nell's lips could be seen to twitch, her guest did not notice. Moll settled herself on the chair which was offered her and took a glass of canary. She looked around the chamber, rather surprised. 'I had no idea you was still settled here in the Lane; I had thought you might have removed some time since. 'Tis so noisy in this part of town, with the Strand but a spit's distance away. I am sure I would sooner *die* than move from Suffolk Street.'

Nell smiled and offered her a large plate of sticky sweetmeats. 'Oh, I don't know, I'm used to it,' she said equably.

'But are you not sadly cramped here? At my house at Suffolk Street, I have three floors, and I swear there is only just enough room. Of course, I have any number of sarvants'—she used the fashionable French pronunciation—'but even so, I can't think how you contrive.'

Nell shrugged. ' 'Tis all a matter of what you're accustomed to, I suppose.' There's only me and Mit and Toby—a little boy I'm looking after—and we don't take up much room. 'Tis a palace compared to the Coalyard, you might say. Have another sweetmeat, they're homemade.'

Moll took one and popped it into her mouth. 'That's true. Of course, I 'ave—*have*—been rather spoilt. My father, Lord Berkshire, gave such a sum to my mother to support me that I've never lived anything other than like a lady. These sweetmeats are uncommon good.'

'Have another,' Nell offered.

Moll took one and looked at her curiously. 'Are you not having any?'

'Lord no! I ate a plateful when I was making them. Tell me, what is Suffolk Street like?'

Moll settled down to regale Nell with a description of the glories that were now hers. As she spoke, her hand constantly fluttered up to her face to display the ring on her finger and she soon brought the conversation round to the subject of the King. 'I can't stop much longer. As a matter of fact, Charles is coming to a little supper I'm giving this evening with the Duke of York and some others. Though I dare say *he* might stay on after the others have gone.' She paused to let the words sink in. 'Of course, he's constantly begging me to give up the boards and I've told Davenant he must not look for me to perform much longer. I only do it now for the novelty—it's hardly a case of needing the pittance I get there.' She simpered, looking at the ring. 'I think I can say I have no worries in *that* direction.'

'You're lucky,' said Nell, refilling her glass, 'to have held his Majesty's favour so well. What a charming gown. Did you get it at Unthanke's?'

Moll thanked her and began to discourse at length on the horrid difficulty of getting the right gowns now that the lacemakers and modistes in Paternoster Row had been burnt out and the Exchange quite destroyed.

Nell gave her half an ear's attention, but her mind returned to Rochester's words on the night of that hideous party at Buckingham's: 'Our Sovereign Lord the King has not the reputation for constancy . . . How long will he love you, my dear? . . .' He was a cynic, she told herself, but how right was he? She thought of Charles. He loved her, she was sure of that, but he himself had said he had loved before and might love again. She did not expect him to stop noticing other women. In her world, men did not stay faithful to only one—already she shared him, with the Queen and doubtless others, but still she knew he loved her. Now. What of the future? An ache filled her heart. How could she expect constancy from him? She had seen the world he had come from, she knew of the years of smooth lies and false promises and deceit he had known. How could a man who had known such a world trust anyone ever again? It was safer not to, safer to hold the world at arm's length and not to admit anyone into a heart that had stopped believing in the permanence of passion. A fierce resolution entered into her: if she loved him, she must fight for him, body and soul; she would show him there was someone he could trust always, someone who truly loved him at all times, no matter what happened. And though he might look at a well-turned ankle or a pleasing pair of breasts, she would fight to possess him, to make him love her and none other.

She leaned forward and her smile was bland. 'Have another sweetmeat, Moll.'

There was a sudden hush in the royal Council Chamber at Whitehall the following afternoon as the Duke of York stood up to address the assembled company. All heads turned, for it was clear that his Highness, heir presumptive to the throne, was about to make an announcement which the Council and indeed all Whitehall had expected for some time.

The Duke's eyes swept along the length of the Council table, over the faces of Clifford and Ashley, Buckingham, Arlington, Lauderdale and Ormonde to the features of his royal brother, who sat at the head of the Council. Charles nodded formally.

James coughed. 'I have to announce to this Council that I, James, Duke of York, have decided to embrace the Catholic faith of the Church of Rome. I wish this fact to be known and for it to be known that my decision to enter the aforesaid Church is an irrevocable one. It is further my wish that I be allowed the freedom to practise my own religion.' He looked at the King. 'Sire, my brother, I regret that I can no longer attend services in the chapel. My confessor has told me that as a Catholic, I must attend no service save the Mass.'

Charles looked disappointed and impatient. 'You are, of course, free to worship as you wish, brother, but the situation is not so simple. You are not merely a private gentleman but my heir and a member of the royal family. While we can have no objection to your worshipping in *private* as you desire, your position as my brother requires that you worship publicly in the Chapel Royal as I do and as our father did.'

James shook his head stubbornly. 'Forgive me, Sire, but that is impossible for me to accept. 'Tis nothing less than hypocrisy. I am not ashamed of my faith. Do you wish to deprive me of my freedom of worship?'

'No one seeks to deprive you of it, brother, but can you not dissimulate a trifle to keep the peace?'

James looked Charles straight in the eye. 'Where is a man if he cannot tell the truth to the world?'

'Oh, James,' groaned the King. 'Truth is like a naked lady. When she shows all, it delights a few, but shocks many. 'Tis certainly a luxury kings cannot afford. Do you realise what effect this declaration and such an intransigent attitude is like to have?'

'I am ready to accept any such consequences. It hath long seemed to me that my immortal soul is of more concern to me than the pomp and worldly glory of earthly things.'

'Unfortunately,' said Charles drily, 'you yet have to live amongst us poor mortals until the time comes for you to ascend to your heavenly reward, and meanwhile I have to seek to maintain peace and order in the realm.'

The Duke sat down with a resentful look on his face. There was a pause while the Council digested this momentous news, which must shortly break upon the Court and could, as the King had said, have dire results in a country which hated Papistry to the point of terrifying obsession.

Sir Thomas Clifford sought to ease the tension. 'I am sure that I speak for the whole Council when I say how deeply one must respect the honesty of his Highness in thus affirming his conversion, a step which cannot have been undertaken lightly and which I am persuaded cannot have been an easy decision to take.'

Charles was silent, but Buckingham's whisper to Ashley was quite audible. 'He would say that; he's a damned Papist himself!'

Lord Ashley spoke. 'Your Majesty, this moment seems an appropriate one to raise the question of the effect the Roman Catholic religion is having within certain sections of our government. I refer in particular to Ireland, where both I and his Grace of Buckingham have been dismayed to find that certain land grants appear to have been made less on the basis of loyal service and more on the basis of the sharing of the Papist religion.' His pale eyes slid round to glance at the Duke of Ormonde. 'Both in these grants and in the recent knightings in Dublin, I feel forced, albeit with reluctance, to suggest that his Grace of Ormonde has acted both arbitrarily and to the detriment of stable government within that kingdom.'

Buckingham nodded. ' 'Tis nothing less than chicanery and I demand—'

'*Demand*, your Grace?' Charles' voice was icy. 'I am sure we must all applaud your zeal, but I misremember that I have asked you—or my Lord Ashley—to meddle in Irish affairs. We are entirely satisfied with the present Lord Lieutenant and I must ask you to drop this topic. No discussion of Ireland is on our list this afternoon and I would rather pass on to more important matters, to whit, the progress we are making towards alliance with the Dutch. My Lord Arlington?'

Arlington fiddled with the stack of papers before him. 'I have this morning received a letter from Temple, who says that De Witt received him most cordially two days ago and said that England's aid has undoubtedly paved the way for agreement betwixt France and Spain and maintained peace in Europe.' He glanced up at the King. 'I feel, your Majesty, that an alliance may be concluded in the near future.'

Charles looked pleased. ' 'Tis news we must all be glad to hear. I feel not only that we have helped secure Portugal, which of course I must have a care for as my Queen's homeland, but that the French must now see that we are a force to be reckoned with. It is to be hoped that we shall find the Parliament better-complexioned when it meets this spring.'

'Your Majesty has become the champion of Protestant Europe!' declared Buckingham. 'With Sweden and Holland at our side, we will be able to dictate to France as we desire.'

Ashley nodded vigorously.

Charles noted their pleased expressions and smiled inwardly to himself. Everything was working out just as he wanted. These overtures to the Dutch would please the Parliament and frighten his great French cousin a little. Perhaps now he would see that England was a power to be reckoned with. And when Louis realised this salient fact, the English and the French together would sweep the Dutch butterboxes from the seas. Charles had not forgotten that it had been the Dutch who had burned his ships and humiliated him in the face of all Europe.

Having formed the Triple Alliance to please Parliament and allay his Council's suspicions, Charles now sought for a means to break it and join in an alliance with France—when the price should be right. It was France that Charles wished to have as ally—France where his beloved Minette lived who was begging him also to embrace the Catholic faith. He knew he could not do so and retain his throne, but he longed for the sway his Catholic cousin held. Both the loyal Clifford and Arlington knew of these secret aims, but the rest of his Council did not. It was Buckingham and Ashley he needed to watch; Buckingham was courting the Dissenters and the old Puritan oligarchs, and Ashley had latched on to him as the rising star of the new government. Charles did nothing to destroy his illusions—Buckingham served as a cover for his own design.

His gaze embraced them all, sitting around the Council table. 'I believe we are entering a new phase in our history, gentlemen. Here we have them—France and Holland, both enemies, both irreconcilable. Whoever can have England for an ally will know she can defeat the other. I declare I feel like a lady awaiting her suitors.'

A loud guffaw echoed around the Council Chamber. Buckingham turned to the King and his voice was silky. 'As you so rightly say, your Majesty, our realm is entering a new era. Does it not seem strange therefore that the Royal Council should still include those whose French sympathies are notorious.' He looked openly and sneeringly at Arlington, very modish in a black velvet coat with great skirts of obvious French cut and design. 'Men,' went on Buckingham, 'who are close indeed to Monsieur de Courtin, our French ambassador, and whose pockets may well be stuffed with louis d'or, for all we know—'

'Damn you!' exploded Arlington, furiously jumping up. 'Don't you dare to question my loyalty! There's no man here done more to promote the Dutch alliance than I have! Why, my own wife is Dutch, which is more than you can say. You've scarcely *got* a wife, and all the Court knows you for an intriguer and an adulterer.'

'My lords!' interrupted Charles wearily. 'This is a waste of words and time. I hardly think wearing a French coat and talking to poor old Courtin can rank as treason. If it does, then I would have to abdicate tomorrow. We're all perfect monsieurs now, brought up to prefer oil and salad to a chine of beef.' His eyes ran down the paper before him. 'I think I can declare this Council meeting closed. Perhaps you could wait on me this afternoon, my Lord Arlington. I should like to discuss Temple's letter further.' The King stood up, doffed his hat to the Council, and the meeting broke up.

As the velvet curtains parted and Charles strolled out of the Council Chamber and down the Stone Gallery a heavy footfall behind made him pause, and he turned and hailed Lauderdale, who was morosely stumping along behind. 'Your Grace looks as if he had just lost a fortune at play.'

The Duke of Lauderdale scowled. 'Aye, weel, ah've no got time tae spend listening to blether o' *that* nature a' day. It's worse than a coven of females, I swear 'tis.'

'Then we won't discuss it,' Charles assured him, eyes twinkling. 'Perhaps you could tell me instead what's this gossip I hear about poor old Shrewsbury and his wife.'

'Faith, she's left him, that's all,' grunted Lauderdale. 'The silly bitch has pushed him too far this time—went and demanded Shrewsbury challenge young Harry Killigrew to a duel because he called her Buckingham's whore, Lord help us! The young fool was in his cups, I gather, and Shrewsbury refused.' Lauderdale chuckled. 'Ah heard old Shrewsbury told her that Killigrew was but speaking the truth and he saw no point in duelling wi' him. So she packed her bags and left him. Shrewsbury's well rid of her. I'd take a horsewhip to her if she was mine.'

'Odsfish! If she was *your* wife, John, even I wouldn't dare give her the eye,' declared the King with a grin.

They walked in leisurely fashion down the Stone Gallery. At the top of the grand staircase a voice hailed the King. 'Charle', wait, I wish to spik with you!'

Tripping lightly up the stairs came the Queen, with a bevy of her ladies making more formal progress behind. Charles stood waiting with hand outstretched and a mischievous smile on his lips. 'I collect Penalva is laid up for her afternoon sleep or else I warrant she would have something to say about a queen who runs about like a dairymaid!'

Catherine smiled back but shook her head impatiently. 'She is. But I shall run as I please—no importa! I have to spik wit' you, Charles, *now*.'

The King descended the staircase with Catherine at his side. 'What's so important, Kate? There's nothing wrong, is there?'

'No, but you have forgotten the grand ball you said was being held next week for the Swedish embassy. If it is to be as spectacular as you want, we must talk wit' the Lord Chamberlain. There are a hundred t'ings to arrange, mi amor!'

'Hmmm . . .' Charles looked thoughtful. 'We must make sure that Monsieur de Courtin comes. I want him to relay back to his royal master how the King of England receives this Swedish embassy. We can't equal Versailles, m'dear, but there must be a show the like of which Whitehall has never seen.'

'Claro. I have ordered new draperies for the Banqueting Hall and the regilding is finished. They have already started building new canopies above the t'rones . . .'

'Lord Chamberlain will deal with it all, m'dear. You have no need to worry.'

But Catherine's eyes were gleaming with the thought of the

splendid occasion to come. 'It will be the greatest dis-s-play of your reign, querido mio. Whitehall will glitter as never before —all the world who matters will be there.'

'All the world who matters . . .' muttered the King. 'Hmmm. How right you are, my dear.'

Mistress Nelly Gwynne received the honour of a royal invitation with horrified amazement. 'Me?' she gasped 'Me—be presented at *Court*? You're raving, Charles!' She was lying in the King's arms in the royal bedchamber at Whitehall, but Charles's casual suggestion made her pull herself up onto one elbow and regard him dazedly. 'You can't be serious!'

'Why not?' The King's tone was light. 'I see no problem. 'Twould be nice to see you coming to Whitehall through the front door rather than just creeping in at night up the backstairs.'

'B-but they'll all know why I've been invited. The King's whore—that's what they'll all say behind their hands. I can just see their sneers as I'm announced and—'

'They'll not sneer. *I'll* see to that. Odsfish, why shouldn't you come?'

'I'm only an actress, Charles. I don't belong at Whitehall.'

His fingers tickled her chin. 'You seem to belong at Whitehall, or at least'—he glanced at the bed—'in a part of it.'

She smiled, but shook her head decidedly. 'I don't want to live in the world of the Court, Charles. 'Tis nothing but plots and intrigues and pretence. It—it *kills* anything beautiful; it sours it and tarnishes it and destroys it. It scares me. If I came here, it might destroy me too.'

'Sweetheart, I want you to come. I'm not ashamed of you. You might be an actress, but I'd rather see your pretty face at Whitehall than most others. Please, Nelly, this is my world, it's *part* of me, whatever it is, and I want you to be part of it.'

Nell did not reply, looking down at her hands and plaiting the corner of the sheet nervously between her fingers.

The King sighed. 'I just hoped that I could show the world how much I cared for you. 'Tis little enough to me that I must take all this trouble to entertain a pack of people most of whom I don't care that for—' He snapped his fingers irritably. 'I just hoped that I could squeeze in amongst all the pompous dreary embassies and court etiquette an invitation to someone I genuinely *wanted* to invite. I dare say I can maintain my kingly state as usual and smile at the lot of them in my usual affable fashion. Cynicism has its uses, after all.' He shrugged.

'You're not a cynic at all, Charles,' she said suddenly. 'You're a complete romantic. You wander through life being permanently disappointed that people are so much less than they should be. That's why your cynicism is written so large on your chest so that no one guesses what tender flesh lies beneath!'

He looked at her in surprise.

'I think you are a fool!' she said in exasperation. But then he saw how she looked at him and felt her hand warm upon his. 'I mean I love you.'

Charles raised her fingers to his lips and a smile crinkled his eyes. 'I was told that when I hold this grand ball, all the world who matters will be there. You matter more to me than all the rest of them put together, my darling.'

She smiled and kissed him gently. 'Pox take you for a cozening rogue. I'll come, Charles.'

He grinned and then dug beneath the pillow. 'I had hoped you would say that, Nelly. Here's something that'll help wipe the sneers from their faces.' He withdrew his hand, clutching a flat box which he flicked open. Lying inside, on a bed of black velvet, lay a pair of exquisite diamond earrings together with a matching necklace and bracelet. 'No one will sneer at this,' remarked the King, lifting the necklace in a long snaky length of flashing fire between his fingers.

Nell shook her head. 'Thank you, Charles, 'tis monstrous pretty, but no.'

'Why not?' he demanded, pardonably annoyed. 'Why can't you take it? What's wrong with it?'

'Thank you, but no,' she repeated quietly.

Charles stared at her perplexedly. 'That's what you always say! I don't understand it at all. Why won't you ever let me *give* you anything? You took clothes and jewels from Buckhurst, why not me? I can afford it; I am the King, after all.'

She threw back the sheet and turned on him angrily, her breasts heaving with the pent-up emotion. 'That's precisely *why* I can't, Charles, can't you see? Don't you see that's the biggest danger to us? If you once started to wonder whether I only loved you for what I can get out of you, then what we have now would be ruined—*killed*! As long as I don't take anything, then you'll know that for once in your life you've got someone at least who's not interested in leeching money or a title from you. You said once that ladies didn't love Charles Stuart the man, they loved Charles the King. I don't. I love Charles Stuart and I don't want to lose him.'

The King gazed at her in dawning comprehension. 'So *that's* why you've refused every—' Suddenly he grabbed her to him, kissing her fiercely. 'Little fool!' he scolded. 'Did you think I could ever think that of you? You're no Castlemaine, my dear, nor ever will be.'

She clung to him, but then remarked with quaint dignity, 'I'm not penniless, you know. I earn a full hundred pounds a year from Master Killigrew.'

She stiffened in affronted fashion as the King collapsed in helpless mirth. She could get no sense out of him, as all he would do was to roll about, moaning, 'Odsfish . . . a full hundred . . . I'm a gazetted fortune hunter, God help me . . .'

'It may not seem much to you,' said Mistress Gwynne severely, 'but 'tis a fortune indeed to me!'

The King sat up, wiped his eyes and humbly begged pardon. 'I must say,' he told her, 'you're the first actress who's ever told me how rich she is.' He paused. 'Talking of actresses, I was entertained to an unusual evening last night at Suffolk Street in the company of Mrs. Davis. A stomach colique or bowel disturbance, I understand. 'Twas the only time I can remember the hostess getting up every five minutes to excuse herself. The evening broke up very early, as Mrs. Davis was finding it nigh impossible to keep still long enough to entertain us! I suppose you can't shed any light on this sad state of affairs?'

'*I*, Sire?' Nell's face was a picture of innocent bewilderment.

'She said,' mused the King, 'that she had spent the afternoon with you and eaten a large number of—ah—homemade sweetmeats of a sticky consistency.'

'Really? I expect she had taken a chill coming in that new town chariot of hers—she said it turned her stomach,' said Nell helpfully.

'I expect so,' agreed the King. 'Do you know, when I was a boy my old tutor the Duke of Newcastle warned me against frequenting the playhouses. He said I'd find only the sort of ladies there who would lie the hind leg off a donkey. What would you say to that observation?'

'Pisspots!' said Mistress Gwynne.

It was just after dawn on a cold misty January morning damp with the fall of a hissing fine drizzle. A small cavalcade of four horsemen crossed the Thames and pushed through the falling branches that drooped across the rutted track of road which led up towards Barn Elms. The horses were forced to follow in single file, splashing along the cart track which skirted a forested incline. A pale grey light was scarcely enough for the foremost of the riders to see his path, but from the determined way he urged his mount onward, it was clear that he was in no mood to dally. From his rich cloak, laced gloves and the breed of his fine mare, it was clear that the leader of the bedraggled party was a gentleman. Indeed, anyone at Whitehall would have recognised in the arrogant set of the chin the person of his Grace the Duke of Buckingham. It appeared that the Duke had brought his page for company, a slender lad in sober homespun with a valise tied to his saddle. Thus it would have seemed until Buckingham turned to address him: ' 'Tis not too far now, my love. I'll have you safe at Cliveden before nightfall. Think you Shrewsbury has any inkling of what's afoot?'

The 'page' behind chuckled. 'I misdoubt whether any news could have reached him yet. I left him a note when I came away last night—but 'twill have to be carried to him at

Hampton Court, as my lord takes his stewardship so seriously he can scarce bear to leave the place!' Her tone was one of bored contempt.

Buckingham laughed. 'I actually believe I have stolen a march on that blackguard Rochester this time. Rochester staged an elopement, but he can't boast he eloped with a married woman *and* when he was married himself!'

Anna Maria began to giggle, but the smile froze on her lips. 'George—look!'

On the top of the knoll above them three horsemen waited, motionless, their outline stark against the winter sky. As soon as they caught sight of Buckingham's party they began to descend, recklessly spurring downwards in a plunging flurry of dead leaves and dull hoof thuds.

' 'Tis Shrewsbury,' muttered Buckingham, surprised. 'I'll warrant there's been a fine betrayal here. Jenkins, Holmes, prepare for trouble.'

The Earl of Shrewsbury's company galloped up to Buckingham's and stopped, their horses sending out clouds of snorting, steaming breath. Shrewsbury's eyes travelled quickly over the assembled group, then they came to rest on Anna Maria. ' 'Tis as I thought,' snapped the Earl. 'You have gone too far this time, your Grace. How dare you abduct my wife?'

Buckingham's brows rose superciliously as he drawled, 'Abduct? My dear sir! To abduct means, I believe, to carry off by force. This lady has come of her own free will.' He glanced at Anna Maria, her eyes flashing fire at the discomfited husband before her. Buckingham's voice was openly insolent. 'I believe *I* have won your lady's heart, but you may by all means try for a reconciliation, my lord, since 'tis no danger to me. They say a husband is a good bit to close one's stomach with when the . . . meal is over.'

With a choked oath Shrewsbury dragged off his heavy riding gauntlet, and spurring up to the Duke, struck it viciously across Buckingham's sneering face. 'You will answer me for this, your Grace—and now!' he shouted, purple in the face with rage.

There was a livid mark on the Duke's face where the glove

had hit home, but for the rest, his features were dead-white and set in a cold mask of rage. 'Shrewsbury,' he remarked pleasantly, 'you filthy little piece of whoreson puff-paste. I am going to kill you for that.'

'No! George, *no*—please!' screamed Anna Maria.

Buckingham ignored her and dismounted from his horse. Behind him Sir Robert Holmes and William Jenkins, the Duke's attendants, did the same.

With a shock of horror the Countess recognised her husband's two companions—his cousin Bernard Howard and Sir John Talbot, renowned swordsmen both. All three now dismounted and began to prepare.

There in the drizzle Buckingham stripped himself of his hat, coat, boots and waistcoat, until he stood in the clearing in his shirt and breeches. With a quick movement he ripped off the lace ruffles about his right wrist, the better to grip his sword, and smiling grimly, looked up at his adversary.

There was the briefest of salutes and then the swords hissed from their scabbards and the silent copse echoed to the ring of steel on steel. Shrewsbury was too beside himself to fight with sufficient skill; his thin nostrils flared in anger, he advanced, attacking Buckingham with the wildest swinging strokes the Duke was able to parry with ease. There was no emotion in Buckingham's fighting; cool as a cat he fought, with a faint trace of a smile on his face as his sword sought the opening that would grant him the kill he had sworn to have. His Grace was a deadly swordsman. Fencing French fashion, his quick wrist deftly turned Shrewsbury's blade and then began to force him back and back until he stood pinned against a tree trunk.

A momentary break in Buckingham's guard appeared to offer itself. Shrewsbury's blade passed over the Duke's, and though Buckingham knocked it hastily upwards, it caught him on the shoulder of his fine linen shirt and a deep-red stain instantly appeared. Buckingham gave no sign and his expression did not change, nor his sword lower for an instant. Now, changing to the attack, his blade lunged at Shrewsbury; again and again, like a gnat, it stabbed, now up, now down, testing the Earl's defence with increasing pressure. Shrewsbury's breath came in gasps and sweat rolled off his brow; seeing the state he was in, Buckingham's eyes shone like agates as he moved in for the kill. He feinted subtly. Again Shrewsbury's desperate eyes thought they saw an opening. He lunged once more, only to have his blade parried carelessly aside. A second later, Buckingham's sword sank deep into Shrewsbury's breast.

There was a tiny gurgling cry and then the Earl staggered back, his eyes glazing, and collapsed in a heap on the ground. Blood trickled dark from his mouth; he gave a couple of twitches and then was still.

Shrewsbury's companions were faring little better. Though Talbot succeeded in pricking Holmes on the hand, a few moments later his blade dropped harmless from his fingers as Holmes ripped open the length of his sword arm, and he cried out in agony and fell fainting against a tree. Bernard Howard had casually spitted the unfortunate Jenkins like a chicken, but then found two blades pointing at his throat. Buckingham and Holmes stood on either side of him. The Duke said politely, 'The day is ours, I think.' With a sigh Howard surrendered his sword.

Buckingham strode over to Anna Maria, still waiting at the side of the clearing. He looked up at her and a strange smile curved his lips as he said softly, 'See, my love, what power you have over men. 'Tis you, not I, that is responsible for . . . this.'

Whatever Buckingham had expected to be the reaction of his beloved, he was doomed to disappointment. Anna Maria gazed coolly down at the two prone bodies, one that of her husband, the other his friend. Talbot leant, ashen and moaning, against a tree trunk, the blood dripping from the long gash in his arm and splashing crimson to the ground. Her eyes returned to Buckingham and a hurt look came into her face. 'But, your Grace,' she reproved gently, 'am I not worth it?'

For once even his Grace of Buckingham was lost for words.

At times Nell began to feel that Mit would drive her insane. No sooner had she heard of what she insisted on calling Nell's 'presentation' than all lucid thought seemed to have gone from her head, to be replaced by an incessant monologue on the rival merits of Genoa or Romane gloves; the lasting qualities of musk as opposed to Hungary water; the advantages of rubbing a paste of almonds, egg yolk and raisins with oil of tartar into the hands at night to make them supple; and a hundred and one other things. It seemed to her distraught mistress that life had become nothing but an endless procession of visits, accompanied by a hectoring Mit, to various modistes, interspersed with rehearsals and performances at the theatre. In vain did Nell point out that she would only be one among hundreds; to no effect did she repeat that the richest women in the realm would be there, whose gowns and toilette she could not hope to equal. This was Mit's finest hour and she knew it.

In the event, Nell was glad of her maid's aid. It was due to Mit that Nell discovered Madame Montaigne, an old and gaunt lady who lived in frowsy lodgings off King Street, a loquacious lady withal but one whose touch with a needle was nothing short of magic. For hour after hour Nell stood while bits of her gown were pinned to her and Madame shuffled round her, her mouth full of pins, commanding her to 'restez tranquille' until each fitting was done.

It was one week later, but Nell felt it had been an age, when one evening she sat in her bedchamber waiting for the coach ordered by the King to call for her. As Mit was brushing her hair, Nell looked into the mirror, and it occurred to her that this little room had seen the beginning of many things in her life. It had been here that she had sat when Charles Hart had stood over her and then carried her off to his bed; it had been in this room that Charles Buckhurst had discovered her and teased and coaxed her into his. And now it had been here that the King himself had come—

'Keep still,' said Mit, dressing her hair with quick strokes of a frowze. 'I can't curl it right if you move all the time.'

Five minutes later Nell stood up in her petticoat, and Mit neatly slipped the gown over her head and then began to button it up the back. Then, commanding her mistress to 'restez tranquille,' with a nervous giggle she stepped back to admire her handiwork. Mit had excelled herself; almost she gasped at the triumph she and Madame Montaigne had made between them.

Nell stood slender and beautiful in an emerald satin gown, long and full-skirted, trimmed with lace point de Gesne over a petticoat of sarcenet, with a black broad lace flounce. An exquisite hand-painted 'landskip' fan, from France—a present from Charles—hung from one fragile wrist. Her face was framed in a halo of red gold, intricately dressed by Mit with cruches of straying fairy curls styled à negligence on her forehead, with 'confidant' strands falling in clusters about her little ears. Charles's other present—the diamonds—glittered and flashed in fiery brilliance. About her neck and wrist they winked and shimmered, so that when she moved, it was as though a hundred lights spun before the eyes.

After a close scrutiny Mit stepped back. 'I never thought to say this, Nelly, but you fair take my breath away. Anyone'd think you were a duchess at least! You'll 'ave ter learn to simper now like a Court lady.'

Nell shook her head decidedly. 'I'll spin my language finer when I'm at Court, haply, Mit, but I'll tell true for all that.'

'Aye, I warrant you will tell the King he was a steaming lump of cow's dung, you would, I know.' She opened a drawer in the table and took out a packet. ' 'Ere,' she said, 'take it—'tis for you.'

Nell unwrapped the parcel and found herself looking at a pair of franzipand perfumed gloves of exactly the same shade as the gown. 'Oh, Mit!'

'I got 'em ter match like. For your presentation. I 'eard my Lady Castlemaine never stirs abroad without 'em. 'Ere now—' Mit interrupted hurriedly as she saw the tears bright on Nell's lashes. 'Less o' that! You'll ruin all that eye kohl you spent the last hour puttin' on.'

Nell laughed a trifle uncertainly and then planted a kiss on Mit's cheek. 'Thank you, they're perfect.'

A banging came on the door below. Nell and Mit both looked out of the window. Down below in narrow Drury Lane stood the most exotic coach either had ever seen. A lozenge-shaped confection of stamped leather, hanging on gilded straps with gold cords and tassels, it waited under the light of a flambeau and in the company of four outriders.

'You need that lot ter keep off the footpads,' giggled Mit. Carefully she picked up Nell's cloak, placed it about her shoulders and propelled her mistress to the door. On the threshold, Nell turned to say goodbye. Mit gave her a gentle push. 'Go on. And, Nelly . . .'

'Yes, Mit?'

'Don't scratch yerself in public, will yer, or they'll think you've got fleas.'

A muffled laugh answered her, and her mistress was gone.

Settled on cushions of crimson plush and with the lackeys trotting at her side, Nell leaned back in the coach and watched while it took her to the Maypole in the Strand and down towards Whitehall. It seemed only seconds before the misty outlines of St. James's Park, which she could see out of her right-hand window, gave way to tall, dark buildings barely distinguished in the gloom, and then the whole equipage came within a pool of light—and Nell gasped.

The tall tesselated splendour of the Holbein Gate loomed over her. Lit with flaming torches in holders along its high wall, the red brick seemed to glow like burnished amber as the coach stopped under the shadow of its great portcullis. One footman in livery hurried forward to wrench open the coach door, while another behind held aloft a flambeau to guide her way. She had arrived.

Descending from the coach, Nell made her way across the cobbles along a line indicated by a seemingly interminable row of royal trumpeters magnificent in their uniforms of scarlet cloaks with silver lacing, and through tall gilt-ornamented double doors which were held open by bowing servants. She passed into a hall dominated by an enormous crystal chandelier that threw the light of a myriad candles over the ladies who now stopped by a gilt mirror on the wall to check that their toilet was in good repair before proceeding further. Her cloak was taken from her, and with her heart beating fast, Nell trod up a great staircase. It was a rare and extravagant creation of pierced panels carved with fruit, flowers, leaves and scrollwork, but such was the state of Mistress Gwynne's nerves, she hardly noticed it at all save to feel sorry when she reached the landing, where she stood irresolute before another pair of doors which stood half open. Strains of music wafted through the opening, together with the murmur of many, many distant voices.

Casually people pushed past her. Nell heard snatches of their conversation as they strolled by. Two gentlemen with gilded swords walked airily past, and Nell heard one say to the other, '. . . dresses her hair about her ears like a virgin bride and wears patches to cover her pimples . . .' before they passed through into the hall beyond. A small plump lady followed, with a tall angular companion. They paused on the portals. 'Jacolatte and cinnamon water—'tis sovereign for indigestion,' said one firmly.

'Nonsense!' retorted her friend. 'Sherris and curds, Lady Appleby. *I* know what I'm talking about!'

With a rustle of silk they were gone at the same second that Nell recognised them as her old friends of Brighthelmstone days. From the doorway she could hear the sound of a voice as each guest was loudly announced. Her heart misgave her. She knew what waited on the other side of that door; she couldn't go in there, she knew she couldn't—

Another couple strolled past, and Nell was close enough to hear them announced: 'My Lord Arlington, Member of his Majesty's Privy Council, Keeper of the Privy Purse—and Lady Arlington!'

With a superhuman effort of will and with knees knocking, she gave her name to the waiting lackey. There was a pause while she stood at the doorway of the Banqueting Hall. The doors opened, and all at once a blaze of colour and noise seemed to hit her and numb her brain.

'Madam Eleanor Gwynne!'

As the voice died away she walked forward, her fingers trembling as they held up her petticoat at the front. Footmen bowed, drawing back, and the throng parted as she went on— the Chamberlain clearing a path with a deft wave of his golden wand. If heads turned or malicious voices spoke, Nell never knew. Her mind was in a haze, registering only odd impressions: the elegant twirl of the Chamberlain's wand, the huge size of the Banqueting Hall and the light of thousands of candles in a line of chandeliers which seemed to stretch away into the distance forever. She followed them, feeling like an ant crawling across the expanse of the vast floor behind the Chamberlain, until he led her down its length and to the royal presence.

There at the end of the Banqueting Hall he sat, gorgeous in white satin slashed with the light blue sash of the Garter, under a canopy of crimson velvet and gold, with the Queen beside him in formal state. Charles the Second. By the Grace of God, King of England, Scotland, Ireland and France, Defender of the Faith. He was a figure distant and misty in majesty. It was not her Charles, she thought in horror. This was not the man she loved; this was a god from another world. It could not be that he was the same man who had lain warm beside her in bed, he who now sat enthroned in such regal splendour.

By the time Nell came up to him her knees felt as if they were turning to jelly. She sank down into the lowest of curtseys, and wondered as she did so if she would ever be able to get up again or whether she would be left forever sprawled on the ground before them all. And then the King astonished his Court. Descending from the throne, as he had never done, even for the French ambassador, he extended a hand and gently aided her to her feet. Whitehall watched while he raised her hand to kiss and a curl of his black periwig brushed her fingers.

'Don't be afraid,' he whispered. 'They all use a pisspot the same as anyone else, you know.' The tension in her relaxed and she smiled at him gratefully while he squeezed her hand. 'I am delighted,' he said gravely, 'that you have come to pay your homage to the King tonight, Mistress Gwynne.'

'Oh, I haven't, Sire.'

He raised questioning brows. 'I am desolated. I had hoped that was why you had come.'

The courtiers saw them draw close together.

She glanced up at him mischievously from under her lashes. 'Indeed no, Sire. Not at all. I have but come to see my Charles the Third.'

The King's deep laughter echoed loud down the length of the lofty chamber.

About the Author

Richard Sumner was born at Leamington Spa, England, in May 1949. He was educated at Maidstone, then the University of Kent, where he took a first degree in medieval history and theology. He subsequently took an M.A. in political history and diplomacy at London University. After teaching for a time in London he began writing, and is the author of a previous novel, *Mistress of the Streets*. He confesses to Jacobite sympathies and a strong interest in the Restoration period, a predilection for antiques and French cooking.